MW00577559

FRESH START

MARK SHAIKEN

FRESH START

A 3J MYSTERY

Published in 2021 by
Mark Shaiken and 1609 Press LLC

© 2021 Mark Shaiken

All Rights Reserved

No part of this book may be reproduced, stored in a retrieval system, or transmitted by any means, electronic, mechanical, photocopying, recording, or otherwise, without written permission from the copyright holder.

ISBN (print): 978-1-7345571-2-1
ISBN (ebook): 978-1-7345571-3-8

Library of Congress Information: copyright registration no. Txu 0-022-489-74

Cover Design and Interior Layout by designforwriters.com

*To all of the broken benches, and the bankruptcy
lawyers in the world
who help debtors to avoid them*

PROLOGUE

IT WAS THE SEASON of sultry, hot and humid in Kansas City. August steamy. Not even the ferocious midwestern thunderstorms could help. When they came and dumped epic amounts of hail and rain, the air didn't cool off; no, it just got hotter and steamier. Like pressing the steam button on a hot iron that had just been filled with cool water. Only the native summertime insects were happy outside in August in Kansas City.

I had received a call from my long-time banker, Warren Hilltop, late in the week before. The message: he and another bank officer would be in Kansas City to meet with me on August 20. Warren was a decent enough sort ... for a banker. My companies were his largest customers, so he was always cordial and I tried to be the same in return. I invited his colleague and him to meet at my office at 1 p.m. Normally, when Warren wanted to meet, he'd ask me if the proposed meeting date was convenient for me. This time, he didn't ask. He told me the meeting date and time.

I knew something was up.

Promptly at one, Warren arrived with a female colleague. I met them in the waiting area and led them to a conference room. Warren was sweating; might've been the heat, but it might've been his nerves. He looked nervous. Warren said they wanted to discuss the $520 million loans I had outstanding to a bank group led by their bank, First Commercial Bank in St. Louis. I figured "they" really meant "she," since Warren could talk to me about the loans over the phone anytime he wanted. He introduced his colleague as Stacy Milnes, head of the bank's special asset group, the department in the bank that handled troubled loans. News to me. There was nothing troubled about my loans. Not at all. I never missed a payment, and the collateral – my high-rise office buildings – were all in perfect condition and fully leased.

Warren said that Ms. Milnes would be in charge of my loans from now on. His voice cracked – definitely nerves. As Warren introduced me to Ms. Milnes, I extended my hand for an introductory handshake. It's the proper thing to do when you meet anyone for the first time; even a banker. Ms. Milnes kept her hands by her sides, looked down at my hand with a curl of her lip. She glanced back at me, stepped too close, stared up into my eyes, and whispered loudly, "I'm not your fuckin' friend."

I assume she was trying to scare me. It was only a moment. If she had scared me, I probably would've thought the moment had stretched out for several minutes. But her message didn't scare me.

I am in real estate. People are in your face all the time. I stared back, with no outward reaction.

She then stepped away, took a chair at the head of my conference table, and informed me I would shortly receive a written demand from the bank for a payment of $30 million, and the letter would explain the grounds. If I didn't pay, she said, the banks would raise the interest rate, call the loan and might start the collection process.

My impression: she was good; she had done this before. It wasn't her first time to set a tone for a borrower. It wasn't her first collection rodeo.

And it wasn't going to be my first time telling a banker "no." Just not today. I had time to let her know my response.

Having finished with her planned comments, she stood, turned, and exited. Mission accomplished. Message delivered. No discussion. No goodbyes. No parting comments. She said what she came to say, and she left. Warren was having difficulty making eye contact with me and finally looked at me after Milnes departed and mouthed the words, "very sorry," put his head down, and followed her out.

Very sorry? Very sorry for what? For not telling me beforehand that the bank would call the loans and try to put me out of business? For not warning me about Stacy Milnes? For trying to ruin my day, while also trying to ruin the rest of my life?

That was the last time I ever saw or spoke to Warren, so I didn't get answers to my questions. Not that I expected any. Warren was a banker. I'm sure he just moved on to servicing other customers whose loans were not managed by Stacy Milnes' special assets group.

Going to bed the night before, I had expected a productive week, providing me with all the joys associated with being the developer of award-winning skyscrapers throughout the country. Now I knew I'd have to find an attorney, probably a bankruptcy attorney, to give me advice, and quickly. Not productive and not joyful. For decades, my affairs had been in order, ready for just such a banker-in-my-face moment as this, but anyone could see that this new, foul-mouthed banker-in-my-face, Stacy Milnes, would be a complication. I needed an attorney on my team to face down this collection bully and back her off. Her bank wasn't getting $30 million, and wouldn't take my buildings either. Milnes needed to understand that.

I am Quincy Gunn Witherman, Quince for short. Everyone has a story, and this is mine.

§

Bankers and Withermans through the ages. That history started with Gunnther Witherman. "Gunn" to his friends. Old Gunn was a prisoner locked away in the Prune Street Debtors' Prison in Philadelphia in 1798. A jail; they called them "gaols" in those days. The banks – his creditors – put him there because he owed them money. And the banks left him there to rot. And rot he did; and crazy, then dead, he ended up. In a miserable, dank, Lilliputian cell, at the end of a long, dark hallway. No light, and no hope, and no dignity; and no honor and then no life.

All he had to do was to pay his banks back, and the payments would have freed him. Simple enough. When his family complained to the banks, a banker, with his coifed hair and gray beard, dressed in his charcoal gray wool suit, his black banker tie, and his black banker stovetop hat, supposedly said, as he gazed down at his banker gold watch and fob, "Gunn has the key to his freedom; just have him pay us. Good day." The banker then spun, exited the room, stepped into his black, shiny, horse-drawn carriage, and sped away.

Gunn never had the coveted key to freedom. He couldn't pay. Not wouldn't: couldn't. He didn't have the money. He lost everything in a real estate scam. Instead, since he couldn't pay the banks back, since his only offense was indigence, he lived and then died in the Prune Street Gaol.

After Gunn died, we Withermans stayed in the real estate business. Over the centuries, we have bought, developed, operated, managed and sold real estate, and then we did it all over again. When people ask, *who am I?* my answer is that I am a real estate developer. Real estate is the Witherman way. Dirt courses through our veins. We have bones made of steel and glass, marble and granite, bricks and mortar, and concrete and wood. Some also say we have balls of steel. All good developers do.

In our business, we Withermans have always borrowed

money from banks. I come from an old, distinguished line of people who owe money – we are debtors. At least they don't imprison us debtors anymore. Right? We've come such a long way. No debtors' prisons, and our Congress has given each of us bankruptcy options. Bankruptcy – the safety net that society provides us when we get in over our heads and the gift of a fresh start – the new beginning of the rest of our lives.

As I sat there and watched the sun set, I thought, I am the direct descendent of Gunn, more than two hundred years later. I'm a student of history; some history is uplifting. Some undermines our faith. We should learn from both. I did. I wondered, what had I learned?

That I would not repeat Gunn's fate – no banker would take me down. So, as you'll learn, I exercised my bankruptcy option. But, you see, I didn't want just a fresh start. I wanted a head start. Just like the origin of the word, debtor – to keep something away from someone – that was my plan.

CHAPTER 1

JOSEPHINA JILLIAN JONES – 3J to everyone who knew her – walked into O'Brien's, a storied old bar in the Westport district of Kansas City. She was the first African American bankruptcy attorney at the venerable Greene Madison LLP law firm, with its headquarters high atop downtown Kansas City, Missouri, offices throughout the world, and influence that at times seemed to extend throughout the galaxy. The first Black partner at Greene Madison. Hell, she was one of the only Black bankruptcy attorneys in Kansas City. A pioneer of sorts. A life full of firsts and onlys.

3J was there to meet her trusted bankruptcy confidant and law firm partner, Bill Pascale, known just as Pascale to his friends. Pascale headed up the Greene Madison bankruptcy group and Pascale and 3J worked closely together on most cases. Pascale arrived at the bar early, having finished an out-of-office meeting, and waited for 3J in the usual place, an old wood booth at the back of the bar. Even in an era of smoke-free environments, 1940s unfiltered Camel cigarette smoke still seemed to ooze from the old booth's oak table and benches.

As 3J made her way to the booth, bar patrons paid attention. They always did. 3J was striking and had been since she could remember. She knew it. But she was much more cerebral than physical, and she mostly didn't care if people looked, and she mostly didn't care what people thought. She was perfectly suited to life as a lawyer – whatever they thought and for whatever reasons they thought it, good or bad, she knew she'd be just fine.

As she arrived at the table, she took off her suit jacket, threw it on the bench, and sat down next to the crumpled coat across from Pascale. 3J ran a finger across her brow as a waitress appeared with her drink: Irish whiskey, neat. The Irish way. One could add water or ice, of course. But why would someone want to do so? It's the rhetorical question one hears in Midleton, Ireland, home to a famous distillery, where the regulars passionately debate the best way to drink whiskey. Golden brown liquor, aged in sherry barrels in a small town in southern Ireland, shipped worldwide to help people wind down at the end of another day. Winston Churchill saved Western civilization from the Nazis in a cramped bunker beneath London with a stogie and a bottle of Scotch. Inspired by Winston, 3J thought she could certainly save the debtors of the world from the evil creditors with the able assistance of an occasional glass of triple-distilled liquor.

George Strait tunes played in the background, George singing about his ex's and Texas. Good ole Houston, Texas honky-tonk twang right there in Kansas City, the country's geographic center while Pascale savored his wheat beer, a local favorite made from golden Kansas-grown wheat. 3J sat down and began to caress her drink. "Hey there, 3J. Tough day at our Greene Madison shop?" Pascale asked.

"Does it show?"

"Not really. I just figured it was another tough day because they're all tough days."

"Ahhh. So true. No, today was fine. I met with a potential new client this afternoon who may need our help. His name

is Quincy Gunn Witherman. He goes by Quince. Ever heard
of him?"

"I think so. Is he that wheeler and dealer real estate guy from
back east – Philadelphia, I seem to remember? If that's him,
I've read some of his profiles online."

"The one and only. Except, it turns out, a few years ago he
moved here."

"Quincy Witherman lives in Kansas City? I wonder why?"
Pascale mused. He took a sip of his crisp beer and said, "He certainly moved here without fanfare. Who would have thought?
Good for Kansas City. We need more rich folks here paying
their city income taxes. What's Mr. Witherman's story?"

3J took a pause after Pascale's stream of consciousness to
relish a taste of the whiskey as she tried to organize her thoughts.
"Well, overall impression – Witherman comes across as an odd
guy, not terribly forthcoming, at least not yet. Probably in his
late forties, early fifties, no family, and he's developed his fair
share of office buildings – maybe more than anyone we've ever
represented. He has a twenty-nine-story building on Walnut
Street near our downtown office, one of his four current high-
rise holdings. One each in Denver, Houston, Philadelphia,
and the Walnut Street building here in Kansas City. They're
all in or near downtown. The construction for all of them
is complete, and they're under his company's management.
Like other developers, he's highly leveraged and owes several
fortunes to his banks. The buildings have pretty conventional
bank loans, and if you add up the total debt, it's pretty large.
He's guaranteed a goodly chunk of that debt personally. So,
even though he was odd, we both know that owing lots of
money can do strange things to people."

Between them, 3J and Pascale had been at the bankruptcy
law game at Greene Madison for decades, mostly representing
debtors. They had long ago learned that debtors come in all

shapes and sizes, but with one salient trait in common – they owed plenty of money, and when the time came to repay it, many either couldn't ... or wouldn't.

"First impression, 3J. Is he honest?" Pascale asked.

"No idea, and like every other real estate debtor we've worked for, we won't likely know the whole story," 3J answered.

Like any experienced bankruptcy attorney, 3J knew you didn't ask your debtor clients if they were honest and telling the truth, the bankruptcy version of "Don't Ask, Don't Tell." Advise them to be complete and transparent, and then accept what they tell you and work with the material they share. At least, until the facts don't sync up with the story.

Pascale asked, "Just how much does he owe?"

"Total debt is something like $500 million, and it sounds like he guaranteed about $50 million of it."

"Wow. A healthy debt load, indeed," Pascale observed with his usual tinge of understated commentary as he lifted the beer to his lips. "But, so far, none of this sounds out of the ordinary or, frankly, even a little bit odd."

"Yeah, that was my initial impression when Witherman and I met and began to talk, but here's the thing. Not too long after he introduced himself to me, he launched into this detailed story about his Revolutionary War-era relative who owed a lot of money due to a real estate venture that turned out to be a big fraudulent land speculation scam. I mean, I know speculation was a stalwart of land development back then. The ancestor's name was Gunn, and his bankers incarcerated him in a notorious debtors' prison in Philadelphia, where he eventually died." 3J took another swallow of whiskey. "Apparently, Gunn's son then also went into the real estate business but managed his affairs better with the help of a financial advisor named Roston, or something like that." Another pause, while 3J looked around the bar and the growing crowd.

"Quince told me this story with a distinct chip on his shoulder; he was almost defensive, as if it's in his ancestral DNA to owe money and not pay it back. Or, maybe because of Gunn, he's hard-wired to believe that all banks are bad. Not sure if he thought I'd find the connection to be interesting as a bankruptcy attorney, or if he told me as a heads-up that his fate would be different from Gunn's."

"Interesting," Pascale offered. "How is his business structured?"

"That part is pretty typical. For each office building project, Witherman sets up a limited liability company. The LLC acquires the land, borrows the money, and builds his high-rise. Then Witherman's management company leases out the building and runs it for a while before he sells it off, makes his money, hits the rewind button and starts over on a new project. He says his return on investment is robust. His buildings are high-end and coveted for their addresses by the elites in the cities where he builds, and he gets a pretty penny for rent. In that way, at least, he seems like a pretty typical real estate guy. Proud of his buildings. Good at what he does in good times; challenged but a survivor when times get tougher."

"Who are his main lenders?"

"Until recently, he said he had spread his debt among many banks, one of which was First Commercial Bank in St. Louis. Then a few years ago, and I'm sure you'll like this, First Commercial approached him for his business and pitched that it made sense to consolidate all of his debt, and he accepted the pitch. Now his lending relationship is with First Commercial, the lead bank in a syndicated bank group consisting of itself, and five other banks from all over. He said First Commercial has the largest piece of the bank debt at about 40%. The other five banks split the remaining 60% of the debt."

"So, First Commercial is in the deal for about $208 million," said Pascale, doing the math. "Yikes. That has to be one of the biggest loans at that bank."

"Correct. Two of the syndicate banks have $78 million each, and the other three have about $52 million each. So not chump change at all."

Pascale nodded his head slowly in agreement.

Experienced, even-keeled, respected. That was the book on him at Greene Madison, and around the local legal community. He was 62 years old. Years ago, he met 3J at a function at her law school, where she impressed him and expressed an interest in bankruptcy law. Back at the firm, he implored the Greene Madison recruiting committee to hire 3J after her senior year in law school to work in Pascale's bankruptcy group because the group needed more manpower and he saw something in the young woman that would revitalize the firm's bankruptcy practice, and, perhaps, his own career path as well. His instincts proved to be money in the bank on both counts. 3J and Pascale were professionally very close, even though they couldn't come from any more different backgrounds.

Pascale was the product of an agricultural family from a small town in western Kansas that, in the Wild West days of the late 1800s before farming took hold, was a place where cowboys ran Texas cattle through town on their way to the slaughterhouses of Kansas City or Chicago. Legendary cattle-drives across Kansas that helped make the West wild. A rough, lawless place where rough, lawless people came to do rough, lawless things and then move on … if they lived. The Wild West's history spawned generations of free-thinking, accept-nothing-on-its-face, question-everything farmers and ranchers.

Pascale had Kansas blue eyes and thinning sandy hair, bleached from working in his parents' wheat and soybean fields.

He went to Kansas State University in Manhattan, Kansas – the Little Apple – on a baseball scholarship. But he hurt his pitching arm during his sophomore year and morphed from life in the athletic dorms to spending the balance of his time at K-State forsaking play time in favor of studying. In his senior year, Pascale took the Law School Admission Test, LSAT for short, and did well. After a K-State Wildcats graduation ceremony, he headed off to the University of Pennsylvania School of Law for an Ivy League education and degree. Suffice it to say there were few wheat farmers at Penn, and while he did well at Penn Law, he never forgot where he was from, and during his three years at Penn, he missed the Midwest intensely. He moved to Kansas City to begin his legal career just as soon as Penn Law finished with him. He joined Greene Madison in 1983 and fell into bankruptcy work almost accidentally, as no one else in the firm practiced that type of law, and no one else wanted to.

3J's background could not be more different. She was a New Orleans kid whose parents divorced when she was four. Her father stayed in her life but her mother raised 3J and her three sisters by holding down two jobs. 3J managed to survive the challenges of living near the poverty line in New Orleans, racial unrest in the New South, and hurricane seasons too numerous to remember, until she ventured off to Whitman College, a venerable liberal arts college in the rural northwest, on a partial scholarship. It couldn't have been further from her life of fried green tomatoes, chicory coffee, beignets, Louie Armstrong and Marsalis family jazz, and the persistent, not-so-repressed, racial biases of the deep South.

3J had never married, and never talked much about her family. She had radiant, smooth, light brown skin, and hair that ended just above her shoulders. Her eyes were hazel with brown, gold, and green tones, the inner portion of her iris lighter than the outer edges. They seemed to capture the light in a room and radiate it back like some kind of superhero from a comic book series. Her looks were memorable, and nothing short of dazzling, but the story of the genes that had gifted her those eyes was an American tragedy repeated, without consequence, all too often. Her great-great-grandmother, a slave on a Louisiana sugar plantation, was raped by the plantation owner's white, contumacious teenage son and the resulting family lineage always incorporated and blended some characteristics of the sugar plantation owner's family: The violent, non-consensual sharing of unwanted DNA to propagate for all generations to come. In 3J's case, it was those striking hazel-colored eyes. History mattered for 3J, and she reaffirmed it each and every morning as she peered into the bathroom mirror and saw her plantation owner's eyes staring back at her. Maybe that daily historical reaffirmation was the reason 3J found her first encounter with Quincy compelling, as he invoked his own historical demon when he related his ancestor's incarceration story. That, and Quincy had his own pair of compelling eyes, the effect of which she would let Pascale discover for himself.

Pascale looked at her and noted that something about her meeting with Witherman seemed to bother her. She was much more distant and deeper in thought than after her usual first meeting with a prospective debtor client. "Penny for your thoughts?" he asked.

3J smiled. "Just a penny?" as she feigned disappointment. As her smile faded, she sighed and said, "Sometimes I think as debtor's counsel, we sit around and wait for that inevitable 'something bad' to happen. We know that some kind of bad moment is in process, but we won't identify it until it's too late to prevent it, and then all we can do is damage control. I have to be aware at all times – prescient – little things I pick up on, a bad feeling here, or an elevated alert level there, none of which can I explain precisely. I just feel them there, lurking. Maybe, the next time someone asks me what I do for a living, I'll just tell them I'm a damage control technician."

Pascale smiled. Sometimes, 3J sped off on a philosophical path of self-awareness that could become overly oblique. *Best to disarm the process,* thought Pascale. He looked into his glass and slowly swirled the remaining beer, and, keeping his eyes on the glass, responded, "Well, I might respond by saying 'you don't know if something will go wrong,' or 'it's much too early to know if something will go wrong,' or 'there, there; something bad doesn't always happen.' But you already know all that." Pascale returned to his glass and this time, drained the remaining liquid but didn't put the glass down. He continued, "And, as an aside, you are more than a technician in the art of damage control. I taught you how to manage the damage debtors can inflict, so you hold a Pascale certificate in the ancient art. You are a certified virtuoso, not just a run-of-the-mill technician. But, no, I'm not going down any of those rabbit holes with you. The feelings will fade, as they almost always do, and then you'll just be Ms. Jones, debtor's counsel." He looked at his now empty glass and returned it to the oak table. "So, instead of all of the abstract, metaphysical, liberal arts stuff that they never taught me at K-State, let me just ask you: where do we go from here?"

3J smiled. Pascale brought her back to Earth. One of his standing assignments. "I guess we have a follow-up meeting to get the usual information from Witherman and give him the initial overview of the process and what he can expect. I've already asked him for cash flow projections and the last two years of financials, which I should get tonight." She paused and added, "Oh yeah, and I forgot. Witherman met with the First Commercial lending officer in charge of the loan a few days ago – a guy named Hilltop. He and Hilltop have done banking business together for years. Witherman said he liked Hilltop as much as he could like any banker. Faint praise. Mr. Hilltop, however, was exiting the relationship and called a meeting to introduce Witherman to his new special assets lending contact. Wait for it – Stacy Milnes."

The waitress brought Pascale another beer. "You're kidding," Pascale responded, his eyes wide with surprise. "The one and only Stacy Milnes. The larger-than-life, combative albeit experienced, bellicose banker. Big loans demand a big personality at the bank. Did she give Witherman her patented, quintessential introductory love tap?"

"Indeed she did. Witherman went to shake hands, and Milnes wouldn't. Instead, she said she wasn't his 'fuckin' friend.' Apparently, Hilltop watched all of this unfold, and looked away. Crashes are hard to watch in real-time, I suppose."

"She said that?" Pascale chuckled. "Good one. Always set the debtor back on his or her heels. She lives out the mantra that you never get a second chance to make a first impression. I imagine that conversation, if you can call it that, will stay with Witherman for a while to come."

"Witherman didn't seem too bothered by it. He's in real estate, after all, right?"

Pascale sipped his beer and then continued, "Milnes certainly is a believer in the 'hit 'em high, hit 'em low, and if they get up, hit 'em again' philosophy of debt collection. Well, at least Witherman understands how this process may go."

From prior deals with First Commercial, Pascale and 3J both knew Stacy Milnes and her special assets group at First Commercial, all too well. Like in most good-sized banks, the special assets group handled loans in default or on a watch-list due to diminishing credit quality – meaning loans that were in trouble and had the bank management worried and the special assets group's attention. As agent for the bank group,

First Commercial owed duties to the syndicate banks to pursue ways to shore up the loans or even begin the collection process – lawsuits, foreclosures, guarantee enforcement, the appointment of receivers, and the like. The Witherman loans were substantial, so they'd be on the bank group's radar.

3J said, "Witherman will find out, though there are no more debtors' prisons, that doesn't mean owing substantial sums of money and withstanding a lender's menu of collection options is at all pleasant in the twenty-first century."

Pascale nodded in agreement.

3J looked at her watch. She needed to head back to her downtown apartment about ten blocks from the office. "Gotta go, Pascale. Can we pick this up in the morning if you have time? I'll send you the preliminary financial information and loan documents tonight as soon as I get them from Witherman."

"Sure thing. Let's circle back in the morning and start plotting out the strategy. Let me walk you to your car."

They settled up with their server and walked across the bar's weathered and creaky, wide-planked wood floors and out into the late summer Kansas City evening, thick with humidity and the constant cacophony of the substantial cicada population. On the street, they encountered growing crowds in the Westport district, the unofficial drinking capital of Kansas City. Students from local universities populated the crowds, using the bars to impede the growth and maturation of their frontal lobes and the development of their executive function skills with "too much drinkin' and too little thinkin'," as Pascale liked to observe in his folksy, Kansas way.

Westport wasn't always the drinking capital, but it featured prominently in Kansas City's history and folklore, settled by the Reverend Isaac McCoy at Christmas time, 1831, ten years after Missouri became the nation's twenty-fourth state as a part of the Missouri Compromise. In the Compromise, Maine became a free state, and Missouri was free to permit slavery. At first, Westport became a hub of commerce given its proximity to the Missouri River and became known as Westport because it was the westernmost entry point to the new frontier. Later, during the Civil War, abolitionists staked out their territory one mile to the west of Westport in Kansas and the southern sympathizers huddled everywhere else. The Confederates and the Union army fought the battle of Westport, sometimes called the Gettysburg of the West, and the conflict ended the Civil War in the West. Today, the city memorialized the battle with plaques and monuments in the park, across from Pascale's large, lonely, stone house.

Now the most famous Black bankruptcy attorney in the Midwest freely strolled down Westport Road toward her car, fully aware that she walked on a street paved over the blood left behind by pro-slavery zealots from the nineteenth century, who died a bloody death just below her feet as they lost their fight for the authority to own slaves. If she was a horror film writer, she could imagine a grizzled, bloody, bigoted hand reaching up through the paved street to grab her free ankle.

But, thankfully, she and Pascale walked peacefully under the street lights, replicas of ninteenth-century gaslights, and her thoughts turned to Quincy Witherman and his view of creditors, the legacy of the death in a debtors' prison of his ancestor, Gunn Witherman.

3J's Whitman liberal arts education caused her to remember something she learned in her freshman literature class that Nathaniel Hawthorne observed: "The wrongdoing of one generation lives into the successive ones." Her English professor called it the sins of the parents returning to persecute the children.

She was not yet aware of just how accurate old Nathaniel's observation would be.

CHAPTER 2

The Debtor recalls Thursday, August 23, 2018

OFFICE BUILDINGS WERE MY passion and specialty. I built lovely, towering, sometimes grandiose but always majestic, buildings. The kind of structures that take a skyline and elevate it to the sublime. Edifices of the sort that stretch upwards towards the heavens and appear to kiss the passing clouds. My buildings didn't compete for air space with the blue skies and billowy clouds. They didn't represent a line of demarcation between nature and man. They cohabited with the skies and clouds. My buildings' facades gracefully reflected the skies and clouds. Nature accepted the presence of my buildings. The other occupants of the heavens welcomed my buildings.

During my adult years, I played a real-life version of Monopoly – I borrowed, bought, developed, leased out my buildings for a while, managed them, caressed them, nurtured them, and then when the time was right, I sold them, and I always avoided the card that read: go to jail, go directly to jail, do not pass "Go." Perhaps I should have been more concerned about my morals and ethics. But I wasn't. I didn't live a mission, visions, and values life: No, I was just a real estate developer.

It was a status thing for lenders to loan me money. When one of my buildings went up, the lenders were there in their shiny, clean, hard hats for the photo op. When a building opened for occupancy, and I cut the ribbon, the lenders were there for the photo op. And the lenders relished the plaque in the lobby that said: "financing provided by XYZ Bank." It made the bankers feel essential, influential, relevant, community-centric, and fulfilled, and, lest we overlook the obvious, it was favorable, free publicity for them. My lenders highlighted me in their public relations materials.

I focused on my buildings. My lenders focused on me. I was always their prized possession, until, one day, I wasn't. My real estate successes were their successes until one recent day, when they weren't.

With each loan document I signed at a closing in a bank attorney's large conference room, I knew I'd have to pay the loan back someday. I always believed that when times got tough and the time for repayment arrived, the banks would squeeze me for every last penny, even if that left me with nothing. They would say, "all you have to do is pay," just like the bankers' ancestors said to old Gunn. A Witherman's fate. Even though the banking industry underwent substantial changes over the centuries – no more top hats and gold watches and fobs, and no more shiny, horse-drawn carriages – nevertheless, the insatiable need for repayment didn't change. Just how the lending world has always played the game, I suppose. And, of course, it's written in the documents that the banks drafted and I signed.

When my time was up, I owed much too much money to a group of banks who I came to despise (Wait, that's not right – I'm sure I loathed them from the start). Truth be told, I firmly believed they wanted all of the money repaid immediately, not just Milnes' demand for $30 million. As Falstaff complained in Shakespeare's *King Henry IV*, "O, I do not like that paying back, 'tis a double labor." I guess for me, it might have been a triple labor.

I had my first meeting with my bankruptcy attorney at the Greene Madison office. Nice building. Not as nice as mine, but serviceable. It was a productive introduction to Josephina Jillian Jones. 3J. I liked her name. I liked the way she carried herself and interacted with me. I liked that she didn't seem hell-bent on convincing me that she was the best at what she did. I liked her eyes. Eyes are something special to me, and I found hers compelling. She was impressive, able to explain complicated legal issues in English. I've dealt with many attorneys in my day, and not many of them can speak in normal English. She gave off an air that she was comfortable with herself and had nothing to prove. That made me comfortable with her.

I felt like she would go to the mat for me. She would throw her heart into my cause. "Hire the brains; get the heart and soul for free," my uncle used to say to me as he taught me the business. 3J was the whole package. I wanted the entire package. I figured I might need it. With 3J, I felt I had a decent chance of restructuring all of my debt – at least as soon as my new banker "friend," Stacy Milnes, stopped swearing and threatening and pounding the table and blustering. Of the firms I interviewed, only 3J had dealt with Milnes before and had even gone toe-to-toe with the foul-mouthed, ill-tempered, eternally unhappy, workout monster on the twenty-second floor of the building First Commercial occupied in downtown St. Louis.

Too bad I didn't build that one. How fitting it would have been if I was Milnes' landlord. I'm sure her presence would constitute some form of default in the standard lease that my tenants sign. My leases contain a clause that the tenant must conduct no business that amounted to an immoral endeavor. Stacy Milnes – synonymous with immoral endeavors. I could dream, right?

I had hired many attorneys in my life. You can't be a real estate developer without getting into some legal scraps. In my business, attorneys are just another category of vendors whose services I bought. Just an unavoidable cost of doing business. As a group, I never really liked them or how they made their living, but I didn't need to like them to hire them. When I studied Gunn's life before he died in the Prune Street Prison, I came across a quote from a man named John Pintard. Pintard was also an imprisoned debtor in the post-revolutionary war era, and he wrote: "a lawyer's trade is Villainy licensed by Law." I sympathized with Pintard's view of lawyers. But I guess my twenty-first-century view of attorneys was a little more mellow than Pintard's eighteenth-century observation – attorneys were just a necessary evil. As for my attorneys, I put more emphasis on necessary than evil, but I certainly understood Pintard's point of view.

But hiring a bankruptcy lawyer did concern me. This engagement would be the first time that any attorney I hired might get real close to the things about my life that no one had ever gotten close to before, and no one should; those few things that were covert and undisclosed. Like the Withermans before me, I had secrets. My own set of hush-hushes. Nowhere to be found in any file I kept, in any Google search, or in any byte that resided on my beloved MacBook Pro. I didn't have many such secrets, but the ones I had were highly classified and not for any lawyer to ferret out. At the meeting, 3J said I'd get a memo explaining the bankruptcy process. She also told me that she *required* transparency and full disclosure from all of her debtor clients, and she gave me a heads-up that the memo would re-emphasize that.

Required. Hmmm. An interesting choice of words. I assumed she said that to all of her clients and she sensed nothing unusual about me that caused her to offer such a directive. I remember thinking as she said it: *We will just have to see.* Transparency and full disclosure were not two of my natural personality traits.

I was a "need to know" guy. I showed others only what they needed to see. Unless something dramatic about 3J and the bankruptcy process changed the course of my life and my DNA, my thinking was that I would be able to say to her, *I hear your words, 3J.* You know, like when someone responded to you by saying, "I hear you," when what they meant was "I'm not going to do that."

I had planned for the bankruptcy moment. I liked to believe I prepared for almost every moment. I intended to stay the course. Part of my Witherman heritage. I didn't see bankruptcy, 3J, or Stacy Milnes, as changing that plan.

CHAPTER 3

Friday, August 24, 2018

3J LEFT HER APARTMENT at 7:30 a.m. for the less-than-fifteen minute walk over to the office. Law school had altered her DNA. As law schools were wont to do, hers took a recent college graduate's laid-back, casual temperament, complete with minimal reliability and predictability, and turned her into a meticulous, predictable creature of habit who thrived on repetition, especially when it came to work-related routines. She entered her office, immediately docked her laptop (habit), and while it powered up, she went for her morning cup of Earl Grey Tea (habit), and returned to her desk (habit) and her trusty laptop (habit). She checked her calendar (habit) and her to-do list (habit), gazed out her window briefly to the city below (habit) and settled into another workday (habit).

This day, she began to draft a memo for Witherman. She had already reviewed the financial information and the loan documents Quincy sent to her the previous night; the memo would not only set out the parameters of the information she and Pascale would need to plan the approach to the Chapter 11 bankruptcy cases, but also some important rules of the bankruptcy game for Quincy.

The "problem" seemed straightforward. The office buildings had solid tenants and a high occupancy rate and seemed to be in vibrant cities: Houston, Denver, Philadelphia, and Kansas City. But the commercial real estate market had taken a small hit, maybe only short term, but a hit nonetheless, and valuations had slumped.

In her review of the loan documents, 3J noted that when Witherman finalized the loans, the loan documents required the balance owed on the loans to be less than 75% of the most recent bank valuation of the real estate. This loan-to-value ratio, or LTV, wasn't at all an unusual provision; but, unusually, the terms of loan documents automatically reset the 75% ratio to 70% four months ago. Based on that adjustment and the softening real estate values, the balance owing on the loans was now more than 70% of the value of the buildings. As a result, the banks wanted a payment of about 6% of the amount owing under the loans – $30 million in cold cash – to get the loans back into contractual and regulatory compliance. Based on her initial conversation with Witherman, she was sure that his empire didn't have that kind of ready cash, at least not without imperiling the ongoing operations' viability. Even if the average real estate developer had that kind of cash lying around in the petty cash drawer, 3J believed that most developers would never readily part with such a large amount of cash – why would Witherman be any different?

The memo contained a trove of bankruptcy information and requested a like amount of background information, financial documents, and data from Quincy and his companies. It explained that Chapter 11 of the Bankruptcy Code protected a business debtor from creditors to give it time to restructure its business and financial affairs in a plan, the debtor's new agreement with its creditors. If the Court approved the plan, the reorganizing debtors received a discharge, which the Court could revoke for up to 180 days after the discharge if there was fraud. 3J concluded by reiterating her comment to Witherman that she required transparency from her clients. As 3J scanned the document, she thought of all the debtors she had represented over the years – smart ones and not so smart ones; local and national ones; big, middle-sized, and small companies; established and start-up companies; ones who waited too long to come in to see her and were now beyond saving and ones who wisely sought her advice before the fireworks began; almost always, ones who owed too much money. Some of her debtor clients presented her with sophisticated financial records and controls, and others gave her aging, crumbling, shoeboxes, which contained frayed records identified in handwriting on the outside of each box simply by the years of the records contained within. She had clients who could answer almost any question about their business, and others who seemed unable, or unwilling, to answer almost every question. She represented old ones, young ones, tall ones, short ones, fat ones, skinny ones, healthy ones, and those who didn't seem they could survive the strain and intense stress brought on by the bankruptcy process.

We're a society of debtors. We run up bills, we buy on credit, and we owe. We spend our lives trying to tread water and navigate the creditors' currents to whom we are all beholden. We are leveraged. The uniquely American way.

And many of the debtors went through some portion of the five stages of bankruptcy death, as she and Pascale liked to call it – debtors who think they can schmooze their way out of debt; then negotiate their way out; then litigate their way out; then beg their way out; and then, for some of them, only to find out there is no way out.

She wondered what kind of debtor Quincy Witherman would be. He came across as very astute, and she suspected he had top-notch records and financial processes. 3J expected to receive no shoeboxes of financial records from the Witherman empire. He seemed like he could operate under pressure and he would need to in order to take on Milnes and First Commercial. He didn't look like the schmoozing kind, but it was too new a relationship to know how he would stand up to the infamous five stages of bankruptcy death.

Back to the memo. 3J re-read it to make sure it addressed Witherman's business, and validated just how much information this was for Witherman to absorb. Bankruptcy was complicated, and the stakes were high. The debtor's counsel needed accurate and complete information – the bankruptcy variant of the garbage-in-garbage-out adage. And the stakes would be high in these cases – bet-the-Witherman-empire high.

Notably, the memo was the first step in her ongoing reminders of the need for full disclosure and transparency. All too often, 3J knew that debtors omitted information, sometimes of no consequence, and other times, critical. Typically, they took the position that they simply forgot something important. Many did forget, but a number came to the process with a "need to know" attitude; counsel would ask for information, and the debtor would decide if, and to what extent, counsel *really* needed to know. A bankruptcy cat-and-mouse game. In 3J's experience, she couldn't overemphasize to her clients the need for full and accurate disclosure.

Early in her career, 3J learned that, for whatever reason, debtors sometimes struggled with full disclosure. Why? Perhaps they were overwhelmed. Or perhaps they just didn't feel comfortable with full disclosure. Or maybe it was experience – when they disclosed something in the past, bad things happened. Or maybe it was just fear. She had no read yet on Witherman to form a view on his level of disclosure. Like with most of her clients, she simply concluded *we'll just have to see.*

She emailed the memo off to Witherman later that morning after asking Pascale to have a run-through for content and form. In the email, 3J asked for a meeting to discuss the memo and formalize the representation. And with that, 3J set the Witherman bankruptcy wheels in motion.

CHAPTER 4

The Debtor recalls Friday, August 24, 2018

3J's BANKRUPTCY MEMO HIT my in-box at about 4:45 p.m. I had just arrived home to my small apartment in a trendy, up-and-coming district of Kansas City, just outside of downtown. While it's true that my buildings were grand, my personal residence was modest. I didn't want a palace. I didn't need to be on the cover of any house and garden magazines. I didn't seek interviews with any lifestyle reporters. I wanted my buildings to be on the magazine covers, and I hoped they would do the talking for me. I didn't require lots of living space. I achieved my goal of a Tokyo-apartment-sized living accommodation in Kansas City's four square blocks between 17th and 19th Streets – formerly known as "Film Row," where, from the 1920s to the 1960s, the area served as a major theater distribution center for most of Hollywood's major studios. It was also home to the Kansas City native sons and daughters who achieved Hollywood fortune and fame, such as Joan Crawford, Walt Disney, Jean Harlow, and Ginger Rogers. No films here today anymore. Just low-rise brick and stone industrial buildings retrofitted for art and artisans and food and music, with an edgy, millennial vibe that I enjoyed … and my small living quarters in a turn-of-the-last-century loft building. All 780 square feet of my comfortable living space, in the Crossroads: its twenty-first-century name, that could either be just a name, or a folklore reference to hoodoo and the place to meet the devil.

I wasn't sure. Maybe the city fathers weren't either.

I moved to Kansas City to stay out of the twenty-four-hour spotlight that is the east coast. I wasn't famous, but I was well-known enough, and that status back east made anonymous living difficult. In Kansas City, I'd found a venue where no one seemed to care all that much who I was and seemed to let me go about my business. That's all I wanted. Sure, it was a cow town in the past, and that was how east coasters still thought of it, but a cow town with an attitude that attracted dangerous, ambitious men with dangerous ways to pursue a means to their end. An exciting place, back in the day, if one survived. I certainly intended to survive, so I found it to be a perfect match. Some of that attitude carried forward into the Kansas City of today, and I enjoyed it.

I learned a great deal about Kansas City's history before I moved here. History was so important to me, and it's how I fit in and how I made sense of things. To borrow from James Baldwin, maybe I was just trapped in history, and history was trapped in me.

The Crossroads was one of those Kansas City nuggets from a bygone era that the locals struggled to keep in their thoughts, lest history was forever lost. It was a city of almost-lost history on so many street corners, like the now-fictional corner of 12th and Vine made famous by Leiber and Stoller's 1952 song entitled "Kansas City." Neither of the songwriters had ever been to Kansas City when they penned the song. Had they visited in the early 1960s, they would have been surprised to learn there was no longer an intersection of 12th Street and Vine; urban renewal had claimed that corner for other uses.

And almost-lost history such as the River Market, former home to mafia families warring to protect their turf; and such as all of the concrete government structures built by the Ready Mixed Concrete Company owned by Tom Pendergast, former boss of everything political and social in Kansas City; and such as the now-gone jazz bars along Walnut Street that in the twenties, thirties, and forties spawned Charlie Parker and provided a haven for traveling jazz bands, offered hookers to anyone with a wallet, saw prohibition as nothing more than a suggestion, and fed fried chicken in the alleyway to all takers, especially the young saxophonist who would become known as Bird. And Crown Center and the Union Station across the way, one developed by native company, Hallmark, and the other built by city fathers as a Midwestern shrine to train travel where outlaws and law enforcement shot it out in the 1930s as travelers hustled through the station to catch the next train.

Many gone but not entirely forgotten, at least not just yet. I liked it.

History should never be forgotten.

I poured a glass of Gifford Hirlinger red wine, my current favorite small vineyard from the Columbia Valley in Washington, and put Grant Green's 1965 post-bop gem, *Idle Moments* on my turntable. Yes, turntable. A good chunk of my 780 square feet housed vinyl records; a musical journey through my life that mirrored, in many respects, my maturation into the world of real estate development. So much of my existence was a throwback filed in the life folder labeled "Never Forget." More history, I suppose.

Immediately I was absorbed in the fifteen-minute opening track from which the album took its name – a slow composition in C minor with Bobby Hutcherson's seductive vibes, all custom made for thinking and comprehending, and reading the memo. As Green opened with the tune from which the album gets its name, written by his pianist Duke Pearson, I read the memo. I thought, *lots of legalese,* but I read it all. My reaction was, *I get it.* No guarantees, the potential for lots of fighting, lots of creditor scrutiny, lots of rules and procedures and hearings, lots of long hours and stress, lots of upside, lots of risks, and with any luck, lots of debt restructuring. Lots of transparency: There was that 3J admonition again. The bankruptcy world portrayed in the memo sounded just like life in the world of real estate development ... except for the transparency part. Also, 3J needed lots of information. I had already sent her a core dump of financial information and loan documents, and I made a mental note to get my folks on the rest of the information requests first thing in the morning.

Interesting. There was nothing in the memo about the bankruptcy judge who would preside over my cases. I needed to find out more about the Judge at our next meeting. A tenant always wants to know something about the landlord before renting space, and I figured I might be a tenant in the Judge's court for a while.

"Time to proceed forward," I wrote 3J back. "I can make myself available for another meeting pretty much any time and place, and we will get you the information you want." I hit send; minutes later, she wrote back and set up an afternoon meeting in a week's time.

Green's touch on the guitar was nothing short of elegant, painted on his musical canvas with his signature single-note palette. As I listened, I could hear the bankruptcy wheels slowly grinding forward in rhythm with the music. *What a dissonant combination,* I thought.

CHAPTER 5

Monday, August 27, 2018

STACY MILNES SAT AT her small desk with papers piled high, a big personality embodied in a small body with a small face and small hands in a small office with one small window overlooking a restricted view. From her office, she employed her two-word, narrow view of banking – "pay up." Sometimes, when she felt talkative, she expanded this to: "pay up, *deadbeat.*"

Milnes was all of five feet three inches tall, slightly roly-poly, with bright blue eyes and nondescript shoulder-length dark brown hair. She had a bump at the bridge of her nose – the consequence of a fight in fifth grade with a boy in the Catholic school playground in the Philadelphia neighborhood where she grew up. She liked to say as an adult, "the bump is nothing. You should've seen the boy." She didn't dye her hair; she didn't doll up her face with makeup, as her father would have referred to it. Milnes had never done anything but special assets work in her banking career. Indeed, internally at the bank, she admitted on more than one occasion that she never took in a deposit or made a loan in her life. When she started her banking career after getting her master's degree in finance from George Washington University, she was one of the few women in the United States doing such work. Women had a long, tortured history working for banks. Sure, historically, banks employed lots of them: typically as tellers, then reluctantly as junior-level lenders, then even more reluctantly, and rarely, as senior lenders, and almost never as special assets officers. Only recently, women had cracked into many of the departments at banks nation-wide, but still not enough at senior management levels. During one of her annual reviews, in response to her male director's comment that he was not sure about further advancement at the bank, a frustrated Milnes said to her supervisor, "Bill, to quote Ruth Bader Ginsburg, 'I ask no favors for my sex. All I ask of our brethren is that they take their feet off our necks.'" Milnes loved the quote and made a career of repelling any attempt by male bankers to place their hooves near her collar, as she liked to call it.

Special assets work was just never thought of as "women's work" by the mostly white, male, senior managers that ran banks from day to day. Milnes was something of an anom-aly. In every special assets group for which she worked in her career, she felt that the male-dominated industry required her to be smarter, bolder, more resourceful, more analytical, more strategic, faster on the uptake, and tougher than any of her male counterparts.

Milnes quickly learned that unless she adopted a carefully forged persona to deal with the mostly male borrowers to whom she was assigned, they would try to run roughshod over her for no reason other than she was a woman. In her early career, she tried many strategies as she developed her style, but the one she found worked the best was to incorporate a certain crassness into her personality. She swore more than her male counter-parts, talked louder than them, and was known to bang on the table if the moment dictated. She had a quick, critical tongue, and she used it. She didn't offer pleasantries. She didn't have any. Privately, she resented that her persona was one acceptable in a man, and considered inappropriate in a woman. But she told herself she didn't care – she got results. The respect she garnered in the industry came from those results.

Milnes had been married and divorced twice. And had concluded some time ago that she must have no need to be loved or liked because, as she did a self-assessment from time to time, she was doing just fine without much of either. She felt that love and like got in the way of special assets work; without either, she was better at her craft.

After successful stints at four different banks up and down the east coast, she landed a position at First Commercial as the head of their special assets group. It meant she had to move off of the east coast, but she liked the neighborhood feel of St. Louis. It reminded her of her blue-collar Philadelphia upbringing.

Her office may have looked chaotic to a passerby, but there was a method to the madness. For each loan that she and her team minded, she had a notebook in which her administrative assistant set up tab-divided sections. The sections contained loan documents, pertinent financial information, a precise analysis of what constituted defaults under the loan documents, contact information for the borrower, valuation experts, and contact information for whichever attorney the bank had hired to handle a particular loan.

Sure, the bank stored all of the information Milnes collected on its servers which she could access from her computer. But Stacy Milnes was still analog and insisted on a tactile approach to relevant information. She needed something she could grab, tuck under her arm, and run to one meeting or another. The notebook gave her confidence that she would always have all of the pertinent information she could ever need at her fingertips.

One of the notebooks she had on the credenza behind her desk was a two-inch binder that stated on the spine, in bold font, simply: "Witherman." Like all large commercial loans, the four Witherman loans were the subject of the bank's credit quality reviews each year. But, as the economy weakened and real estate values began to drop in many markets, and then failed to quickly rebound, First Commercial's brass became concerned. The bank regulators reviewed the loan portfolio and labeled the large Witherman loans as problematic because the collateral lost value. The cyclical ups and downs of real estate values were part of the American real estate industry and always had been. Banks tried to navigate the boom and bust nature of real estate by profiting in the booms and mitigating losses during the busts. First Commercial was a favorite lender of the real estate industry because it had a history of working with its borrowers. But the bank had a new chief credit officer, whose perspective of loans was that there was something "wrong" with *every* loan the bank made, and his job was to uncover what that was and then decide if the loan should be handled by the special assets group. This new CCO also felt the regulatory review pressure and knew that the bank had to take some action on the Witherman loans. Consequently, at the behest of the CCO, the Witherman loans moved quickly into Milnes' special assets group.

The notebook under her arm right now was the Witherman binder. A few days ago, Milnes had her first get-to-know-you meeting with Quincy Gunn Witherman – *what a name*, she thought. When she met Witherman, she neither liked nor trusted him, but truth be told, that was her normal reaction to most borrowers. The Witherman move to her group had prompted Milnes to call a meeting at the bank with her new customer – standard operating procedure for a loan newly transferred to the special assets group, and what she sometimes affectionately called the "Come to Jesus" meeting. The meeting wasn't to get to know a borrower and establish a relationship.

It was to send a message and set a tone. She felt good about the tone she set and considered the short meeting a success.

Before the Witherman meeting, Milnes had pondered the best path for the banks to collect the loans. The four buildings had dipped somewhat in value, but that might very well be temporary, and if so, the value loss would self-correct, and probably quickly. The recent reset of the loan-to-value to 70%, and the softening in the real estate market, meant that the buildings' values were insufficient. Consequently, the value dip triggered a clause in the loan documents that fifteen days after written demand, Witherman would have to come up with a cash payment, which Milnes calculated would be roughly $30 million. If Witherman and his companies failed to make the payment, they would all be in default. Then Milnes' options ranged from implementing a default rate of interest, here 5% higher than the current variable rate of 4.8%, at one end of the spectrum, to the commencement of collection proceedings – foreclosure, receivership, suits on the guarantees. Consistent with her approach to bad loans, and based on her review of the loan documents, she wanted to get the clock running on the cash payment and the potential for a higher interest rate.

But while Milnes thought the Witherman meeting was a success and she was confident about her collection strategy, she was beginning to realize that she had another problem to contend with. First Commercial was not the only lender on the loans. Because of the size of the aggregate loans, Commercial had brought in other banks and divided the loans between the banks. First Commercial was the lead bank of the bank group, the Agent. But Milnes had to answer to StarBanc from Houston, Wall Bank from New York, Wertz National Bank of Washington, D.C., Telfair National Bank of Denver, and Silvermine Bank Limited of Durban, South Africa, who collectively held 60% of the total loans to the Witherman entities. This kind of loan syndication was a popular way for banks to make big loans, and it required the banks in the group to work together toward a common goal – payment.

Milnes was bothered by the structure of the bank group. She didn't like bank loans where the agent bank had less than 50% of the loan. *Bad lending practice*, she thought. Hilltop had obtained approval up the chain to put the bank group together, and obviously, the Witherman loans were large. Perhaps First Commercial wasn't comfortable with owning more of the loans. It wouldn't matter until the loans defaulted. But as a rule Milnes always wanted to be in control of the bank group and the collection process. With less than 50% of the loans, she could see that might be a problem in the future.

Popular as loan syndications might be, Milnes didn't like the bank group context. She was a lone ranger in the special assets world. She neither appreciated the nuances of seeking the syndicate banks' approvals with politically correct communications nor did she practice the art of consistently obtaining permission from the syndicate banks before she acted; her style was to assume the syndicate banks were on board. Better to seek forgiveness than waste time with approvals, was her approach. Milnes didn't seek input from anyone about anything. She exuded that she knew what she was doing, and, to her credit, she had proven over the years that she did.

The five other syndicate banks knew each other well. None of the syndicate banks, however, had worked with Milnes before. They listened to Milnes explain that her strategy was an exit plan to get Witherman to find other lenders to take over the loans – get the borrower to move the loans to other banks and pay off First Commercial and the syndicate banks in the process. Moving the loans, of course, would be more than acceptable, but none of the syndicate banks were so sure it was feasible for Witherman to do so. In the bank group meetings, Milnes could feel the tension in the air as she explained her strategy and they seemed interested in exploring a more conciliatory tone with Witherman.

If Milnes cared about the tension between the syndicate banks and First Commercial, she didn't let on. She viewed the syndicate banks, to the extent they disagreed with her, as an annoyance to ignore. Milnes considered the strategy set; the syndicate banks considered the matter still open for discussion. That could be a problem, but she didn't dwell on it. She was Stacy Milnes, and the syndicate banks would know that, fall in line, and follow her lead. They would have no other option, or so she thought. For their part, the syndicate banks were not at all interested in uttering a pledge of allegiance that in Stacy Milnes, they put their trust. So, while Milnes appeared to plow forward on the loans without approval from or consideration of the views of syndicate banks, the syndicate banks each decided to take a wait and see attitude.

§

Milnes' next task – hire a law firm to represent the banks in dealing with Witherman. She knew Witherman would lawyer up and wondered who he would turn to for the help she knew he was going to need. She had many attorneys from which to choose, and, like Mr. Phelps at the beginning of each *Mission Impossible* episode, she mentally went through her dossier of possible hires for the team. She would need to hire more of a litigator than a pure bankruptcy attorney, and someone she could pressure into doing her bidding. She settled on Dennis Sample, with whom she had worked before. Dennis not only had the distinction of being good in court but in other matters he had handled for the bank, he had shown a willingness to accept her vision of the collection process without a great deal of proselytizing or hand-wringing. *Just do what I say*, was the relationship she wanted with her attorney on the Witherman files. Sample had proven to have a subservient, weak personality, which was exactly what Milnes wanted. *Sample would fit the bill nicely*, she thought.

She wondered, *what would the Witherman approach be in response to the pressure on him to move the loan?* Because she certainly did not genuinely expect Witherman to stroke a $30 million check to the banks. In this day and age, what experienced real estate developer would do so?

CHAPTER 6

Friday, August 31, 2018

PROMPTLY AT 1:30 P.M., 3J and Pascale entered Conference Room 27A, where Quincy Witherman sat with his chief financial officer, Ronnie Lindsay. The "A"-designated conference rooms, one on each floor that Greene Madison occupied, were the large power conference rooms, with high ceilings and ornate décor. Attorneys typically used the room to try to impress prospective or new clients, execute closing documents in large deals, or intimidate deposition witnesses in litigation matters. The rooms made one feel that the law indeed resided in and permeated the space occupied by Greene Madison and that the firm handled important, weighty matters every day.

3J greeted her new client. "Quincy, meet my partner, Bill Pascale." Pascale and Quincy shook hands, and Quincy's appearance immediately struck Pascale. At their O'Brien's meeting the other night, Pascale failed to ask 3J what Quincy looked like. Now he knew.

The younger man looked under fifty years old, about five feet eleven inches tall, maybe one hundred and seventy pounds, fit and lean. He had brown curly hair and piercing eyes. But they were two different colors: one icy blue and one light brown. Pascale thought back to his happy hour with 3J and how she omitted mentioning anything about Quincy's eyes. Pascale tried hard not to directly inspect Quincy's eyes, but they were arresting; his gaze lingered too long, and before he could look away, Pascale felt flustered.

"Heterochromia."

"Excuse me?" Pascale replied to Quincy's one-word statement with a touch of remorse. He knew Quincy had caught him staring.

"Heterochromia Iridis. Complete heterochromia. The fancy words science assigned to describe when a person has two completely different colored irises — no big deal. Native American tribes called them ghost eyes — they believed that a person with ghost eyes could see into both Heaven and Earth. Not sure I have ever managed to see past Mother Earth. I usually just tell people what they're looking at, so they don't feel self-conscious as they look. Some people can't make eye contact, and others lock their gaze on my eyes. Not that they ogle. They just look, not at me, but my irises. In my experience, it can be a distraction, and it can interfere with their ability to focus on whatever I'm saying. Either way, sometimes it's all people see, at least for a while when they first meet me. So, every once in a while, I break the ice. Heterochromia."

Ice broken, Pascale noted to himself, hoping the diversion wouldn't adversely affect the attorney-client relationship. 3J smiled to herself. At O'Brien's, 3J intentionally failed to mention to Pascale that Quincy's eyes were two different colors. She privately enjoyed watching the always-in-control Pascale get momentarily flustered and then recover.

Quincy barely paused for a breath, pivoted to the matters at hand, and said to both 3J and Pascale, "Ronnie has put almost all of the financial and corporate information you requested on a server for you to download. I think you'll find it all quite comprehensive, and if you have any questions, you'll have full access to Ronnie. Just keep me in the loop. Ronnie will also get you the retainer you requested by wire transfer so you have the money before we meet with the ever-animated Stacy Milnes and her merry group of banker capitalists."

"I hope the bank meeting will be productive, but we'll be ready to file the bankruptcy papers if we can't make progress toward an agreement at the meeting," 3J said. "We have two trusted associates who can work with Ronnie to put together all of the bankruptcy papers in the required format for your review and execution. Quincy, any questions about the bankruptcy overview memo we sent you?"

"Not now," Quincy said. "I'm sure I may as we get into the cases."

Pascale took the floor. "To review the structure to make sure we have it correct, Quincy: You own 100% of a holding company, which owns 100% each of the four property entities. Looks like the holding company use to be a Pennsylvania entity but when you moved here, you reconstituted it as a Missouri entity.

"The holding company guaranteed 100% of each property entity's debts, and you guaranteed 10% of the holding company's debts. You also personally own Witherman Management Co. LLC, which manages each of the properties, is paid a management fee of 6% of the entities' gross rents each month. Management Co. collects the rents, pays the bills, and retains for its account the management fee. You're paid from the management company each month. Your bank group has as collateral for the loans, mortgages, or deeds of trust, on each building to secure that building company's loan. To secure the holding company's guarantee, the bank group has a security interest in the holding company's ownership interest in each building company, and to secure your guarantee, the bank group has a security interest in your ownership interest in the holding company."

Quincy and Ronnie followed carefully, and when Pascale finished, Quincy simply said: "Correct."

"Anything we missed, or anything that you want to flesh out?" 3J asked.

"No." Quincy could be a man of few words, after all. Pascale half-jokingly always warned 3J to watch out for the debtors who gave short, efficient answers. He thought debtors should be nervous and as a result, talkative.

"Quincy, the loan documents automatically adjusted the loan-to-value ratio from 75% to 70% a couple of months ago," 3J noted.

"Correct," Quincy agreed.

"Other than that provision and the substantial default rate of interest, we didn't identify anything else noteworthy in the documents," 3J concluded.

Next, they moved on to the topic of asset valuation. "Quincy, how comfortable do you feel with the bank's recent valuations, which, along with the 70% reset, triggered the demand for a $30 million cash payment?" Pascale inquired.

"Unfortunately, my team and I believe the banks got the valuation mostly right. A couple of years ago, the office building market dipped in each building's city to different degrees. We believe it's a temporary supply and demand situation; too much square feet of office building rental property came online, and the market needed time to absorb the new space. The glut of available space drove down the rental rates somewhat. With rates down, values had a corresponding dip. It's nothing new in the industry, and we don't think it's long term; it's just part of the natural ebb and flow that's always been the commercial real estate market in America since the Revolutionary War days.

"In past slumps, and indeed during most of most recent dip, First Commercial and other of our prior lenders noted a potential drop in valuations but refrained from making a cash call. Now that I've met Milnes, my feeling is that she's using this as an opportunity to grab a significant amount of cash. If I don't pay, she'll call a default and increase the interest rate five percentage points under the loan documents as she implements the default rate of interest. We couldn't handle the increased payments resulting from such a significantly higher interest rate."

3J and Pascale nodded their understanding as Quincy expounded on his view and the predicament. Some special assets groups had a reputation of "working with" a borrower to find something that would work during a finite time period. Milnes didn't have a reputation of working with anyone at all, let alone a bank customer assigned to her group.

"Do you work with an appraiser you trust?" 3J asked.

"We do – George Herndon. He offices in the Livestock Exchange Building in the West Bottoms area. He's solid. If you haven't worked with him before, you'll like the experience."

"We've worked with him before, and he's very good on the witness stand. We'll reach out to him after this meeting. Quincy, do you believe the value of each of the properties has now stabilized, or do the values continue to slide?"

"Stabilized, and probably on the cusp of appreciating again," Quincy responded. "I believe George agrees, but make sure to ask him for his view when you reach out."

"Will do," 3J assured him.

Quincy continued, "The interest rate increase in the loan documents requires a fifteen-day written notice before the banks can implement it, and we've not yet received that notice."

"How would you describe the quality of the tenant population in your buildings?" 3J asked.

"Top notch. The buildings are all A-plus properties in or on the edge of viable downtowns, and the rent per square foot we get for our space is at the highest end of the market rent for each city. That high rental rate pretty much excludes tenants with their own financial and cash flow issues. As a result, the tenant default rates we experience are minuscule. We're lucky that way. No, the problems here are market forces beyond our control and the reset provision in the loan documents. The market forces will self-adjust just as suddenly as the value slippage occurred, but we can't fix the loan documents. We're stuck with the reset."

Ronnie nodded in agreement as Quincy gave his high-level analysis of the situation. 3J watched Quincy as he spoke and used his explanations as an opportunity to assess how he would play on the witness stand in bankruptcy court. She quickly reached the conclusion that Quincy Witherman would play very well. He was mostly soft-spoken, yet commanded the room and the topic when he spoke. He was completely comfortable with the facts and seemed to be able to master the art of testifying in court. He was disciplined and didn't appear to have the habit of talking too much. He didn't give long answers, and answered just the question asked. *Perfect for the courtroom.*

"I think we should let the bank group know that we're ready to file for bankruptcy relief for the four building entities, the holding company, the management company, and for you personally," 3J said. "We'll propose a term sheet setting forth the conditions under which we would forego bankruptcy filings. Pascale?"

"Correct. Here's the draft term sheet we put together with the wish list of what we'd like to see," Pascale explained as he handed Quincy the draft term sheet. "Frankly, it's not all that much different than what will happen if we file. Hopefully, the banks will recognize that and not force a bankruptcy filing. The term sheet addresses these points. Interest payments, but not at the default rate of interest. A smaller principal payment to match what you can afford and not jeopardize the buildings' operations. An extension of the maturity date of the loans. And an openness to enhanced reporting requirements. Look over the term sheet when you get back to your office and give us your thoughts."

"Quincy, do your companies, or do you, have your depositary bank accounts at First Commercial or any of the other banks in the bank group?" 3J asked.

"No. We bank at Kansas City Federal Bank & Trust. We've gotten good service from KC Federal, and when we moved our loans to First Commercial, I didn't want to move any of our operating accounts. It would have been a big hassle. I spoke with my prior loan officer at First Commercial, Hilltop, and he agreed he wouldn't require us to move the accounts. They've remained at KC Federal at all times since."

3J took some notes and said "good" as she wrote. "We don't want the banks to be able to freeze your accounts or even take the money in the accounts," she explained as she finished writing on her pad and looked up. "Not to change the subject, but why did you decide to hire Greene Madison as bankruptcy counsel?"

"I didn't. I don't hire law firms. I hire lawyers. I hired you." No darting eyes; no booming voice. Just direct. 3J liked that about him.

"Ok, then, why me?" 3J probed.

"You know real estate. I don't want a neophyte attorney who I'd have to train in the ins and outs of commercial real estate in a crash course that would amount to on-the-job training. And I'd have to pay that lawyer while I provided the training. You also know Milnes and can stand up to her and her bank." Quincy didn't see any reason to tell her he was comfortable with 3J and her style. That might come later, but it was too early for that kind of thing. "That's about it."

"Ok. I hear you. Thanks for putting your trust in us. Do you have any other questions?"

"Yes. Tell me about the judge that will likely preside over the cases."

3J responded, "There are three judges, any one of whom might handle our case. The system assigns cases mostly randomly to the judges. Luckily for us, they're all good, fair-minded, usually patient, and, at least in the beginning months of the cases, any of them will have a predisposition to side with the debtors on most matters related to money and cash flow. Judge Robertson is the newest. He hasn't presided over any significant commercial cases yet. But word on the street is that he's now gained experience on the bench and will begin taking complex commercial Chapter 11 assignments. So, we might get him. That would be an interesting assignment for us; my sense is that he'd be a good fit. He did debtors work when he was in private practice, and my best guess is that he wouldn't be inclined to make any controversial rulings against us that would impede our reorganization efforts. But it's truly tough to predict which of the three will get these cases."

"No way for us to affect the judicial assignment?" Quincy asked.

"No way," 3J confirmed as she nodded her head.

"Understood," said Quincy. "Thanks. Just thought I should ask."

Pascale inquired, "Quincy, have you testified in court before?"

"Sure."

"In business matters?"

"Pretty much exclusively in business matters. I'm in real estate development. At times, I've wondered if I was in the courtroom business and just built buildings on the side; real estate can be a full-contact sport of sorts. Lawyers are a necessity, and effective courtroom appearances are a tool of the trade, so to speak." Quincy paused to see if the lawyers followed his explanation and then added, "I'm not bothered by the need to testify."

"Good," Pascale said. "The bankruptcy court is a trial court. While it sometimes has the reputation of doing things without evidence or live testimony, we think there will likely be some evidentiary hearings in these cases. The banks may very well be contentious, and if they are, I can safely predict that you'll have to testify and spend some quality time with us preparing. Herndon as well."

"Understood, and not a problem. Mention that to George, please. I can give you as much time as you'll need. Anything else?" Quincy asked.

"No, I think that's all for now. Much more to come," 3J declared. "Oh wait, one more thing. Along with the papers we'll need to file to start the bankruptcy cases, we'll have to file an affidavit you'll sign in support of the things we'll ask the Judge to approve as the cases begin. It's a good chance to make an initial favorable impression with the Judge. You know, to get our story out there. We'll get you a copy for you to review and edit. But just like the bankruptcy schedules and statements of affairs, the affidavit is under oath, so we always want to make sure it's all absolutely correct and you're comfortable in signing it."

"Ok. Understood. I'll read it carefully and get you any comments or edits I may have."

They all stood as the meeting wound up, and Quincy said, "Thanks to both of you for the meeting. Lots of work we all have to get to if we're going the bankruptcy route. So, let's get ready to file and then meet with the banks. I don't have high hopes for the bank meeting, but you never know."

3J responded, "Agreed. We all have work to do, so let's get to it."

CHAPTER 7

The Debtor recalls Friday, August 31, 2018

WHEN OUR MEETING WITH the bankruptcy team at Greene Madison ended, I headed home, telling Ronnie that she knew how to get ahold of me if she needed me. I didn't often go home early, but the bankruptcy matters were coming to a head quickly, and I needed to think through one more time my commitment to my private plan – that undisclosed blueprint I had inherited from my ancestors that I had stuck with and continued for many years in the expectation that, at some point, a day like the impending bankruptcy day might be upon me. I needed to test one more time if I was willing to continue to lie. I thought I knew the answer … but one more run-through couldn't hurt.

I threw *Chet Baker Sings* on the turntable, resolved not to worry about whether Chet was a singer who played trumpet or a trumpet player who sang. I just knew that whether he was singing or blowing, Chet would help me sort through my analysis, as he always did. Music just helped me think and process – it gave me focus and calm.

The blueprint had started simply enough after Gunn's death. It must have been horrific for Gunn's son, Gunn Witherman, Jr., to watch his father die in the prison forced upon him by his bankers, after losing everything to a land investor con artist.

Then Gunnie Jr. got involved in the real estate business, in particular a new land fraud scheme dubbed infamously as the Yazoo Land Fraud, named after the Yazoo River in Georgia. The complicated, government-sponsored swindle involved the transfer of tens of millions of acres of land to innocent purchasers who unwittingly agreed that they would make no claims if the land had defective title ... and it did. When the Yazoo dust settled, each investor had lost their money and owned no land.

Ultimately, after years of wrangling, the Federal Government set up a significant reparation fund for swindled purchasers. Gunnie received $400,000 from that fund in 1816, a fortune in those days, the equivalent of more than $7 million in 2018 dollars. It was as if God looked at the Witherman ledger and determined that the only way to right the wrong Gunn suffered was to take care of Gunn's son, just as Gunnie started to wonder if the American real estate trade cursed every Witherman.

Gunnie took his reparations and turned those funds into yet more gold. At the end of his life, Gunnie Witherman directed the establishment of a trust using Swiss bank accounts to pass the wealth to the Witherman generations that followed. Some Withermans cashed out their inheritance and spent it on one venture or another. Others just let the wealth sit and grow. My particular Witherman ancestral line let it grow: My share was $17 million when my parents died. As it turns out, generations of Withermans had failed to report the Swiss accounts: Far be it from me to change that family tradition.

The Swiss had perfected the art of bank secrecy and discretion. As a result, Switzerland became a legendary haven for all walks of life to place assets out of the purview and reach of the taxman and creditors, and the occasional lawman and angry spouse, and, early in Swiss history, the Withermans were right there to help the Swiss grow their reputation. Because the Witherman clan had used the Swiss bank account process almost since its inception, there was no obvious trail to show the assets had been handed down from generation to generation unless one went all the way back to Gunnie. Even then, it would be nearly impossible to trace assets from the early 1800s. Therefore, unlike others trying to hide assets in Swiss banks, I had no paper or electronic trail for a suspicious creditor to follow into the land of the Swiss confederation. The assets would remain hidden.

But I did more than hide the secret assets – you could say that I enhanced them.

Every time I sold a building, in each transaction, the proceeds of the sale paid off my existing lender. That lender, happy to receive payment in full, did nothing to monitor the use of the proceeds above and beyond their own remuneration. I, however, did. In each such transaction, and there were many over the last twenty years, the closing statement had one line item for a disbursement to a company I formed named The Yazzoo Finance, LLC, a Bermuda limited liability company. A subtle nod to Gunnie. My Yazzoo was a shell company that invoiced my management company for consultations performed in the ordinary course of business, and the escrow agent paid the Yazzoo invoice at closing. Yazzoo deposited the proceeds directly into the Swiss account or used the proceeds to purchase cryptocurrency on the dark web where crypto wallets existed that didn't comply with normal domestic record-keeping requirements, and in effect acted as an anonymous mechanism to hide crypto assets. Banks were paid in full at closing so none of them raised an eye-brow that Yazzoo received a fee.

I wouldn't label this multi-pronged process "money laundering" because it wasn't illegal money. All of the money and crypto were legitimate. I just hid what was mine and then failed to disclose the money or the process. I never listed my Swiss bank account or my crypto tokens on any financial report I provided to my various lenders. Of course, I never shared the process with the Internal Revenue Service or state taxing authority, and I never told anyone the story of the Witherman secret set-asides in Switzerland either. Well – almost no one.

So by the time of the Greene Madison meeting, the balance in the Swiss account was something like $25 million. The crypto value depended on the significant ups and downs of the market, but was worth as much as $3 million. I hid all of this away for a rainy day, and now, I could see the storm clouds hovering high above and the potential for significant rain coming soon.

I never allowed myself to believe that what I did was wrong, any more than Gunn's banks thought it was wrong to jail him for non-payment. I knew I couldn't claim I was Robin Hood robbing the rich to pay the poor; I didn't rob anyone to get the money, and I had no intention of giving it away, either. But Robin Hood decided for himself what was right and fair, and then acted on it. I liked to think that I had decided what was right and fair and then acted on it, as Withermans had done for centuries. So, in that sense, I felt a little like Robin Hood … or at least I liked to think so.

That evening, after reviewing my assets following the meeting with 3J, I had the same thoughts I always had. Stay the course. Continue to hide the assets. Continue to lie about the plan.

"Catch me if you can," my business card would say in my dream world, and no one had yet. And now that I had met Stacy Milnes, I was confident the banks wouldn't either.

INTERLUDE

Thursday, November 8, 1798

To Gunnie Witherman

My dearest son,

Here I sit, destitute. Freedom-less, hopeless, helpless, and soon, I fear, lifeless. No one genuinely knows despair until they find themselves in this hellhole called Prune Street Prison. I know the man who designed this place. He is a prominent architect here in Philadelphia, and I used to call him my friend … before my incarceration. My friend, whose gaol design ensures the loss of my freedom with such efficiency and permanence. Damn you! May you manage your money more carefully than I did, and may you never be a resident of this evil structure you created.

They call this place a gaol. Did you know, my son, gaol comes from an old, northern French word, gaole, which in turn comes from caveola, a diminutive form of the Latin term cavea, which means cage? But it is not a cage. No, it is a funeral home just waiting for deaths. The design of the cells and corridors of this God-forsaken place prevents prisoners from communicating with each other. I use the word "prisoners" with disdain. I committed no larceny. I committed no murder. I am a prisoner because I am penniless – no other reason. I am penniless because another soul-less person bilked me out of all of my wealth.

The windows here are high up, and my cell has what I estimate to be a nine-foot-high ceiling. My single window – I use that term generously – is grated and louvered and as a result, I cannot look onto the street. I can perceive neither Heaven nor Earth, even as I now reside in Hell, and the walls are so thick that I hear no sounds emanating from my fellow prisoners.

I have a ratty mattress, a leaky water tap that delivers brownish water to me sometimes, and a privy pipe. And I have this diary, a pen, and some ink that a somewhat sympathetic guard snuck in for me. This diary is my sole outlet for communication. When I die, I know not what will happen to this record I have created, but I have made it clear to the guards that I want you, my son, to have it.

The guards permit no discussion among the prisoners. The guards permit no singing or laughing, in the unlikely event that anyone in here had any inclination to sing or laugh. I make little eye contact with other humans and thereby share none of my inner feelings and thoughts – the only thing shared by fellow prisoners is disease, which begets a trip to someone who calls himself a doctor. He says he is a man of science and medicine. I see no science in him. I doubt that his forte is biology; he appears to have a specialty only in culling prisoners from the ranks. He returns far fewer prisoners to the prison population than the number who go to see him for a cure. He is no healer. He thins out prisoners from the rolls of the living and thereby feeds Heaven and Hell with new residents.

Stale bread and cold potatoes keep me barely alive, if you could bring yourself somehow to describe my existence as a state of living. Mush. Foul, cold mush, and nothing more.

Supposedly, there are women in this prison, but the guards keep the men and women separated. My clothes are not my own. They are made here in prison – linen and wool shirts and trousers as coarse as sandpaper, perhaps to provide a chafe to my daily existence to remind me of how soft and refined and dignified life used to be.

The guards try to promote that they preach morality and religious improvement. But neither morality nor religion is cause for my incarceration, and neither morality nor religion will occasion my release. No, they have nothing to teach me, and I have nothing to learn from them.

My home is now a penitentiary. The Quakers expect me to seek salvation through penitence, self-examination, or any other means. But my only possible salvation would be a payment to my banks that I cannot make, and as a result, I live out my days with no salvation and with the day-to-day prospect of death close-at-hand. I will die because some bank let me die, watched me die, caused me to die. I am likewise confident that my path to the afterlife will cause no bank to seek salvation through any means whatsoever.

Some say that imprisonment in a debtors' prison, instead of the death penalty for failing to pay, is a sign of society's progress, and civility. Still I am convinced beyond all doubt that confinement will shortly lead to my death, so I fail to see the progress or the civility in this type of incarceration.

Is this nothing more than my grievances? I think not. This is my gospel – facts as cold and hard as the Prune Street Gaol floors and walls where I will live out the abbreviated remainder of my life.

I record all of this for you, my son, and your offspring, so they will forever know that Gunnther Witherman committed only one true indiscretion in his life – that of indigence. Indigence is a crime in the great Commonwealth of Pennsylvania, county and city of Philadelphia. The city of brotherly love … unless one owes a debt. No love from any brother, then.

Imagine – a crime for nothing more than the status of having nothing. I fought for freedom from the King. We won. I generously helped those in need. I prayed each Sunday. I lived outside of Center City Philadelphia in a wondrous house and was a person of influence. Important people sought me out for my guidance, my opinion, my solace, my wisdom, my instincts, and when I had it, my money. But all of that came to an end when my money disappeared because of worthless scurrilous hucksters. Then I became a prisoner in my house, where the law prevented my creditors from serving me with a writ of incarceration. But they watched with their beady little eyes from afar. And, when I left my house and saddled my horse, process servers descended upon me and handed me the dreaded writ of incarceration, and the authorities took me against my will to Prune Street.

This course of events must have been satisfying to my creditors. Perhaps the more vindictive among them found contentment, justice, and even delight at my freedom loss. But none of these proceedings could possibly generate a single penny toward repayment of the debts I owe. My incarceration will in no way rehabilitate me because I lack any mechanism to repay my debts, the sole method of rehabilitation in this Gaol.

My only hope would be to generate money, an impossibility from the confines of Prune Street. So I have no hope as long as I rot in this cell!

The only question is, which will rot faster – my small mattress or me? I fear I know the answer to that question all too well. But perhaps I shall not rot my way to the afterlife at all. It is almost winter here now, and a wave of yellow fever now passes silently from prisoner to prisoner. And I fear my passage out of this gaol will be the progression from yellow skin and eyes to pain, to fever, to delirium, and to an ultimate resting place in a pauper's cemetery with no headstone even to mark

FRESH START | 57

my stay on this Earth. Such a terrible end will, frankly, come as a relief.

My Quaker friends have the inner light so fundamental to their faith, but the only light my creditors have is the light from the lantern necessary to craft the writ of my incarceration. No light shines inside of these evil beings. No true light shines inside the confines of this penitentiary. There is no presence of the Lord in the hearts of my creditors, just the inner, dark faculty to calculate the amount I owe and the interest that accrues on that debt for every moment I breathe. Damn them!

Gunnther, I am sorry. I am sorry for bringing such inevitable shame on you and the family name. I am sorry we will not see each other again. I am sorry I am not there for you.

I love you, my son.

CHAPTER 8

Tuesday, September 4, 2018

BACK IN HER OFFICE, 3J collected her thoughts, made a few notes, and then called Stacy Milnes. She had Milnes' direct dial number from the last deal they had together, though "had together" was completely the wrong way of describing their previous go-around. The phrase sounds so chummy, as if they were partners in a project working toward a common goal. No, there was no common goal and nothing friendly about the last encounter. Perhaps it would be more accurate to describe the last deal merely as "when their paths last crossed." In that deal, while the bank and the Debtor were fighting in and out of court, 3J's client, a private airport shuttle service that operated a fleet of high-end vehicles, suddenly lost its license to operate because of a lack of proper safety protocols. 3J could never prove how her client lost the license, but she had always privately wondered if Milnes had something to do with it.

Bankruptcy couldn't save her client from the sudden shutdown and a complete loss of revenue. "Bankruptcy cain't help if you ain't got no cash and no prospects for cash," Pascale said to 3J to cheer her up using his best Wild-West-Marshal-Earp-of-Dodge-City impression. Milnes won that one – if you could call it a win – and the bank wound up with a fleet of used, albeit fancy, vehicles to sell to recoup whatever it

could. 3J had wondered ever since just what the extent of the
bank's recovery was and how much of a financial bath the
bank ended up taking as it liquidated used airport limousines
to pay down the debt.

3J dialed the 314 St. Louis area code exchange, and Milnes
picked up on the second ring.

"Stacy Milnes," she stated in monotone cadence to identify
herself, sounding like a distant recording of someone bothered
that the phone call had interrupted her train of thought. Her
tone was one of annoyance as if to say, "this better be good."

"Stacy. This is Josephina Jones. Quincy Witherman has
engaged us to represent his companies and him – I think you
met him recently. We want to set up a meeting with you and
your bank group as soon as possible. Can we make that work?"

No "hello." No "how are you doing?" No reason for it with
Milnes, who would have undoubtedly responded with something like, "Since when did you get so fucking friendly?" From
past encounters, 3J knew well that one of Milnes' favorite
modifiers was "fuck," whether used as a verb, adverb, or
adjective.

Milnes was quiet for a moment and then said, "Give me a
couple of days, and my assistant will set something up for us
to meet."

"Has the bank engaged an attorney for this file?"

Milnes replied, "We'll be hiring Dennis Sample, like on the
last dance you and I had together."

Ah, there's the Stacy Milnes we all know and love, thought 3J, as
she cringed at the very notion of an actual dance with Milnes
in which they stood uncomfortably close to each other as the
music played. 3J almost shuddered. It wasn't a mental image
she wished to dwell on. "Very well. I'll reach out to Dennis
tomorrow, and maybe we can all use his firm's office for the
meeting."

Milnes said, "Fine," and before 3J could end the call with the traditional "goodbye," the line went dead. Milnes was a woman of few words, and when she had used them all up, she would terminate the communication.

3J chuckled as she put the desk phone back in its cradle. *Vintage Milnes*, she thought. She would've been disappointed if the call had gone any other way.

§

Pascale went back to his office after the meeting with Quincy and Ronnie ended and called George Herndon. Herndon took his call straightaway, and after the initial pleasantries, Pascale explained that Quincy Witherman had engaged Greene Madison to represent the Witherman companies. "George, when was the last time you did a formal appraisal of the four buildings owned by Quincy Witherman's companies?"

"Let's see. 'Bout a month ago, so my reports are all current." George spoke with no regional accent, like so many Midwesterners.

"How long have you been appraising the properties?"

"For at least four years now."

"Can you email over the current appraisals?"

"Sure thing."

"In the latest appraisals, did you conclude any loss in value year over year?"

"Not year over year. The buildings suffered a small value loss, but it happened maybe two years ago, and certainly after the banks made the four loans. In my opinion, it was a loss due to an economic downturn we all lived through, but as the economy comes back, as it's doing now, so will the value. These are superb properties."

"Do you foresee any further erosion in the values?"

"I just really don't. In fact, I predict the exact opposite. I see the value of these properties appreciating in the near term."

"What's your prediction based on?"

"Seems to me that the slight downturn was due to some very isolated market adjustments – price of oil decline that has now recovered; tick up in the Fed's rate of interest, which the market has now absorbed; slight increase in unemployment; overabundance of office space and the resulting temporary softening demand for office space, which has now reversed. Nothing systemic or long-lasting and nothing in the relevant real estate markets themselves."

Pascale took notes and then said to George, "Very well. Thank you. That's all I have for you for now. George, I can't share with you where this is heading just yet but …"

George interrupted him and said, trying not to chuckle, "Oh, not to worry, counselor. I can pretty much guess. No need to fill in the blanks for me."

Pascale smiled to himself. "Good enough, George. Thanks for your time and the reports. I'll be in touch."

After the call, Pascale rang up 3J and reported his conversation with Herndon. 3J listened and then said, "That's good news. We want a stable value when we file. No further erosion of value is music to my ears. Potentially appreciating property is too much for even me to ask for. We don't see that all too often in this line of work, do we? I'm trying to get a meeting set up with First Commercial and the syndicate banks, and then we're off and running."

"Agreed. It should be an interesting one."

§

Pascale received an email from George Herndon with the appraisal reports attached shortly after his call ended. Herndon was an MAI appraiser, the highest designation a commercial appraiser could achieve in the United States, and Pascale expected a thorough and thoughtful analysis by Herndon in the reports. He wasn't disappointed.

Pascale went through the appraisals carefully and took some notes as he did. Pretty standard valuation process, using generally accepted methods – income approach, replacement cost, and comparable sales. Pascale focused on Herndon's income approach, which determined the actual and projected income from the rent generated by each of the buildings. Herndon then applied a discount rate to that stream of income to determine the current value of the properties. The higher the discount rate, the lower the value. A higher discount rate reflected what the appraiser might perceive as a riskier investment. Here, when the economy faltered, Herndon used a slightly higher discount rate to reflect the market uncertainty and wrote about that decision in the body of the appraisal.

Of interest to Pascale, the loss of value in the buildings was not due to the loss of tenants, which would have yielded less rental income. Indeed, the report noted that the dip in rental rates hadn't occurred in the Witherman buildings because of the high instance of long-term leases and high occupancy rates. Instead, as Herndon had alluded to in the phone call, he attributed the loss entirely to non-Witherman building economic factors, which resulted in Herndon's conservative decision to apply a higher discount rate than he had in previous appraisals.

Pascale looked up from his desk, where he was deep in his thoughts about the loss of value, to discover 3J leaning on his doorjamb with a cup of her signature Earl Grey tea in her hand. He motioned her to come in. After removing a pile of papers from her favorite chair in his perpetually messy office, 3J deposited herself in the cushy chair.

Pascale said, "I spoke with the appraiser and these are his current appraisals. Excellent reports and pretty plain vanilla stuff." He explained the higher discount rate, and she nodded in agreement as he talked. Pascale then said, "This will be an interesting issue once we're in front of the Bankruptcy Judge. We'll ask for permission to use cash to continue to pay the bills. When the banks object, we'll be able to show that not only is the value of each property stable, but they are showing signs of an increase in value as these other economic hiccups resolve and stabilize. As they do, the appraiser will consider moving back to a slightly lower discount rate in the next round of appraisals. The Judge wouldn't normally preside over a real estate bankruptcy case where the collateral is likely to go up in value. Agreed?"

"Agreed. We've both heard rumors that Judge Robertson will start taking commercial Chapter 11 cases. If we get Judge Robertson, how do you think he'll react?"

Pascale responded, "Gazing into my trusty crystal ball … I think he'll buy our argument that the use of cash is safe because the values are steady, if not rising. We may even get away with not paying the banks for a while to ratchet up the pressure on the banks to cut a deal with us."

"Sounds good. Do you have time to oversee one of the associates who can write the motion to use the cash that we'll file on the first day and suggest no payments to the bank for the first month or two until we stabilize in bankruptcy?"

"Sure thing. Did you talk to Milnes?"

"Yep. Fun times. Short, and whatever her version of sweet might be."

"Are we meeting?"

"Yep. Her assistant will call me back with the date and time."

"Any hints from Milnes as to her thinking?"

"Negative. She was her usual thoughtless," 3J joked with a little smile. "Look, Milnes is smart. Since I called, she knows we're preparing to file bankruptcy papers. I can't believe she thinks things will go well for the banks in a bankruptcy court. She said she'd hire Dennis Sample to represent the banks."

"Sample? That should be fine. I didn't find him offensive in the last case we had with him," Pascale said.

"Agreed," 3J concurred.

"Milnes aside, we know what we need to do. So, we just press forward and implement?" Pascale said.

"Roger that," 3J agreed.

"3J, I have a hunch we're going to get Judge Robertson as our judge if we file," Pascale revealed.

"How do you figure?"

"I was over at the courthouse today on another matter, and I overheard one of the clerks saying that Judge Robertson would likely get the next big case filed."

"Interesting. We'll just have to see how that shakes out, I guess," 3J replied.

§

Daniel Robertson: *Hear ye, Hear ye, the Honorable Judge Daniel Robertson, United States Bankruptcy Judge for the Western District of Missouri presiding,* to attorneys appearing in his courtroom. Judge Robertson was one of the three bankruptcy judges, appointed by the Federal appeals courts to a fourteen-year term, in the Western District of Missouri where Kansas City sits.

Not particularly tall; not particularly young (at least not anymore), but not old yet. Not particularly profound (at least not during his time as a private practice attorney), but insightful enough. Not particularly commanding, but respected enough. He more than lived up to his reputation as a very hard worker, a savvy, effective lawyer, and thoughtful, very thoughtful. That was Daniel Robertson.

He lacked any particular life plan as he entered college, and shortly before his scheduled exit from college, that hadn't changed much. He went to law school because that was all he could think of to do during his senior year in college. Law school was fine, but over his career, he realized that he had felt no particular passion for it. He needed a job when he finished law school, so he joined a private law firm practice in Kansas City. That was also fine, but as time went on, he came to believe that he may never have had a passion for private practice either, or, if he did, he lost it long ago. When he applied for the open bankruptcy judge slot, he had quiet hopes that an appointment to the bench would reinvigorate his interest, if not his passion, for the law.

Robertson was pretty sure the circuit court selected him to sit on the bench because of the things he was not. He was not controversial. He was not flashy. He lacked skeletons in his closet. He was not a heavy drinker. He was neither a Democrat nor a Republican. He was not a malcontent. He was not a gossiper. He traded in no black market scuttlebutt. He was not loud. He was not famous. And … he was not hard to like.

Neither the sitting bankruptcy judges nor the court of appeals had any interest in filling the open slot with even the potential for controversy. Judges' rulings might very well be news, but judges themselves should not be: Hence, Daniel Robertson. A married white male, of average height and build, brown eyes and thinning brown hair, well-known to the other bankruptcy judges on the bench and to the court of appeals judges, with a respectable education and career, who lived with his statistically average wife and two kids in an old English Tudor house in Kansas City's Romanelli Gardens neighborhood on a side street just off the fabled winding, tree and fountainlined Ward Parkway.

Who, most importantly, had no sharp edges and no pointy elbows. The perfect jurist, or so he strived to be.

In his brief time on the bench, he had received high marks from the lawyers who came before him, but he had yet to preside over a major commercial bankruptcy case. While the assignment of cases to the three judges was "random," that randomness translated to the assignment of cases to a judge who had experience handling cases of that type. At first, for Robertson that meant consumer cases and smaller commercial matters so, as one of the judges explained to him, "he could get his chops on the bench," like a lead guitar player building his experience by playing small gigs each night. At the same time, he could pay his dues by taking the less desirable cases filed in Kansas City. Robertson's docket of experience-building cases freed up the other judges to handle the more complex matters. But the Chief Judge recently told Robertson that his name would now be thrown into the mix for all cases, and he would get the next complex commercial case filed, so he knew his time had come for a big case in which he could immerse himself. Robertson looked forward to the opportunity.

He sat at his gleaming, mahogany wood desk in his chambers on the sixth floor of the beautiful Western District courthouse. From his office, he looked out through floor-to-ceiling windows north across the Missouri River, the Mighty Mo, to Kansas City's Northland and beyond as he carried out his routine work. As the Midwestern sun drifted from right to left across his windows, occasionally his thoughts drifted too, and he wondered what that first big case might look like.

Little did the Honorable Judge Daniel Robertson, United States Bankruptcy Judge for the Western District of Missouri, know what was coming his way.

CHAPTER 9

The Debtor recalls Friday, September 7, 2018

I RECEIVED WORD FROM 3J's team that the bankruptcy filing papers were ready for me to sign. I left my apartment and headed to the Greene Madison offices. On the elevator ride up, I noted sickening background music droning on. That wouldn't happen in my buildings. The ride was for transportation to a destination, not for bad renditions of Top Forty hits of days gone by. As soon as the elevator doors finally opened, I escaped into the welcome silence of Greene Madison. I met 3J's paralegal, who had printed out all of the bankruptcy petitions, schedules, and statements of affairs for me to review. The petitions were short, just as 3J predicted, and all of the action was in the schedules and statements of affairs. My schedules and the schedules for each entity listed all assets, debts, and contracts. The schedules also set out my view of the values of each asset and the addresses for the creditors and contracting parties. Using the information provided by Ronnie, the Greene Madison team condensed, categorized, and organized everything into these approved forms.

The statement of affairs asked numerous questions that my team answered, including where we banked, where we kept our records, who we used as our accountants, and any transfers and payments made during specific periods. The real moment of truth would be the information in my personal papers.

I rented an apartment – true.

I owed the bank money – true.

I had assets – true.

But did I list all of my assets? Not quite. And I had no intention of doing so. I was ready to sign.

For many, the decision to tell less than the whole truth may very well be agonizing. For me, it was just part of the plan, and just the way I am. That's my character. I spent no sleepless nights struggling with the legal and moral decision or wrestling with the ethical dilemma of hiding assets.

Yes, it was a federal crime to fail to list all my assets on the schedules – a quick couple of Google searches revealed the criminal laws and all of the horrors that constitute the penalty for not playing the bankruptcy game straight up. Section after section listing of all the potential felonies of concealing assets during a bankruptcy proceeding, making false oaths, filing a fraudulent bankruptcy petition, or any other fraudulent document in a bankruptcy case, or making any false representations; each punishable by fines and up to five years in federal prison.

I had always been eminently careful to leave no trail, and the failure to divulge the hidden assets on the bankruptcy papers seemed to me to be nothing more than a natural extension of what I had already been doing for years. Once I had committed to my plan to hide assets years ago, I had no choice but to remain all-in.

Only one person in the entire world knew of my blueprint, and her credentials for secrecy were impeccable. Michaela Huld: My London trusted financial adviser, confidante, and, yes, my love.

Lastly, I reviewed the affidavit in support of the first-day motions we would file. The affidavit did a nice job explaining the situation, the banks' demand for $30 million, our need to continue to use cash, and the need for a moratorium on payments to the banks for a short period. I liked the storyline. I liked that this would play out before the banks could impose the default rate of interest and more than double our interest payments. That "truth, *the whole truth*, and nothing but the truth" thing was the significant elephant in the room, but when the elephant lumbered around, only I felt the floor shudder. The presence of the elephant that only I could see was a necessary risk to get the monkey that was Milnes and the banks off of my back, to mix my metaphors … without remorse.

In any case, I didn't flinch as I reviewed and then signed the bankruptcy papers under oath, thereby swearing that everything in the papers was true and correct, "so help me God." Kind of an odd phrase; what an unusual reference to God's help. Maybe the phrase should have been, "everything is true and correct, and I affirm I know I am on my own when I say that." I certainly didn't expect help from God, any more than God reached out to help old Gunn.

CHAPTER 10

Monday, September 10, 2018

As promised, on Monday morning, 3J and Pascale spoke to the bank's newly hired attorney, Dennis Sample. Sample was a seasoned attorney whose practice was mostly limited to representing banks.

One of his better clients was First Commercial. 3J often wondered if there was someone she could pay to be a fly on the wall when Sample and Milnes talked privately – he the steady, predictable, even-keeled personality; she the volatile, interpersonal-skills-be-damned powder keg. Did she treat the bank's attorney any differently than how she treated the rest of humanity? A question to ponder the next time 3J got together with the bottle bearing the name of the man who made Irish whiskey famous.

Sample was an interesting selection by the bank. He certainly knew enough of the Bankruptcy Code to call himself a bankruptcy attorney, but he was much more of a litigator than a traditional bankruptcy geek, in 3J's view. He always seemed more comfortable cross-examining witnesses than at the courtroom podium pontificating about different Bankruptcy Code sections. Did it signal some of the moves Milnes might make in the bankruptcy cases? A fight at every turn, even on issues where normally the debtor and creditor would find agreement and common ground? That type of strategy certainly would not sit well with any of the three judges who might preside over the cases. Any bankruptcy judge would expect the parties to bring negotiated agreements to the Court for approval; every judge in the Western District would frown on a party forcing contested hearing after contested hearing, consuming large chunks of court time with numerous testifying witnesses.

Sample was business-like on the call. The lawyers discussed a meeting time and place, and agreed to a morning meeting a couple of days later at Sample's offices in downtown St. Louis.

That gave 3J's team just two days to prepare first-day motions – seeking court authority to maintain the bank accounts, hire counsel, hire the appraiser, and to operate the businesses under the cash budget prepared by Quincy and Ronnie. The timing was good. It was mid-month, so the management company had already received virtually all the rent due from tenants, and had already paid most of the recurring monthly bills.

They had a straightforward plan: meet with the banks and present the proposed terms of the workout agreement for discussion. Assuming they made no real progress, they would have the Greene Madison team back in Kansas City file the bankruptcy papers shortly after the meeting with the banks ended, immediately identify the assigned judge, call the Judge's chambers and try to get a first-day motions hearing in front of the Judge set for the next morning or as soon as the Judge's calendar would allow; the break-neck pace of almost every new bankruptcy case.

3J couldn't say she was looking forward to renewing old acquaintances with Stacy Milnes. No one who had met Milnes ever could. Milnes was the special assets occupational hazard that went along with representing borrowers. All 3J could do was prepare, as she always did, and in that preparation, find satisfaction that her team was ready for whatever came next.

CHAPTER 11

Wednesday, September 12, 2018

VERY EARLY ON WEDNESDAY, 3J, Pascale, and Quincy met at Executive Airport, just north of downtown Kansas City, where the airport's runway ended at the curve in the Missouri River near the confluence with the Kansas River. A small airport with a short runway and no excess real estate for expansion. Hard to believe that at one time, this airport served all domestic air travel in and out of Kansas City before the construction of the spacious international airport nineteen miles north of downtown. Shortly after they arrived in the waiting area, they exited to the tarmac and boarded a small charter flight arranged by Quincy to fly to St. Louis.

3J was not a fan of small propeller planes, especially in the Midwest where the wind and weather were famously unpredictable. She remembered her mother's stories of the "day the music died" in the very early morning hours on Tuesday, February 3, 1959, when Ritchie Valens, Buddy Holly and J.P. "The Big Bopper" Richardson, along with their pilot Roger Peterson, died in a small plane crash that took off from Mason City, Iowa in bad weather as they tried to get to their next gig. 3J's gigs were court appearances and meetings and every time she boarded a small plane, she silently hoped the flight wouldn't be the day her music died in her last act on Planet Earth.

She rarely talked about her small plane aversion, but, luckily, the famed Midwest jet stream that at times can move air like a wind tunnel was on its best behavior, and the flight was smooth. The flight took about an hour, and the travelers had little in the way of conversation. 3J used the time to collect her thoughts for the bank group meeting. Pascale and Quincy reclined with closed eyes and ignored 3J's white knuckles and the iron grip she had on her armrest.

From above, the plane roughly followed the Missouri River east from Kansas City into the rising sun. The river below cut through farmland and gently rolling hills, past Lexington and its courthouse with a civil war cannonball still embedded into its facade; past Boonville, home of riverboat gaming; by Columbia, home to the the University of Missouri Tigers; and onward to the confluence with the Mississippi River a few miles north of the City of St. Louis, near the border of St. Louis and St. Charles Counties.

The plane then headed southeast to a small airport in East St. Louis, Illinois, just across the Mississippi from downtown St. Louis, Missouri, where it landed without incident. As they exited the plane, 3J exhaled slowly and looked west across the tarmac to the Mississippi River and the city of St. Louis beyond, on the western banks of the Mississippi. The iconic and famous Gateway Arch, the majestic six-hundred-forty foot stainless steel gateway to the American West, grounded her as it glistened and reflected the newly-risen morning sun.

After a quick ride-share, the threesome found themselves outside the Laclede Gas Building, an older, thirty-one-story office building near 7th and Olive in downtown St. Louis. They entered, passed through security, took the elevator to the twenty-eighth floor, where they checked in with the law firm's receptionist and silently followed Sample's legal assistant to the conference room. Quincy was glad to see 3J shed the nerves from the plane and resume her cool, professional demeanor as if it had never slipped. Entering the room, he noted that it was modest in size and décor and significantly smaller than Greene Madison's war room, where he met with Pascale and 3J not more than several days ago.

Already in the room were Sample, Milnes, and StarBanc's troubled loan officer, Brian Chimes. At the head of the conference room table was a large screen where other bank group members were piped into the meeting across the internet, appearing in boxes on the screen, like the boxes from the old game show, *The Hollywood Squares*, 3J thought. The only difference between the *Hollywood Squares* stars, who occupied the game show boxes, and the bankers on the big conference room screen was that the bank group members looked decidedly humorless. Nothing funny about a debt of half a billion dollars, give or take, after all. But their faces all had a single, recognizable expression – a grave one, reserved for the fear of an upcoming non-payment default, perhaps taught to them by a body language expert at a banking school they all attended when they began their banking careers.

Milnes took control of the meeting immediately and introduced her counsel and the other bank group members. Pascale did the same for the three attendees, then 3J began to talk.

Milnes promptly interrupted, holding up her hand in the stop position. "Whoa there, cowgirl."

Milnes' tactic was effective and 3J stopped in mid-sentence, her mouth in mid-formation of her next words which never came. She had been called a lot of things in her career, but "cowgirl" was a first. It might have been a fun moniker at O'Brien's and there, maybe even a compliment. From Milnes, however, it was an aggressive put-down. 3J knew that Milnes was making her play for control, but decided not to respond in kind. Milnes might shut down, and 3J wanted to keep her talking.

Milnes continued, "Slow down. If you're here to do a work-out, you're in the wrong room. This is the payment room, not the let's-make-a-fuckin'-deal room. We don't see that you have anything to sell us that we have any interest in buying, and we think your companies need to file for bankruptcy relief. The Bankruptcy Court can sort out our differences."

It was clear immediately to 3J that none of Milnes' comments had been discussed or approved by the bank group. She saw Brian Chimes attempt to keep his best poker face, turning his gaze out the window rather than looking down at his empty pad, but the tightness of his face as his jaw clenched gave away his surprise at Milnes' comment. The bankers on the video conference looked down at their desks.

Chimes returned his gaze from the window, but made no eye contact with Milnes or Witherman. He just looked down at his pad and twirled his pen aggressively as if it was a fidget spinner used to curb anxiety. To 3J, he looked like he needed the spinner.

3J took in the reactions, then responded without any emotion or anger in her voice. "Stacy, we flew here with a proposed term sheet for you to consider, and we were expecting a discussion of the terms. If you're saying the banks don't want to use our time to discuss it, we're disappointed, but that's *your* choice."

"It *is* my choice, and yeah, that's what I'm saying," Milnes declared forcefully, emphasizing that she alone made the nego-tiating decision. The other bankers tried again to hide their surprise and irritation.

"Does anyone else want to say something?" 3J asked the other bankers. No response. 3J felt that Chimes' body language suggested he wanted to take the meeting in a different direction than the tone being set by Milnes, perhaps having the common courtesy to review the term sheet and foster a discussion. She stared directly at Chimes, her eye contact giving Chimes the license to say something. But he looked away, unwilling to air any dirty bank group laundry in front of the Witherman team. 3J could respect that, despite her frustration.

Based on the lack of banker willingness to talk, she decided not even to broach the topic of the $30 million payment. She had every belief the banks harbored no legitimate expectation that Quincy would make such a large payment based on a temporary loss of value. Instead, she shrugged her shoulders and stood up to leave. "Very well then. I guess we'll see you on the other side, in bankruptcy court." Taking their cue from 3J, Quincy and Pascale stood to leave as well. It was an awkward moment; it would have been politic to offer to shake hands, but all three decided to forego doing so in acknowledgement of Milnes' tone. Pascale looked at Sample and said, "Dennis, we'll be back in our office by noon at the latest, so if you want to talk, give us a call."

As they turned for the door, Quincy offered the non sequitur to Milnes, "Be well." She said nothing in response. End of meeting.

No substantive discussion; no term sheet; no politically correct pleasantries. Bad karma. Another Milnes meeting completed and in the record books. Milnes would rate the meeting a success. The other bankers would rate it a category five unnatural disaster.

During the ride-share back to the East St. Louis Airport, 3J called her team and instructed them to file the bankruptcy cases as anticipated, directing them to call her when they completed the filings electronically using the Federal Court's electronic case filing system.

They boarded the small plane for the short trip back to Kansas City and buckled in. Once aboard, Pascale vented. "Well, that was a complete, God-damn, flat-out, 100%, total waste of our fuckin' time. I have no idea what they're thinking

– or maybe they aren't. The beginning of a bankruptcy case won't go well for them; surely they know that?"

3J gave a small, tight nod of agreement. She knew it was always better to let Pascale air his feelings without egging him on or trying to stop him, and she was too busy taking air-travel-induced subtle deep breaths to debate anything. Quincy surprised them, however, and said with a hint of a smile, "Oh, I don't know. I've traveled further for less."

"How much less than God-damn-nothing could we possibly get? 'Cause nothing is what we just got out of that meeting. And I'm being generous when I call it a meeting," Pascale complained.

Quincy smiled.

Abandoning his need to continue to rant, Pascale calmed himself, lowered his decibel output, and asked, "Ok. I'll bite. How do you figure?"

"Two reasons. First, I expected so little, and Milnes met my expectations with flying colors, so I left the so-called meeting without any feeling of disappointment – I feel validated." Quincy paused, and Pascale grimaced in acknowledgment. "Second, I used our brief time to survey the body language of the bankers in attendance. For all of her bluster, Milnes made no eye contact … with anyone. When she spoke, she looked at her yellow pad. When she didn't speak, she looked at her pad. When she raised her hand for Ms. Jones to stop, she looked at her pad. Quite unlike my first meeting with her, when she tried to stare me down."

3J looked at him. "You can call me 3J, Quincy."

"Her lawyer, what's his name, Sample? He pretended to take notes. What notes could he possibly have taken? No one said anything that was worthy of a single note. No, Sample used the subterfuge of note-taking to give himself something to do other than make eye contact. The other bankers looked fidgety to me.

So much so that I could even see it in the ones that appeared on the big screen. Usually, you can't get much of a body language read on a video conference. But on this one, the read was clear. And like Milnes, none of them made eye contact."

The lawyers looked at each other, quietly impressed.

Quincy continued, "3J, when you looked directly at Chimes, he was in no mood to lock eyes, and he looked as far away as he could. I also thought I saw a moment of anger flash in his eyes before he looked away, and I choose to assume he found nothing we did worthy of anger. Folks, I could be wrong, but I always try to get a read on the room, and that room oozed discomfort."

"So your read is that not everyone in that room wants us to file for bankruptcy protection?" 3J asked.

"Could be," Quincy said. "Could very well be. Or, not everyone in Milnes' cavalry is committed to the war she wants to wage."

"Well, if the banks are bluffing, we may still be able to call off the filings, but we'll need to call my team immediately," 3J said, the concern in her voice suggesting she was not sure she could rein in the filings at this point.

But she didn't need to worry. Quincy said, "No. Proceed. Let's file and get this show on the road. I don't want to give the banks any more time to send me that letter they threatened jacking up the interest rate. We won't get anything worth negotiating from the banks tomorrow or the next. Their fearless leader just told us to file, so let's file, and then we can see what they're packing."

While 3J, Pascale and Quincy reached 10,000 feet, 3J's team back at command central in Kansas City filed the cases electronically. By the time they landed in Kansas City, 3J learned that their judge was the Honorable Daniel Robertson. *Good*, she thought. *A great group of cases for him to cut his Chapter 11 teeth.*

3J called chambers and learned that the Judge set hearings at 11 a.m. the next day to consider their various motions.

She ended the call and passed the update along to Quincy, urging him to return with her to the office to prepare for the hearings, ensuring he was ready if Judge Robertson required his testimony.

As soon as 3J sat down at her desk, she emailed Sample a set of all the filed papers with the case numbers and the affidavit, advising him that her team filed the cases, and that Judge Robertson would hold the hearings the next morning. She ended the email by inviting Sample to call her if he had questions. 3J didn't expect Sample to have questions for her, but reflected wryly that perhaps he might have a few questions for Milnes.

In any case, game on.

3J wondered what the banks' game plan could possibly be, thinking back to Quincy's comment about finding out what the banks were packing. She wouldn't have used a firearm reference in the same sentence as the word "banks;" even metaphorically, she wouldn't want to arm the banks with weapons. Were all the banks on board with Milnes' insistence that the Debtors should file for bankruptcy relief? With that banker, one just never knew.

§

When the meeting with Witherman ended – no deal because Milnes didn't want a deal – Milnes and Sample lingered in the conference room to talk.

While Milnes retrieved her voice mails and made some phone calls, Sample had time to contemplate. He met with Milnes in person the day before the short meeting with the Witherman team where she had made it clear she wouldn't even look at any proposal for an out-of-bankruptcy settlement if the Witherman team brought one to the meeting. Sample knew Milnes was a master at creating tension as a tool to collect a loan, and her refusal to look at a proposal would ratchet up the tension dramatically. True enough, without even looking up from her pad, Milnes delivered the terse message – keep your damn proposal. Not interested. Won't even read it.

Sample knew how experienced and effective Milnes was, but, on a professional level, he disliked that tactic. It was disrespectful of the Greene Madison team, who were likely strapped for time and had better things to do than to travel to St. Louis for a crass, non-event. Of course, Milnes showed no interest in entertaining a discussion of his concern. She rarely asked for Sample's input, and when he offered it, she typically batted it away like a quick tennis volley back over the net without consideration of his comment.

Sample understood Milnes' strategy to exert pressure on Witherman until he either ran out of cash to pay his attorneys or crumbled under the pressure and decided to move the loans. Milnes wanted this approach to play out in the harsh spotlight of a bankruptcy case where almost everything that happens is in the public eye, but he wasn't a fan of the tactic. In Sample's experience, the path to achieving the "move-the-loan" goal was never straightforward. It always had its share of obstacles and crossroads. And some borrowers had a much higher tolerance for pain than others. He wondered how much discomfort Witherman could withstand.

There were the many debtors who were no longer creditworthy and couldn't refinance; there were those who liked the terms of the existing loan documents and didn't want to risk the potential for new, more onerous terms and conditions that might appear in a new bank's documents. But Sample also knew there were debtors that saw no reason to be bullied by the banks and used bankruptcy to stay in the loan for the thrill of the fight. The "see-you-in-court" debtor who would battle with the "see-you-in-court" banks: good for the various law firms' bottom lines, but not necessarily a good business decision by the debtor or the banks.

It was unclear which of these types of debtors Witherman would turn out to be.

Sample also knew that implementation of Milnes' tactics would bring heat on the banks in court as most bankruptcy judges would expect some level of cooperation between the parties, even if they were skirmishing, to pursue a path to a resolution. Once the Judge recognized this was not a resolution case, but rather what some might call a scorched-earth case, he would undoubtedly be unhappy, and if that Judge directed his unhappiness at Sample, as the mouthpiece for the banks in court, it could get ugly quickly. More importantly, it could empower Witherman, whose thought process might then be, *hey, I don't need to cut any deals with these banks. Let's just steamroll them and get a plan approved over their objection in a contested confirmation hearing.* Not only was the scorched-earth method risky and costly, its rate of success was fairly low. That type of case could quickly spiral out of the control of the banks as they wait for the debtor to crack under the pressure. Sample didn't know Witherman well enough to assess whether he would fray, crumble, or crack, or alternatively if the Debtors could weather the psychological storm and come out on top as the winners.

As Milnes returned to the conference room, Sample asked her, "What is it that you suspect, Stacy?"

"Hiding assets. I think Witherman's hiding assets."

"Based on … ?"

"Based on, I think he's hiding assets," she answered bluntly, without attempting to mask her annoyance.

He ignored her tone and continued, "Don't you have financial statements from him presented over the years?"

"Of course. I mean assets *not* listed on the financial statements," she answered quickly and dismissively.

Sample decided to turn his attention and preparation to the usual nuts and bolts that arise in newly filed bankruptcy cases, concerned about the valuation and use-of-cash issues paramount at the beginning of almost every case. For Witherman, the valuation issue was the cornerstone of the bank's demand for a large cash payment.

"Did the collateral diminish in value recently?" he asked.

"No," replied Milnes. "But the buildings went down in value, the loan-to-value-ratio reset to 70% in the documents, and the loan documents permit the banks to make the cash payment demand."

Sample knew that. But just to make sure he and Milnes were on the same page, he gave her a by-the-book look and said, "Stacy, you know the bankruptcy law doesn't care about a prior loss of value. It only cares about whether the collateral has stabilized in value or if it continues to lose value and thereby harms the banks' position going forward. So, is the collateral continuing to lose value?"

"Not according to our appraiser," Milnes responded.

Bad answer, thought Sample. "Then we won't fare well at the beginning of the case. The Judge will let them use the cash and may even let them defer monthly payments to the banks for a while," he said without raising his voice or sounding frustrated.

"I get that. Right after the Judge rules on the first-day motions, I want you to set up examinations of the debtors. Document production requests. Depositions. Keep the requests coming. Keep them more than occupied. I want to uncover every rock and find out what's been going on behind the scenes with Witherman. Every debtor has secrets, and I want to know what Witherman's secrets are. We have lots of information about the buildings but I want to know more about Witherman and the management company. The prior loan officer had a very chummy relationship with Witherman, and as far as I can discern, the banks know very little about the management company and Witherman personally."

"So we are going scorched-earth right out of the box?"

"Correct," Milnes quickly responded.

"That may very well sour the Judge's view of the banks very early on in the case," he pointed out.

"I hear you."

I hear you, he thought. Hmm, did she? Did she really? Did Milnes hear Sample at all? Did it matter? He hoped she had considered her options. He wasn't so sure. He was sure, however, that Milnes wasn't asking for his advice and thoughts. She had already determined the course of the bankruptcy cases and, with her usual high degree of clarity, she had conveyed it to Witherman and his Greene Madison team, who were exceptionally experienced and conflict-seasoned. They didn't need to fight in every case, but Sample knew they could and would to protect their clients. While some bankruptcy lawyers didn't like courtroom battles and guided their clients away from such conflicts, the Greene Madison team knew how to settle, but had no problem litigating a case in court, and were well known for those courtroom skills.

"So, you want us to focus on Witherman," Sample asked as he nodded.

"Correct," said Milnes. "We can always have discussions with him under the bright bankruptcy lights of disclosure, but only after we gather some more information, press our thumbs on what might be some open wounds, see how much he winces, and then assess where we are. Capisce?" Milnes asked.

Understood.

As Milnes departed, Sample thought, *This case will certainly be good for business.* But he knew it would be stressful, at least in the short term. Not necessarily good for his health, but then, he had learned that much of the practice of law could fall into the category of things potentially bad for your health. Unlike cigarettes, however, the practice of law didn't come with the hazardous warning from the surgeon general. Maybe it should. Perhaps the eight by eleven-inch law license given to him by the Missouri Supreme Court many years ago should have contained that disclosure on the back. Not only that, but maybe there should also have been a health warning in the partnership agreement he had signed many years ago, when the firm offered him partnership status and handed him a sixty-page partnership contract to sign.

Oh well. Enough deep unanswerable lawyer musings for one day. Sample dutifully recorded his time entry for his meeting with Milnes in neat, one-tenth of an hour increments: "Meet with client regarding case strategy and analyze same" – 3.6 hours. *Living each and every day by the point ones.* Also hazardous to one's health. *What an existence,* he thought with an all-knowing grimace.

§

After they arrived back in Kansas City from the unproductive bank group meeting, 3J, Pascale, and Quincy made their way to the Greene Madison office where they met Ronnie in Conference Room 27B. *So this is the blue-collar conference room they use to get actual work done,* Quincy thought to himself. It was much smaller than 27A and more modestly appointed. He could still feel the law in the air, but in this room, without any pretension.

On the table laid three identical notebooks prepared by the Greene Madison paralegal which contained each motion the Judge would consider at tomorrow's hearings and outlines of the arguments the Greene Madison team would make. 3J took the lead to explain to Quincy the motions and their purpose in bankruptcy. She had done this countless times before and shifted to autopilot to explain the mostly perfunctory documents, predicting with the highest degree of confidence that the Judge would grant their requests to allow the companies to continue in business.

Next, the trio turned to the *Motion To Use Cash Collateral.* As 3J said, "Cash is king in bankruptcy, and we need permission from Judge Robertson to use it." As she began to discuss the cash collateral motion, she turned off autopilot and grabbed control of the bankruptcy instrument panel. The motion proposed spending money under a comprehensive budget prepared by Ronnie and attached to the motion. Under the budget, the Debtors would pay the monthly bills for the next sixty days from the buildings' cash, including wages and benefits to employees.

The motion set out the buildings' current values and stated that the current values as of the filing date were both stable and likely to increase. Thus, the monthly spend would not adversely affect the banks, as they would always have the value of the buildings to look to for protection. In the budget, the Debtors didn't propose to make monthly payments to the banks. The Debtors asserted that since the building values were stable, bankruptcy law did not require them to make such payments at this time. The motion suggested that the Court could revisit the decision not to pay the banks in sixty days.

"We expect the Court to approve the use of cash collateral on an interim basis and set another hearing to consider a more permanent approval to use cash. At the next hearing, I'm betting we'll get some push-back from the banks since we aren't paying them." 3J paused before giving her advice. "I'm inclined to hold fast on the 'no payment' approach; let the Judge decide how to handle the issue. For that next hearing, we'll need to make sure that George Herndon is ready to testify as to the value. You'll be ready to testify the Debtors will hold any money not spent on the budget in the operating account subject to the banks' lien and pending any further order of the Court. How does that sound to you, Quincy?"

"I'd like to try to stretch out the period of non-payment to the banks as long as the Court will allow. Not so much for revenge or vindictiveness. Those feelings are a waste of time," he responded. "But right now, it's the only economic leverage we have over the banks that I see. It could remain something we might trade if the banks ever come to their senses and decide to engage in any workout discussions. Even if Milnes is playing a longer game of ratcheting up the pressure on me, the syndicate banks may feel the pain and want monthly payments. After all, they're banks, right?"

"Understood," 3J agreed. In their first meeting, Quincy's comments were short, almost staccato responses to questions 3J had raised. Now, however, Quincy had shifted to business-savvy comments and his statements were more communicative and substantive. She liked the businessman better than the staccato Quincy, and hoped that the more narrative comments reflected Quincy's growing comfort with her.

The three then went over testimony Quincy might have to offer. 3J and Pascale practiced with him to make sure he was ok with his direct testimony if they had to call him to the stand. They practiced his answers to some likely questions the banks' attorney would ask him on cross-examination. They had already agreed that 3J would handle the presentations needed from the podium, and if the Court wanted to hear live testimony, Pascale would handle that chore. All in all, their initial impression of Quincy was spot on. *He'll be a great witness*, both 3J and Pascale thought. It always surprised the non-attorneys of the world how much preparation went into trial work. The world expected that the courtroom drama unfolded as it did every week during the *Perry Mason* episodes of old. All examination from the seat of Perry's pants, as conjured up by the non-attorney scriptwriters, with the penultimate leading question to sway the jury that always began with, "Isn't it true?" Not in the real world at all: preparation made the difference, not slick lines of questioning thought up on the fly in the courtroom, crafted by a room full of non-lawyer Hollywood writers.

They finished up their meeting at around 6:30 p.m., and Quincy and Ronnie departed, leaving 3J and Pascale to gather up the papers and retire to their offices for additional preparation. Both were ready.

They were ready. 3J knew Judge Robertson would be ready as well.

As the evening progressed, she felt the usual exhilaration as the first hearing approached. The first time in front of a judge after a new Chapter 11 filing was always an exciting time; it never got old for her. This time was even more thrilling, because she had the chance to start the process of giving the banks a symbolic black eye. While the affidavit laid out the background in detail, 3J would let the Judge know all about the demand for the $30 million payment, which the Debtors could not make, and which triggered the need to seek bankruptcy protection. *The Judge should start to get the lay of the land early and often as the bankruptcy cases developed.* 3J liked Quincy's comment that he had no use for revenge or vindictiveness. Nevertheless, she hoped that Milnes and some of the other bankers would be in the courtroom so the Judge could get a glimpse of the devil-banker and some of her band of evil merrymakers.

CHAPTER 12

Thursday, September 13, 2018

"YOUR HONOR, JOSEPHINA JONES and William Pascale of the Greene Madison law firm representing the Debtors. The Debtors appear by their Chief Executive Officer, Quincy Witherman," 3J announced from the courtroom podium. She returned to the table on the right side behind the podium and took her seat next to Pascale and Quincy. At the beginning of her career, 3J would have to consciously struggle to control her nervousness as she began a new case from the podium, but her presentations were now confident, assured, and she was completely comfortable speaking to the Judge. She commanded the courtroom when she spoke, and her effectiveness was beyond question.

"Good morning, and thank you, Ms. Jones. Who else do we have with us in the courtroom today?" Judge Robertson asked.

Dennis Sample walked to the podium, buttoned his gray suit jacket, and tugged on the cloth to straighten it. "Your Honor, Dennis Sample representing First Commercial Bank, the agent bank for the bank group consisting of StarBanc from Houston, Wall Bank from New York, Wertz National Bank of Washington, D.C., Telfair National Bank of Denver, and Silvermine Bank Limited of Durban, South Africa. I believe the bank group is the principal secured creditor of the Debtors. The bank group also appears by Stacy Milnes, vice president of First Commercial Bank and head of its special assets department."

Brian Chimes was also present in the back of the courtroom. He had no attorney representing StarBanc, so no one pointed out his presence to the Judge.

Other parties then entered their appearance through their attorneys, who introduced themselves and their clients in a similar fashion. When everyone finished explaining who they were, Judge Robertson looked to 3J and said, "The floor is yours, Ms. Jones. What do we have today?"

3J had her usual outline of points to cover, but she didn't read her remarks from a prepared written speech. She was there to have a dialogue with Judge Robertson, the sole subject of her attention. "Thank you, Your Honor. My clients commenced Chapter 11 bankruptcy cases yesterday to protect themselves from the bank group that was in the process of demanding an immediate $30 million cash payment. We have seven related Chapter 11 Debtors who appear before you, Your Honor. Four companies that each own an office building, a holding company that owns the four building companies, Mr. Quincy Witherman, who owns the holding company, and a management company that runs the buildings on a day to day basis. Mr. Witherman owns 100% of the management company. The four office building companies each built a high-rise office building. Those buildings are high-end, class-A space in or near the downtowns in Houston, Denver, Kansas City, and Philadelphia. They are all more than 95% occupied with first-rate, paying tenants."

As 3J outlined the situation, she maintained her eye contact with Judge Robertson to assure him that the new bankruptcy cases were under control and in good hands; no distracting paper shuffling at this courtroom podium. She explained the temporary loss of value and said, "Of importance, Your Honor, the diminishment in value occurred some time ago, but the banks never took action until Ms. Milnes took over the file. It merits repeating: as the agent bank, First Commercial never made the cash payment demand until the loan moved from the loan officer to the special assets group. The Debtors made their business decision to seek bankruptcy protection rather than try to figure out how in the world they would come up with $30 million without risking the stability and integrity of their operations. Mr. Witherman explains all of this in his affidavit that we filed in support of the first-day motion."

3J paused almost imperceptibly. It was time to start the process of getting Judge Robertson to buy into the proposed course of the cases. Her presentation was going well, as if she were in the midst of a casual conversation over a cup of coffee. "I want to share with the Court the Debtors' overriding strategy in these cases. We are ready to accelerate our process and quickly file a reorganization plan and seek prompt approval to restructure our debts. We anticipate that the plan will provide for payment in full of the banks' debts, with some modifications of the loan documents' terms, which we believe the Court will not find controversial even if the banks object."

As 3J spoke, Quincy watched the Judge intently to see if he had any reactions to the plan. What he saw was a sense of assurance in the Judge's eyes that he was untroubled by, even in agreement with, everything that 3J said.

"Our team is well aware that in so many cases, the debtor delays and delays the plan process, while the principal secured creditor becomes more and more frustrated. Perhaps the Court becomes frustrated as well. In this case, we will not frustrate the banks or the Court through delay," 3J continued. "These are fast-track cases. We hope that by fast-tracking these cases, we will all, the banks included, keep our eye on what is important to confirmation and not use the bankruptcy process to derail a quick confirmation effort."

Throughout 3J's presentation, the Judge comfortably maintained eye contact with her, refraining from looking around
the courtroom to observe any reactions to the presentation
from the other attorneys. He broke eye contact at this point
to nod as he glanced over to his law clerk, Jamie Li, sitting
in the courtroom in front of the bench. "Thank you for the
background, counselor."

Stacy Milnes watched the events unfold. As a special assets
officer, she regularly attended court hearings and saw nothing
unusual about the process in the Witherman cases. She was,
of course, unmoved by 3J's presentation, and made no effort
to hide a look of disdain and boredom on her face. She was
used to bankruptcy attorneys standing before the court and
saying their clients were honest, angelic, downtrodden debtors
and that the big, bad banks were in the wrong. Milnes knew
that in Quincy Witherman's case, she was in the right and that
Witherman was more than likely gigging the system. She was
Stacy Milnes, and her gut was almost always right.

Brian Chimes also observed the proceedings, and was struck
by the interaction between 3J and Judge Robertson. It was only
the second day of the bankruptcy cases, but 3J and Judge Robertson seemed to be in the midst of an impromptu conversation,
not immersed in a courtroom presentation. Chimes hoped
that the Judge would refrain from aligning with the Debtors
at this early stage; hopefully Dennis Sample would have the
courtroom presence to remind the Judge that the banks had
done nothing wrong and Witherman owed a significant amount
of money that he had to repay.

3J continued, "If it pleases the Court, next I would like to
address the motions filed by the Debtors."

"Before we get to that, counsel, does anyone else wish to be
heard on the matters touched on in the Debtors' introductory
presentation?" Judge Robertson inquired.

Silence from the attorneys in the courtroom. Chimes was surprised by Sample's silence. Milnes was unconcerned.

"Very well. Hearing nothing, Ms. Jones, please proceed," said Judge Robertson.

3J then went through each of the non-controversial motions. After explaining each motion, Judge Robertson asked, "are there any objections to the requested relief?" No one advanced an objection, and the Judge simply said, "Motion granted," for each, and asked 3J and her team to submit a proposed order granting the relief requested in the motion after sharing the proposed order with the other interested parties.

"That brings us to the *Debtors' Motion To Use Cash Collateral* pursuant to § 363 of the Bankruptcy Code," 3J said.

"Proceed," repeated Judge Robertson.

"The Debtors obviously need to use the cash generated in the operations. The source of that cash is rent paid by the many tenants who occupy the buildings. That cash is collateral to secure the banks' loans based on the mortgage documents we have reviewed. Attached to our motion is a proposed budget setting out, in detail, the cash we expect to receive each month and the expenses we anticipate we will need to pay. As set forth in the motion, the buildings are not diminishing in value. Indeed, they may have begun to appreciate, on a path, we believe, back to their original value, as the markets where the buildings stand pull out of the economic dip that occurred two years ago. To protect the bank group, we offer the continued stabilized value of their collateral, liens on each month's rents, and a lien on whatever cash remains after paying the bills. The Debtors will hold the excess cash in the management company's operating account pending further order of the Court. We have also set out a portion of the budgeted amounts that we would need to use in the next fifteen days and request approval of the motion on an interim basis. We further ask the Court to set another hearing, evidentiary if necessary, at the end of those fifteen days, to consider more permanent relief."

"Counsel, I reviewed the motion last night, and this morning. I note the Debtors are not proposing to pay any money to the banks under the *Cash Collateral Motion*. Did I read that correctly?" Judge Robertson observed.

"That is correct, Your Honor," 3J agreed.

"What is the Debtors' thinking on this issue?" Judge Robertson probed.

As 3J began her explanation, Stacy Milnes began to doodle on her pad, showing no interest in the issue whatsoever. Brian Chimes, however, sat up straighter in the courtroom pews. He hadn't read the *Cash Collateral Motion* until his plane fight from Houston to Kansas City early that morning and was stunned to learn that the Debtors were proposing to make no payments to the banks. No syndicate bank had authorized Milnes to agree to a no-payment budget, and he expected that Dennis Sample would vigorously object when his turn to speak arrived.

3J continued, "The Debtors would like time to make sure the rent stream remains steady before we commit to paying the banks. The money is safe, and if the bank group wants to ask this Court to direct the Debtors to make a payment to the bank, that is their right."

"Very well, counsel. I understand the Debtors' position. Mr. Sample, what does the bank group have to say about the *Cash Collateral Motion*?"

Sample stood and again adjusted his suit as he reached the podium. Many attorneys have a nervous courtroom tick: Sample's was the lay of his suit. He leaned closer to the microphone, his hands grabbing each side of the podium's square surface. "Thank you, Your Honor. The banks understand that the Debtors must spend cash to keep their operations running. The Debtors say the value of the buildings is now stable. The banks need to finalize their thinking and position on the value issues. Therefore, the banks will reserve their comments on value until the next cash collateral hearing."

No objection to the proposal to use cash and not pay the banks. Not even a mention of payments. Judge Robertson noted the absence of an objection, filed it away under the category of "strange," but decided to ask no questions for now. *If the banks didn't care about getting paid, that was their business,* he thought.

Chimes, however, was again stunned. *What's Milnes up to, and how the hell can she let the Debtors avoid payments without bank group approval?*

Sample continued, "If I might, Your Honor – we need to take discovery, both to prepare for that upcoming hearing and to better understand what has been going on in the Debtors' businesses, including, in particular, the management company and Mr. Witherman personally. I'm told by the banks that, frankly, we seem to have limited information about both Mr. Witherman and the management company in the banks' records, and we would like permission to take such discovery on an expedited basis. While the banks may, of course, seek payment from the Debtors, in the short term, we can defer that issue.

"As to the final hearing, Your Honor, we think we will need a bit more time than fifteen days to complete discovery, exchange appraisals, and the like. The banks suggest we should hold a hearing October 10, if the Court has time that day."

The Judge nodded. "Anything else, sir?"

"No, Your Honor," Sample replied.

"Very well. Thank you, Mr. Sample," stated Judge Robertson. "The Court grants the request to use cash collateral pursuant to the budget. Based on Mr. Sample's comments, the period for initial use of cash collateral will run through October 10.

On the tenth, beginning at 9 a.m., we will have a hearing to consider any pending objections. If there are none, the Court will merely extend the Debtors' right to use cash collateral pursuant to the budget thereafter without a hearing. Ms. Jones, please have your team submit a proposed order consistent with my ruling after sharing that with the parties in the courtroom today as well." As 3J nodded, the Judge looked around the courtroom. "Mr. Sample, please file any objection to the use of cash collateral by September 21, close of business, so we know what we are arguing about, and we can frame the issues. If we are going to have a valuation dispute in the context of cash collateral, I need to know that by close of business on the 21st as well. If there will be a valuation dispute, I want the parties to exchange their appraisals by September 24 and make their appraisers available for expedited depositions immediately thereafter." He fixed both 3J and Sample with a firm stare. "To both counsel involved, please follow our local rules and timely submit witness and exhibit lists. Mr. Sample, if you want to take discovery, let's break it up into two phases: first, discovery directly pertinent to the cash collateral issues. Second, discovery about the Debtors' business operations, assets, and liabilities. For the first phase, submit discovery to the Greene Madison team consistent with our local rules for discovery in expedited matters. For the second phase, file your Rule 2004 application, and we can go from there.

"Any questions ..." There was nothing but silence in the courtroom. "Ok, hearing none, Court is adjourned."

"All rise," commanded the clerk of the Court. As everyone in the courtroom stood, the Judge left the bench, and he and his law clerk exited the courtroom.

§

Judge Robertson and Jamie Li returned to chambers and as the Judge removed his black robe and hung it on his coat tree, he asked, "What do you think, Jamie?"

"Sounds like these will be fun cases," Jamie replied.

"Did it bother you at all that the banks didn't press for payments?" the Judge inquired.

Jamie Li had been Judge Robertson's law clerk for more than a year now, and he knew the Judge's penchant for teaching by gentle questioning without ever revealing any answers – kind of like law school's Socratic teaching method but without all of the drama of a professor in front of the classroom putting terrified students on the spot. Unlike law school, it was a collaborative process with Judge Robertson, and Li knew the proper response was not, "I'm not sure," but to instead enter a process of dialogue to get to the answer. He usually enjoyed this process, so he engaged and said, "Most banks want money. It's what they do."

"Indeed."

"These banks want information," Jamie offered.

"Indeed."

"You would think a group of banks would have much, if not most, of this kind of information already in their voluminous files."

"You'd think. It'd be impossible for the banks to survive regulatory review each year if they didn't have the information in their files. So why do they say they want information?" the Judge asked.

"You would also think that the banks know full well their current view of the value of the collateral; how else did the banks know to ask for a $30 million payment?"

"Exactly. They know – oh, there's no question that they know," Judge Robertson said. "My bet is that some sophisticated appraisal work went into that kind of significant demand."

Jamie said, "Then my guess is that the information dump will significantly stress the Debtors' team at the beginning of the case. Sounded like the Debtors' team was ready to turn to the plan process and proceed quickly to restructure the debt, and the banks want to slow that down."

"Agreed. Ok, good job. Let's look very carefully at the banks' records and information requests and see if they're overly burdensome. The banks are entitled to information, and to some degree, they are entitled to a bit of a fishing expedition. But I shouldn't sanction their use of a records dump to derail what otherwise might be a quick and successful reorganization."

"Do you want any research, Judge, on the information request issues that are looming?"

"Couldn't hurt. Thanks, Jamie."

Jamie departed for the Judge's library to start his research, and the Judge made his way back to his desk.

Judge Robertson continued to think about Dennis Sample's short presentation. The Judge was familiar with 3J and Pascale but didn't know Sample. He made a mental note to ask the other two bankruptcy judges to give him their impressions of Sample.

As he thought about the hearing, Judge Robertson found it surprising that the banks didn't pitch to him the notion that payments to them were a critical component of their protection and should begin immediately. Sample seemed to be much more focused on discovery – documents and depositions – than cash. *We'll see how long the banks stay silent during the payment drought.*

He turned his attention to the never-ending pile of motions and orders for him to review. Not his favorite part of the job. Before he took the bench, Robertson had appeared in front of judges who, over time, seemed to become disenchanted with life as a judge, and as their disenchantment grew, they found it harder and harder to hide how they felt. Those judges sometimes sounded like a prisoner scratching out the days remaining in the sentence on the concrete cell block wall with a dirty, bent spoon, handle. Robertson remembered those few judges well, and he had made a promise to himself that he would try like hell never to be that kind of jurist. Never. Even in the face of the endless motions and orders.

Most days, it was easy to keep that promise. Still, on more than the occasional day, he had to work hard to be true to the underlying reason for the promise – he was lucky to be a judge, and he never wanted to forget that or have it lost in the darkness of the judicial isolation. He looked back at his pile of documents to read, as he sat at his desk and surveyed the stacks. *Don't complain,* he smiled to himself. *You wanted this life.* And, he did.

§

After the hearing, 3J and Pascale collected their papers, packed their trial bags, and headed for the elevator with Quincy. Once out on the street, 3J asked Quincy if he had any questions or comments about the proceedings.

"No."

"Quincy, are you concerned about the banks' investigation of you and your assets?" 3J asked. She tried not to exude concern over the potential investigation, but she wanted to highlight for Quincy that the request for documents sideshow could gain a life of its own and become the main event.

"Not especially," said Quincy.

"Do you believe the banks lack information about your business affairs and the management company's operations?" 3J continued.

"Not especially."

"How so?" 3J asked, trying to coax a more robust answer from Quincy. Something about his abbreviated answers bothered her, but she couldn't put her finger on it.

Quincy obliged and elaborated, "The banks have all of the financials I've delivered to them over the years. They haven't done an audit of the management company or me over the past few years, nor have they asked many questions either. The relationship was pretty simple – we made timely payments, and they took the money happily. But over the years, whatever information they asked for, we gave them. Their focus has mostly been on the operations of the buildings."

3J was satisfied with the answer, but noted to herself the dichotomy in the detail, or lack thereof, in Quincy's answers. *Sometimes he doesn't seem too willing to provide detail,* she thought.

Quincy asked, "What do you think they're looking for?"

"No idea," 3J responded. "But I would think that at this point, since they led with the investigation notion in their first appearance before Judge Robertson, they either know or suspect something and are looking for some form of ammunition to use against us." She watched his face for any sign of a guilty response.

"They can look. There's nothing to see. I don't lead all that complicated of a life," Quincy said. *There I go again,* Quincy thought. Trouble with that second truth – *the whole truth.*

That was a good answer, in 3J's estimation, but she wasn't sure Quincy appreciated the risk that the document requests could derail a quick path to plan confirmation.

By now, the threesome had reached the front of the Greene Madison building. Pascale said, "I'll head up to get going on those orders and let George Herndon know we'll need him for the next hearing ... maybe."

"Ok, be up shortly," said 3J. "Quincy, I want to get the process underway to develop a restructuring plan we can file quickly.

Our Judge has a notion that cases over which he's presiding should move expeditiously, even the big, complicated ones. I'm sure he'd consider it a feather in his Chapter 11 hat if his first big case quickly confirmed a plan. I want to use that to put pressure on the banks. Normally, banks want cases to move more quickly, and debtors try to apply the brakes in the early days of the bankruptcy cases. We want to press on the gas, and my sense is that the banks may try to slow the process down. I hope that's the banks' game plan, because it won't play well with Judge Robertson at all. Let's have a meeting to go over the plan process and how we get to where we need to be in these cases."

"Sounds good. Let me get back to my office and figure out when we can meet. It should be soon."

"Good." 3J continued to look at Quincy and said, "It seems to me that the banks are looking to start a fire. They have the gasoline can and are just looking to pour it on something combustible. I don't think there's anything combustible in the schedules or statements of affairs, so what are they looking for, Quincy?"

"Unclear," said Quincy. "It'll be fine, 3J."

Another abbreviated answer, 3J thought.

Quincy continued, "I gotta head back to my office. You can get me there if you need me. Thanks for the good work." He shook 3J's hand and turned and walked away.

The hearing had gone well – even better than expected. The Debtors would use cash and not pay the banks, at least for a while. But as 3J watched Quincy walk away, she couldn't help wondering why she continued to feel a twinge of concern … about Quincy.

§

After the hearing, Sample and Milnes hailed a ride-share to the Kansas City International Airport. The thirty-five-minute ride took them north across the aging Buck O'Neill Bridge, past the downtown Kansas City airport, and north, past tall cliffs that rose from the Missouri River and served as the bedrock for multi-million dollar glass facade houses facing the downtown skyline, and new developments on either side of the Broadway extension. They headed to the intersection with I-29 North, the Northlands of Kansas City, and eventually, the KCI airport.

During the ride, Milnes discussed the Judge's discovery comments and focused on how broad the requests could be without ending up in front of the Judge again in a discovery dispute that would delay any documents production. Sample explained that he should draft the discovery narrowly and the requests should seek things the bank did not already have.

"Tell me about the information the banks already have from Witherman over the years," Sample asked.

Milnes said, "Every six months, on schedule, Witherman presented his financial statement to the banks. As I told you when we met, I don't believe him."

"Have the banks ever audited Witherman?"

"Two years ago, and it revealed nothing."

"Stacy, you know this better than I. If Witherman is hiding something, he isn't going to produce any thing that can be used against him. He's too savvy for that. Won't you have to find the concealed assets some way other than through Witherman?"

"Just get me the draft of the application for the document requests, and then we can talk about next steps. I want the application to set out my suspicions in as much detail as possible and ask for as many documents as possible. Broad requests, not narrow."

Milnes was an expert at cutting off a conversation, like a roller derby jammer reaching for her helmet to cut off the jam. Sample felt like he just got knocked off of the track.

Rather than protest any further, he simply said, "will do." Sample knew his capitulation was a mistake. He should have pushed back on the notion that Milnes' mere suspicions could form the backbone of the application but he was not in the mood for more Milnes-style communication.

Silence followed as the ride-share made its way to the terminal for the drop-off. As they exited, Sample looked at his watch. They had about an hour before they would have to go through security. They went to the bar, and ordered a beer each.

When the drinks arrived, Milnes asked, "If you were one of the Greene Madison crew, what would you do in this case?"

Sample answered quickly, "I would race to push a plan through to confirmation and do everything I could to make sure the banks couldn't dictate the course of the case. I would fight discovery requests about issues other than confirmation."

"What treatment would the plan give the banks?"

"Maybe stretch out payments, reset the interest rate at the current market rate, alter the provision for a payment in the event the values diminish. Generally, pay the banks in full but under different terms."

"How many of those could they get approved by the Judge?"

"Pretty much all of them. The Bankruptcy Code permits a debtor to make all of those kinds of loan document modifications."

Silence again. Sample drank. Silence was often a good thing in conversations. Like in music, not every beat in a measure needed a note to be played on an instrument. But with Milnes, silence had more significance. She was smart and methodical, but she was also volatile, and she knew it, and she used silence to build tension and create doubt in a nervous audience as to whether she would erupt or remain calm and seemingly under control. Sample knew she had an outstanding record of success in special assets, but her unorthodox aura and methods kept people, including him, on edge. Unorthodox might be an understatement – at times, she seemed to enjoy inflicting pain. Not the kind of client he relished, but at least she promptly paid the invoices.

Milnes broke the silence. "Can we force them to move the loans?"

"It's a noble objective, Stacy, but I don't see them doing that willingly, or even at all, in this marketplace. The quest to secure financing as one exits Chapter 11 is hard to achieve in good times; it's likely to be close to impossible in the current environment. That's also why their tactic of racing through Chapter 11 as quickly as possible makes great sense for the Debtors in these cases. No wasted time looking for a holy grail take-out loan. Ride the horse they have."

Milnes said nothing in response.

Sample inquired, "What do the other banks say?"

"They're on board." She had no idea if the syndicate banks were on board, because she had no intention of asking them. What Milnes meant was that she was implementing her plan, and the syndicate banks would go along because that was just how it was going to be.

Silence again, as they finished their beers, until, finally, Milnes said quietly, "Let's go to the gate and get through security."

Before they boarded, Sample emailed the associate who worked with him on the file and directed him to draft the application for permission to seek the documents from Witherman. Sample directed the associate to focus on Witherman and to emphasize the suspicion that Witherman was hiding assets.

The attendant called the passengers to board; they lined up, and less than an hour later, the plane touched down at St. Louis Lambert International Airport west of downtown St. Louis.

Milnes and Sample didn't talk on the plane; issues of attorney-client privilege and the chance someone would overhear the discussion always made meaningful conversations between lawyer and client problematic in any public transportation setting. Besides, Sample wasn't sure what they would talk about. It was hard to make small talk with Stacy Milnes. Instead, they both put on their headphones and listened – for Sample, to an uplifting podcast he downloaded about the resiliency that humans exhibit in the darkest of times, and for Milnes – *who knows what she's listening to,* thought Sample.

When they landed, they parted company. Milnes headed for the garage and her car, and Sample made his way to the MetroLink train station to head back to his office. On the train, he tried to gather his thoughts. How could he devise a strategy to implement the banks' goals when this file seemed to cry out for a negotiated resolution? But Milnes' business decisions were already baked into the plan of attack, and not likely to change. From Sample's experience, Milnes' most significant weakness was her inability, or perhaps it was her unwillingness, to alter a plan of attack once implemented. *That could prove to be her undoing in this case,* he thought.

§

Brian Chimes found a coffee shop near the courthouse when court adjourned, and called Stephanie Bonde of Silvermine Bank, one of the syndicate banks. He and Bonde had worked together on other troubled loans in the past and he had a great deal of respect for her. It was past quitting time in South Africa, but Chimes was certain Bonde would be at her desk plugging away after hours. Bonde picked up the phone on the second ring.

"Stephanie Bonde."

"Steph, this is Brian Chimes calling about our favorite high-rise office developer, Quincy Witherman."

"Hello, Brian," Bonde said in her best South African accent. "How goes the battle?"

"Listen, Steph, I flew up to Kansas City for the first day of hearings in the Witherman cases and I learned two things today. First, the Debtors won't be paying the banks during the case, at least not in the first couple of months, and second, First Commercial wants lots of documents from Witherman and seems primed to have a big fight over discovery right out of the gate."

Bonde had come to appreciate Chimes' South Texas accent in previous deals they had worked on together, and despite how different Texas English was from the South African, she found it soothing.

"When did we all agree to that approach?" she asked in surprise.

"That's the thing. We never did. I shoulda seen this coming after that B.S. meeting we had with Witherman just before he filed the bankruptcy cases. I gotta say – I ain't too damn happy about this."

"No, neither am I," Bonde concurred.

"I'm running for my plane back to Houston. Let's talk about this when I get back and maybe we should rope the other syndicate banks into the discussion."

"You mean talk amongst ourselves without First Commercial?" Bonde asked for clarification.

"Exactly," Chimes said.

"Normally I wouldn't want to have break-out discussions, but on this deal, I am ok with that," Bonde said. "Travel safely, Brian."

CHAPTER 13

Monday, September 17 to Monday, September 24, 2018

MONDAY MORNING, 3J AND Pascale ran through the recommended plan outline before Quincy arrived at the office. The Chapter 11 bankruptcy plan was all about power: Power, power, power, all residing in the Chapter 11 debtor. The strategy decisions all addressed harnessing that power to match the bankruptcy law with the debtor's business needs and then how to sell the plan to the Judge so he would approve it, as smoothly as possible. 3J and Pascale were ready.

Quincy arrived, and they got right down to it. The game plan – ram through a plan and get it confirmed by the Judge to cut off the banks' right to harass the Debtors with irrelevant document production requests. Change the narrative from what the Debtors did before bankruptcy, which the Debtors believe was nothing improper, to how the Debtors will operate after bankruptcy. To do so, 3J and Pascale recommended altering the loan documents to better account for the current economic times.

"We'll change the current floating variable interest rate to a fixed interest rate to match the lower market rates that are currently available," 3J explained. "The loans are currently due and payable in full in three years. We should move that date back to six years to give your organization a better chance to refinance your way out of the First Commercial world. Just promise us, Quincy, you will find a bank where Stacy Milnes doesn't work."

"I'm with you there, guys," Quincy agreed.

3J continued, "We'll reset the current amortization to be twenty years commencing as of the date the plan becomes effective. You'll need to check our math here, but we think the combination of a reset amortization and a lower fixed interest rate will save the Debtors significant amounts of money each month." Quincy nodded in understanding.

"As to the cash call, the plan will reset the loan-to-value--ratio from 70% to 75% and eliminate any automatic adjustments to that loan-to-value ratio in the future. We'll also adjust the documents to defer any cash-call payment for eighteen months while we all see if the market valuations rebound. In other words, the next time to measure the loan-to-value-ratio will be in eighteen months. If there's a shortfall under the new formula, the Debtors will pay that out over time, hopefully with the savings from the lower monthly payments."

"Can we do that?" Quincy asked as he raised his eyebrows high into his forehead.

"We think so," said 3J. "The Judge is new, and likely he'll be cautious, but at the same time, he'll be inclined to approve the plan and put his first confirmation notch in his judicial six-shooter. So, yes, we think so."

"Alright, then. You'll need projections and financial information from us, I assume?" Quincy asked.

"We will – five years of past financial information and five years of projections. We'll need to put together something called a disclosure statement to go along with the plan to explain where we've been, how we got here, and how we get out of bankruptcy," 3J explained.

"It's going to be a lot of work in a very short period of time, but the prize at the end is always worth the short term pain," Pascale chimed in.

"Understood. Ronnie and her team are yours full time as you need them. Ronnie knows this is coming, and she and her team are the best. They'll be your resource," Quincy said.

"Good. Let's turn to the cash collateral issues," 3J said. "We still don't know if we're going to have a valuation trial or not. We'll know that by this Friday … I hope. So, for now, we'll have to assume we are. We have to disclose George Herndon's expert report that day. We'll use Herndon's testimony to establish that the buildings' value is stable and perhaps appreciating. We'll need testimony from the Debtors to support the budget. Will that be you or Ronnie?"

"I would prefer that I testify," Quincy answered. "Ronnie is great with numbers, but she has minimal experience in a courtroom setting. Will that work for you?"

"Yes. That's fine. The questions will be straightforward and reasonably brief. We'll prepare your examination for you and send it over for you to review. Then we can schedule a practice session."

"Thank you. Should be fine," Quincy said.

"Quincy, not to beat a dead horse here, but I'm thinking ahead to possible avenues of cross-examination. Over the years that the loans have been with First Commercial, I assume you and the companies have completed financial statements for the banks and submitted them?" 3J asked.

"Yes, of course."

"Are they consistent with the schedules and statements of affairs?"

"100%."

"Got it," 3J said. "Ok, let us get started on the papers, and pretty soon now, we'll begin our quality time with Ronnie and her team for the plan and with you for the cash collateral issues."

"Questions?" Pascale asked Quincy.

"None at this time, counselor," Quincy responded.

They shook hands, Quincy thanked them, and left to return to his office. 3J watched him depart, still unable to shake off her unease.

On his walk back to his office, Quincy thought, *I truthfully answered those financial statement questions posed by 3J. The financials submitted to the banks and the bankruptcy papers were identical in all respects. 3J asked if I submitted consistent information and I had. So, my answer was truthful and nothing but truthful, albeit incomplete, omitting mention of the hidden assets.* Quincy acknowledged to himself, *there was that recurring "the whole truth" problem again.*

§

Over the next week, the Greene Madison team worked at a frenzied pace to prepare the bankruptcy plan. In addition, they crafted the disclosure statement with more historical and current information than any creditor could ever hope to review, as well as projections into the future, confirming that the cash flows worked. With the loan adjustments, the Debtors could feasibly make all payments and the revised cash call payments over time, if they became necessary in eighteen months.

On Friday September 21, the banks objected to the Debtors' use of cash, and filed their application seeking permission to take discovery. Their blueprint began to emerge from the banks' discovery filing: the principal focus of the requests was information from Quincy Witherman, personally. The discovery application was lengthy and set out the history of the loans and the type of financial information provided by the Debtors to the banks as required by the loan documents.

As 3J read the application, she noted with interest – and concern – that it also contained a carefully drafted, extensive section that suggested the Debtors had not fully disclosed all of their assets to the banks over the years, and that the bankruptcy schedules and statement of affairs likewise failed to disclose all assets. While the application used the phrase "on information and belief" repeatedly to make it clear that the banks had no hard proof and wanted documents to build their case, the damning implication was that the Debtors had lied to the banks and the Court.

The application seemed materially short on facts; it read as if someone at the banks had a gut reaction to Quincy Witherman and a bad one at that, and sought to act based merely on intuition. Someone like Stacy Milnes. 3J was surprised by how far out on a limb Sample was willing to go. She could only hope the application would leave as bad a taste in Judge Robertson's mouth as it had in hers.

As the Greene Madison team completed their work, they were keenly aware of the information sought by the banks. In discussions with Quincy, he continued to exude an air of calm and a complete lack of fear and apprehension. Indeed, he explained that he would have no problem producing the necessary documents in response to the request. He sounded almost boastful when he explained that the documents were utterly consistent with information given to the banks over the years. He was adamant that the documents would show nothing different from the information set forth in his schedules and statement of affairs filed on the first day of the bankruptcy cases.

3J didn't know it, but all of Quincy's statements were true simply because the lie about his assets had been in play for so long that it made it easy to now say that the current documents were all consistent with financial documents submitted to the banks.

Yet, despite Quincy's serenity, 3J continued to worry about the diversion created by the document requests. Because the plan proposed to pay the banks in full with interest, the side-show that was the banks' fishing expedition seemed to border on irrelevance. Even if the requests produced inconsistencies, the plan still proposed payment in full nevertheless. This issue of relevance was more a silent complaint that 3J harbored. The Bankruptcy Code allowed for investigations by creditors, and she knew it. The Bankruptcy Code and the Federal Criminal Code required complete honesty and transparency in all bankruptcy filings. A plan that paid a hundred cents on the dollar to creditors did not somehow insulate a debtor from, or cleanse the bankruptcy process of, either the requirement for honesty and transparency or the investigations to determine compliance with those requirements. The integrity of the entire bankruptcy system was at stake. The system afforded relief to honest debtors – those who followed the rules. The penalty for straying from the rules could be severe. A bankruptcy penalty – the loss of a discharge. And a criminal penalty – fines and incarceration. Period. Quincy must know this, and would surely conform as any honest rule-follower would. At least, that was 3J's hope.

After a long week of drafting the plan and the disclosure statement, 3J and Pascale found themselves at O'Brien's again nursing their favorite alcoholic beverages, Irish whiskey and Kansas City-brewed beer. Both were light on discussion as they sat at the usual worn-wood table. 3J watched as the dim lights refracted through the caramel-colored liquid in her standard-issue bar glass. It was as if the condensation and the refraction each reaffirmed that another week had come to a close and, despite the practice of law, the laws of nature and the universe remained intact and unaltered … at least, mostly.

Pascale watched as condensation formed on his beer bottle and slowly, methodically, meandered down a random path on its way to the paper coaster. While some believed that the practice of bankruptcy law could alter time and space, that notion was, of course, false. The trick was to remember that nature and the universe always won out. Always.

3J broke the silence. "How do you think the Judge will react to the discovery application? Pretty broad, don't you think?"

"The breadth of the requests is enormous, but more than that, the application goes way over the line. It virtually states as a fact that Quincy's been hiding assets from the banks for years. They don't know that at all. Rather than just ask for the documents, they wrote a complete work of fiction and publicly smeared Quincy," Pascale complained. "It's as if the smear was the principal purpose of the filing."

"It's a hatchet job. There can be no doubt that the personal attack was the principal purpose. But that's how you and I reacted. How will the Judge react?" 3J probed.

"I have to hope the application and the breadth of the requests will offend him. The discovery has nothing to do with the plan at all, and I think the Judge will see that and not derail the train as it makes its way down the tracks to the confirmation station."

Pascale smiled at the analogy offered by 3J. "Confirmation station, eh counselor? Reminds me of a story I don't think I ever told you."

"Uh oh. Here we go," 3J said with mock anguish. In reality, she liked Pascale's war stories, especially when told at O'Brien's.

Ignoring 3J's comments, Pascale pressed on with the story. "When I was a mere associate pup, I found myself in the chambers of my favorite non-Kansas City bankruptcy judge. The Judge had finished examining a global settlement proposal agreed to by all the major players in a Chapter 11 case, save one – my client – who refused to sign on to the deal. Instead, my client sent me to court to deliver the message – he would fight the good fight to the end. The Judge, a wise jurist of many decades in the judicial trenches, looked at me without anger or disappointment, and in a soft, measured voice, said: 'My friend, the bankruptcy train has just left the station and is rolling down the track. You and your client can either board the train or get run over by it, but you can't stop it.'" Pascale paused for a sip of his beer and continued, "I absorbed the message and advised my stubborn client of the Judge's communiqué after the meeting with the Judge. 'Fight to the end,' my client demanded, and that is precisely what I tried to do. But the end came swiftly, and, as the Judge had predicted, the confirmation train ran me over, and my client as well – figuratively, of course. One loud whistle toot from the Judge in chambers that day, to clear the tracks, that the client ignored." Pascale swirled the beer in his bottle as he watched the golden liquid travel round and round and concluded, "Just one of many useful lessons a young Pascale learned in the bankruptcy case foxholes. This one was simple: clients sometimes make bad decisions, but it is their right and prerogative to do so. It was a lesson that stood that young counselor Pascale well in his years of representing debtors at Greene Madison."

3J smiled at Pascale. As always, she endured his affinity for parables because they were instructional, and truth be told, fun to listen to.

"But, back to the matter at hand, 3J," Pascale said. "I need to think about this some more. Seems that the best play is to tell the Court that we're here to reorganize, and the Court should recognize that the banks are not contesting reorganization but rather trying to disrupt the process. You laid the groundwork for that theme in your opening remarks, and I think that theme will resonate with Judge Robertson." 3J murmured agreement. "But I also don't want to lose sight of just how offensive the application is, and I want to see if we can make some hay out of it before Quincy starts collecting and copying documents. I don't want to hurt Sample, but he signed the pleading and, to my read, he went way over the line of advocacy into the land no lawyer wants to go – a lack of substantiation and good faith belief," Pascale concluded.

3J nodded her head and replied, "Let's try to bring our analysis to a conclusion and advise Quincy. Anything exciting planned this weekend?"

"You mean other than attending to all my other matters that are not Witherman-related? You mean other than that jealous mistress we call the law whose company we both frequent every minute of every day of our pathetic lives?" Pascale grinned and continued wistfully, "Nah, not really. I'll take some more walks and live in my lovely, lonely house that's too large and feels empty and wait for the epiphany that will light my path to whatever comes next for me."

3J listened intently but said nothing. She had the deepest respect for Pascale. She often thought it was nothing short of a miracle that he could get out of bed each morning and show up to work these days. A testament to the human capacity to find inner resiliency in the face of horror and resulting hope-lessness. Just two years before, both his wife and daughter were tragically killed in an automobile wreck four blocks from their house by someone with a drinking problem who had somehow escaped forfeiture of his driver's license. Every day since the crash, Pascale worried that wherever they were in their after-life, his wife and daughter didn't forgive him for living on. But, during his darkest moments, he knew they forgave him and it was he who didn't forgive himself.

Pascale's life path emphasized something that 3J was quite aware of: Different people handle tragedy differently. Pascale's version was to bury his family, stay in the same house border-ing Loose Park, and take walks around the park's perimeter hoping to to find peace and purpose in his new normal. She knew that he drank, but not to excess. He prayed for answers

at church each Sunday, but without conviction, not expecting
to divine answers. He walked, but without purpose or direction.
He drifted through each day, but without direction except
for work. He just existed, waiting for whatever came next.
He didn't present as a tragic figure. He presented only as a
corporate bankruptcy attorney who was good at what he did.
In fact, most of what made him Pascale didn't present itself
at all unless one knew his background. Even then, he didn't
display tragedy on his shirt sleeve for all to see, and many, if
not most, didn't even know the story. While the story was just
one Google search away from disclosure, most people didn't
run Google searches on William Pascale and as a result, most
people never read the *Kansas City Star* stories that documented
the tragedy befallen the family of a storied local bankruptcy
lawyer.

3J felt a responsibility to be there for him but had learned
that being there could take many forms. With Pascale, being
there meant not discussing the past and being a good listener
in those rare moments when the tragedy bubbled to the surface and he referenced the car accident or the fallout from it.
Not the role that she wanted to play, but it was the role that
he assigned to those few who knew the story.

"Another beer, Pascale?" 3J asked.

"Sure," said Pascale. "Why not?"

3J waved her hand in the air, and the bartender brought
another beer and a whiskey without further communication.
Good to be a regular, thought 3J.

She raised her glass toward Pascale and said, "Here's to the
maiden Chapter 11 voyage for the Honorable Daniel Robertson. Let's hope he gets it right. I have faith that he can."

"Can, not will?"

"We give them the tools to get it right. Then, we step back
and hope they do," 3J analyzed philosophically.

Pascale and 3J clinked their glasses together, and Pascale said softly, "Hear, hear."

§

Late in the day on Monday September 24, the Court set a hearing on the banks' document requests for October 10, the same day as the continued cash collateral hearings. That same afternoon, the Greene Madison team filed the plan and disclosure statement, and Sample apprised the Court that the banks reserved the right to have a contested valuation hearing. Neither 3J nor Pascale could figure out whether there would be a valuation dispute. Judge Robertson had asked for a yes or no answer on the valuation hearing issue and Sample instead said "maybe." *The reservation of rights probably won't endear Sample to the Judge,* 3J thought.

She knew that a misstep by the other side could always work to the Debtors' advantage, so in that sense, she was happy to see the reservation of rights. But it caused 3J to wonder what exactly the banks' strategy was. If it was not obvious to 3J, it certainly would be a mystery to Judge Robertson. *Very odd.*

CHAPTER 14

Sunday, September 30, 2018

THE PAST WEEK HAD been hell for Sample. Milnes had gone off the grid. Completely non-responsive to Sample's needs and the deadlines that were coming and going. From the start, Sample had been careful to make sure that Milnes knew of the cash collateral deadlines. The first deadline – the exchange of expert valuation reports – came and went, and Sample still had no access to the banks' appraiser. So, to try to protect the banks, Sample filed a reservation of rights. He knew it was suspect – rather than telling the Judge definitively whether the banks would challenge valuation, Sample wrote that the banks might or might not mount a challenge. He worried that his filing would likely irk the Judge but he saw little choice. Sample called Milnes several times, and she didn't answer the phone and didn't return his calls. He texted her. No response.

The entire case has turned into the worst possible situation – a non-responsive client, with a deadline that's passed, and an upcoming courtroom hearing that I'll lose, hands down. Sample didn't like to lose. Who did? But, more than that, he was diligent and always prepared, and he felt Milnes was sacrificing his excellent reputation for whatever her scheme might be.

So, unshaven and dressed in his favorite Sunday ratty and tattered gray sweatshirt, Sample made his way into his office, sat down at his desk, and began to draft another email to send to Milnes; this time, an ultimatum:

> Stacy, I have left you several emails and voice mails, and I have texted you. You have not responded. I have emailed you the cash collateral deadlines and the timeline, and you have not responded. Now, an important deadline has passed – the Court's requirement to reveal if we are contesting valuation. A cornerstone of the attorney-client relationship is communication. I can't represent the banks if you won't respond, nor can I represent the banks if I have no direction regarding strategy, witnesses, exhibits, discovery, etc.
>
> I do not want to do this, but I see no alternative, so please be advised that I will have to file a motion to withdraw as counsel for the banks if we can't rectify the communication problems outlined herein immediately.
>
> Sincerely, Dennis.

Sample reviewed the email and hit the send button. With a swoosh sound, the email was off, and delivered to Milnes. He wondered how long it would take her to read it and respond; whether she even would. Recent history left the answers to these questions less than obvious.

Five minutes later, however, the phone rang. Like most special assets officers, her mobile phone was at her side 24/7 and chirped regularly, even on a Sunday. She was anxious and, as was her custom, less than pleasant.

"Don't do anything. I don't want to authorize you to withdraw the cash collateral motion yet."

"Stacy, this case is getting away from us. What are we doing?"

Milnes gritted her teeth. Everything about Sample's email and this phone call was over the line. She used attorneys, and she, not they, decided their role and what they needed to know. They served her needs. They were not her partner with a seat at the strategy table. "Dennis, if you want off the case, file your motion to withdraw. Otherwise, that's all for now." And she hung up.

Sample wondered, *How much more of this shit can I take?* Then he answered his own question. *You're an attorney. You'll take as much shit as a paying client can dole out.*

CHAPTER 15

Monday, October 1 to Thursday, October 4, 2018

ALL THE BANKS MET weekly, typically by video conference. But after the pre-bankruptcy meeting with Quincy and his lawyers in St. Louis, and First Commercial's revelation at the first day hearings that the banks wanted documents, not payments, the five syndicate banks that owned sixty percent of the Witherman loans began to have phone calls that excluded First Commercial's Stacy Milnes. The banking industry generally frowned on this type of "sub-group," and certainly agent banks, like First Commercial, disapproved of these kinds of group communications that excluded the agent bank. In the best of cases, it made the agent bank upset; in the worst of circumstances, it made the agent bank suspicious and paranoid. Then again, anyone who knew her would classify Stacy Milnes as the worst of circumstances.

In emails to each other that excluded First Commercial, the syndicate banks complained about First Commercial's strategy and felt Stacy Milnes had been out of line on several fronts at the pre-bankruptcy meeting.

The syndicate banks had a litany of grievances about First Commercial and Stacy Milnes. Foremost, none of them approved the approach she had started to employ. Milnes had asked none of the syndicate banks to approve her "no negotiation" blueprint.

She had consulted with none of them to seek their input. Each of the syndicate banks expressed that Milnes and her unmistakable style chafed them significantly. They objected to the complete exclusion from the decision-making process.

None of the syndicate banks saw a reason to start things with such caustic, almost inhuman, interplay. None of them believed that a special assets officer's portrayal as a collection specialist with a hard, callous, and rude personality had any place in the sophisticated commercial lending area. Gone were the days that special assets equated with the phrase "junkyard dog." Except, perhaps, for Stacy Milnes. None of the banks saw any productive reason to employ such unnecessary posturing. In their private calls, the syndicate banks agreed Quincy was too sophisticated a real estate investor and too savvy in his dealings with banks over the years to succumb to threats, bullying, foul language, or pressure. The syndicate banks thought that Milnes was dead wrong in her belief that such conduct would adjust Quincy's strategy in any meaningful way. As Brian Chimes of Houston's StarBanc put it so succinctly, "that dog just ain't gonna hunt in this deal." The syndicate banks didn't see Quincy wilting under Milnes' pressure. Therefore, they didn't consider it likely that Quincy would move the loans to a new group of banks, even if he could find another group to take over the lending relationship.

The syndicate banks also couldn't believe that First Commercial capitulated in the Debtors' proposal of no payments. They wanted to continue to receive payments as any bank would. Several of the banks expressed concern that the current strategy would just run up the legal bills and turn the Bankruptcy Judge against them early in the case.

After the syndicate banks read the discovery application and saw the unauthorized use of their names on the pleading Dennis Sample filed, they convinced Stephanie Bonde of the South African Silvermine Bank to reach out to Milnes on behalf of all of them and express the group's concerns. Bonde was the head of Silvermine's special assets group, and, like Milnes, had made her way and her name in a mostly male-dominated industry of bad loans. Unlike Milnes, Bonde was soft-spoken and rarely pounded the table, even when she wanted to.

Many parts of South Africa are a melting pot of different cultures and influences, which affected the dialect. Bonde's dialect was part British, part Dutch, with a healthy dose of local Bantu. The mix resulted in a beautiful, almost melodious banter, easy to understand, and soothing in its rhythm. Perhaps Bonde could soothe Milnes into a state of rationality and draw Milnes into performing and acting like … well, like an agent banker should act. Or so hoped the syndicate bankers.

The risk was significant. Of course, her call would tip-off Milnes that the syndicate banks had excluded Milnes from their meetings. This revelation, coupled with Milnes' propensity to explode, might render the call worthless, save for one issue. The syndicate banks wanted to hold a full bank group meeting immediately. Because they held sixty percent of the total loans, if Milnes said no, they could still call the meeting without her and vote to remove First Commercial as the agent bank. It was within the syndicate's rights and powers, and removal would be a black eye for First Commercial in lending circles. In future deals, banks might decline to purchase a portion of a commercial loan syndicated by First Commercial for fear that if the loan went bad, they too would be subjected to Stacy Milnes. If the revelation of the syndicate banks' phone calls was likely to upset Milnes, the threat of removal would send her into orbit.

Bonde called Milnes first thing on Monday, October 1. She would later report back to the syndicate banks that she made the call and that Milnes answered her phone, but those were the only things that went according to plan. After the call concluded, Bonde wrote an email to each of the syndicate banks:

> All, I connected with Stacy Milnes today at 9 a.m. her time. It didn't go well. She took the call, then took offense at the call, the message, and as expected, our side-meetings. She was aggressive, and dismissive, as expected. I resolved nothing substantive or positive during the call. She certainly showed absolutely no interest in adjusting her conduct or strategy. We will need to call a meeting ASAP and take this matter to the next level. I can send out an email invite to everyone including Stacy. Stand by for whatever comes next … Best regards, Steph.

Bonde scheduled a video conference meeting for all bank group members for Wednesday, October 3. At the appointed time, all of the bank representatives logged on, including Stacy Milnes and Dennis Sample, who logged on together from a conference room at Sample's offices. They stared at the big screen and the deadpan, cold sober looks on the bank representatives' faces. Sample swallowed. *This group has the collective power to control the banks' approach in the Witherman bankruptcy cases. This is going to be a shit storm.*

"We've already set the game plan for how to move these loans out of our respective banks, ladies and gentlemen," Milnes led with her customary style as she addressed the syndicate banks. No "welcome" to the call. No introductory remarks.

Bonde responded: "With all respect, Ms. Milnes, this is not your meeting with us; it is ours with you. What you characterize as 'the game plan' was never presented to the bank group for a discussion and a vote, and if it had been, sixty percent of the bank votes would reject that kind of plan. In other words, we set the case strategy as a group. You do not set the strategy as a dictator. We need to know if you have an issue with that?" she asked, with no emotion and without raising her voice.

Bonde had succeeded in doing what most cannot – brush Milnes back.

On her heels, not a familiar position for Milnes, she began her answer too quickly, growling out, "I have a big issue with that. A real big issue." Her tone bordered on belligerent. "First Commercial has the biggest exposure to these loans, clocking in at $208 million, and we won't be held hostage by a group of banks, not one of which has exposure greater than $78 million."

"We have one of the $78 million pieces, Ms. Milnes," Bonde countered. "I'm sure you and Mr. Sample have read the loan and credit agreement that governs not only our dealings with Witherman but the interaction of the banks with each other, including how First Commercial is to conduct its business with us. I believe your bank's lawyers drafted the document, so I trust you are familiar with the terms." She waited for a response which didn't come, then continued, "Those terms do not grant additional rights to First Commercial just because you have the largest share of the loans. Instead, the documents require us to vote on proposed decisions. Then we tally the votes, set the course of action, and that's how we manage the loans – all based on votes. Your bank holds forty percent of the loans; the rest of us hold the remainder. In any vote where we vote as a block, First Commercial will lose. We expect you to respect that state of affairs and adhere to the credit agreement precisely."

"This is total bull…" Stacy blustered, but Bonde spoke on without pause.

"Any pleadings you propose to file on behalf of the entire bank group must be submitted to us first for review and comment. For example, the discovery application Mr. Sample filed is over the top. Way over. You never reported any of the discovery application's information to the banks. That's because it isn't factual – you don't know most of the facts alleged in the application, and our bank's in-house attorney is so upset by the content of the application that she may need oxygen to calm down. Your attorney, Mr. Sample, signed the pleading on behalf of First Commercial, and wrote 'as agent for the bank group consisting of …' and then listed each of our bank's names. He has no inherent authority to do so, and you should direct him to withdraw that pleading as soon as this call is over."

Milnes was so uncharacteristically quiet that Bonde was uncertain if Milnes was even listening. She sternly asked, "Do you understand what I am saying, Stacy?"

Sample thought, *Oh, she understands. I've told her.* But he also knew Milnes tended to do what she wanted, and the world judged her on what she did, not what she thought or understood.

Milnes looked at each banker's face. They all were perfectly willing to make eye contact with her, unlike their demeanor in the pre-bankruptcy meeting with Quincy. Mustering all of the control at her disposal, Milnes said slowly and deliberately, and through clenched teeth, "I hear you. What approach do you folks propose?"

Bonde responded, "We want to contact Witherman and offer to resolve any differences through negotiation. We do not see it as a viable strategy to pressure him with document production requests to obtain documents we all have received from him over the years. If he has other documents, if he has hidden assets, if he has been lying to us for extended periods of time, if he is committed to a course of conduct that does not play things straight-up, he isn't going to reveal those lies and deceits all of a sudden just because we ask him to do so in a bankruptcy proceeding. So we want to withdraw the document application."

Just as I told Milnes, Sample thought.

Bonde then added, "And we want to withdraw the cash collateral opposition as well. We have no evidence to offer that the budget is inappropriate and our own expert agrees with Witherman's expert as to values. I am informed by my in-house attorney that we already missed a Court-imposed deadline. Simply and utterly unacceptable." She continued, "In our estimation, it is not a sustainable, winnable 'game plan,' as you called it. And we think – no, we know that Quincy and his team know that. We should immediately explore how to get the best deal available to us through negotiation and close the books on this matter until the revamped loans next come due. After we negotiate and reach a resolution, if any bank wishes to pursue the storyline that Quincy Witherman has committed fraud for a very long time, and conduct, at their own expense, a surreptitious fraud investigation, they should have at it. But, just to be sure you hear and understand me, let me re-emphasize in the strongest terms: Any investigating bank will do so on its own and, in your case, any investigation will be on your own nickel."

Brian Chimes, whose StarBanc held $52 million of the loans, cleared his throat. In his deep Texas drawl, as far removed from Bonde's melodious accent as possible, he added, "We completely agree with Stephanie. Alternatively, Stacy, First Commercial can, surely enough, buy us all out at par, and then do whatever it wishes with its $520 million of loans."

Chimes thought it was too easy to push Milnes' buttons and send her over the edge. He knew he would enjoy what came next; he wasn't disappointed.

"My bank is not buying your goddamn fuckin' loans!" Milnes smoldered and howled each word slowly and methodically into the video screen. Her face was beet-red, her pulse had accelerated, her palms were clammy, and despite the separation occasioned by the video conference, all of this was readily apparent to the syndicate representatives. Chimes exulted silently, *High five! Touchdown!*

"Good, then we have eliminated that potential option," Chimes said, making no effort to hide his sarcasm. "Unless Ms. Milnes wishes to share with us a provision in the credit agreement that permits her to make all these decisions unilaterally, I do believe, ladies and gentlemen, that we have agreement and we have settled the matter. We can vote and the tally will be 60–40. Going forward, we'll handle the loan in the manner outlined by Ms. Bonde, according to the letter of the credit agreement from now on. And, Stacy, y'all should please direct Mr. Sample to develop the suggested tactics to negotiate with Mr. Witherman and submit it to all the banks ASAP. We'll all look over Mr. Sample's handiwork and figure out where we can go, as a group, from there."

Chimes paused as if he had finished his comments, but he had not: "Stacy, a little piece of unsolicited free advice from down here in the good old Lone Star State. You might give some serious thought to adjustin' your mindset on this one, my friend. Might add some valuable years to your life and certainly will maintain First Commercial's stellar A+ reputation in the banking community, which I am sure is important to your bank's brass. Once your brass figure out what's been going on – meaning your course of conduct on this one – my Houston intuition tells me they'll be all-in on the new normal for how we're gonna handle this loan from now on."

More button pushing by Chimes. Milnes knew it. She knew he was trying to get a rise out of her. She knew she should control her reaction to his comments. But she couldn't. Instead, she thought she could feel steam leaving her body through her ears like the steam leaving a pressure cooker through the valve. She had more to say, much more, none of it planned, none of it productive, none of it civil, none of it designed to defuse the charged comments hurled at her by Chimes and Bonde, none of it profound, and none of it of a nature that would change the outcome. She thought, *Dressed down by a not-so-tall Texan on a loan to a fraudster during a bankruptcy case pending in Kansas City. What a bunch of shit.*

She remembered to breathe, if erratically, and as she returned to some more acceptable level of oxygen delivery to her brain, she thought, *if I say something, these bastards might take a vote to silence me! What a dysfunctional, steaming mess.*

The bank group voted, and as predicted by Brian Chimes the vote was 60-40 to change course, withdraw the discovery application and the cash collateral objection, and sit down to negotiate with Quincy Witherman. As the voting finished, Milnes looked at Sample and uttered, mostly under her breath, "fuck," drawing the word out for several seconds in a long exhalation of air. Uncharacteristically, Milnes decided to hold her tongue and not give the group the satisfaction of further deliberations. They got what they wanted. Instead of engaging in any more video conference minutes, she clicked on the "leave meeting" button on the lower right-hand portion of the screen and terminated the video get-together. No "goodbye." No "good day." Just an instant video termination. Instant fade to black. It was, after all, Milnes.

Looking at the blank screen and shaking her head in disbelief, Milnes said to Sample, "Well, you heard them. Draft up a fuckin' outline of how negotiations might go. I can supply business points when my blood pressure returns to something below 200 over 120."

"We'll need to withdraw the application I just filed to seek permission to take discovery, and the opposition to cash collateral. When I do that, it'll spark a call from Ms. Jones."

"File what you need to file; don't take Jones' call. Get me the fuckin' outline. Show me my fuckin' options." Not "our" options, "my" options, Sample observed. He just saw Milnes listening to Stephanie Bonde's comments on the video call, but he wondered if she heard anything Bonde said.

"Based on the vote, I need to get the outline to all of the banks, Stacy," Sample corrected her.

"Whatever," Milnes said, like a scornful teenager. "Just get the outline done."

With that, Milnes closed up her notebook and left Sample's conference room in a huff.

§

On her walk back, Stacy Milnes found herself particularly bothered by Brian Chimes and his damn Texas drawl, a far cry from her native Philadelphia accent that surfaced when she was stressed, angry, or both. *Chimes — Ten percent of the loans; ninety percent of the mouth.* She felt sure that Chimes felt the same lack of respect for her. She needed to develop another strategy with three goals: save face; prove she was right about Witherman; prove the syndicate banks were wrong. Oh, and a fourth goal – diffuse any concerns raised by the First Commercial brass when they learned about all of this.

As she walked, Milnes considered what Bonde said about an investigation of Quincy after the bank resolved the issues through negotiation. Milnes was ready to commission a deep dive into everything Witherman now, though, not later. She had taken enough orders from the syndicate banks already, and she had no intention of waiting to get started on a Witherman investigation. *And I know just the person to help.*

§

Sample returned to his office and prepared to advise Judge Robertson that shortly, the banks would withdraw the cash collateral opposition and the discovery application.

He knew the decision to withdraw the opposition to the use of cash collateral was the right one. During the short life of these cases, Milnes had provided Sample little in the way of ammunition against the Debtors' request to continue to use cash. Witherman's management company maintained the buildings and had a stellar reputation, the buildings were highly desirable, and in top-notch condition. Moreover, the Debtors' budget contained nothing that would cause the Judge to raise an eyebrow. In a trial, the Judge would likely reject any budget opposition raised by the banks.

Sample also knew the Debtors' appraiser George Herndon and, based on past experiences, he was confident that Herndon was solid both in his written analysis and witness stand performance. He assumed that the Debtors would call Herndon as the first witness, and after that testimony, the cash collateral issues would be over for all intents and purposes.

No, from Sample's review of the matter, the banks had less chance to successfully oppose the Debtors' request to use cash than George Armstrong Custer and his Seventh Cavalry Regiment had to defeat Crazy Horse and his Lakota warriors at the battle of the Little Big Horn. So it was a relief that he wasn't being sent into the Bankruptcy Court version of the Little Big Horn to try to fend off Witherman's Lakota warriors.

Sample picked up the phone, called Judge Robertson's chambers, and the Judge's law clerk answered the phone. Sample explained that the banks would withdraw their cash collateral opposition and the discovery application in the afternoon. With much relief, it was a quick call, taking less than thirty seconds. He felt mad at himself for allowing Milnes to browbeat him into filing such an incendiary pleading. The statements had no real basis in fact and had come from Milnes. He had done no independent investigation to assure himself that Milnes' version of the facts were true. He well knew that even if clients sometimes conflated beliefs with facts, it was his job in the federal system to be the gatekeeper and investigate before filing a pleading based merely on beliefs. He hadn't done that in this instance and he knew it was wrong. He knew that could get him in hot water with Judge Robertson. He hoped the withdrawal of the application would provide some salve if the Judge was angry.

Sample drafted and finalized the withdrawals in less than ten minutes, and he filed it electronically in less than forty seconds. Less than five minutes later, the phone rang, and the caller I.D. revealed it was Josephina Jones. As instructed, he didn't take the call. He let it roll to voicemail.

He retrieved it a minute later. "Dennis, this is 3J. Could you please give me a call? I thought perhaps it would be productive for us to talk and see where these cases are heading. Thanks."

Sample considered 3J's message for a minute or two. He respected 3J. He even liked her. Talking to her, at this point, would be normal. But Stacy Milnes had directed him not to speak to 3J, and not talking was what he intended to do. Sample wasn't sure that the silent treatment made a lot of sense, but obediently he sat down to draft an outline of negotiating points for the meeting with Quincy that the banks had now decided, democratically, would occur.

§

Judge Robertson sat at his desk and looked over an email from his law clerk recounting the telephone call received a few minutes ago from First Commercial's attorney. During the past week, the Judge had three trials in other cases, and didn't have the time to read the Witherman discovery application. The trials were over now, however, and the Judge had just begun to review the Witherman files, when the Banks withdrew the discovery application and the cash objection. The question bothering the Judge now was, what's the game plan unfolding here?

Judge Robertson finished reading the lengthy discovery application, and what he read disturbed him. The whole application seemed designed to discredit the Debtors. Rather than just ask for documents, the application was full of innuendo that the Debtors maintained hidden, undisclosed assets, and had done so for years. The problem was, the allegations were made on "information and belief" and failed to disclose the referenced information or the basis for the belief.

If the banks had a plan in mind that was designed to get documents, it seemed flawed, and now that there was no longer an application for the Court to consider, all that was left was the tarnish of the allegations, and Judge Robertson didn't like it at all. He urged his law clerk to contact the attorneys for the interested parties and set up an hour status conference in the Judge's chambers.

Jamie scheduled the meeting for Friday, October 12, 2018 at 10 a.m.

Judge Robertson reflected on the strange goings on in the bank group, and the over-the-top application he just read. Though the Witherman cases were shaping up to make good cocktail party conversation, he knew he would never have that conversation over cocktail party drinks.

When he became a judge, he quickly learned that his life had changed from one of professional companionship to one of isolation. Attorney Robertson's private practice of law consisted of many daily contact with clients, prospective clients, partners in his firm, associates and staff who worked for him, judges, and attorneys at other law firms with whom he had cases. He liked the social part of his practice.

By contrast, life on the federal bench was a cloistered, hermit existence, and at times profoundly lonely. Judge Robertson's interactions were limited to his law clerk, Jamie, a legal administrative assistant he shared with another judge, the other judges in the Western District, and the attorneys who appeared in front of him in court. Upon donning the judiciary's black robe, his circle of friends shrank from whoever he wanted as a friend to, mainly, other judges.

He had decided to apply to be a bankruptcy judge, because he believed that a life as a judge was a way to cast off the jealous mistress that was attorney work, and take control of his daily existence. Attorney Robertson had many bosses in private practice – partners for whom he worked; clients for whom he worked; judges for whom he worked; experts he hired; even sometimes opposing counsel. Then there were also the law firm's marketing directors, chief operating officers, recruiters, managers, and information systems people for whom it seemed more and more like he worked. He came to believe that he worked for just about everyone and, in the information age, every one of those bosses could and did reach out to him at any time of the day and night, and expected an immediate response. He often thought he heard the jealous mistress cackling after another 10 p.m. text; every lawyer could agree that the mistress had a sick sense of humor.

As a judge, he saw the possibility of mostly just working for himself, ditching the jealous mistress, and asserting control over his daily existence. He liked that prospect. He liked it a great deal. Shortly after he was picked to be the next judge, he fulfilled his dream of serving the mistress with a cease and desist order and telling her to get the hell out of his life for good.

So he knew there would be no Witherman cocktail stories; he would have to leave the cocktail stories for those private practitioners still serving the whims of the jealous mistress. He sighed and returned to the work on his desk.

CHAPTER 16

The Debtor recalls Thursday, October 4 to Saturday, October 6, 2018

FIRST THING THAT THURSDAY morning, my mobile phone rang: 3J.

"Hey, 3J. What's up?"

3J explained to me that the banks withdrew their discovery application and their opposition to the use of cash.

"Hmmm," I said. "That's good, of course, but did you expect that? What do you make of it?"

"I didn't expect it. I don't know what to make of it. I'm stumped."

"No analysis for me?"

"None."

"Well, let's not look a gift horse in the mouth."

3J said nothing for a few seconds. Then, "Yes, sorry. I just don't like a turn of events that I can't explain."

"Maybe it all goes back to the pre-bankruptcy meeting and the body language I saw," I said. "Either way, it seems they have given me a chance to proceed with all speed toward confirmation. So, let's."

"Agreed. I'll get hearing dates from Judge Robertson, and we'll press this along to conclusion, Quincy. I'll be in touch."

After the call, I didn't know what to think. But the path to get out of bankruptcy just opened up, and the only thing that made sense to me was to race down that path to the finish line and push across before there was another unexpected event.

§

I awoke on Saturday, confident that the plan for my bankruptcy case was well on its way to successful completion. Sure, there would be some bumps in the road, but I felt good that the team I had chosen had the matters well in hand, and I continued to believe that I had my private matters equally well managed and that they remained highly covert.

I shuffled to my front door, opened it to retrieve my daily *Wall Street Journal*, and returned to listen to a Michael Franks album I liked to enjoy in the morning – *The Art of Tea*, with one of my favorite new age Jazz songs – "Nightmoves." I gently lowered the needle onto the vinyl disc, and Franks sang about his far away love confined in a prison of wishes. As I relaxed to Franks' gentle rhythms, I opened the *Wall Street Journal* and found a headline that had the potential to change everything: "Switzerland to Share Information."

I froze. *How is that even possible?* I read the article intently. Suddenly, I heard none of *The Art of Tea*, none of Michael Franks' sly lyrics, and none of Joe Sample's electric piano. Instead, I fragmented between the words on the page and the racing, random thoughts in my brain that focused on the implications of secret Swiss bank accounts that would no longer be secret. In typical *Wall Street Journal* efficiency, the article reported that Switzerland had signed a convention to share information with sixty countries, including the United States. And on Friday, October 5, 2018, for the first time ever the venerable Swiss Federal Tax Administration agreed to begin to exchange bank account data that had been formerly camouflaged with foreign tax authorities. The article ended with a proffered opinion that this momentous event marked the beginning of the end of Swiss banking secrecy.

The article traced the history of the secret Swiss banking industry. I knew that the Swiss banks had been under pressure for years, more likely decades, to release information. I was aware that in 2007, Switzerland had said it would release funds belonging to the late Congolese dictator Mobutu Sese Seko, who was reputed to be a regular at Swiss banks. At that time, I had considered "relocating" the Witherman inheritance that had been in the custody of Swiss banks since the 1800s. But I had decided not to do anything at that time that could create a trail of the hidden assets, protected from scrutiny for centuries behind the veil of Swiss secrecy like a science fiction cloaking device, favored in outer space movies.

The article reported a rumor that the United States Department of Justice had prepared a lawsuit against a fabled Swiss bank. The article quoted an anonymous source who predicted that the DOJ would accuse the bank of defrauding investors in the sale of mortgage-backed securities. The source said the DOJ based its suit on secret information previously held behind a formidable Swiss shroud that had protected those who banked at the internationally renowned Swiss banks for centuries. The article concluded by opining that individuals could no longer safely hide assets in Swiss accounts because Switzerland and its banks would now share that information with other countries, including the United States.

Maybe I should have moved the account to Singapore, a growing haven for hidden Asian assets. But I didn't focus on that thought for very long; I knew it was too late for such a move in light of the pending bankruptcy cases. I assessed that the odds were still quite low that Milnes would find a way to access information about my hidden account, but the odds were no longer quite as close to zero as I hoped all of a sudden, and that caused me anxiety. I needed to control my emotions because I saw no viable alternative but to stand firm at this point.

I moved from my couch to my desk. In the back of the top drawer was a burner phone that I used to call Michaela.

Michaela Roston Huld, a graduate of Trinity College in Dublin and of the Tuck School of Business at Dartmouth College's master's program. Michaela, who, upon graduation from Tuck, had entered the same profession as her great-great-uncle Francis Marion Roston – asset protection advice. Michaela, who lived in London and offered her services to clients worldwide. Michaela, who had always advised me to stay the course and keep my account where it was – hidden in the Swiss Alps' foothills, in as discreet a setting as existed on the planet. Michaela, who officially served as an asset advisor, and unofficially as a guidance counselor, a philosopher, an armchair psychologist ... and my love.

I had a custom of seeing Michaela several times a year in London. We used those times for economic and philosophical discussions, a chance for her to listen to me talk about my hopes and dreams for new buildings, and to catch up on that part of my life that was mostly unfulfilled: Love. Yes, I was in love with her. All five foot four inches and a hundred and five pounds of her. I loved her auburn hair, her blue eyes, her hands, her graceful fingers, and every other part of her athletic body. She was the living being in the present that served as my organic tie to the past.

I dialed her number – her own burner phone – and said, "Michaela, m' love. How is London in the fall?"

"Wet, m' love. Wet and gray. Always wet and gray. It builds character."

"I miss you. I always miss you."

"And I do you."

"Michaela, I'm calling because I have a business concern." I always called my hidden assets a "business concern." The fact that I had hidden assets was just business, after all.

"What is it?"

"My concern is on the front page of the *Wall Street Journal*. Have you seen the article?"

"Indeed. We should discuss this in person. Are you still able to come to London and be with me in ten days?"

"Yes. Counting the days."

"Then, let's talk as we walk the Thames."

"Love you."

"Same."

The call ended. As I replaced the phone in the back of the drawer, I looked at my prized bronze statue of a broken bench and found myself in deep thought. I had filed for bankruptcy relief. I had navigated the process so far. I was heading down a lighted path to the exit. In the shadows, to the side of the bankruptcy path, was my Swiss account, and I intended for it to stay in darkness.

As was my custom, some years before, I had learned a bit of history about the bankruptcy process. "Bankruptcy" derived from the Italian, *banca rotta* – broken bench. Medieval Italian merchants who didn't pay back their debts found a broken bench outside their establishment, and with it, the judgment, ridicule, and shame of the world for failing to pay their creditors. That merchant debtor also had to run naked in a public place like the piazza and strike his backside three times against the Rock of Shame while crying out, "I declare bankruptcy." Fun times, in the olden days. I guess we humans have always held a special place in our hearts for people who owe money.

Outside of my door there was no broken bench. And, of course, I could no longer go to prison if I failed to repay debts. Oh, how progressive America had become since the eighteenth century. But I kept the small replica of a broken bench on my desk to remind me of Gunn and how ugly it could get when the day came that I could not – my lenders might say, would not – pay back my debts.

We come from nothing, and we return to nothing – earth to earth; ashes to ashes; dust to dust. As dust, we take no legal tender with us when we pass on to whatever, if anything, comes next. I thought of Gunn and how he ended his life with nothing. But I didn't begin my life with nothing, thanks to Gunnie's good fortune after the Yazoo Land Fraud. I had no intention of ending my life with nothing and thereby repeating the tragedy of Gunn.

Oh Gunn, if you're watching all of this unfold from the great beyond, and you have any enlightenment you can offer, give me a sign. Otherwise, the plan must proceed quickly. Restructure the debts – quickly; get the confirmation order from Judge Robertson – quickly; and get the hell out of Dodge, or in this case, the Bankruptcy Court in Kansas City – quickly.

CHAPTER 17

Saturday, October 6 to Monday, October 8, 2018

IN HER ONE-BEDROOM TOWNHOUSE, Stacy Milnes poured a cup of French-press coffee, sat down at her table, and flipped through her morning *St. Louis Post-Gazette*. Milnes shared her townhouse, coffee, table, newspaper, and her life with no one. She found nothing of interest in the national and international sections, nor in the sports section. Milnes turned to business news and read the Swiss Bank news story picked up by the *Post-Gazette* off an international wire service.

Milnes paused, considered, and then slowly smiled. A small smile, and then it grew from ear to ear. She was not particularly religious, despite her Catholic school upbringing, but she couldn't help but think that good fortune had just shone down on her from the heavens. There could be no other explanation. Did she *know* Quincy had a Swiss bank account? No, of course not; not yet. All she "knew" was the information in the plain vanilla financial statements that Witherman presented to the banks every six months, and a deep-seated feeling that the information failed to include all of Witherman's assets. She knew the voice in her head and the feeling in her gut that alerted her to beware of the financial information. Every fiber in her body told her that there was something more to the Witherman empire than he reported to the banks. Those instincts had guided her through a successful career, and she wasn't about to ignore them in Witherman's case. Was she jumping to conclusions? Maybe. But she allowed herself to see this development of the end of secret Swiss bank accounts as a form of credit providence.

She knew what she wanted to do. On Monday, she would pick up the phone and call an old acquaintance in New York City, Moses Aaronson. Moses was in the business of collecting discrete information. He quietly promoted himself as someone who finds the unfindable, identifies the unidentifiable, and uncovers hidden secrets. *He'll be perfect for the Witherman problem,* Milnes thought.

§

Early on Monday morning, Milnes phoned Moses Aaronson.

"Moses. Hi. Stacy Milnes."

"How is Ms. Milnes today?" Moses asked, exuding deference and respect.

"Good, good. Actually, excellent. And how are you? It's been a while."

"I am as good as any of the aging homo sapiens who wake each morning to discover they are still a bipedal primate, spinning daily on planet Earth, can hope to be, I suppose. So I can't … or won't … complain."

Milnes laughed. Classic Moses. A simple, *I am well,* was just not in his constitution, but his way of answering questions was part of what made him compelling.

"How can I be of service, my friend?" Moses inquired.

Milnes did not know Moses' exact age, but she guessed he was approaching eighty years old. She had last seen him several years ago in Manhattan at a special assets officer function. She had used him on several matters in the past, and

Moses always seemed to be able to dig up the goods on one borrower or another. She tended to reserve his engagement for the very special assets, as she liked to explain to colleagues. His reports were like nothing else in the collection business. Detailed; thorough; honest; attention to process; written in the King's English; and, most importantly, revealing. Very revealing. A private eye's private eye, as one of her former colleagues in New York had referred to him.

Moses, however, bristled at the notion that he was a private investigator. "No, no," he would say when anyone suggested that P.I. work was his vocation. "I am neither a sleuth, nor a detective, a dick, a Pinkerton, or a bloodhound," he would explain. "I am not coarse. I don't hang out in an alleyway under a dim street light with a cigarette dangling from my lips like a 1930s pulp fiction character. I am cultivated – a student of society and human nature." Then, with quiet confidence, Moses would explain what he did. "I shine light on that which is dark. I illuminate. I am an illuminator." By this point in the conversation, many in his audience often thought he was just an old rambling coot, short on remaining years, and long on comedic hyperbole. Milnes knew Moses was not comedic in the least. She also knew that she very much needed Moses' services to shed light on Quincy Witherman's dark underbelly.

Moses was old school – a throwback. In his office, he sat at an old, weathered, oak roll-top desk, on an old wooden chair with a seat whose cushioned pad had changed slowly from smooth leather to suede over the many years Moses occupied it. Old School. Outside, he wore a dark, navy wool French beret. Old School. He had manners, respect, and deference. Definitely Old School. He spoke with a notable New York accent, albeit one that suggested education, elite social circles, and status. He had never married, but could be seen in his younger days at any number of New York City society events with a sophisticated, stunning, plus-one on his arm. In his younger days, he had enjoyed the attention. He seldom raised his voice. He simply rarely found the need to, or the purpose served by doing so. He had a gravelly voice that he often cleared before speaking.

He lived in Manhattan's Flatiron district, not far from the famous Flatiron Building, at the convergence of Fifth Avenue and Broadway, and near Madison Park, where he was a frequent visitor. He used the park benches to sit in solitude, focus, and sort out the narrative of whatever his current engagement might be, as he tried to eliminate the dead ends and identify the paths to illumination.

Milnes explained the situation to Moses, that the focus of her "curiosity" was her guarantor, Quincy Gunn Witherman. After Milnes finished, she asked Moses if he was interested in the assignment and said, "I'll send you the Witherman financial statements. I want you to find something significant that's not on the statements. That simple."

"Ahhh, simple," said Moses into the black telephone receiver. His small rat terrier mix dog, Emily, had jumped into his lap and sat there quietly with her eyes shut in ultimate dog bliss as Moses slowly stroked her sleek, brown ears and the silky underside of her chin. "Ms. Milnes, we humans are anything but a simple breed. We take the simple and turn it into the complex with every breath we take, each and every day, without fail. I am reminded of something one of my music heroes, Charles Mingus, once said: 'Making the simple complicated is commonplace; making the complicated simple, awesome simple, that's creativity.'"

"Moses, in whatever manner you do it, whatever music you listen to as you do it, and with whatever means you must employ, please find me … no, sorry, please shine your light on something that's not on those financial statements."

"Indeed, Ms. Milnes." Moses then asked, "What precipitated your inquiry, if I might ask?"

Milnes paused, then said, "Good question. I was sitting here at my kitchen table. I flipped through the newspaper, and there, in the Saturday business section, I found an article about the new law in Switzerland that seems to do away with that country's fabled bank secrecy. I don't believe in mysticism but it was as if the article was put there in the newspaper for me to find. To use your word, it was an illumination. And I wondered, 'what if Quincy were one of those businessmen, who's taken advantage of Swiss bank secrecy for years?' And then, of course, I thought of you. You'll answer that question for me. My hope is that you'll answer it in the affirmative."

Moses smiled. *Ms. Milnes knows precisely what I do. She values my methods, and this is why I like working with her.* "Do you have any specific reason to suspect Mr. Witherman hides assets in a Swiss Bank account?"

"Just my gut," she replied.

"Ahhha! Intuition. Instinct. A premonition. A hunch. Our sixth sense. But, not *just* our guts; no, our *elan vital*, Ms. Milnes. Our essence. The gray areas we humans rely on to assess. Although we cannot explain them, we depend on them, and most importantly, we know they work. I understand. Ms. Milnes, it would be my honor to be in your employ again and work to find something in the Witherman — shall we call it, portfolio? upon which I can shine a light for you. I will report weekly as per our past affiliations. Is that correct?"

"Exactly. Call this number. It's my mobile phone."

"Send me the information, and let me get started tomorrow morning, Ms. Milnes. Good day," said Moses and then gently placed the old New York Bell Telephone and Telegraph Company black receiver back on its cradle. Old School.

Milnes liked and respected Moses. She valued a professional relationship in which she could turn off her adopted, hyper-aggressive persona and just get to work in a collaborative effort to solve a problem. She thought back to the admonition she had received from Stephanie Bonde about finding assets and smiled to herself. "Finally, my nickel, my rules," she proclaimed softly to herself. *Maybe when this is all said and done, and Moses has performed his magic, Ms. Bonde and the other syndicate bankers will extend an apology to me, and in fact, thank me for going the extra mile to out our common adversary, Quincy Gunn Witherman.*

After the call ended, Moses looked down at his yellow pad on his desk and further down to Emily, who had curled up in his lap and seemed as content as any creature could possibly be. He circled the name Quincy Gunn Witherman on his pad. *What an interesting name,* he thought. He wondered about Witherman's family history and if any part of Witherman's name was a part of that history. One of Moses' mantras: One cannot solve the mysteries of the day without understanding the accounts of the past. He liked to say that to people in the private investigation industry. They heard him, but he was certain few listened to him. No matter. He would delve into the Witherman name first while he awaited information from Ms. Milnes. He gently placed Emily in her bed, which had just begun to attract the afternoon rays of the sun, said goodbye to her, and told her to be good and to guard the flat in his absence. He donned his beret and headed down to the street for a walk to collect his thoughts. Emily sighed deeply and curled her head into her front paws as she settled into a satisfying afternoon of dog naps and dreams.

Tuesday morning, bright and early, Moses decided he would head to the New York Public Library, the largest marble structure ever constructed in the United States, where all of the world's information that matters resided. Old School. He envisioned spending some hours in the dusty recesses of the library's stacks as he felt a little Witherman-history-exploration was in order. He wondered if First Commercial had looked at all into Witherman's past before extending loans to his companies.

There are many things of which a wise man should be ignorant, Ralph Waldo Emerson wrote. *Not in my line of work; history is so important,* Moses thought. Little did he know that on this topic, he and Quincy Witherman were in complete agreement.

§

After her call with Moses, Milnes headed into the bank and when she reached her desk, there was a voice mail from Stephanie Bonde simply asking Milnes to call Bonde when she could. After talking with Moses, Milnes was in such a good mood that she didn't think further discussions with a member of the bank group, especially Bonde, could ruin her day. She dialed Bonde across the ocean and two continents. Bonde picked up on the second ring.

"Hello, Stacy," Bonde said. "Thanks for calling. We would like to start the plan discussions with Quincy Witherman's team and would like Brian to be the point person for those discussions. Any objection?"

"You want a bank that's not the Agent to take the lead in the negotiations?"

Bonde stayed silent, allowing Milnes to process the situation and vent if need be.

"Well, I don't like it, but I suppose if I say no, the rest of you folks will just take another God-damn vote, and then Brian will be the negotiating point person whether I like it or not."

Bonde continued her silence.

After a few moments, Milnes conceded. "I won't raise any objection at this point. But, at the meeting with Witherman,

Chimes should clarify that he has no authority to bind the banks until the banks vote on whatever deal comes out of the discussions and then agree in writing. Will he have a problem with that?"

Bonde found the "no authority" request ironic. Not a week ago, Milnes would have thought nothing of agreeing to a deal without bank group authority. Bonde decided against a conflict with Milnes, however, saying instead, "No problem. We discussed that point. Brian Chimes is very experienced, and he is fine with setting those ground rules. I would take the lead myself but it makes little sense for me to fly all the way from South Africa when Brian is right there in the States. I'll ask Brian to reach out to Quincy and set up a meeting in Kansas City. Stacy, we also want First Commercial to be present at the negotiations."

"I don't know about that," Milnes hesitated as she responded. "What purpose would be served?"

"All the banks will have a representative at the discussions, as you would expect. Most will be on a video feed. You wouldn't have to fly to Kansas City. You could just appear by the video feed. Your presence would be an important message to Witherman; you're tough and you're very involved. Why is that a problem?"

"I'm not going to commit to an appearance at this time. I'll let you know how I feel about that later," Milnes responded with a huff.

"It is important that the members of the outside world not, shall I call it, 'take part' in the banks' disagreements. They have no place at the banks' private table. It's not their place, it's not their table, and it's not their business. No good would come of it. If you don't attend, we will invite them into our private disagreements and deliberations. We don't want that. Why would you?"

"You don't like how I run the loan strategy; you don't like how I communicate; you probably don't like me either. You all voted. Congrats. That's where your power ends. Don't you dare lecture me about the table. I'll let you know if I think it's important for First Commercial to appear at the discussions. Anything else?"

"Well, I disagree that is where our powers end. I don't want to know if you think First Commercial's appearance is important. I want to know your decision about attending before the meeting. Is that going to be a problem?"

"No," Milnes said begrudgingly.

"Very well, then. I will look for you to communicate your attendance decision to me before the meeting convenes. Anything else you want to discuss?"

"You called me. I've got no agenda items to discuss," Milnes said harshly.

"Very well," Bonde replied in a sing-songy, upbeat kind of way, and hung up. As she replaced the receiver on her desk phone, she looked at the phone and said to herself, "Always a pleasure, Stacy."

§

Bonde next rang Brian Chimes at StarBanc, who answered, "Y'ello, Brian Chimes." Chimes had a habit of adding a "Y" to the beginning of hello, and Bonde thought that the "Y" coupled with his Texas accent made the greeting almost charming, at least in an American New South kind of way.

"Brian, Stephanie Bonde here. I spoke with Stacy Milnes, and she signed off on the decision for you to run point in the plan discussions with Witherman. She hedged when I told her we wanted her to participate, and my takeaway is that she's not likely to appear at the discussions. I doubt she'll send a representative either. Not much we can do about that, I'm afraid, but maybe it's for the best. If she came, she might be inclined to try to take over the show, and we don't want that," Bonde cautioned. "If you have time today, please reach out to Mr. Witherman and let's see how quickly we can set up a meeting and then reach an agreement. How does that sound?"

"Sounds just fine to me, Stephanie," Chimes said in his Texas drawl.

"We will need to come up with something to say to Mr. Witherman when he asks why Milnes is not at the meeting."

"None of his business, don't you think?"

"Is that what you suggest we tell Witherman?"

"Not in so many words, but the message will be that the rest of the banks will participate in the negotiations, then there'll be a vote, and then we'll inform Witherman of the results of the vote. I can be pleasant in telling him he doesn't get a seat at the bank group table. He'll be fine with it."

"Sounds good," Bonde agreed.

"Did you see the outline from Sample?" Chimes asked.

"I did. It looked comprehensive to me. Good work product," Bonde said.

"Agreed. He seems like a good lawyer, especially when he's answering to *all* of us banks," Chimes observed, pausing momentarily on the word "all" for emphasis.

After a few pleasantries, the call ended.

§

Chimes dialed Quincy Witherman's mobile number, and he answered straightaway.

"Quincy? Brian Chimes of StarBanc here."

"Mr. Chimes. Good afternoon. To what do I owe the pleasure?"

"Quincy, my father was Mr. Chimes. I'm just plain old Brian, please."

"Got it."

"Quincy, the banks had a meeting, and we've decided that what we want to do is to negotiate some of the plan provisions with you, and then if we can reach agreement, we'd support the confirmation of the plan. You know, we'll all join arms and sing Kumbaya together in front of Judge Robertson and the world, and make the good Judge just happier than I could ever imagine a newbie judge could be. How does that sound as a course of action?"

"Well, frankly, I'm more than a bit surprised, Brian. We could've done an iteration of this when my team and I flew to St. Louis to meet with the banks. The banks forced us to take the bankruptcy route because of their posture at the meeting. You may recall that meeting wasn't at all productive, and in fact, you guys wouldn't even look at our term sheet. Heck, many of you wouldn't even raise your heads to look at me."

"Yeah, I remember it well. I surely do," Chimes said quietly and cautiously as he paused and then continued, "Look, Quincy, here's the thing. I don't want to go into a bunch of details, but I'll just observe that we are where we are, as my teenage son likes to say to me when he doesn't want to explain something he did last night that he shouldn't have. Quincy, we're willing to meet. Hell, we want to meet. I'll be the point for our side. As far as we can tell, Milnes may not even be at the meeting." Chimes let that point sink in and then continued. "There's nothing to lose but a little time; we think it'll be – as they like to say in the movies – mutually beneficial. So what'd'ya' say? We're happy to meet at the Greene Madison offices if they can brew us up some of that good Kansas City coffee they offer to guests. I think they serve Filling Station coffee in the big conference room. That'll be just more than fine."

"I hear you, Brian, and I appreciate the call and your perspective. Let me talk with 3J, and I'll get right back to you."

"You got it, Quincy. Have yourself one of those good old days."

§

After the call ended, Quincy sighed deeply. He wondered if each of the banks' special asset officers were off-beat characters or just the ones he was unlucky enough to have to deal with directly. On the other hand... *A meeting with the bank group without Milnes. We might genuinely get something accomplished.*

He called 3J and got her voice mail. He left a short message. "3J? Quincy. Brian Chimes of StarBanc just called me. Wants to meet with us to negotiate the terms of an actual plan. I assume I'm awake and not dreaming and that I'm not all of a sudden living in some kind of computer simulation. Just call me when you free up. Bye."

Minutes later, 3J returned to her desk with a fresh cup of Earl Grey tea, listened to Quincy's voice mail, called Pascale, and when he arrived at her office, the two attorneys called Quincy and put him on the speakerphone.

3J said, "Quincy, any details besides what you said on your voice mail?"

"Apparently, Chimes thinks Milnes won't attend. Chimes also said he'd lead the negotiations for the banks."

Pascale whistled. "Really?" he exclaimed. "Wow. No Milnes. What a productive meeting that might turn out to be. I wonder if that's her choice or if she's sitting in the corner of her office facing the wall in a bank group time-out like a misbehaving three-year-old?"

"Yeah. Really. When I tried to whine a bit about the pre-bankruptcy non-meeting we had in St. Louis, Chimes deflected and said, 'we are where we are.' I guess that's hard to argue with. So what do you guys think is going on in our favorite bank group?"

"Hard to say," 3J replied, "but I have to agree with Chimes' inarguable truism and add my Pascale-like observation that we are *always* where we are. In any case, it seems clear that there's been some kind of power or influence shift. The syndicate banks can out-vote First Commercial under the credit agreement. Maybe they backed Stacy down. Or just had enough of her. She's incredibly effective but I can see her style wearing thin with bank group members, and perhaps quickly. If so, I'm sure she's having the time of her life."

"I assume we take the meeting?" Quincy asked.

"Why not?" asked Pascale rhetorically. "Will they meet in Kansas City?"

"Not only will they meet in KC, but they also offered to meet at your offices," Quincy explained. "Chimes wants a cup of your firm's Filling Station coffee."

"Let's tell them we can meet in a couple of days at our offices and ask them to send us a term sheet with the plan points they want to negotiate. We'll brew a pot for him. Sound ok?" asked 3J.

"On it, boss," said Quincy, and they disconnected.

§

Quincy called Chimes back and arranged the meeting day and time, delivered the term sheet message, and Chimes was his amiable self again. He almost seemed to enjoy himself. *Ahhh, the things that can brighten up an otherwise bleak, gray sky, special assets day.* Quincy thought. Chimes was a breath of fresh air, and nothing about him seemed to say, "I'm not your fuckin' friend." What a trade-up from Milnes.

§

When Chimes finished his call with Witherman, he leaned back in his chair and considered a little analysis and self-clarification of his views. Chimes wasn't saying that Milnes was wrong; that her instinct was off-base. In Chimes' view, Milnes mostly had good instincts and indeed, Witherman might not be at all honest. Hell, with many borrowers, honesty was not the first word that crossed Chimes' mind as he considered their fate and his collection strategy. No, Chimes was just asking, *why go down that path if you don't have to?* And in this matter, Chimes saw no reason to go down an expensive path to test Witherman's virtue. Especially if the banks won and put Witherman out of business, the winner's "prize" would be to take back the office buildings and run them. *What a freakin' disaster that would be,* he thought. A better plan was to assume Witherman lacked an honest character, know the devil across the table, cut a new deal, and then trust little and verify a lot as you see fit.

Nevertheless, Chimes wondered about Witherman's level of integrity. After all, Chimes was a banker, and bankers, especially special assets veterans, always thought about the level of a borrower's integrity. Unavoidable. Too many years of disappointment at the hands of people who owed the bank money. *I do wonder about Witherman. Yes, indeed, I do.*

Chimes was a fan of Warren Buffett, and one of Buffett's observations in particular always stuck with Chimes. Buffet said, "We look for three things when we hire people. We look for intelligence, we look for initiative or energy, and we look for integrity. And if they don't have the latter, the first two will kill you, because if you're going to get someone without integrity, you want them lazy and dumb." Bankers should look for the same three things in their borrowers, Chimes believed. Chimes knew Witherman was intelligent and had energy, but he wasn't sure about the integrity piece of the equation. He also knew that Witherman was neither lazy nor dumb, so, as

Buffet would say, that made Witherman a problem. That and his companies owed the banks $520 million. So, a *problem indeed that owes us a ton of money*, thought Chimes.

Better to paper a modification and get as far on repayment as possible before any of Witherman's potential lack of integrity issues surface and impede the payment process in any fashion. Chimes certainly liked the buildings that Witherman created, but he didn't want his bank to own or run any of them. He just wanted repayment in good old Uncle Sam currency. Negotiation presented a much greater opportunity to reach that goal than a fight.

Once we negotiate a deal and the bankruptcy cases conclude, the banks will all fade back into the shadows of what banks do − collect money each month and use it to make new loans. As long as they received the timely payments, the banks will return to a bank's state of suspended animation − passivity − no more Witherman special assets time. Or so Chimes thought.

INTERLUDE

Thursday, May 15, 1828

GUNNTHER "GUNNIE" WITHERMAN, JR. was the son of the infamous Gunnther Witherman, disgraced debtor now deceased at the hands of the Prune Street Gaol. Gunnie was ill, and he knew his time drew near. His life was about to conclude. He had developed a nasty persistent cough, and his doctor's diagnosis was consumption, later to be known as tuberculosis, for which there was no cure. The doctor advised Gunnie to get his affairs in order because his life would be over soon. As he looked back on the different unplanned paths his journey had taken, he counted himself a lucky man. He didn't end up in a debtors' prison. He lobbied for reparations from the Federal Government for the Yazzoo Land Fraud debacle, and after many years, the reparations came. He took the reparations, and through luck, good fortune, savvy, and skill, he grew the reparations into a goodly sum, some might say a fortune. Along the way, he came to distrust lenders as his father had, and as he hoped future generations of Withermans would too.

He had no will, but needed to draft one … quickly, as he felt he was living on borrowed time. So, late at night, in front of his fireplace, by the light of his oil lamp and in between uncontrollable coughing fits, he drafted his last will and testament, stating truthfully that he was still of sound mind, and that he was also of sound body though he knew that was not the case. The will introduced the establishment of a trust for future generations to benefit from Gunnie's good fortune. The trustee would be Francis Marion Roston, a savvy Philadelphia financial advisor, and one of the few men of finance that Gunnie had in his inner circle of acquaintances that he could trust.

Francis Marion Roston was a trusted advisor to his clients, including Gunnie. Roston was a graduate of Harvard College, who, upon graduation, found employment working for another Harvard grad who had carved out a living assisting those with money to get more money and, importantly, secure it from creditors. Asset protection. A financial advisor to the wealthy. A noble profession? Not especially. But a necessary one, or at least the wealthy believed so, and the profession represented a quintessential American offshoot of capitalism, wealth, and money.

Once he was established in Philadelphia, Roston met Gunnther Witherman, Jr., son of a prominent, now deceased, real estate developer and a real estate investor himself. They struck up a friendship, and it grew into an enduring role for Roston as a trusted advisor. Roston helped Gunnie amass significant wealth and then helplessly watched as it vanished in the investment known as the Yazoo Land Fraud, only to reappear later in the form of government reparations. He was a regular when Gunnie was moneyed and stayed a regular when Gunnie had none. A loyalist, to be trusted with Gunnie's life if need be. It was Roston who lobbied Congress for the better part of a decade to set aside funds to pay those who were bilked by the Yazoo Land Fraud. Roston's motivation was simple: he couldn't bear to see another Witherman end up in as vile a place as Prune Street.

In many respects, Gunnie felt that Roston single-handedly saved him from the same debtors' prison fate as his father, Gunn.

When it came time for Gunnie to consider the bequest of his fortune to future Witherman generations, who better than Roston to call upon for help? Gunnie's goal was not only to leave the bequest but to structure it in such a way that future Withermans were safe from creditors who might swarm when economic times turned difficult. It was Roston who revealed to Gunnie the protections afforded by the secret Swiss banking industry and advised him how to use the Swiss industry for the benefit of future generations.

It was Roston who told Gunnie how to bequeath his fortune, first to Gunnie's two children, Adam and Betsy, and then their offspring. Roston advised Gunnie that he could leave his assets in a way that could help those yet-to-be-born Withermans to not only receive their share of the fortune but to keep and shield it from their creditors beneath the concrete facade of the Swiss system.

Thus, when it came time for Gunnie to draft his will and name Roston as the trustee, no further instructions were necessary. Roston not only knew what Gunnie wanted him to do; Roston was the architect of the plan Gunnie had decided to employ. Gunnie gave Roston specific, oral instructions about how he wished the funds to be handled, drafting the will broadly to provide power to Roston to invest as he saw fit. Gunnie had no personal experience with the Swiss but verbally directed Roston to place the trust assets in one or more accounts in Switzerland and thereby begin what would be almost two hundred years of hidden Witherman assets just outside the purview of their lenders.

The year was 1820.

Roston was there at his bedside as Gunnie slipped away, and then died within days of completion and execution of his will. Roston filed the will in the Philadelphia courts, and the Court awarded him the power to administer Gunnie's assets.

Not two months later, Roston had established a labyrinth of Swiss bank accounts that would serve the Witherman offspring for generations, spanning centuries. One of those accounts passed down to Quincy Witherman. There is no escape from history, nor would any Witherman wish it so.

CHAPTER 18

Tuesday, October 9, 2018

BRIGHT AND EARLY TUESDAY morning, Moses arrived at
the library and began some preliminary research on the Witherman family history. He made his way to the library's recesses
where he could review documents and conduct his searches in
quiet solitude. Moses liked quiet solitude. He believed it freed
his brain to collect data and organize it without the intrusion
of outside interference.

Moses had reviewed the initial bank files Milnes emailed
to him, including the loan write-up. There was a write-up
by the loan officer for the loan committee's review in every
new proposed loan. The First Commercial write-up contained
all the financial information Moses would expect to see, but,
not surprisingly, included minimal history about Witherman
himself. In every new engagement, Moses always wanted to
start at the beginning and learn what the bank's files failed to
include. What he called the "genuine history."

Occasionally, his quest for history yielded very little because
he found nothing of historical significance about the borrower.
But far more often, his searches uncovered interesting nuggets.
Knowing little about Witherman from the First Commercial
write-up, the volume of information he generated in a short
period surprised him; information about the Witherman clan.

Their many intersections with important moments in American history yielded many research hits. By mid-afternoon, Moses learned that Gunn Witherman died a pauper in Philadelphia's Prune Street Jail, where Robert Morris, financier of the American Revolution, also ended up when he could not repay his creditors. Morris managed to survive the ordeal and claim his rightful place in American history; Gunn Witherman, however, was not as fortunate.

He learned that Gunn made, and then lost, what in those days amounted to a fortune in the real estate business. When his lenders surrounded him, literally and figuratively, they committed him to prison until he repaid his debts. He never did.

Moses learned about Gunn's son and his own adventures. Unlike his father, Gunnie lucked out and Uncle Sam awarded him a large sum of money to make up for his losses. Gunnie died a wealthy man, and after that, many members of the Witherman clan made their own living in the real estate business. *Fascinating*, thought Moses. An entire multi-generational real estate dynasty.

Moses acknowledged that the Withermans seemed to do pretty well for themselves over the centuries. *And then came Quincy Gunn Witherman*, ostensibly named after his great-great-great-grandfather. Not only did he join the family legacy with the Witherman surname and Witherman vocation, but he also joined it as the keeper of the patriarch's first name as well.

There wasn't much that the public records could say about the family's wealth. Real estate, after all, was an up and down industry. The ups were soaring and exhilarating, providing the highest of euphoric highs. The downs could be epic, invoking terms like bottoms, drops, slips, slumps, cascading losses, and depressions, like – well – like Gunn, and the payment of the ultimate price – life itself.

Moses was interested in reading any wills recorded by Gunn or Gunnie. He learned that Gunn appeared to die in 1798 intestate. It wasn't surprising that his thoughts from the Prune Street Jail near the end of his stay on planet Earth did not turn to the distribution of his wealth. He had none, and therefore no use for a will. But Moses learned that Gunn's son Gunnie owned assets when he died, and, as it turned out, his executor probated his will. Moses was hopeful that the Gunnie will would provide a lead, and wrote a to-do item on his yellow pad – see if he could secure a copy of the Gunnie will from the ancient Philadelphia records.

Based on newspaper articles he read and the information he gathered on day one of his inquiry, the generations of Withermans certainly seemed to come from resilient stock. Resiliency was perhaps the most critical characteristic to have in the real estate business. Moses, a proud resident of New York City, thought, *just like New Yorkers who had been abused, beaten down, challenged, tested, and attacked, to still find a way to meander through life gracefully, testily, forcefully, meaningfully, tastefully, pointedly. We will see if the Withermans managed a similar path.*

CHAPTER 19

Thursday, October 11, 2018

THE BRIGHT, MIDWESTERN SUN shone through the east-facing window of conference room 27A at Greene Madison. Seated on one side of the conference room table were 3J, Pascale, and Quincy, and on the other side, Brian Chimes. Chimes had his notes and a cup of coffee in a Greene Madison mug, steam drifting upwards. He took a sip of the coffee – Filling Station as he requested – and savored the flavor.

No other banker attended in person. On the video screen, Stephanie Bonde appeared as well as representatives of Wall, Wertz, Telfair, and Silvermine Banks. Neither Stacy Milnes nor Dennis Sample appeared.

Five banks out of six, and no agent and no lawyer, Stephanie Bonde thought. *What a piece of work Milnes is.* She was sure that Milnes must have barred Sample from attending.

The night before, Chimes had provided the Debtors with the points in the plan the banks wanted to discuss and an indication of how the banks wanted those points resolved. The meeting got underway with those points, and the tone was business-cordial.

How far the world's come, thought Quincy.

Chimes made it clear that he was there to negotiate a potential deal but that he couldn't bind the banks to a deal today.

Rather, his goal was to reach terms that he could recommend to the full bank group that they should accept. Standard operating procedure in the special assets world, even though sixty percent of the banks would participate in the meeting.

The parties moved through the banks' points of contention: appropriate interest rate, loan-to-value-ratio, maturity date, and if, when, and how much the Debtors would pay if the value of the collateral diminished. Surprisingly for the entire Witherman team, as Chimes laid out the banks' reasoning, he emphasized that *everyone* present was there in good faith. He was hopeful the collective negotiating group could bridge any gaps between the banks' asks and the Witherman offers. Quincy smiled thinly. *Encouraging from a bank group who previously acted, through Milnes, more like a small terrorist organization.*

Over the next four hours, only Chimes spoke on behalf of the banks, and he showed his primary negotiating skills: preparation, efficiency, persuasiveness, and a steady demeanor. To the Witherman team, he sounded earnest. What a change from the Milnes approach. Several times during the negotiations, the Witherman team stepped out of the conference room so the banks could talk among themselves about a sticking point. Each time, when everyone returned to the conference room, Chimes had a reasonable suggestion at the ready to bridge the negotiation gap that worked for the Debtors.

By the end of the four-hour session, the parties had tweaked provisions of the plan to the satisfaction of both the Witherman team and the banks present at the meeting, and had agreed to the resumption of partial monthly payments in thirty days. Chimes announced he would take the revised terms back to his full group to further discuss, and, if appropriate, seek approval.

Quincy, ever the student of body language, watched the video feed to observe the bankers' mannerisms. This time, they seemed relaxed and engaged. They regularly nodded their heads in the affirmative and seemed to be in agreement as Chimes negotiated the points. Those banks plus StarBanc could vote to accept the revised terms even over First Commercial's objection. But the Witherman team understood that they would not witness the bank debate or vote.

Chimes confirmed that the next step was to seek approval from the entire bank group. *Seek approval,* thought Quincy. *What a surprise to hear those words in the context of the money my companies and I owe to the banks.* Not a phrase that would have been uttered by Stacy Milnes. Certainly not in the context of reaching an agreement with the Debtors.

"Anything else to cover today? Or have we hit all the discussion points?" Chimes asked.

"I believe that's everything," Quincy said.

Chimes collected his papers, shook hands firmly, and said to Quincy, with all seriousness and gravity as he held Quincy's hand in the extended handshake, "I do believe that I've enjoyed our time together as much as the coffee." He followed the comment with brief silence that seemed to resonate as he released Quincy's hand, and then slowly smiled. Not a toothy grin, but a mature, wistful smile involving only his lips, cheeks, and eyes.

He looked at the screen, told Bonde he would call her tomorrow; the video feed faded to black, Chimes exited the conference room, and 3J, Pascale, and Quincy were once again alone in the flagship conference room.

"Am I missing something? Are any of the plan changes that we considered here today controversial?" Quincy mused.

"Quincy, they're all business points, so you'll have to take the lead in answering your own question. But from our perspective, the changes appear to be minor in the grand scheme of things," 3J said. "They're all things we hoped to agree to before filing for bankruptcy protection."

"Minor, easy changes to make, and once the Judge knows we've worked through issues with the banks, he'll speed these cases to confirmation," Pascale added.

"I want Ronnie to run through the numbers again, but my gut is that the negotiated business points are all fine with me. More than fine," Quincy stated. "Pascale, when you say 'speed to confirmation,' just how fast can we move?"

"If everything clicks perfectly, you and your companies could be out of bankruptcy in maybe seventy-five days or so."

"We won't be paying the banks their full monthly payments during that period, so that seems fine. If there's any way to go even faster, we should, because that would be even finer," Quincy said.

"We'll need to see if the Judge has any appetite to shorten the required periods. He's so new to the Chapter 11 game as a jurist that he may just want to follow the time periods set out in the rules without adjustment," 3J said. "Quincy, if it's ok with you, I think we should go ahead and start making the plan changes discussed today. The banks are meeting simply to deal with Milnes and comply with their credit agreement requirements. Whether she votes yes or no, however, shouldn't matter – Chimes has over half of the vote in his pocket already."

"The path to confirmation is neither linear nor is it the same in every case, but then neither is the path through life," Pascale philosophized for Quincy and 3J. He enjoyed his role as sage philosopher.

Ignoring Pascale's liberal arts approach to bankruptcy, Quincy agreed with 3J and said, "Yes, please start on the plan modifications so we can be ready to go as soon as we hear from Chimes."

"Say, Pascale and I are probably going to get a drink at O'Brien's in Westport after work today if you want to join us," 3J offered to Quincy.

"Is that an Irish honky-tonk bar in the Midwest's drinking capital?" Quincy asked skeptically.

"Definitely in the drinking capital, definitely formerly Irish, and probably a honky-tonk at different times, depending on whose dollar powers the jukebox and your definition of honky-tonk," Pascale admitted with a wry smile.

"Definitely honky-tonk in my book. How about this? Drinks, sure. But can we go to the Street Hotel Club in the 18th and Vine District, and catch up on some jazz while we talk? Maybe a little less honk and more Monk, if that's ok," Quincy countered.

"Monk?" Pascale asked, feigning ignorance as he furrowed his brows and looked at the ceiling to emphasize the fake confusion he tried to convey.

"Thelonius," 3J said as she shook her head in disbelief and grinned at Pascale. "We can dress you up, but can we take you anywhere at all?"

Ignoring the ribbing, Pascale responded, "Sure. I knew that. How about 6:30 at the Street Hotel Club?"

"Done," said Quincy. "See you there."

§

As Quincy arrived at the 18th and Vine District, he inhaled deeply and took it all in. He did that every time he came to the District. Home to the American Jazz Museum, the Negro Leagues Baseball Museum, the Gem Theatre, food, drink, jazz … and history. Lots of history. The racial dividing line of Kansas City's not-too-distant past. Once a thriving hub of segregated Black commerce, followed by terrible urban decay that some linked to baseball's integration and the resulting demise of the Negro Leagues.

Now, the District was in the throes of slow but steady revitalization and revival, driven on the backbone of the Kansas City

African American community's strong cultural roots, immense pride, art, community, baseball, barbecue, booze, and jazz. Historically segregated, but always shared by Black society. How different from the White society whose historical dividing line began just blocks away. Also historically segregated, but rarely shared. Quincy could almost hear the crack of the bats swung by the Kansas City Monarchs of old, the premier Negro League's baseball club. He could smell the sweet hickory aroma of brisket cooking low and slow for twenty-four hours. He could imagine the spattering sounds of fried chicken cooking in the alleyways of old. If he closed his eyes, he could see a rotund and jovial Jay McShann tickling the piano keys, a child-like Charlie Parker mesmerized by the sounds he coaxed from his saxophone, and a dapper Count Basie leading his big band through some exhilarating Kansas City swing sets from behind his piano.

3J and Pascale already had a table in the club, not too close to the stage, so they could hear each other as they talked. Quincy joined them. He didn't socialize all too often with his attorneys. Not a hard and fast policy, just the way it had seemed to work out over the years. He liked some of the attorneys he hired, but none made it to his inner circle; they had their place, and usually, that place didn't include social events he attended. So jazz with 3J and Pascale was a rare exception for Quincy.

"Have you been here before?" Quincy asked to get the conversation going. 3J had her whiskey, and Pascale had his beer. Quincy waved a hand in the air to catch the waiter's attention so he could order a glass of Merlot.

"Years ago," Pascale said, leaving out the part that he would come here with his wife on their date nights. Back when he had someone with whom to share a date night. Back when jazz and his life seemed to have more connections than his life of solitude had with jazz or anything else after his wife and child died.

"Not as far as I can remember," said 3J. She just seemed to have so little time for stepping out after work. But, for the record, if asked, 3J would always answer that she liked jazz. She was from New Orleans – jazz was in her blood, so she liked some jazz a great deal.

"It's pretty historic. This club used to be in the State Hotel in the 1930s and was home to many of the greats. A real part of Kansas City's history – the good and the bad," Quincy explained. "And, if you like jazz, the music here these days ain't too bad at all," he added, smiling.

"Do you come here often?" Pascale asked.

"Not as much as I'd like to," Quincy answered.

"How long have you lived in Kansas City, Quincy?" 3J inquired.

"It's been a little more than two years now – and please, call me Quince."

"Not too many big-time national real estate developers choose to make Kansas City their home. So why did you?" 3J probed. "Kind of fly-over territory for most Northeasterners."

"Look, I can do what I do from pretty much anywhere that has an airport and an internet connection. I'm pretty location-agnostic these days when it comes to my work. And, when I'm building, I'm never home. I was just tired of the east coast life. Get up early, walk to the trolley station. Take the trolley to the subway. Board the subway, shoulder to shoulder with hundreds of people staring at their phones in one hand while they hang on to a pole with the other hand as the subway careens and screeches around subterranean corners. Everyone was just doing what I was doing. Rocket on the subway to Center City. Get off the subway. Walk to my office. Etcetera, etcetera. Don't get me wrong. I like mass transit, and I liked much of what makes Philadelphia an interesting place to live. But I wanted some more anonymity. I learned about Kansas

City when I spent some significant time here as the Walnut Street building went up. I don't have roots in Philadelphia anymore, or anywhere for that matter. So, here I am, and so far, here is good."

"I would've thought with your pretty significant nod to all things historical that history would have had something to do with your decision," Pascale observed.

"You'd have thought right. When it comes to history, Kansas City isn't Philadelphia, but then, few places are. But Kansas City has a rich history that lets me dive in and learn about things I don't know about, and, yes, I do like that. But the real draw is: I can just be me and not that semi-famous developer who changes skylines around North America," Quincy explained.

"I heard George Brett say something like that once when asked why he stays in Kansas City now that his hall-of-fame-baseball-days are over. He said he stays in KC because here, he can just be himself, and no one bothers him," Pascale said. "Not being famous, I guess I never gave that much thought. It could be an interesting calling card for the next iteration of the 'Visit Kansas City' economic development campaign. 'Visit Kansas City and lose yourself among the Midwestern masses. We won't care who you are, and we won't bother you.'"

3J changed the subject. "When we first met, you told me about your great-great-great-grandfather who died in a debtors' prison in Philadelphia. Why the fascination with all things history?"

"It's a good question, 3J. I learned that you couldn't know where you're going unless you know where you've been. Where I've been includes all the Withermans who came before me. It includes Gunnie Witherman, who was defrauded out of all his money in a land speculation scheme down south gone bad and got his money back a decade or more later from the Federal

Government. It includes all the Withermans who were in the real estate business in one form or another. For me, where I've been also includes the history of the place I live. So, it includes an attempt to understand Kansas City's sordid history of 'us and them' groups: Black and White, Italian and Irish, Jewish and Christian. All perpetuated and stoked by boss politics and institutional segregation. History helps me appreciate that with all of the bad can come an incredible amount of good, like jazz and the Negro League, and of course, barbecue. Good from bad. The human existence. The not-often-enough-achieved American dream."

3J smiled. Long answer. Seemed genuine. "Ok, Mr. Kansas City, since you're here and steeping in our richness, what's your favorite barbecue?"

Quincy considered. "Well, I haven't tried them all, but I seem to go back to Joe's and Bryant's the most for different reasons. I like Joe's fare the best, but you can't beat Bryant's for the history," as he smiled broadly. "I would swear that the old, skinny guy at Bryant's who works the meats in the smoker behind the counter has been there since Leroy Satchel Paige was spinning screwballs from the Monarch's mound at Municipal Stadium across from the restaurant. Oh, and I like to go to BB's Lawnside on 87th for ribs and live gritty blues. What an authentic juke joint. Low and slow. Loud and proud. And you?"

3J answered, "You know that Kansas Citians argue about their rubs and their smoke frequently in open verbal warfare, right?"

"I have indeed learned that."

"For me, I'm a Jack's Stack gal. BBQ'd salmon. Heaven."

"You're both wrong," Pascale interjected. "Q39 for me, any day, any time."

"And there you have it. A look under the hood at some classic Kansas City food-debate dialogue with no resolution. Just positions staked out," 3J said as she chuckled.

As they talked, the early band took the stage. A completely integrated melting-pot ensemble of professionals who were so good that they were about to play together for the first time seamlessly even though they had just met an hour ago. Drums (White), upright bass (Asian), piano (Black), and alto sax (Latino). *The perfect lounge band for a perfect lounge. Jazz certainly has the power to bring out the best in the melting pot experiment we call America,* thought 3J.

"Did you always want to be an attorney, 3J?" Quincy asked.

"Not sure I have ever *wanted* to be an attorney. It just sort of happened. Did you always want to be a real estate developer?"

"Mostly, but not always. There was a point in time where I thought it would be great to be an FBI agent. But guns scare me, so I had designs that I'd be a forensic accountant for the Bureau. You know – catching bad guys through numbers analysis. But real estate's in my blood, I guess – a family thing. My uncle took me in when my parents died, and he was in the real estate development business, so I was in it with him as well. Artists talk of a moment when they discover their artistic voice. I have no artistic skills. My moment was when I discovered my business voice. My bard to make money," Quincy said as he smiled at the lawyers.

"You really seem to like your jazz," 3J observed.

"All music," Quincy said, "but jazz in particular."

"It's good to have music in your life."

"It is. I don't easily let people see the inner me," Quincy said, "but music appreciation is a way I can express myself and if people are paying attention, my music will give a hint of how I am feeling, I suppose."

"I'll try to take note," 3J said, and then smiled, "no pun intended."

They all turned to the music for a few minutes and abandoned the Q&A.

As the song was ending, Quincy said, "So let's talk about the cases and our favorite bank group. Your best guesses. What's up with our friends on the other side of the bankruptcy table?"

"Best guess," Pascale offered, "sixty percent of the loans didn't warm to forty percent's attempt to turn this into a fishing expedition, and they simply out-voted First Commercial. I'm sure there's more nuance to the story, and secret spice and flavor, to borrow from the BBQ world. But I figure it's just simple math. It's interesting; many agent banks won't syndicate loans like these if they'll own less than half of the deal. With more than fifty percent, they avoid the 'majority rule' syndrome of potential revolt since they can control the vote each time. Here, my guess is that it was a stretch for First Commercial to have even that much of the loans because of this size of the debt, and someone in the bowels of the bank just decided to approve the loans and, in doing so, ignored the revolt issue."

3J had her glass to her lips, and just before the glass took precedence over the conversation, she added, "Yeah, I agree. We won't ever know for sure, but all the JooJoo that we've observed here in the last few days says that the majority has taken over."

"Still not our friends, as Milnes so eloquently told you at the outset, but we can work with them, and they can work with us," Pascale said. "That's all we need, and frankly, that's all they need as well."

"I posed this question back at your offices and just wanted to follow up again. Can we now get out of bankruptcy quickly?" Quincy asked.

"Yes, but I still have to put 'quickly' in quotes," Pascale said. "It's up to the Judge. We have to change the plan and disclosure statement, send them out for review by creditors, get the disclosure statement approved, send out ballots, count the vote on the plan, and then have the plan confirmation hearing. I just don't see Judge Robertson's inclination to shorten time periods significantly in a case of this size. I'd count on an end-of-year exit from bankruptcy."

"Not that I haven't enjoyed your collective company or the stay in bankruptcy, but I'll be most happy to have a deal with the banks. I want to get the new documents signed, sealed, and delivered, and be on my way with my discharge as I return to civilian status and start to think about my next project."

Quincy seemed to put on a good face as he heard again about the timing of the bankruptcy case. But for a moment, his eyes flashed exasperation with the length of time still left, and 3J caught the momentary look in both his different-colored eyes. Just a moment, but she caught it. Sure, Quincy was anxious to be free of the bankruptcy process. Who wouldn't be? Yet – maybe it was nothing, but 3J thought she saw not just exasperation, but concern. Exasperation was understandable. Concern, however, was not. She wondered why a bankruptcy debtor who had just received great news would be concerned with the fresh start finish line now clearly in sight.

"It's been an unusual case, that's for sure. Let's get that discharge order so you can frame it," 3J said.

The band was just finishing their nod to Kansas City jazz with a cover of Count Basie's and Ray Brown's "Sandman" from the album *For The Second Time*, performed by what the Count called "The Kansas City Three." The addition of the fourth instrument – the live saxophone – added a nice touch to the cover: pure Kansas City. No need for explanation. "It is what it is," as only the Count could say in his smooth-as-velvet voice when asked to talk about his music.

Good tunes, they all thought, even Pascale.

Quincy insisted that the drinks were on him, and settled up with the Club, thanked the lawyers for the invite, and then 3J, Pascale, and Quincy departed, clapping for the band as they headed for the exit.

CHAPTER 20

Friday, October 12, 2018

3J, PASCALE, AND SAMPLE arrived at the courthouse for the chambers conference with Judge Robertson. They exchanged pleasantries with the Marshals who guard the courthouse, went through security in the courthouse lobby, and took the same elevator up to the Judge's chambers. At the Judge's chambers, they pushed the buzzer, identified themselves, and the locked door electronically opened for them to enter.

The level of federal courthouse security had increased incrementally over the years as federal judges had become the targets of threats in a more and more polarized society. The marshals and technology protected the judges. Lawyers who were regulars at the courthouse had come to take the security for granted. But every once in a while, someone, somewhere in the United States, tried to get into a courthouse with a gun, which served to remind everyone just how vital the security was.

Once inside Judge Robertson's chambers, they didn't have to wait long for the Judge and his law clerk, and they made their way into the Judge's conference room for the meeting.

"I have read the plan and disclosure statement, counsel," the Judge said.

"Your Honor, as soon as the banks approve the deal discussed yesterday with representatives of the banks, we will file amendments to the plan and disclosure," 3J explained.

"Mr. Sample, are you in agreement with Ms. Jones' comments?" the Judge asked what he thought was a routine question.

"Your Honor, I was not at the negotiation meeting, so I will need to await the full bank group meeting and see if the parties have a deal. If they do, then I agree that Ms. Jones and Mr. Pascale will need to amend the plan and disclosure statement to reflect whatever it is that the parties have agreed to," Sample said.

Expecting a simple "yes" for the answer, the Judge was surprised by the wordy response. "So, you don't know what was discussed at the meeting?"

"Correct, Your Honor," replied Sample.

"Who was at the meeting on behalf of the agent bank?"

"It is my understanding that in attendance were Mr. Witherman, Ms. Jones and Mr. Pascale; Brian Chimes, a special assets officer from StarBanc in Houston – and perhaps some other syndicate bank representatives appeared by video conference."

"I asked about agent bank attendance," the Judge said, annoyed, as he pressed Sample.

"First Commercial did not attend."

"Why not?"

"I can't answer that, Judge."

"Who could?"

"Pardon me, Your Honor?"

"Who could answer my question, Mr. Sample?"

"I suppose Ms. Milnes could, but she and I have not talked since the meeting between the Debtors and StarBanc concluded."

"Did the meeting with the Debtors occur with First Commercial's knowledge and consent?" the Judge probed.

"First Commercial was aware of the meeting."

"And what about the consent, Mr. Sample?" the Judge inquired, unwilling to let Sample dodge the question.

"I would have to talk to Ms. Milnes, Your Honor."

Judge Robertson exhaled audibly and sharing his exasperation, said, "I am finding this all highly unusual, counsel. Am I pleased that some of the parties in these cases got together for a meeting to try to work through the Debtors' plan and disclosure statement? Of course. Chapter 11 provides the opportunity to negotiate a business deal, and I always support that effort. But am I pleased that the agent bank's attorney is sitting here and can't seem to tell me whether that was a sanctioned meeting or if several of the bank group members went rogue? I am *not*." Sample nodded his head to convey understanding and sympathy with the Judge's points but said nothing. The Judge took the head nod as a patronizing, unnecessary gesture and continued, "I asked you here today, so I could determine if this case was going to explode into a big discovery dispute followed by litigation. I read over the discovery application. It is quite a pleading. It suggests that the Debtors failed to disclose information to the banks over a series of years before the commencement of the bankruptcy cases. It seeks enough documents to fill a warehouse; many, maybe most, of which I have to assume the banks already have in their possession. Then, literally as I was reading the application, Mr. Sample, you called the Court, told my law clerk of an intent to withdraw the application, and withdrew the application before I even got the email from my law clerk about your call. I find all of this a most curious turn of events. Most puzzling. You led me to believe that we would have an involved, contested cash collateral hearing. But you withdrew the cash objection as well. I don't know, counsel. You want documents, and then you don't. You oppose the use of cash, and then you don't. I am trying to understand whether we are going down a litigation path or a consensual plan. Are you able to address that for me, counsel?"

The Judge didn't hide his frustration with First Commercial. No lawyer likes to be on the receiving end of a grilling from a frustrated judge, and Sample was no different. He had enough experience, however, to know that he just had to weather the judicial storm. All he could hope for was to survive as unscathed as possible while at the same time fulfilling his duty to advocate zealously for his client. He had once described a lawyer's hope of riding out the uncomfortable ire of a judge as akin to a boxer's tactic of laying on the ropes and covering up while he waited for the bell. Here, however, there was no bell coming, and the Judge's body blows were starting to hurt.

"Judge, I think all that I can confirm is what you already know. We filed the discovery pleading; it set out our views, and we withdrew the pleading. I am sorry I can't tell you more at this time." He knew this explanation would neither satisfy the Judge's curiosity nor quell the Judge's growing frustration with First Commercial and Sample himself. Body blow; body blow. Pain.

"Counsel, my read is that you signed the discovery pleading on behalf of all the banks, not just First Commercial. Were the views set out in the pleading reflective of those held by all the banks or just by First Commercial?"

"I was apprised that the pleading represented the views of the banks."

"Who apprised you?"

"First Commercial, your Honor."

"So you personally never talked to the other banks before you filed the discovery application," the Judge stated as a fact, not a question. Then, almost imperceptibly, Judge Robertson shook his head east to west and back again, just like an angry parent dealing with a teenager who decided to stick to a story the parent didn't buy, no matter the level of the parent's ire. "Ok, counsel. This is what we are going to do. Ms. Jones, Mr. Pascale, please email my law clerk on or before next Friday, October 26, and let me know if the banks and the Debtors agreed on the terms of a plan. Usually, I would, of course, ask the agent bank to let me know that. But this discussion leads me to believe that I should get my information from the Debtors on this question, at least until Mr. Sample's answers to my questions start to sound a bit more like substantive answers and a little less like the answers of a politician engaged in a debate that isn't going well." 3J nodded. "If there is an agreement, you will then have two weeks to revise the plan and disclosure statement and file it. Once you file the plan, we will set a hearing to consider approval of the disclosure statement. If I approve the disclosure statement, we will establish the time line for you to mail the plan and disclosure statement to all creditors and parties in interest, obtain the votes for or against the plan, and have a hearing to consider approval of the plan. Does that make sense, Ms. Jones?"

"That works for us, Your Honor."

Judge Robertson decided that he didn't care to know if Dennis Sample thought the timeline made sense, so he didn't pose the question.

3J and Pascale remained sitting at the conference table, getting the feeling that the Judge had more on his mind. Dennis Sample, thinking that the conference had concluded – and that he had weathered the storm – largely because Judge Robertson had abandoned the inquiry, rose to say his goodbyes, and began to return his papers to his briefcase.

"Mr. Sample," the Judge said. "We aren't quite done." Sample sat down. "Since you are not able or willing to let me know if there will be another discovery application filed that would, of course, tend to disrupt the disclosure statement and plan process, please know the following – and please, share my comments with Ms. Milnes. I don't know what First Commercial has in mind, but I view all of this with plenty of skepticism. The bank had a fair chance to go down the scorched-earth path and, at least for the moment, has backed away. If First Commercial wishes to reactivate that process again, I may not have a great deal of time or, frankly, interest in halting the plan process to account for First Commercial's whim *de jour*." The Judge glared at Sample to emphasize his direct message. "Those comments are directed to your client. Please share them with Ms. Milnes. The following thoughts are directed to you as an attorney practicing law in my Court. I find myself troubled by the allegations made in the discovery application that you signed and filed. If it is true that the Debtors have not disclosed assets to the banks for some time, then that path should be pursued by First Commercial, and, I would think, should be pursued now. If it is untrue, then that pleading pushed the envelope past the line and may very well be frivolous.

"You've been around the block. So you know the drill, counsel. As a lawyer in this Court, you had a duty to make an inquiry reasonable under the circumstances, and thereby determine whether you had a good faith basis for making the claims you did. You know the requirements: You should file nothing that is presented for improper purposes. You should file nothing frivolous. What you write in your pleadings must be likely to have evidentiary support. You signed and filed the pleading, and I have reservations about what you filed and its compliance with these rules. That you withdrew the pleading has no impact on my reservations. You filed it, and there it sits on the Court's ECF system for all to see and read. It reads like an unsubstantiated smear. Rest assured, I will give that some considerable thought. To reiterate: I don't at all view the withdrawal of the pleading as a resolution of my concerns. I trust you get the gist of my message here, counsel."

The Judge retained his composure even as he poured scorn on Sample and the banks. He then collected his papers and, without looking up, said, "Mr. Sample, we are now done. Thank you, counsel, for coming over here on such short notice."

With that, the Judge stood and exited the conference room, followed closely by Jamie, and headed for the Judge's office, all before any of the attorneys could utter the customary, "thank you, Your Honor."

In the office, it was just Judge Robertson, Jamie, and their thoughts. This time, the Judge showed little interest in playing Socrates with Jamie. The exchange in the conference room was not a bankruptcy law teaching opportunity; at least, not right now. Instead, it gave Jamie the chance to put a pin in the conference and post it on his mental cork board for future reference. Jamie had not seen this side of Judge Robertson before. He had not seen the Judge transform from soft-spoken jurist to a hardened, taskmaster drill sergeant. The one-sided exchange could not have been fun for Sample. Sample was a seasoned attorney and tried not to squirm, but he was human, and it had to be an unpleasant experience. But, as the Judge told Jamie from time to time, the practice of law is a full-contact sport, and the Judge had just flexed his judicial muscles as he made an open-field tackle.

Jamie imagined Sample moving swiftly for the elevator and the courthouse exit the minute the conference concluded, for fear the Judge might recall him for a further lashing. On this point, Jamie was correct.

§

After the testy conference with Judge Robertson, Sample walked a block away from the courthouse and ordered a ride-share. Once in his ride back to the Kansas City airport, he phoned Milnes. He had two goals – let her know the timetable, and have an honest discussion about the Judge's frustrations. She was an adult. She could handle it … he hoped.

"Stacy? Dennis here. The Judge is very frustrated with the banks. His frustration is not going to help us in this case."

"I'm not overly concerned with the Judge's state of mind, to be truthful. Just manage him," she said, deflecting Sample's concerns.

"I don't have any tools to quote, *manage him*, unquote, Stacy. He made it very clear he would not entertain future emergency applications to rekindle document productions, and he was very suspicious that First Commercial wasn't at the plan negotiation."

Milnes spat back, "I'm pretty frustrated as well, but the syndicate banks can out-vote First Commercial. I can't change the group vote. You can't change the vote. The Judge can't change the vote. The syndicate banks wanted to negotiate, so they did. Not a damn thing I can do about it."

"I'll email you the timetable, but it will be pretty quick to plan confirmation, and since the group will vote to approve the deal struck by StarBanc, the process will proceed forward consensually. I will just need to understand what you want me to say in Court and to the Debtors."

"The Debtors get to know nothing. I see no obligation to communicate the inner workings of the bank group to Witherman, even this crazy group. My inclination is that the Court is likewise entitled to know nothing of the bank group deliberations."

"I understand your position about the Debtors. But your position as to the Judge isn't sustainable. To be candid, I can tell the Debtors to fuck off. I can't tell that to the Judge. If the Judge wants to delve into the bank group process at the confirmation hearing, I don't think either you or I can just look Judge Robertson in the eye and tell him it's none of his business. It won't work that way at all."

"Well, it should work that way," Milnes complained, maintaining the mistaken view that she was in charge even when the Judge was the one calling the shots. "Let me think about this a bit more, and then we can talk again. By the way, when are the banks going to meet to discuss and vote on StarBanc's proposed deal with the Debtors?"

"Tomorrow afternoon."

"Alright. We can discuss that meeting and vote tomorrow morning as well."

§

Moses operated on a system of trust and faith. To shed light, he needed to employ operatives who offered leg work in their areas of specialty, often in different places throughout the country. He could travel to each location and perform his own research, but he had established a group of trusted helpers who could find things out for him and be discrete in doing so. He called his collection of helpers "The Moses Team." They ranged in skill set from what he might call analog information gatherers to digital-savvy information collectors.

One such trusted analog helper was Dale Stoops, a tall, slender African American who lived in West Philadelphia just beyond the University of Pennsylvania campus on a street lined with trees, many of which looked like they dated back to the end of the Revolutionary War. The trees were majestic and had fared much better than the neighborhood, for which the trees provided a canopy and protection from the elements. Stoops' greatest asset – he knew the Philadelphia public records system better than anyone in the world, including the elected and appointed officials charged with managing the records. Those records dated back to 1682 when William Penn first arrived in Philadelphia, and Penn's Quakers were notorious record creators and keepers, so the records were substantial.

Moses reached out to Stoops, who answered his mobile phone as he finished his breakfast at a diner in the Reading Terminal in Center City, Philadelphia. Stoops was a regular, or a repeat offender as his waitress liked to call him – eggs over-easy, bacon, scrapple, and a cup of La Colombe coffee, a Philadelphia treasure. Scrapple: literally from the word scrap and made of scraps of pork that would not be good enough for a pork sausage ... hearts, kidneys, livers, and skins. Fried up in butter or oil, generating a surprisingly rich aroma. A Philadelphia delicacy for the natives, and an acquired taste for non-natives, many of whom just never seemed interested in putting in the time and effort to develop the taste.

"Dale, my good friend," Moses said.

"Moses, how are you these days?" Stoops asked.

"I could complain, but I won't," Moses replied.

"I hear ya'. Every part of me hurts these days. Just the day-to-day grind in the City of Brotherly Love, I guess. What can I do ya' for?"

Moses explained his need to review the Gunnther Witherman Jr. will and any other related information that Stoops could dig up.

"About what year are we talking here, Moses?"

"I'm not entirely sure, but I'd guess the early- to mid-1800s. You should be able to determine the exact year from a public record revealing when Mr. Witherman Junior passed over the great divide, and I believe a court would have probated his will shortly after that."

"Ahhh. Moses, my friend. If it were just that simple, you wouldn't need me," Stoops chuckled.

"I will always need you, my friend. Always. Keep me apprised," Moses said, and the call ended.

After soaking up the eggs and finishing the last bite of scrapple, Stoops dropped a twenty-spot on the counter, thanked the waitress, and headed out to the street.

Stoops made his way to the Office of the Register of Wills located in the iconic City Hall building in downtown Philadelphia, which the locals called Center City, the slightly off-white, circular structure that interrupted Market and North Broad Streets, and atop of which stood William Penn, or at least his likeness, overseeing the city he founded. Once inside, Stoops made his way to the counter where he found his favorite assistant clerk. They had their usual short discussion about her kids, work, the weather, the just-completed disappointing Phillies baseball season, and the upcoming hopeful Flyers hockey and remaining Union soccer seasons. Stoops then made the ask for the Witherman will. She was part clerk, part record keeper, and part historian. Together, they were able to figure out when Gunnie died, and from there, with a little luck, they were able to locate the digitized historical probate records. Eventually, they found Gunnie's will. The clerk printed out a copy of the will for Stoops, who tipped his hat in thanks, and sat down in the reading area to absorb the handwritten will. *Short and pretty standard,* he thought. He quickly found the reference to Francis Marion Roston, who would serve as trustee of a trust with the discretion to invest the trust assets where and how he saw fit. There was no record of a filed trust document. Stoops decided to do some quick research on Mr. Roston as well for Moses. *A walk will do me some good after that breakfast,* Stoops thought.

He left City Hall and headed down JFK Boulevard to North 19th to Logan Square and the Philadelphia Free Public Library on Vine Street. He liked to walk. He cherished that Philadelphia was such a walkable city. He figured that the walks cleared out his arteries for tomorrow's breakfast at the Terminal. Once at the Library, Stoops made his way to the microfiche records, and after several searches, he found references to Roston. Articles from the *Philadelphia Inquirer* newspaper, then called the *Pennsylvania Inquirer*, described him as a trusted economic advisor to the Witherman family. Stoops read and copied the articles and included them in his email package to Moses.

Roston sounds like an interesting fellow, Stoops thought. He wrote: "Moses, here is the will and a little bonus research for you on this guy named Roston. The will expressly mentions him. An interesting chap from my quick read of the article. Note that the will merely refers to a trust document, but there is no trust filed of record. I don't think the failure to record the trust document is unusual. Also, note that the will gives Roston the power to invest trust assets in whatever manner Roston sees fit, so Gunnie granted Roston very broad powers. I suppose that's not too unusual for a trusted advisor like Roston. Note that the will references the termination of the trust, which has probably happened by now, and the distribution of trust assets to the beneficiaries and their heirs. So, my assumption is that if there are assets left and heirs who own then, the heirs own the assets outright today, free of any restrictions imposed by the trust. Let me know if there is anything else I can do to help you. Be well, my friend."

Stoops sent the email off to Moses and now felt his entire afternoon had freed up. As always, his thoughts turned to his next meal – perhaps a cheesesteak hoagie at Jim's? Happy with his decision, he headed out for a long walk to South Philadelphia and the land of cheesesteaks. Between breakfast and lunch, and the effect each would have on his cholesterol levels, he figured he shaved a few months off his life each time he dined. *But if you can't go out with a happy belly, is life even worth living?*

CHAPTER 21

Monday, October 15, 2018

ON MONDAY, OCTOBER 15, the banks convened an afternoon group teleconference meeting to discuss the StarBanc negotiations with Quincy Witherman and to vote on acceptance. All of the banks dialed in for the call, including Stacy Milnes and Dennis Sample. Brian Chimes took the lead on the call and explained his discussions, the plan points negotiated with the Debtors' team, the resumption of payments to the banks, and his recommendation to accept the plan modifications. Of course, everyone on the conference call was aware of the negotiations because they had all attended – all except Sample and Milnes.

After Chimes' presentation, Stephanie Bonde asked, "There was a chambers conference with Judge Robertson and the Debtors' counsel last week, correct?"

Sample responded, "That's correct."

"Can we have a report, please, before we vote on the plan issues?"

Sample provided a report of the chambers conference and the details of the Judge's questions that he could not answer.

"It sounds like our Judge is frustrated with the banks. Is that a fair read?" Bonde asked.

Sample responded, "That's fair, Stephanie. He expects the agent bank to run the case, and gets the sense that the banks are divided. He made it very clear that if the banks approve the StarBanc settlement proposal, he'll focus the Court's time and efforts on confirmation and won't entertain non-confirmation motions that would slow down the confirmation process."

Chimes jumped in: "What I hear from your report is that the Judge is frustrated with First Commercial, not all the banks. And the Judge's frustration could spill over on the rest of the banks by association. I think I speak accurately for all of us when I say that we don't like getting skewered just because our agent bank has gone rogue."

"I've tried accurately to portray what happened at the chambers conference. You will draw whatever conclusions you wish, Brian, I suppose."

"I've drawn no conclusions," Chimes shot back. "The Judge poured us out. Plain and simple. The blood-spatter from the tongue-lashing landed on the rest of us."

"Ok. Ok. Unless anyone else wishes to speak, let's vote on the plan settlement, and then figure out what our approach will be," Bonde said. "Can the agent bank please call the roll and record the voting?"

Stacy Milnes asked Sample to call the roll. When he called each bank's name, every representative responded with "accept," except for First Commercial. For First Commercial, Milnes said, "abstain." As expected, sixty percent of the banks accepted, and a hundred percent of the banks who actually lodged a vote accepted. Either way, the banks were on the path to a consensual plan confirmation.

Now, what to do with Stacy Milnes.

Stephanie Bonde led off the discussion and returned to Chimes' points before the plan vote. She was pointedly critical of First Commercial. She didn't blame Dennis Sample. He was just the lawyer. Bonde directed her comments to Milnes to make the issue personal. "Stacy, it is beyond disappointing that

First Commercial decided not to attend the negotiations with the Debtors. On so many levels, it sends a terrible message to the Debtors as well, now, as to the Court. Besides, I had your express word that you would let me know First Commercial's position on attendance before the meeting, and you failed to do so." Milnes merely rolled her eyes. "Am I surprised? No. But so I am clear on behalf of my bank, from the beginning, your conduct has compromised our position, and it puts at risk a payment-in-full-settlement over a reasonable period. Not only is that unacceptable, but it also is not the role of the agent bank." Bonde paused to gather her thoughts and then said slowly, "Fellow banks, my management has instructed me to move for the removal of First Commercial as the Agent in these syndicated loans and to substitute StarBanc."

Milnes squirmed in her chair. As Bonde delivered the damning remarks, Milnes thought, *Who does this banker think she is?* But before Milnes could fashion a response, Wall Bank and Wertz Bank seconded Bonde's motion, cutting off discussion and setting up an immediate vote.

Milnes had no opportunity to lobby for the retention of First Commercial as the Agent. Nor did she have a chance to try to bully the syndicate banks and defend her actions, if there was a defense. It wouldn't have mattered. She wouldn't be able to talk, negotiate, browbeat, domineer, or beg her way out. Not this time. Nor did she have a chance to try to put Bonde and Chimes in their place, if she could even do so at this point. If she had tried to speak, Chimes and Bonde would shut her down; none of the syndicate banks were in a mood to listen to Milnes. It was apparent that the syndicate banks had lost all faith in Milnes, and even more so, the syndicate banks had no intention of letting Milnes retain a position where she could continue to take actions on behalf of all of the banks without a vote. The syndicate banks were ready to vote and, taking a page from the Milnes playbook, implicitly told Milnes that if she wanted a discussion, she was in the wrong room.

In a matter of minutes, the banks all voted. First Commercial didn't abstain from this vote, but it didn't matter. The syndicate banks voted First Commercial out of its role, and StarBanc in, as the Agent.

Milnes should have been concerned for her continued employment at First Commercial. It would've been a natural reaction, and anyone else would be. But all she could think of was accelerating the Moses Aaronson process to a conclusion as quickly as possible. She needed a status report from Moses and to push the process forward. Moses needed to go to the next level to feed Milnes' hope that a positive development in his investigation would cause First Commercial to move past what was about to be a significant black eye in the banking industry.

If she could coax a report from Aaronson that supported her intuition, maybe the First Commercial brass would thank her instead of firing her. And, perhaps, she could take the hoped-for Aaronson report and shove it across the table to Bonde and Chimes and see if they had any further smart-ass comments that they cared to share.

§

Sample returned to his desk. He'd seen a lot of things in his days as counsel to banks. But nothing quite like this. If he was honest, he felt a measure of relief. He had represented First Commercial in the past, and his contact had been Milnes. She had always been professional with him, albeit her tone was never warm, and she had a stellar record as a special assets officer, even though she could be erratic and unpredictable at times. But not to the degree he had experienced in the Witherman loans. Her strategy had been elusive; *no,* he thought, *elusive is too generous.* The word "elusive" suggested Milnes had a strategy she could cogently articulate. She could not, because there was no strategy. No, she seemed to be flailing in her quest to take down Witherman.

His mind returned to the just-completed meeting, and, he thought, *that vote!* In his entire career, he had not witnessed a meeting like that. For whatever reasons, Milnes had decided in the Witherman loans that she would be a separatist and as a result, she had seemed hell-bent on seceding from the bank group from the outset. From the beginning of his representation of First Commercial in the Witherman cases, Sample had been concerned that if Milnes kept up her tactics and style, her wish to be on her own would be granted. He foresaw that the syndicate banks would assert their station as the majority in the bank group, and they would remove Milnes and her bank as the agent. With such a move, the syndicate banks would impose on her a sentence of permanent isolation. Now, it had all come true.

None of it made any sense to Sample. Not Milnes' tactics; not her bank group death wish; not her lack of communication not only to the bank group, but also to him as First Commercial's counsel; and, most importantly, not her contentious personality. *There's a time and a place to be disagreeable,* Sample thought, *and for her, the time and place in the Witherman loans seem to be always and everywhere. Not particularly selective.* She wanted to be a separatist, and now the syndicate banks granted her wish. *What a complete mess.* From the lender's perspective, Chapter 11 cases required a game plan consistently applied from the outset. The only thing consistent about Milnes' strategy was the lack of a defensible strategy that could be intelligently articulated to anyone at all.

As Sample considered what came next, the phone rang, and it was Brian Chimes.

"Dennis Sample here."

"Dennis, this is Brian Chimes, StarBanc."

"Yessir, good afternoon."

"Quite a fuckin' meeting, don't you think, Dennis?"

"I was just sitting here thinking that. I've never seen anything quite like it, Brian."

Chimes chuckled and said, "Well, Stacy has been deposed, and not in the way you lawyers put people under oath and ask a bunch of questions, if you know what I mean. Look, Dennis, the reason for my call is that the banks, minus Milnes, talked, and we'd like you to finish this case off for us as counsel for StarBanc. I reached out to Milnes to see if she was ok with that switch, and I'll clean up and shorten what she said: 'Fine.'"

"Thanks for the opportunity to finish the case for you, Brian. I'll confirm with Stacy in writing, and then I can get going for StarBanc promptly."

"Excellent. Let's bring this case to a conclusion before anything else bizarre and off-the-wall happens, eh?"

"Agreed," Sample said. "Thanks, Brian."

The call ended, with both Sample and Chimes thinking the same thing: *Surely nothing else off-the-wall could possibly happen now.*

CHAPTER 22

The Debtor recalls Monday, October 15, 2018

MY PHONE RANG.

"Quincy? Brian Chimes here. Look, I wanted to call and let you know that the banks met to discuss the terms you and I negotiated a few days ago, and based on the vote of the bank group, I'm authorized to tell you that we agree, and we have a plan deal. We should proceed forward to draft the necessary papers and push this thing through the Bankruptcy Court."

"Brian, thank you very much for the prompt call and the message. I appreciate both."

"Look, don't thank me. It's just business, and speaking just for my bank, we think this is the right time to move on without fighting World War III over this deal."

"I understand. Can you share with me if the vote was unanimous?"

"No."

"You mean no, it wasn't unanimous, or no, you won't share the vote with me?"

"The latter. The deal's approved. I think that's all you need to know. Ok?"

I said nothing.

"One other thing, Quincy. You're entitled to know this under the credit agreement. The banks decided to make a change in the designation as agent bank. StarBanc will fill the agent's role from now on. So I'll be your point of contact."

I said nothing for a moment, which seemed more like an eternity. When that moment finally passed, I asked, "I assume you're not going to answer any questions to elaborate on that revelation either, Brian?"

"Correct."

"See, Brian, we *are* getting to know each other," I humored him.

Brian chuckled softly and asked, "Quincy, do you have any additional questions?"

"No. I'm sure we'll be in touch."

"Say, before we hang up, can y'all do this? Have the Greene Madison folks reach out to Dennis Sample, and let's hope the lawyers can work together with a minimal amount of posturing to secure a confirmation order quickly. Sample will continue on as StarBanc's attorney."

"Will do," I said.

"Good. Now that we have a deal, I don't want these damn lawyers getting in the way of a swift conclusion."

And the call ended. *Another one of those fly on the wall moments,* I thought. I wondered what the meeting among the banks was like. I wondered if Milnes talked to the banks the way she spoke to me. Did she treat them in the same way as she treated me? Did the syndicate banks initially stand for her bullying? Or was the bank group a single, continuous, contentious exchange of ideas before the syndicate banks decided to remove First Commercial as the agent? Did the banks remain businesslike, or were words exchanged? Or was the removal the ultimate weapon they used to put her in her place? All good questions, the answers to which I'd never know. And I didn't need to. But I'm human; I just wanted to know.

My meeting with Chimes was a productive one. It was a good negotiation session, followed by a brief, positive call. Maybe the tide had turned. While Chimes didn't have Stacy Milnes' particular style, he made it clear nevertheless that he wouldn't be my confidant, informant, or my anonymous source for bank group information. That would be fine. I didn't need information from him.

I knew he'd be proper, and I knew I'd be proper. For his part, he'd say please and thank you as his momma taught him, and for my part, I'd continue to channel my most sincere sense of gratitude along with a healthy dose of deference and just leave it at that. We'd shake hands to show that our word was our bond and to display our good faith. But even when we shook hands, I resolved to keep my eye on the prize – the discharge, my fresh start, and access to my Swiss assets and crypto; my head start. I didn't need Chimes for any of that.

Next up, I had to call 3J and Pascale and see how they were doing on the plan revisions.

CHAPTER 23

MOSES READ GUNNIE'S WILL and found the sole reference to Francis Marion Roston, just as Dale Stoops had written he would. Moses read the newspaper articles provided by Stoops and learned bits and pieces about Roston. In his line of work, bits and pieces added up to the development of a profile, like the small pieces of a large puzzle. Bits and pieces that combined like LEDs to bring the picture to light – how to solve any mystery.

As Moses sipped his cup of Pu-Erh tea, unsweetened, un-creamed, strong and smooth, he stroked Emily's velvety fur and decided to take her for a walk to the park. He put on her harness. They made their way to the street and the press of New Yorkers going about their daily business, each adding incrementally to the tumult that was the intersection of Broadway and Fifth Avenue in Manhattan, where the iconic triangular, twenty-two-story Flatiron Building sat. Incredibly, neither the level of the activity nor the decibels that assaulted her sensitive ears seemed to concern Emily.

Moses watched as Emily bobbed along at his side and saw her rhinestone collar sparkle as it caught and reflected the afternoon sun. Emmy, as he liked to call her, was his little Rhinestone cowgirl. She didn't need or require much in life, but Moses was happy to provide whatever she wanted. In his long life, he had many best friends, man and beast, but Emily was the one that was the best of the best. He adopted her from a rescue shelter and saved her from who knows what fate. She seemed to understand that, and she committed that she was his for life.

As long as she was by Moses' side, she was content and safe. She had a sense of loyalty and safety commonly found in a rescue dog saved from a terrible fate. Emily knew who saved her.

Moses and Emily arrived at Madison Park and sat on their favorite bench. The park provided some measure of protection from New York, as so many of New York's parks managed to afford. The dividing line between commotion and tranquility, pandemonium and serenity, and a place of refuge as long as one remained within the park's defined boundaries.

As Moses rubbed Emily's ears, he pulled out the article on Roston to reread. He didn't find it unusual that a dying man's last will and testament would single out a trusted advisor to protect and grow wealth for future generations. Not unusual at all. But the article that Moses read about Roston fascinated him. It wasn't just a newsworthy article about a favorite son of Philadelphia. It was a detailed interview of Roston that traced his history, beginning with parents who fled England and landed in the port of Gloucester, Massachusetts, with no money and no belongings except for the clothes on their back.

Roston was born as the Revolutionary War raged on. As new colonists, the Rostons read articles about the war in the Boston area newspapers and were enamored with one particular colonist war icon from the southern battles – Francis Marion, nicknamed the Swamp Fox. When their son was born, they honored the war hero by naming their son after him. Then, Roston's father left to fight the redcoats and lost his life to the bayonet end of a British musket. Roston's mother had to fend for herself, so she and Roston moved to Boston's developing metropolis, where she worked as a seamstress. He managed to find himself a path to education and eventually, against all imaginable odds, Harvard College. Roston's intellect was apparent as a child. Even as a product of the working class, and even in the late 1700s, the system somehow identified him. It steered the prodigy to higher education and away from the Boston streets or the docks, or another form of manual labor.

Roston was drawn to economics and money even as his mother had little need for economics because she had even less money. At Harvard, he continued his interest in such matters, and upon arrival in Philadelphia, he forged a career in which he tended to other people's money. Moses paused and thought, *Interesting journalistic article for the times.*

Moses replaced the article in his worn, leather satchel that served as a briefcase and cajoled Emily out of her park bench nap to a path back to the apartment.

Once Moses returned Emily to the apartment, he went back down to the street and, this time hailed a taxi and headed to the New York Public Library again for a more exhaustive search of Francis Roston. The thorough search yielded a surprising number of hits for Moses to review. Most were nothing more than references to Roston's time in Philadelphia. One hit in particular, however, provided a heightened degree of interest. The reporter had apparently set out to write an article about the developing American banking system and became interested in comparing the Federal Banking System with other banking systems throughout Europe. To make sense of the comparisons, the reporter needed to interview someone knowledgeable, and the trail led to Roston.

In the interview, the reporter conveyed that Roston spoke confidently about the still-developing American banking system and several different European systems, including the Swiss system. Roston shared information with the reporter about how the Swiss system of secrecy worked. The reporter also asked Roston if he utilized the Swiss system for his clients. Roston answered that while he held his clients' information in the strictest of confidences, nevertheless, he felt comfortable generically telling the reporter that the Swiss banks could be used effectively by an appropriately positioned client depending on their particular investment plan, strategy, and goals.

Moses took the answer as a wordy way of saying, "yes."

Roston's comments about banking and the possible uses of Swiss Banks were so forward-thinking that Moses had to remember the interview didn't occur in the twenty-first century, but rather in 1819. He read the article carefully and deliberately. He let the import of Roston's comments sink in as if Roston had explained the Swiss system to him as they sat in a coffee house sipping espresso across the table from each other. He knew he had not uncovered the ultimate answer to the question posed by Stacy Milnes. Not at all; instead, he found a flickering light up ahead on a path that might lead to insight and knowledge.

Next, Moses would have to figure out how to connect Roston's knowledge and apparent use of secret Swiss bank accounts to Quincy Gunn Witherman, if there was even such a link. Looking for a needle in a haystack was hard enough; looking through the haystack without even knowing if there was a needle within was – well – it was what he did.

Moses still had a problem. Even if there was a way to show that hundreds of years ago, Gunnie Witherman, near his deathbed, instructed Roston to establish one or more secret Swiss bank accounts for his legacy, there was no nexus to future generations of Withermans, including Quincy Witherman. That lack of visibility to a nexus was precisely how the Swiss intended their banking system to work, at least through October 2018.

Moses printed out the various articles and information he discovered that afternoon and hailed a taxi back to his apartment and his patiently waiting four-legged companion. Moses had often thought that if there was an afterlife in which deceased humans return to Earth as another creature, he fervently hoped he would return as a canine assigned to a household in New York City like his. In other words, he wanted to come back as Emily with an owner like himself. He told Emily this often, and as long as Moses stroked her neck while he told her his plan, Emily was perfectly fine with the suggested future course of action. Emily never seemed to take offense that Moses wanted her life. Not as long as he provided her food, love, ear and belly rubs, and companionship.

Sometimes, the research identified many locked doors that he had to open. Other times, a single locked door led to the revelations of the past and the solution to the mysteries of the present. Roston was an important clue, and Moses wondered if it might be the key to unlock doors to what might be the Withermans' centuries-long secrets. The Roston clue was evident in the will, but its importance was not at all obvious. But one of Moses' many credos was that if all one looked for was the obvious, one would miss much of what comprises life. He would pursue the clue because he pursued all clues. He traced, tracked, followed, and hunted down. He rejected the obvious, and he focused on the obfuscated. His methods were dependable and time-tested. It worked for Dashiell Hammett's Sam Spade in the 1930s, and it worked for Moses Aaronson in the twenty-first century. Spade had his personal code of conduct; Moses had his methods. Of paramount importance, he needed to find the link to Quincy Witherman. He needed to convert the interesting and the curious into the relevant. He needed to find the confluence of what he knew and what he needed to know. He needed the link.

He had some thoughts on how to pursue linkage. One, in particular, might work. Milnes could use one of his digital assets on The Moses Team. But it involved the darker side of what Moses did, and many clients would not let him drift to the dark side on their behalf. He understood why. The dark side had risk; it could lead to consequences. Unpleasant *legal* consequences. Some of his clients wanted to find the answers they sought through Moses' services and were willing to undertake that risk. Those clients knew that without the risk that the dark side carries with it, there might be no light. Moses believed that few bankers were comfortable with the dark side of what he did for a living. They were not skilled as dark side risk-takers.

In the end, he always presented the dark side investigation option to his clients, and then he would step back and let his better clients decide how much risk they were willing to take. It was almost time for him to report to Stacy Milnes. He would see just how dark of a path she was willing to travel.

CHAPTER 24

Wednesday, October 17 to Monday, October 22, 2018

BASED ON HIS REVIEW of background information, Moses wanted to know more about the Withermans and the Roston family who came after Gunnie died. One of the members of The Moses Team was Hillary Lockton in Denver, Colorado. Hillary was a fifty-something widow who spent the better part of her professional career serving as a paralegal in a large regional law firm headquartered in Denver.

After Lockton's husband died, she left the large law firm world and set up a business in which she investigated family trees in America. She worked out of her four-level townhome in Denver's Washington Park neighborhood, Wash Park to the natives. On her top level, if she craned her neck, she could see glimpses of snow-capped mountains. While Denverites can't always get a good look at the mountains, they always know the Rockies are there. Her clients were ordinary people curious about their past and professionals, like Moses, who wanted to develop background facts for people they investigated. Hillary was good at what she did. Very good. She knew her way around ancestry.com and other online services and used them to develop an ancestral skeleton, and then if her clients wanted more information, she used her considerable on-line research skills to fill in the blanks to put more historical meat on the genealogy bones.

Moses and Hillary had worked together in the past, and he had great confidence in Hillary's skill set, her accuracy, and the speed with which she worked. He contacted Hillary and explained that he wanted genealogical information for both the Witherman and Roston families and provided Hillary the background information. In particular, he wanted to see the ancestry tree that connected Quincy Gunn Witherman – date of birth circa 1969, to Gunnie Witherman, date of birth circa 1772 – and provided the background information. He also wanted to see the lineage of Francis Marion Roston's descendants, date of birth circa 1778.

After several days of research, Hillary developed the essential family tree for Gunnie Witherman and Francis Marion Roston, tracing all the way down to Quincy Gunn Witherman and Michaela Roston Huld.

For her written presentation to Moses, she focused on the direct ancestral line from ancestor number one (information provided by Moses) to the subject of Moses' inquiry. She didn't trace the lineage of other brothers and sisters, just the ones that led directly to Quincy Witherman and Michaela Huld. Essentially she created an ancestral tree trunk and eliminated most of the branches to focus the analysis and discussion. She emailed the trees to Moses and suggested a follow-up call to discuss her findings.

Moses studied the trees upon receipt of the email, and on Monday, he called Hillary to discuss the findings. Hillary explained that the Witherman tree was straightforward. Gunnie had two children, Betsy, who never married, and Adam. She found the Witherman tree interesting because of the consistency of male offspring between Gunnther and Quincy. The surname, Witherman, was present from Gunnther in the 1700s to Quincy in the present.

Hillary explained that the Roston tree was likewise simple to trace, although female offspring meant potential surname changes along the ancestral line. But she found it interesting that Michaela's middle name was Roston, suggesting Michaela's parents understood and honored their historical, genealogical roots. Hillary likewise learned that Michaela traveled before settling down, first to Dublin, Ireland, and eventually to London, England. Hillary also discovered that Michaela held a finance degree from Trinity College in Dublin and a master's in business from the Tuck School at Dartmouth in Hanover, New Hampshire. Michaela had since established her own financial advisory firm in London named NOIRAM Advisors, Plc.

Moses stared at the name of Michaela's advisory firm – the name Marion spelled backward. A transparent inversion and tip of the hat to the past.

Hillary said she would email Moses a report to help follow along with the more detailed trees by mid-afternoon. Moses thanked Hillary for her usual thorough and prompt work, and ended the call.

Moses enjoyed the engagements in which he called upon Hillary for genealogical assistance. He was a great believer in the idea that while we all exist – we have little choice in that – how we exist, however, is up to each of us. Are we authentic; are we a fraud? Do we decide to go down a life path hoping to give life meaning, or do we drift, undefined? Do we honor our past, or do we ignore it? Do we respect our history or do we deface it? The trees developed by Hillary always sparked these existential thoughts.

CHAPTER 25

The Debtor recalls Thursday, October 25 to Sunday, October 27, 2018

I SAT BACK IN my Boeing 787 Dreamliner business class United Airlines seat, closed my eyes, and thought three words: Michaela Roston Huld. Eyes like sapphires – but that description sold her eyes short. There were so many different blues in our world: Sky blue, baby blue, azure blue, navy blue. So much of the world was the color blue as the blue sky meets the blue sea, covering the vast majority of the Earth. In our reverence for the color, we gave it unique names like azure and ultramarine and midnight.

With so much blue in the world, Michaela Roston Huld's eyes still stood out. They were royal blue, akin to the color of Princess Diana's engagement ring, which now encircles Kate Middleton's finger. But even that description sold them short. Michaela's eyes were even bluer than the royal engagement ring, and therefore, I more accurately described them as royal, sapphire blue. Unlike commonplace blue eyes, Michaela's had little gray or yellow mixed in. They were largely just blue. They also seemed to glisten and radiate light – they sparkled with catch-lights that would make a photographer proud. They seemingly sparkled even when there were no lights to provide the sparkle and the reflections. As the plane gained altitude after takeoff, I thought of her eyes. With my dual-colored eyes closed on my way to London, I now had more than three words on my mind: Michaela Roston Huld with royal, sapphire blue eyes that sparkle with catchlights.

I first met Michaela at a real estate developer conference in New York City some fifteen years ago. She introduced herself as Michaela Huld. I was unaware of her middle name, and she was unaware of the intersection of our bloodlines. She was at the conference on a client development mission to find wealthy real estate developers who needed high-end financial guidance. She and I had a connection as we tried to talk over the band's din, and the noise of the mingling and drinking. The next night, we escaped the conference for a small neighborhood Italian restaurant in the Tribeca area of Manhattan. Candle lights flickered as we dined on the best Mediterranean branzini in the world and the best red wine from Sicily – a medium-bodied vintage grown on the volcanic soils of Mount Etna. As she talked, the candles' dim glow hit her eyes, which amplified the light and reflected it back into my gaze.

As we shared the chef's decadent take on panna cotta, I started down a familiar path for me – a discussion of my family legacy. Back to 1798 and Gunn, and then the early 1800s and Gunnie. I mentioned that the United States saved Gunnie from a life of destitution by the reparations it made. Those reparations would've never happened but for the tireless efforts of Francis Marion Roston, who became Gunnie's close friend and advisor and the trustee of old Gunnie's trust legacy. As I explained my interest in history and uttered the name Roston, Michaela's eyes widened, and she looked astonished at my history lesson; perhaps even distressed or overwhelmed. I instantly went from elation to dejection and asked her if I had said something wrong; I was both sorry and perfectly willing to talk about anything else. My historical diversions could sometimes sound like prattle, I acknowledged, and I was sure I was boring her anyway.

She regained her composure, dismissed that I bored her, and as she sipped her glass of wine, she explained who she was and revealed her middle name.

She said that family lore, passed down orally over the generations, recounted the life and legend of Francis Marion Roston with reverence and pride. After his death, the Rostons fanned out across America, with many heading west as the railroads pushed from the eastern seaboard to the Pacific Ocean, but no one in the family took up Francis' vocation. Certainly, none shared his interest and skill in delivering financial advice and his knowledge of the art of hiding assets for clients behind the curtain that was the Swiss banks.

She traveled and ended up at Trinity College and found an interest in economics and history – her family's history. Upon graduation, she moved to Hanover, New Hampshire, and obtained her master's degree from Dartmouth. Eventually, she ended up in London, first learning the financial advisor trade in a storied and venerable London firm, before leaving the firm to embark on a new venture – her own firm: NOIRAM Advisors. And yes, the name was the tip of her metaphorical hat to her Francis Marion past that led her to a specialty – helping the wealthy invest and shelter assets; yes, sometimes in Switzerland.

I had just started to make a name for myself in the office building development game at that point in my life. I had the proceeds of the trust fund traced back to Gunnie and entrusted to Francis. In Francis' hands, the value of the trust fund had grown substantially. Some of Gunnie's other relatives decided not to stay with Francis, opting instead to cash-out their bequest; they did with the money whatever they did with it. But the descendants down a direct line to me did not. Sure, they drew funds out of the Swiss account from time to time, but they kept the assets where Francis had placed them – in Swiss banks and beyond the knowledge and reach of any authorities in the United States. It was the rainy day fund access to which, impressively, they ultimately never seemed to need. So it grew, hidden away far beyond any attempt by creditors to discover, if creditors were even looking.

I had never shared the story of the account with anyone. But the bewitchment that was Michaela Roston Huld immediately drew me in like a magnet and engulfed me. I decided first to share with her the existence of the account emanating from the Gunnie Witherman trust, and, later, to allow her to manage it on my behalf. She seemed to have the same legendary touch as her great-great-grandfather, Francis.

At first, our relationship was a shared past, then a business relationship, but then her eyes took over. She later said that my eyes first attracted her to me as well; the dual-colored ghost eyes and the supposed ability to see into Heaven and Earth, which I admitted to her was a nice myth and made for a good cocktail party story, but not a vision I had ever been able to access. If I could somehow, someday, summon the power to see into Heaven, I was sure I would see no one there as enchanting as Michaela.

Our lives were in different hemispheres, and we were both slaves to our trades. Somehow, we maintained that rare monogamous relationship between adults separated by an ocean, eight hours of air flight, and over 3500 miles and 5700 kilometers. Few adults could make such a relationship work, but we did.

Sure, the sex was beautiful, loving, tender, satisfying, amazing, epic, sometimes explosive, a mutual act of reverence and compassion. As sex can be, though, it could also be average, modest, even middling, and perhaps that's how companions know they're meant for each other, when they remain companions through the middling. We weren't in the relationship just for sex.

Sure, the companionship when we were together was carefree, spontaneous, comfortable, secure, even cozy. But it could also be distant and unfocused, and perhaps companions know they are meant for each other when they stay close together even when they're distant. No, we learned we weren't in the relationship for companionship.

We were like the attraction of positive and negative electrical charges simply drawn to each other. But why? A shared history, and a belief that if there was an afterlife, then maybe our chance first meeting was arranged by Gunnie and Francis from far beyond the grave. We were not as far apart as far must have been for those beyond the grave, but even from our worldly three and a half thousand miles apart, we could both feel the pull of the other. We could honor both of our ancestors only by honoring each other. So, we did. Nothing was better for a lasting relationship than honoring each other as the years go by and the precision and form of youth, looks, vigor, and passion fade and blur and dull and then sometimes vanish. Honor need not fade. Ours did not.

And now, I was on a United Dreamliner about four hours outside of London and looking at my screen as the icon of an airplane slowly, painstakingly made its way across the Atlantic to the British Isles. Once I landed, Michaela would meet me at the airport. Was it too childish for me to think, *I can't wait?*

Finally, I landed on time, made my way through customs at Heathrow Airport, and found my way into the general airport population, many of whom waited to meet someone from the plane flight. My ride was there with her blue eyes, dressed in a light tan-colored raincoat and we hugged and headed for her car, a medium blue, slick 1971 Austin-Healey AAN10. A classic, driven by a classic, on the streets of the city of London. Once in the car, we headed for our special place where we holed up when we met in London.

No, we didn't stay in The Rosewood London or The Lanesborough. Instead, we stayed in a little bed and breakfast not far from the Shadwell Station named the School Mews Inn. Built in 1790, the inn was a restored former ale house comprised of three bedroom suites with private bathrooms located in old London's fashionable East End not far from the Thames. We had both stayed in the Rosewood and the Lanesborough, but, we enjoyed the working-class streets near the inn, the gardens where we could stroll, the nearby historical neighborhood English pubs, complete with Cockney accents, beer warmer than most Americans were used to, dartboards, and televisions tuned to one football match or another. And we relished the proximity to the Thames for our daily walks together. We were like an old married couple, aging gracefully and gradually out of our midlife.

That first night, we took the overbridge train at the Shadwell Station to the famous Bank Street Station, exited, and headed for a favorite, quiet French restaurant and an evening of catching up. Michaela was aware of the bankruptcy case but had few of the details. So, unlike other dinners we shared at *Chez Boucherie*, this one found me focused on the bankruptcy story, the bank group, Stacy Milnes, and the newly minted exit plan. Michaela listened intently, and when I finished, she asked, "What of the Swiss account, and the crypto?"

"I didn't list either in the bankruptcy schedules."

"The penalty?"

I smiled and said, "Well, none if I don't get caught. If the alternative occurs, nothing good, I'm afraid."

"I figured. I'm worried. And this Milnes creature sounds dangerous."

"Don't be worried. I'll be fine either way. As to Milnes, she's mostly a vulgar annoyance, a caricature of a bad-loan banker who fancies herself bigger than life. The other banks will manage her. They don't want to fight. They want a business deal and a solution."

Michaela listened, concerned, and, after a few moments, asked, "Are we careful enough?"

"We have been and continue to be as careful as we can possibly be," I reassured her.

"When this is all over, it may well serve us to find a new, safer venue to house the account. Something less civilized, less scrutinized, and less prone than Switzerland to cooperate with Western authorities," Michaela said quietly, reverting to her role as trusted financial advisor.

"You are undoubtedly correct, my dear. But, those are matters we'll address after my companies and I have exited from bankruptcy. Agreed?"

"Agreed."

For our first evening, that was the totality of our discussion of everything I had temporarily left behind in Kansas City. Instead, we focused our few days together on our favorite things to do in London. We walked and held hands and talked. We walked across the Wobbly Bridge, officially the London Millennium Bridge, and back. We walked to the Borough Market. We bussed and walked to the Chelsea Market, our destination for fresh Ethiopian coffee, roasted at an outdoor food booth one cup at a time in a copper pan over a single flame. The most flavorful and aromatic coffee in the world. We also met-up with the Chelsea Market vendor who crafted beef bourguignon sandwiches, the most decadent sandwich we had ever tasted.

We walked along the Thames at dusk to seek the guitar players and the man who blew gigantic bubbles for the kids to romp in. We double-decker bussed to Abbey Road and walked the famous crosswalk like first-time tourists. And we journeyed to our favorite, the Diana Princess of Wales Memorial Walk. A seven-mile-long walk, charted by ninety plaques set in the ground, that took us within sight of famous buildings and locations associated with the Princess during her life and through four of the eight Royal Parks. We were lucky. Mostly, it didn't rain. The weather service said it was partly sunny. Of course, in London, that meant the sun peeked out from behind the clouds for ten minutes.

That first night, we laid next to each other. Quietly. Listening to old Fleetwood Mac when it was a blues band and before it reached mega-success levels as a straight ahead pop band. A favorite of Michaela's: "Love That Burns" – it was as if Peter Green had us in mind when he penned the lyrics, and when he sang the song, it was as if the only audience was Michaela and me.

Each morning, we went to a coffee shop not far from the inn. It was a favorite custom of Michaela's to frequent a coffee establishment each morning and sip an espresso before the day began. Espresso and the internet on the coffee shop WiFi. As a matter of course, we each used a Virtual Private Network, a VPN, to maximize our internet anonymity. We never used public WiFi to send emails or access any sensitive data, but we did like to catch up on the business news of the day before the day got started and used our VPNs so that no one could know what exactly we were searching for or reading. We knew we couldn't be too cautious in this crazy world.

All too soon, it was Sunday and time to return to the States. As we drove back to Heathrow, Michaela said, "Please be careful. Very careful. I know you believe that anyone who builds skyscrapers is a natural risk-taker, and you are. But you understand and manage the construction risks. I am quite concerned that the risk associated with the Swiss account is not one you can ultimately manage and control."

"Indeed." I paused and repeated, "Indeed."

We traveled in silence for several minutes, and then I asked, "Why not visit me in Kansas City?"

"Until the bankruptcy cases are over, I don't think that would be a good idea, Quince. My connection to the Swiss account is much too great. While an occasional rendezvous in London seems anonymous and reasonably safe, I don't think I could say the same about a Kansas City meeting, no disrespect intended. Let's keep it safe and simple right now."

"You're probably correct," I conceded as we arrived at Heathrow. And, like an old, married couple, we kissed. Not a passionate, sex-crazed, teenager kiss. But a comfortable, contented, warm, luxurious kiss. The kind of kiss that says, *I'm sad to leave, but I have to.* A John Denver, "Leaving On a Jet Plane" kiss. And then I was off on that jet plane to finish off the bankruptcy case, earn my discharge, secure my fresh start, quietly revel in my head start, and move on.

CHAPTER 26

Friday, October 26, 2018

JAMIE LI KNOCKED ON Judge Robertson's door and entered. He waited for the Judge to finish approving an order and then said, "Judge, the Witherman cases have gone radio silent."

Judge Robertson rolled his eyes and said, "Not a big surprise, I suppose. I am hoping to hear from Ms. Jones that the Debtors and the banks agreed to a plan, and we'll all then rocket toward confirmation. Odd case, indeed." After a moment of contemplation, he continued, "Jamie, let's do this: See if Ms. Jones and Mr. Sample can be on a conference call with me at 4 p.m. today so you and I can hear them say that they take the *pinky swear* that we're on the road to confirmation of a consensual plan. Hopefully, Mr. Sample will have the good sense just to say 'yes' and nothing more," the Judge said as he smiled.

"Will do, Judge."

At precisely 4 p.m. that afternoon, then, Judge Robertson, 3J, Pascale, Dennis Sample, and Jamie Li were on a conference call. Judge Robertson said, "Counsel, thank you for getting on a call with me on such short notice. I understand we have no further cash collateral disputes, correct?"

Sample and 3J both said, "Correct."

"Have the banks approved the terms of a consensual plan?"

Sample and 3J again both said, "Correct."

"We're therefore on track for an uncontested confirmation hearing?"

3J responded, "We believe so, Your Honor."

"Will it be a joint plan proposed by both First Commercial as bank group agent and the Debtors?" the Judge inquired.

Sample cleared his throat and then spoke slightly slower than his usual cadence. "Your Honor, First Commercial is no longer the bank group agent. That role has passed to Star-Banc of Houston, and I will now represent StarBanc through confirmation. So, lots of shuffling of pieces on our end, I am afraid. To the Court's question, at this point, I am unclear whether it will be a joint plan or just the Debtors' plan that the bank group supports. I can try to get clarity on that point for Your Honor."

By now, Quincy had reported the news of First Commercial's removal to 3J and Pascale, so they weren't surprised. The Judge, however, was not expecting the news and had a look of surprise on his face as he processed what he just heard. He rarely liked the lawyers to see emotion on his face, so it was fortuitous that this was a telephone conference call and not a video conference. He composed himself quickly, however, and, without emotion in his voice, said, "That won't be necessary, counsel. I was just curious. Ms. Jones, are you still ok with the timeline we set out in our last chambers conference?"

"Yes, Your Honor."

"Ok. Very well then. Unless either of you has any other items you wish to cover, I will say goodbye."

3J and Sample each said, "Nothing further, Your Honor," and the Judge ended the call.

Jamie lingered in Judge Robertson's office. Judge Robertson looked at him, slowly shook his head left and right, and said softly, "Short-lived tenure as agent bank for First Commercial and Ms. Milnes. Damndest thing I've seen or heard."

"I'm glad you said that, Judge," Jamie said with relief. "I thought maybe I was missing something here. I thought maybe these kinds of strange things happened in all Chapter 11 cases."

"Bankruptcy can certainly bring out the bizarre; take the mundane, and make it interesting when you least expect it. But, based on my years in practice, the banks in this case are testing the waters for new levels of kooky." The Judge paused, and Jamie said nothing. The Judge continued, "Look, let's do everything we can to get this to confirmation quickly before any of those folks on the call with us or their clients change their minds."

"Certainly," Jamie agreed as he left the Judge's chambers.

Alone in his chambers, Judge Robertson gazed out of his windows. Fall had progressed. It would shortly finish its annual appearance in Kansas City. The leaves on the many trees along the river had turned orange, red, yellow, and gold, and had begun to drop and carpet the ground below as the temperatures diminished and the days grew shorter. Always a gorgeous sight. It was often a surprise to a first-time visitor to Kansas City just how many trees called Kansas City their home and how many sat on the hills and the bluffs that rose out of the Missouri River banks. Not the flat, barren Midwest that so many mistakenly believed comprised the thousands of miles west of Pennsylvania. Oh, there were great expanses of flatness to the west of Kansas City – the Midwestern Plains and the High Plains beyond. But flat was not how anyone who knew Kansas City would describe it.

Even as the Witherman bankruptcy cases had become unpredictable, Robertson thought to himself, *At least you always know what's coming when fall arrives, and a harsh, wet, gray, icy Kansas City winter is just around the corner.*

CHAPTER 27

Friday, November 2 to Monday, November 5, 2018

AS STACY MILNES EXPECTED, Moses set up a phone call with her to give her an update on his status. She had no idea yet of the significant personal risk she'd have to consider by the end of the call.

In advance, Milnes received from Moses his written preliminary report explaining methods used and information reviewed. The report also set out what Moses knew, what he believed, and what he suspected: His suspicions that Michaela Roston Huld was in the same business as her ancestor, Francis Marion Roston and that like the Roston of old, she used Swiss accounts to hide assets for her clients. In addition, Moses reported that he suspected Quincy Witherman and Michaela Huld had at some point connected, he was her client, and now they were potentially an item in certain European high-society circles. Moses concluded that Quincy was likely Michaela's occasional "plus-one" at London society events.

Milnes noted that Moses stopped short of writing that he suspected Huld had continued to assist Witherman in hiding assets in Switzerland. She needed no prodding and no power of suggestion to conclude that Witherman hid assets, and that Huld helped him do so.

§

On Friday, November 2, Dennis Sample informed 3J that the banks agreed to the terms of the revised plan. At the end of the day, 3J's team filed the revised plan and disclosure statement.

3J and Pascale then sent a memo to Quincy outlining how they would ask the Court to confirm the plan. They wrote in the memo:

> The Court will first consider whether the disclosure statement contains sufficient information to permit a creditor to decide whether they will vote for or against the plan. Given that the banks have agreed to the plan and the plan proposes to pay all creditors in full with interest, we do not expect any opposition to the disclosure statement's approval. We do not anticipate the need for your testimony at the disclosure statement hearing.
>
> Assuming the Court approves the disclosure statement, we will then mail it along with the plan and a ballot to every creditor and party-in-interest in the seven cases for them to vote. As the votes are returned to us, we will tally them and file a ballot report. We assume the creditors will vote to accept the plan since they will be paid in full. You will need to testify at the confirmation hearing, although we believe your testimony will be quick, and we do not expect that anyone will cross-examine you. We simply need to make a record, so the Court has the necessary information to approve the plan.
>
> If the Court approves the plan, it will enter a confirmation order, which will include the discharge afforded to each of the Debtors. The plan provisions will then become the operative agreement between the Debtors and all of the creditors. After the Court

enters the confirmation order, you will sign revised and restated loan agreements with the bank group documenting the new deal terms.

In many bankruptcy cases, any one of these steps could engender a significant court fight by creditors who oppose the plan. But, where the principal creditors and the Debtors agree to a negotiated plan, we expect the process to move swiftly and without incident.

Let us know if you have questions.

Judge Robertson's chambers gave them a hearing date of November 27, 2018 to consider the disclosure statement's approval.

§

Monday morning, Moses dialed Milnes' mobile phone number, and she answered before the second ring finished.

"Good morning, Ms. Milnes. Top of the mornin' to ya', as my friends in Dublin like to say to me."

Milnes laughed as Moses greeted her – she had an unusual tolerance for Moses' greetings that she eschewed with everyone else, and found it odd to hear the usually prim, proper and very New York Moses take on a working-class, Irish accent, preferring his customary college English literature professor cadence and New York City dialect much more. "Same to you, Moses. I see you've made progress?"

Moses dispensed with his contrived Irish accent and laid out for her what he had discovered, and in particular, he focused a great deal of historical attention on Francis Marion Roston.

"Roston was the trusted financial advisor for Gunnie Witherman. We know this from Gunnie's will that sets up a trust for future generations and expressly establishes Roston as the trustee. Of interest, the will made no mention of exactly how Roston should administer the trust assets. There is no trust filing in the Philadelphia Government offices, so we are left to guess a bit about its terms and provisions. But we do know that the will simply relegated investment decisions to Roston." Moses paused and asked, "do you have any questions so far?"

"Not yet, Moses," Milnes replied. "Go on."

"Very well. At the same time that Gunnie installed Roston as the trustee, his financial advice business flourished. From the contemporaneous newspaper articles I read, colonists from all over the United States sought Roston's advice. So much so that the *Pennsylvania Inquirer* sought out Roston for insights on financial articles its reporters wrote. As well, the *Inquirer* sought out Roston for an extensive interview about his financial advisory practice. In the course of that interview, we learn that Roston believed that in some circumstances, he felt it was appropriate to use the secret Swiss banking system to shelter assets without actually admitting that he did so for his clients."

Moses paused to let that point sink in.

"Roston's advisory firm closed its doors when he died. But of interest, a new firm named NOIRAM Advisors has sprung up and operates today with its base in London, England. The firm's principal is one Michaela Huld. The Roston genealogy chart is interesting. It reveals that Michaela is a direct descendant of Francis Marion Roston, and you will note the relation between the new firm's name and Francis Marion's middle name. It seems our Michaela has rekindled the family business in present-day London. Of particular interest, we located society photographs of Michaela and Quincy Gunn Witherman dressed in formal wear in attendance, apparently together, at one charitable event or another.

Last, we know from public Department of Justice reports that NOIRAM has assisted clients in hiding assets in Switzerland."

Milnes listened to Moses spin the facts and suppositions he had amassed so far with such intensity that Moses thought he could hear the bones in her neck creak.

He continued, "So, Ms. Milnes, what facts have escaped our grasp to date? First, just because Michaela and Quincy know each other and have been seen in each other's company does not mean that Quincy uses her financial services. Even if he did, it does not mean that Michaela is carrying on her family's tradition of hiding Witherman assets as her ancestor did for Gunnie Witherman. We suspect, but we do not know.

"Second, we still do not know if Francis Marion Roston used the Swiss banking system to shelter Gunnie Witherman's assets in the 1800s. While we are free to surmise and suspect, we do not know. Third, even if Roston did, we don't know if those assets remained hidden over the approximately two hundred years before Quincy came on the scene or if Witherman clan members who came before Quincy cashed in the assets and thereby removed them from the cloak provided by the Swiss bankers. On this point, I don't know, and I am not ready to suspect.

"Make no mistake, Ms. Milnes. These are significant questions. Plainly put, we need to find a critical connection, the nexus between the Swiss banking system and Quincy Witherman. The key to the success of this project is that nexus. It would be eminently helpful if we could connect Michaela Roston Huld to Quincy Gunn Witherman and each to Witherman assets held in the Swiss banking system."

Silence. Moses thought he could hear more cracking of joints. Milnes spoke finally and said, "Finding that nexus could be time-consuming. How much time?"

FRESH START | 221

"Most definitely, it can be time-consuming. Given the nature of what we are seeking, it could take months or longer. Even then, there is no guarantee that we will draw that nexus we seek."

"Months or longer is too long for this project, Moses. I'm under some significant pressure here at the bank on this one." She didn't explain why she felt under pressure. No need to burden him with the consequences of the shortcomings of her difficult personality. "Have you considered any other investigatory alternatives?"

"I am glad you asked. I have, Ms. Milnes. Indeed I have. The alternative I have in mind has no guarantee of success, but it will speed up the inquiry to a matter of weeks, not months."

"I like the way that sounds," said Milnes with anticipation in her voice. "What is the alternative?"

"Ms. Milnes, the alternative is certainly not within the protection of the law. It will involve an intrusion into Quincy Witherman's or Michaela Huld's technology."

"Before we get into an assessment of just how risky the intrusion is, tell me how we could accomplish it."

"You know about The Moses Team, correct?"

"Yes."

"The Moses Team includes a member skilled in the art of technological intrusion. This team member is a master of the bits and bytes. Even as a tech wizard, the team member I have in mind is a firm believer that even in this sophisticated digital age, the successful intrusion is a combination of digital technology and an analog old school operation.

"Now, I should be clear about the terms of engagement of this team member. While I will make the introduction, you would be responsible for the engagement. I will not be the middle-man who engages this team member. I will not be your interface. You will interact with this associate directly. Are you clear on this?"

Moses would not involve his intrusion virtuoso without a clear understanding with Milnes on the engagement protocol. Especially with Milnes, he viewed this potential engagement as a modern-day version of the Greek myth of Icarus and his father, Daedalus. Father and son wanted to escape the isle of Crete, and Daedalus, a master craftsman, created a pair of wings made of feathers and wax for Icarus to fly away from Crete. Daedalus warned Icarus neither to fly too close to the sea, for fear the moist air would clog the feathers, nor too close to the sun, for fear the heat would melt the wax. Icarus ignored his father's warnings, probably because of his youth and hubris, and flew too close to the sun. The wings melted, and Icarus fell to the sea and drowned.

Moses knew that Western civilization depicted the lesson of Icarus in many forms. Ironically, one such depiction was a relief of Icarus at the bankruptcy chamber entrance in Amsterdam's Royal Palace, which he understood to represent the risks of high-flying ambition. He sensed that this particular depiction of the Icarus myth captured the essence of the project consuming Stacy Milnes, and he expected Milnes would ignore his admonitions, filling the role of Icarus as she pursued her Witherman obsession. Moses would create the construct for her to implement the intrusion by introducing her to his team member, and as he stepped away, he would, of course, warn her of the dangers of the project. Hopefully, she could manage her ambition and steer clear of both the sea and the sun.

Milnes said nothing during Moses' explanation as she engaged in her own silent thought process. She broke the silence and said, "Yes, I'm clear, Moses. Who is it, and what does he do?"

"My team member's real name will remain a mystery to you. You will know the member only as Parker Romero. Code name, "Rome." Rome's specialty is technological intrusion. I cannot speak knowledgeably as to the methods that Rome employs. Sadly, I long ago concluded that those in my age bracket lack the vital DNA strand to comfortably and accurately address many elements of the technology world. So, I explain Rome's task to you merely as obtaining information from Witherman's or Huld's technology to attempt to show the nexus we have discussed today. You know that such an intrusion is likely a crime, correct?"

"I do."

"And you know that the consequences of the commission of such a crime could easily reach your doorstep."

"I know that, as well."

"I have known you for many years, Ms. Milnes. I value our working relationship, and I consider you a friend. Therefore, allow me to speak forthrightly as a friend, and offer you this sincere caution. My strong suggestion is that you should take in all of what we have discussed today, organize it in your mind, and find some quiet time to think through the implications of a technology intrusion. Implications for the bank. Implications for you, my friend. Implications for the successful conclusion of your Witherman project. To ensure that you think this through, I will require a cooling-off period for contemplation before I will allow you to accept the darkness and proceed with Rome. If, after a day or two of introspection, you still want to contact Rome, please communicate with me, and I will arrange for the delivery of contact information to you, and I will let Rome know that you may be calling."

"I'm ready to decide now, Moses."

"Perhaps you are, Ms. Milnes. Perhaps you are. But if you are about to tell me that you've decided to proceed, I would not accept that decision today. I require you to go through the introspection process I have outlined, focusing on the potential criminal nature of the venture we have discussed. The decision could affect your life. *Adversely* affect your life. Please consider carefully if the darkness is worth it. Clear?"

Milnes realized that nothing she could say would change the way Moses wanted the next phase to proceed. So, rather than argue, she said, "Clear, Mr. Aaronson, sir."

"Very well. We will communicate in a day or two. Thank you for your patience, Ms. Milnes, and have a good day."

Moses looked down at the sleeping Emily. She had found a ray of sunlight that fell on his bedspread, and she curled up on his bed in the warm sun, her long, graceful toes tucked under her chin as a pillow. *Oh, what a wonderful, simple life you lead, my lovely Emily,* Moses thought. *No intrusions. No technology. No Greek mythology. No data. No crimes. Nothing hidden. No need for contemplation before you act. I can only hope that your life will be the life for me when this one ends, my darling. I very much look forward to it.*

Moses moved to his bed and sat next to the dog so he could stroke her ears. She rolled on her side signaling that she was open to a belly rub as well. As he attended to Emily's wishes, he continued to think about the Witherman project and his client. He doubted that Milnes would avail herself of any meaningful periods of introspection and he felt concern for her. *Her penchant for gut decisions doesn't bode well for her to avoid the sun,* he thought. *In this matter, she is simply not presenting as a person of reasoned reflection.* He recognized Stacy Milnes as a creature of passion. He was concerned that Milnes would charge ahead without proper thoughtfulness and pursue her own crime of passion.

Emily stirred, rose, and stretched. "Time for our lunchtime walk, m' dear?" Emily trotted to the front door and awaited her friend. Moses put her harness on, and down to the street level they went. He had an uncanny ability to turn off his work, like an on-off switch. As Emily and he exited his building for the streets, Moses hit the off switch, and he and Emily proceeded to enjoy another wonderful day in Manhattan, free of plots to commit crimes in a foreign country to acquire information. Even with all of the chaos, the streets of Manhattan presented such a simpler, predictable alternative to his day job.

CHAPTER 28

Monday, November 5 to Tuesday, November 6, 2018

MILNES LEFT HER CALL with Moses feeling unsettled. Even though she had expressed a desire to proceed forward with the next stage of the investigation, in doing so, she masked her concern for the next phase. To find out if Witherman had committed a continuing felony for years, she would have to cross over a line even she never crossed before in all of her years in special assets. Every special assets file had a theme. Was the Witherman's file theme, to catch a felon, Milnes had to be a felon? She recognized the gravity of what came next. She was about to put in motion the commission of a crime.

Milnes knew she was not a criminal. But if she was to prove her point to the other bank group members, if she was to take down Witherman rather than just capitulate to the deal struck by Brian Chimes, she saw no alternatives. None. She spent no time with the facts and suppositions outlined in Moses' call because from the beginning, she assumed the truth in everything he outlined; all he did in his work, and he did it well, was move some of the suppositions to the fact column and thereby identify what was left to nail down.

Milnes didn't expect to spend a great deal of time with introspection either, despite his advice. Even with her concerns about the criminal nature of the next phase of the project, introspection was not her strong suit. She felt that introspection would lead to wallowing in self-pity and she had no interest in pursuing that tangent. Instead, the only introspection she engaged in was a brief but accurate analysis of her view of herself. A short, psychological system self-check. It was a quick process as she knew herself well. She considered herself neither an ideologue nor a pragmatist. An ideologue believes what is right will work. A pragmatist believes what works is right within the bounds of social norms. No, she was neither. Instead, she considered herself to be one who believed that whatever it takes is what she was willing to do, and since that works, that is right even if norms are ignored. She had long ago adopted this view of herself in her efforts to forge a career as a female special assets officer in a man's world of bad loans. But, in all her years as a "whatever-it-takes" bank officer, the one norm she had never violated was the law – she had never committed a crime. So, now, the only decision she had to make was whether she was willing to deem as right the commission of a crime to catch a criminal.

While Moses felt there was a dilemma for Milnes to resolve, for which she appreciated his concern, she didn't consider what she was about to do as a significant violation, and therefore the only answer she could reach was to engage Mr. Romero, code name "Rome." She had a sense of anticipation for the engagement.

Out of respect, Milnes would reluctantly wait out Moses' required twenty-four hour period, and then she would promptly inform him of her decision. She hoped he would accept her decision without further commentary, criticism, parables, or annotations. Not that he did it on purpose, but from time to time, Moses could be a little like a father trying to steer a child in a particular direction without coming right out and saying what was on his mind – that the child's current path was a tremendous mistake. She didn't want or need that tone or message right now. She just wanted to reach the end of what was about to become a sordid affair.

She was more than a little curious about Parker Romero and exactly how he would intrude, and she wanted to get that part of the process underway as soon as possible.

§

"Moses, this is Stacy Milnes. Do you have a moment to talk?"

"For you, always, my dear," Moses replied. It had been precisely twenty-four hours since they last talked.

"Great. Thank you. I'm calling to let you know my decision."

"Go on, please."

Milnes hadn't slept well the night before. She usually didn't lay awake after a contentious day of debt collection. She had always been able to separate the job from what little life she had outside of the job. But she'd known Moses for many years. While they had a strictly professional relationship, they were friends within that relationship; Moses had always given off the vibe that he was concerned about her day-to-day life. In some respects, whether he intended to or not, he applied some paternalism to the things he said and asked of her. She sensed that he would disapprove of her decision to engage Rome. So she was apprehensive as the conversation started.

"Yes. Thanks, Moses. I'd like to engage Rome. How do we make that happen, and how soon can we begin the process?"

"I am not surprised. I have no editorial comment to offer. You are a grown up. I trust what we discussed yesterday was not lost in your decision-making process. I expect you were thoughtful and comprehensive in your analysis of risks and rewards." Truth be told, Moses believed that Milnes made her decision hastily with little, if any, analysis and thoughtfulness.

But he was a gentleman and was merely stating his hope, not his true expectation. His hope for Milnes' introspection was only aspirational, and not an expectation. He knew he wasn't her father and it was time to step back and let her own the consequences of her decision.

"Ms. Milnes, Rome has been informed that you may reach out, and I have provided Rome with sufficient background information to facilitate your call. Rome is sometimes located here in New York City, although currently, Rome may be in London. I will text you the contact information. And, Stacy ..."

"Yes, Moses?"

"Please take care."

Paternalism? Concern? Just an older man ending a call? No matter. Milnes felt no anger toward Moses. She could never be peeved with him.

"Understood," said Milnes. "Always. Thank you."

"Good day," Moses said, and the line went dead.

Milnes was grateful for the call's brevity and immensely relieved that Moses refrained from assuming the role of parent. *Moses probably knew I would hire Romero when we finished talking yesterday, so my decision was likely no great surprise.*

§

As promised, within a minute, Milnes received a text from Moses with Romero's phone number. She texted the number and asked when they could talk. A response came straight back that they could talk on Friday, November 9. Milnes confirmed the appointment, and exhaled.

§

Code name, Parker Romero. Real first name, Belita, meaning one who is beautiful. Last name, Davies. No particular meaning.

Schooled at Bryn Mawr College in Main Line Philadelphia, west of Center City, a campus of gothic, castle-like architecture hidden about half a mile north of the Paoli Local train tracks. An all-women's college. An intellectually stimulating institution for a native of Britain. While in secondary school, she had expressed a desire to her parents to attend university in the United States, and Bryn Mawr was by far the best school to accept her.

Once at Bryn Mawr, Belita focused on all things technology. Yet her undergraduate major in anthropology had little to do with high tech, instead celebrating non-electric, non-computer worlds and cultures of long ago. She was thoughtful, quiet, and at times reclusive.

After college, Belita returned to London and fell into an underground group of drop-outs, outsiders, and loose cartels of tech-oriented odd-person-outs, as she struggled to find a path for the rest of her life or at least the immediate future. In the underground, she learned and perfected her skills in the art of hacking. But hacking, while interesting, was not her true passion. Instead, like anthropology, she enjoyed sleuthing. She wondered if there was a way to combine her interest in high-tech with her training in the low-tech sleuthing that drew her to an anthropology major and somehow forge a career of sorts.

After a chance meeting with Moses in New York City, Belilta's tenure as a member of The Moses Team began with engagements to obtain data for clients of Moses who might need to use methodologies that were not necessarily sanctioned by society. And that became her specialty.

Moses gave her the code name Rome. She became so fond of the code name that she introduced herself as Rome more often than she used her given name, Belita.

The rest, as the saying goes, was history.

CHAPTER 29

Friday, November 9, 2018

ON FRIDAY, MILNES PLACED the call to Rome. The number Milnes called was, in reality, a burner phone – a prepaid, anonymous mobile phone not bound to a carrier contract and without any registration requirements – that Rome used for just these types of engagements. Typically, both parties to this kind of call make use of a burner phone; Milnes, however, used her regular iPhone.

After the first ring, a female voice answered, "Yes?" with a tasteful British accent, which might explain Moses' comment that Rome might be in London.

Milnes was startled that the voice was female. She had assumed Rome was male. Milnes had called Rome "he" in her conversation with Moses, and he hadn't corrected her. The code name, Parker, also sounded male, but she now realized it could be a woman's name as well. Momentarily, she thought she had dialed the wrong number, so she asked, "Is this Rome?" failing to mask her surprise.

"Yes. Who is this?"

"Stacy Milnes."

"Ah, yes. Moses said I might hear from you. Good morning."

"Are you Moses' technology operative?" Milnes asked with a slightly derisive tone. "I thought Moses said you were a man."

Rome detected the surprise in Stacy Milnes' voice and attributed it to disappointment. She had heard this type of surprise
before when the client was male, and she had little patience
for anyone who thought that hacking and computer intrusions
were the province of males only. She decided to get the issue
on the table immediately. "Ms. Milnes, if I might momentarily
digress before we get started? I hear bewilderment in your voice.
You are surprised, perhaps disappointed, I am a female, no?"

Silence.

Rome continued, "You are not the first, but Moses led me
to believe that you were a special assets banking officer who
admirably forged a successful career as a tough woman in a
man's world. So, candidly, I am disappointed by the level of
surprise I hear in your voice."

Milnes thought to herself, *Not a good way to start. Shit. Am I
now going to have to start off this engagement by being contrite?* She well
knew that she neither liked to apologize nor was she good at
it. She was comfortable with a life decision never to say she
was sorry and as a result, she had little practice in the art of
falling on the sword to keep a relationship going.

"I *am* surprised," she exclaimed too quickly, too loudly, and
too awkwardly. She was still flustered and spoke without any
regard for the political correctness of her comment. She
sounded like she was unhappily surprised when all she wanted
to do was to convey the bare minimum of an apology and move
on to the substance of the impending operation. As she heard
the words come out of her mouth, she grew more agitated with
the direction the conversation was taking.

"Ms. Milnes. I feel one of those walls. Unlike what I hear
about you, I don't have to spend my days trying to fight my
way through this type of wall. Given what I do, I have the
luxury to move on from such fights and seek other engagements that … well, that lack the wall. So, your surprise – it

is of no moment to me. Perhaps you would like to terminate our discussion and regroup with Moses. If so, please apprise me now of that decision, and I will return to the engagement I left to take your call."

Milnes thought, *shit, shit, shit! Now what?* She knew that her stereotyped reaction was about to sour the not-yet-begun engagement with Rome. What a disaster that would be. *What a fuckin' disaster!* And to have the Witherman investigation end on an issue of implied bias unintentionally dished out by one who spent her banking career on the receiving end of white-male-delivered, implied bias daily. How awful would that be? A complete debacle.

So she tried once again to apologize, this time forsaking a lifetime belief that only weak people said they were sorry. In her next attempt, she said too much. "No, no. I apologize. I assumed something that I shouldn't have. I'm embarrassed that I did so. You *are* right. I've lived this issue my whole life, and I should know better. I'm *pleasantly* surprised and want to work with you. Please accept my apology, forgive me, and let's proceed." As she heard the words leaving her lips, Milnes thought, *if that doesn't get the job done, I've got nothing else left in the tank.*

This time, she hoped she had hit the right chord and things could move forward. Since she was not practiced in the craft of considering the feelings of others, she had no idea if her latest attempt would work. She also felt complete discomfort in having to essentially beg Rome to join the team on the Witherman project. While Milnes was a do-whatever-it-takes banker, she was not one who ever begged for forgiveness. That was not part of the "doing whatever." So, having taken the extraordinary step of asking for forgiveness, she now found herself enmeshed in what seemed to be an unnaturally extended period of silence and hoping to herself that she wouldn't have to take a third shot at soothing Rome's irritation.

For that extended period, Rome said nothing and Milnes said nothing. Rome was wondering whether Milnes' comprehensive awkward attempt at an apology was a sign of insincerity.

"Very well," Rome finally said. *Moses was right,* Rome thought. *Milnes is a difficult creature.* She hoped there would be no further discussions like the one they just had.

"If we can move on to the matter at hand, has Moses briefed you?" Milnes asked. No "thank you." No "great." No "welcome to the team." Just Milnes back in command and pushing forward to the matter at hand.

"Yes."

"Then you know the mission?"

"Yes."

"I'd like to understand a little bit about how you propose to accomplish your mission. Is that ok?"

"Certainly. Let me just give you an overview, and let's see if that will suffice."

Silence from Milnes, so Rome continued.

"I am here in London. Michaela Huld is here in London. Moses apprised me that Huld is a creature of habit. She frequents the same coffee shop each morning. She arrives at the same time and leaves at the same time. She buys the same coffee drink and pastry each morning. With her coffee and pastry in hand, she sits at the same table each day and briefly surfs the internet, although I assume that at the coffee shop, she does casual surfing and shies away from business-related internet activity under the belief that she is safe on the public Wi-Fi as long as she refrains from business-related, sensitive information.

"My current plan is that I will follow her for a couple of days to confirm these habits, and if I am correct, I will use the coffee shop setting to – shall we say – get some information about her … let's call it browsing and internet access information.

FRESH START | 235

Once I have that information, I can determine the next steps and report to you in more detail."

"No hacking into her phone or laptop?"

"We will be in London for this operation, Ms. Milnes, not Hollywood," Rome responded with a small smile on her face that Milnes, of course, couldn't see.

Rome paused for this explanation to sink in. Silence from Milnes.

"Ms. Milnes, is there anything about the mission you would like me to amplify?"

More silence.

Rome probed, "No questions or concerns?"

Milnes thought for a moment, broke her silence, and responded, "I *do* have questions which lead to many concerns; while I have them, I'm also trying not to focus on any of my concerns. I'll just have to manage them. So, I have no questions right now that I think I want or need to know the answers to." An uncharacteristically long answer for Milnes. She could simply have said, "no," but the length of the answer reflected her continuing discomfort with the process, rather than any qualms about her decision to proceed.

"Good. Then the details of how I acquire actual data will be something I can share with you later. Yes?"

"Yes."

"We will come back to the details."

"Yes."

The two then discussed Rome's fee, and Rome advised Milnes, "Ms. Milnes, I can begin the mission as soon as I receive 50% of the fee. The rest will be payable at the conclusion of the mission. If that is agreeable, I want you to download an app for your phone called *Flag* and set it up for use on a burner phone. It is a messenger app that encrypts and then destroys texts and does an excellent job of protecting our communications. I will use that to communicate with you; you will not reach out to me. I will limit the content of my *Flag* communications to topics such as the fee, or if I need to advise you that we should speak and when I can talk to you. We will both use burner phones when we speak. Do you understand?"

"Do we need all of this cloak and dagger?" Milnes asked.

"We do. It is how I operate. It is what I require if you want to work with me. Once you acquire the burner phone, you will let me know the number so we can communicate. So, again, do you understand?" Rome asked.

"I do."

"Very well. I will use *Flag* to inform you of the payment information and once I confirm I have received the deposit, then give me a few days, and you can expect we will talk again," Rome said and disconnected the call. No pleasantries. No "goodbye." *Just like me*, Milnes thought.

Even as she realized she had no details of precisely what Rome was planning on doing, nevertheless, Milnes found herself intrigued by the little bit of the proposed methodology she conveyed. Since Rome made it clear she would not hack into Michaela's laptop or mobile phone like in the movies, then it stood to reason she would employ some other methodology. Moses said he lacked the DNA strand to allow him to speak in detail about such tech issues. Milnes had the same DNA deficiency, and so she would just have to wait. Her feeling of uncomfortableness about the process and the secretive method of communicating persisted. Intrigued and uncomfortable. Not a great combination of emotional conditions. But she would just have to power through any concerns and await the next report. Waiting was not one of her strong suits, but hopefully, the reward after the wait would make the pain worthwhile.

As for the payment, Milnes felt lucky that First Commercial didn't have the best-in-class secure system for senior officers to make payments to vendors in open cases. As the head of special assets, Milnes had significant discretion to hire experts, investigators, and consultants and arrange for payment of their fees without requiring a second set of bank eyes to approve such payments. A second-set-of-eyes requirement might have doomed Milnes' entire inquiry as her explanation of what she was after could very well have sounded so far-fetched and alarming to someone else at the bank that they would have declined approval of the payment. While Milnes was pushing the envelope in what she paid Moses and his team, she was nevertheless still within her significant approval level.

If this inquiry doesn't yield information to use against Witherman, the payments I authorized will eventually come to light, and bank management will summarily escort me from the bank. Fired. Undoubtedly unable to secure another special assets job at a different bank. That thought was cause for concern, and Milnes was not immune from those types of employment concerns. But, given her conduct on the Witherman loans and her negative interactions with the other bank group members, she figured that only the kind of information she was after would save her job and her career in special assets. She viewed the downside as a no-sum game. She either needed to get her hands on information that could be used against Witherman or find another way to make a living.

CHAPTER 30

Tuesday, November 13 to Monday, November 19, 2018

AFTER HER CALL WITH Milnes, Rome knew she would have to explain her methodology in a way that someone less technologically savvy could understand. It was often challenging to explain technology to the uninitiated, so in Rome's other assignments, she had learned to put the time in to make her explanation understandable and break the operation down step by step.

In Rome's experience, drawing an analogy between the physical and the virtual helped people understand the basic workings of the internet, so in this operation, the trick was to imagine computers and websites as buildings with addresses. Every computer had an address like the street address of a person's house, a "MAC address." Similarly, every website also had an address like the street address of the addressee's office building, an "IP address." In the physical world, the letter sender would write its return address on the envelope, which was addressed with the addressee's street address. On the internet, the process worked in much the same way. A person surfing the internet used its browser to navigate to a website – the surfer's computer sent a communication from its MAC address to the website's IP address.

In the physical world, a letter sender might instead write a number of letters, but put them all in one large envelope addressed to a forwarder who would act as a conduit with instructions to open the envelope and mail the enclosed letters. Anyone seeing the envelope would have no way of knowing the addressees of each of the enclosed letters and it would appear as if the sender wrote only one letter in one envelope. In the virtual world, a virtual private network, VPN, acted as a fowarder conduit. To connect with a website, the user's MAC address would communicate to the VPN the website it wished to visit. The VPN then connected to the website, acting as the conduit between the user and the website. Once connected to the VPN, no matter how many websites the user visited, its MAC address would connect to just one IP address – the VPN's.

Rome's operation had three phases: intercept, match, and compromise.

In the intercept phase, if Rome was in the physical world, to know the addressees to whom Michaela sent her letters, Rome would have to intercept the envelopes before they reached the post office, read the envelopes for the names and addresses of the addressees, and then return the envelopes to the post office for delivery. If Michaela used a forwarder, Rome would have to intercept the single envelope, and then try to match the addressee to a list of known forwarders.

In the virtual world, to intercept, Rome would employ a man-in-the-middle attack, in which she would use an app called *Bivouac*. The app would intercept the communication from Michaela's MAC address to the IP addressee, and record the IP address for Rome in a log before sending on the communication to the IP address. With *Bivouac*, Rome would know the websites Michaela visited. In a normal surfing session, a user might visit dozens of websites and if so, *Bivouac* would log each of the websites' IP addresses. Or, if Michaela used a VPN, *Bivouac* would log only one IP address – the VPN's – no matter how many websites she visited.

Rome hoped that like many business people, Michaela used a VPN service. If Rome could determine that Michaela connected with only one IP address, phase two would be for Rome to determine if Michaela used a VPN by trying to match the lone IP address with a VPN service. If she could, then phase three would be for Rome to try to compromise the VPN service and gain access to all of Michaela's internet activity that she ran through the VPN, including all of Michaela's email traffic.

Rome knew that people used VPNs in the belief the private network provided anonymity: since their only connection was to the VPN's IP address, no one – except, of course, the VPN company – knew the actual IP addresses the user visited or the email traffic, just like only the forwarder knew what letters were in the large envelope. People believed that all of their internet activity – such as website data and emails – was private, anonymous, and confidential. Not true.

Anonymous? Sort of, but not exactly. While the VPN hid the data from third parties, such as the user's internet service provider, advertisers, and the government, that data still resided with the VPN company. Rome knew that some VPN companies stored the data – surfing history and web-based email contents – and some dispreputable companies even sold the data. And she knew that even in the reputable companies, humans ran operations, and some humans could be compromised – paid to improperly provide her with the data. If Michaela used a VPN, Rome hoped in phase three of the operation to compromise someone who worked for the VPN company and, for a fee, acquire Michaela's data.

§

Rome learned that Michaela's go-to coffee shop was the Espresso Habit and quickly located the small purveyor of caffeine. On the operation's first day, she arrived early at the Espresso Habit and took a seat with a cup of cappuccino and a pastry as she awaited Michaela Huld's arrival. Her hair was tucked up under a charcoal gray knit hat. It always amazed her how hats could affect the look of a person's face.

Rome opened her Sony Vaio laptop, logged on to the insecure coffee house network, and bided her time. She observed no camera security system at the small shop. Michaela arrived at 10:30 a.m., bought an espresso, and settled in with her MacBook Pro to surf the internet. To be precise, she logged on to the coffee house network at 10:36 a.m. – duly noted by Rome at her own table.

Rome repeated the exercise the next day to assure consistency. On the second day, she wore a black porkpie hat with a feather, and her hair cascaded out of the hat and down to her shoulders. She looked completely different from the previous day. Michaela reappeared at the same time, and performed the same routine.

Based on her background research, Rome planned to implement the man-in-the-middle attack on Thursday, November 15. Rome again arrived at the Espresso Habit before Michaela, this time wearing a navy blue French beret and round, John Lennon-style, wire-rimmed glasses. She enjoyed her ability to shape-shift. Once she got her coffee and sat down, Rome opened her laptop and activated *Bivouac* as she awaited Michaela's arrival.

Her target arrived on schedule at 10:40 a.m., ordered her usual espresso and a biscuit, sat down at a small table for two, opened her laptop, and, at precisely 10:46 a.m., logged on to the coffee shop's Wi-Fi. There were only a few other customers in the coffee shop with computers, and those customers had been surfing the internet for some time.

Rome watched surreptitiously from several tables away as Michaela logged on to the internet. The *Bivouac* log showed only one new log-on at 10:46 a.m., and as a result, she instantly knew the new log-on was Michaela's laptop. By design, so as not to cause any suspicion, Rome was too far away to see Michaela's keystrokes or her screen, and she was careful not to stare. But she didn't need to see the particulars of Michaela's computer activity; all she needed to see was the *Bivouac* log in real-time. She watched the log to see if Michaela's MAC address surfed to many IP addresses, or just to one. Lo and behold, Rome quickly saw that as Michaela clicked her way through different web pages, her MAC address connected to a single IP address: 98.990.160.187. Could it be that Michaela was using a VPN to hide her browsing activity? Rome would have to do further research to try to determine if the sole IP address Michaela visited was associated with a VPN company.

In short order, Michaela finished her espresso and biscuit, turned off her computer, checked her watch, and hurriedly left to begin her workday. As Michaela exited the coffee shop, Rome gazed into the remains of her cappuccino. After Michaela exited, Rome peered out the coffee shop floor to ceiling window to see another gray, drizzly day in London, and planned out her next steps.

Before long, she closed up her laptop and headed back to her flat to discover the owner of the single IP address visited by Michaela.

§

98.990.160.187.

With real estate, anyone can go to the keeper of the local public real estate register and determine who owns the land associated with a street address. In the internet world, however, there was no public register and most VPN companies didn't necessarily want the world to know which IP addresses they owned. Another layer of secrecy and anonymity they could use to promote their services to potential clients.

But, despite the attempts at anonymity, there were still ways to associate an IP address with its owner. For example, the world's law enforcement agencies had been successful in associating IP addresses to VPN service providers. In addition, internet hobbyists published lists and keys to link IP addresses to VPN providers. Similarly, private anti-fraud companies sprung up around the globe who, for a fee, linked IP addresses to VPN companies. Rome hoped that one of the hobbyists would have already provided the link between the IP address she had discovered and the VPN owner. With that connection, she could instantly identify Michaela's VPN provider.

She sat cross-legged on her bed and searched to see if someone had already matched the IP address in question to a VPN owner. She started with general internet Google searches to see if she could link the IP address with an owner. The results were disappointing. Each search turned out to be a time-consuming wild goose chase. Her man-in-the-middle attack had successfully yielded the information she sought, but so far, she was stymied, frustrated by an inability to find the next level of information she needed. It was as if she had picked the lock on a door which led to another door with a new lock she couldn't pick.

She then turned to a search on Reddit. Reddit organized its posts based on topics that users could create, called subreddits. Not that she minded putting the effort in, but she was hoping for a bit of that Romero luck as she began looking through subreddits for IP address keys. But, once again, her efforts yielded no subreddits with IP lists posted, and she was again discouraged by the paucity of information.

She decided to put out an information request to her extensive network of underground tech drop-outs who she had met after completing her studies at Bryn Mawr and with whom she always stayed in touch. Rome was a life-time member of the network, revered in some circles for her success in monetizing her skill set while still managing to stay beneath the prodigious radar of government and law enforcement.

One acquaintance got back to her the next morning and suggested she search on a website called NetHub. She learned that NetHub was a developer's website with a wealth of information available. Her NetHub searches revealed a hobbyist who had posted several IP lists. Rome researched the hobbyist, and found several posts in which he proclaimed the need for full transparency in all things internet-related. Finally getting a promising gut feeling, she returned to his posted lists on NetHub. Finally, in the fourth list, Rome struck pay-dirt and connected the IP address to its owner, a British company named Sueden, plc.

Punching the air in victory, Rome navigated to LinkedIn and located Sueden's profile: It was indeed a VPN company, located in London. In the LinkedIn profile, Sueden reported that it had nineteen employees and described itself as follows:

> Protect your online privacy. Assure your privacy when you are online from third parties, such as your ISP, advertisers, and governmental entities.

Rome knew the description was an advertisement, but when she read the word "assure," she rolled her eyes and thought, a bit sarcastically, *well … maybe.* Further research revealed that Sueden maintained servers.

From the LinkedIn information, she quickly identified and cross-referenced Sueden's list of employees, especially those she could determine claimed London as their home. She identified twelve such employees. With her list of twelve, she was ready to gather information on each to see if she could find a weak link in the chain of corporate secrecy, someone at Sueden who could be compromised and would be willing to share with her Michaela Huld's precious data, in violation of every corporate policy that Sueden had on the books.

To find that weak link, she again reached out to her underground network. On the private message board the network used to stay in touch, she posted several questions. First, did they know anyone on the attached list of names? Second, what could they tell her about anyone they recognized, such as age, family situation, personal finances, debt structure? And third, whether they thought the people identified would be willing to enter into a financial transaction for an information exchange. She did not need to spell out the last category of information she sought. Everyone on her list of contacts would immediately know what she was after.

Within a few hours, she had two responses that satisfied her information request, each discussing a different name on the list. Two identifications: Wyatt Smithyman, a 34 year-old family-man VPN specialist, and Basil Hargrove, a database technician in his early forties at the end of a divorce, and now owing alimony. She organized the information about each so she could compare them.

Rome studied the information and refined it based on information in each prospect's Facebook and LinkedIn pages. They both needed money. Who didn't? But for different reasons – Smithyman for his growing family and Hargrove to fund his divorce. Her contacts also reported that Hargrove was a gambler and cocky. Certainly, it was not an in-depth dive into Smithyman and Hargrove, but it was a start, and it gave her a flavor of each of them. From the information she gathered, Rome leaned toward Hargrove. She just had a sense that with Hargrove's recent divorce and no family, he would be more willing to consider the transaction – information for a fee.

Before she proceeded, however, she felt this was the time for her next call with Stacy Milnes. She found Milnes quirky, awkward, unpredictable, and potentially even difficult, as Moses had warned her. Impossible to predict how Milnes would take the need to generate funds to make a significant payment. *Surely the woman wouldn't think a compromise of this nature would be free?*

She used the *Flag* app to message Milnes that they needed to talk and suggested a call on Tuesday, November 20 at 10 a.m., St. Louis time, using Milnes' burner phone.

Within minutes, she had a one-word response: "Agreed."

CHAPTER 31

Tuesday, November 20, 2018

AT THE APPOINTED TIME, Milnes was restlessly awaiting Rome's call. When the burner phone rang, she answered immediately, grateful for the clear, international connection. Rome explained the operation so far: the decision to target Michaela, not Quincy; the coffee shop, the man-in-the-middle attack, the discovery of the VPN used by Michaela, and the significance of the discovery, using her analogy to letter mailing and physical addresses to help Milnes understand how the operation worked. As predicted, Milnes groused that it all sounded so complicated. Rolling her eyes, Rome ignored the comment.

Rome then revealed the preliminary research that Sueden maintained servers, and that she identified two VPN employees who were possible weak links she could try to approach and compromise. If one of the VPN employees cooperated, she explained, she could get actual data and determine if any of it concerned secret Swiss accounts.

"And I will have to pay an employee for the plan to work, of course," she finished.

Milnes listened closely and asked, "I can still see significant hurdles in front of us, correct?"

"Correct."

"What do you need from me?"

"Two things. Your approval for the analog part of the operation, and the funds necessary to pay the employee for the
service he will perform."

"In English?" Milnes demanded.

"I need the money and permission to try to turn one of the
subjects," Rome explained.

"Permission granted," Milnes authorized quickly without
giving any thought to the question. "I noticed as you described
the next steps that you didn't use the word, 'bribe.' That's
certainly how I'd describe what comes next."

"I find 'bribe' to be such a harsh word. One of the Sueden
employees will perform a service and deliver a product to us; in
this case, data. We will pay for that service and the data. I could
just as well call the transaction, if you will, a perk, a reward,
an inducement, a purchase that we will make; but I stay away
from emotionally charged words like bribe or payola because
they have connotations that we just do not need."

Even though much of Milnes' persona revolved around the
power of emotionally charged words, she viewed the distinction between a bribe and Rome's explanation of the process
as nothing more than semantics. She was getting frustrated
with what she viewed as a potentially long road ahead. To get
to this point, she had to commit a felony – authorizing the
infiltration of Michaela Huld's laptop on her behalf – and so
far, all she had to show for the crime was a bunch of numbers
and dots that was the virtual equivalent of a street address. She
needed more results, more quickly. She reverted to her crass
personality and asked gruffly, "How much money?"

"Twelve thousand pounds, sterling."

"Geez! Is that the going rate?" Milnes exclaimed as she grimaced, taken by surprise at the size of the payoff.

"Honestly, Ms. Milnes, there really is no going rate. Our
target employee will take a chance, and if he gets caught, he

will most certainly lose his job, or worse. Twelve thousand pounds should cover the risk-reward metric, in my estimation. We can expect that he will, of course, be nervous, so I don't want to encourage a negotiated rug trade with him. We need to offer him enough of a remuneration to catch his interest immediately. A protracted negotiation with him will not be in our best interest. Do you see my point?"

"Listen, I come from the land where everything's both negotiable and negotiated. But I don't want to waste a lot of time on what might be seen as nickels and dimes, so if that's what it's going to cost, then that's what it is," Milnes replied, still conveying a sense of unhappiness at the size of the payment. "How will I get the money to you?"

"I will *Flag*-message you with instructions. Do you want to think about it before you commit to the proposed low tech path and the price?"

Rome didn't require Milnes to think about the decision for twenty-four hours as Moses had. For that, she was grateful. At this point, she was either all-in or all-out; there was no middle ground. She was, and continued to be, all-in. No waffling. But there was now some legwork to do at the bank to get the funds to pay for the operation. "I'm committed," she said bluntly. "But I'll need a few days here to be able to transfer the funds per your instructions."

"A few days is fine. That will give me a little more time to develop any further information about our target employees to see which is a better fit for our needs."

"What else do we need to discuss?" Milnes asked to try to conclude the conversation.

"Ms. Milnes, I want to be sure that you understand there are no guarantees. I cannot promise that I can compromise either target. We have been lucky so far, but we have yet to learn about the targets' personalities and whether they need the money badly enough to take a paid walk with me on the dark side. I do not want you to leave this call with the belief that we have a lock on the data. We do not, and the next phase of 'approach and convince' will be critical to the operation's success. Do you understand?"

"I understand," Milnes said as she rolled her eyes. *Sounds like something my lawyers would say to me.*

"Very well. Do you have any questions for me, Ms. Milnes?"

"None."

"Excellent. Please watch for my next message to you," Rome said, and terminated the call.

CHAPTER 32

Friday, November 23 to Monday, December 10, 2018

MOSES WARNED ME THAT Milnes could be difficult, even galling at times. But the warning and the real life experience were two different things. Rome decided to chalk it up to a learning experience. *Dealing with Milnes will make me a better operative.* Nevertheless, she was unsure if she would receive the necessary funds. But the money arrived on November 23, just as she'd instructed Milnes in her *Flag* message instructions. *Game on.*

In the meantime, she settled on Basil Hargrove as the better candidate to approach to obtain Michaela's data. Upon receipt of the funds from Milnes, she set in motion her plan to meet Hargrove. One of her contacts knew a few of the Sueden employees and reported that after work, of late, their target liked to frequent The Grosvenor Victoria Casino – the Vic – in the heart of London. In particular, he liked to play the blackjack tables.

Rome did some background work on the Vic and learned that the casino attracted gamblers from all over the world, had one of the largest poker rooms in the world, and attracted not only high-rollers but small-bet customers as well. She was not at all a gambler, but she dressed herself in a millennial sheik outfit and headed for the Tube and the Edgware Road Station, which was also near the Sueden office, for a chance to hang back in the shadows and get a feel for Hargrove and his routine.

Rome was nervous. She had little to no experience in the art of seduction, and this phase of the mission would challenge her natural instinct to observe the world from a distance.

She was lanky; five feet, ten and a half inches tall, with slender everything – legs, arms, fingers, nose … everything. Overall, she paid little attention to her looks, and she didn't need to. She was one of those people who inexplicably conveyed an air of mystery and intrigue. But she was not a mingler. Just like when she attended Bryn Mawr, her comfort zone was hanging back in the shadows, which she did well. Rome was an observer from selected vantage points that allowed her to stay in the shadows if she so chose, as, usually, she did. A wallflower. Stepping out of the shadows made her anxious and self-conscious.

To calm her nerves, Rome focused on the reality that the next phase involved no actual seduction. More of a meet and greet. Rome wasn't living out a James Bond movie plotline, and, there would be no bedroom scene; no super-spy love-making would be needed to get what she wanted.

When she arrived, she registered at a small front porch and entered, noting as she walked in that The Vic was a much higher class establishment than she would expect someone of Hargrove's likely means. Perhaps it was his post-divorce "break-free" place.

She noted six blackjack tables in the glitzy but classy gaming room, and she bought a glass of white wine and found a wall near the tables and waited. She didn't have to wait long. Hargrove entered and went to the bar. Hargrove was six feet tall, 165 pounds, with an angular nose, a trimmed brown beard, and a quiff haircut. She recognized him from his social media. Rome saw the bartender hand Hargrove what appeared to be a scotch, neat. With scotch in hand, he made his way to table number four. Since he didn't hesitate in his table selection, she figured table number four was his good luck place to play blackjack. She altered her outpost position slightly to have a better look at the man, his mannerisms, and his playing style. He seemed conservative but knowledgeable; quiet, not brash. Despite the intel that he was cocky, Rome didn't observe that. From her vantage point, as the evening progressed, Hargrove seemed to win and lose hands, and overall, he seemed to hover at the break-even point. He didn't seem bothered by a losing hand; he didn't seem particularly excited by a winning hand. After a few hours, Hargrove called the evening and headed out. He had valet-parked his late-model, white Camry and called for the attendant to retrieve it. Shortly, he was in his car, speeding away.

§

Rome followed the same protocol for the next evening, and nothing in Hargrove's routine or mannerisms varied. Table number four, confidence at the table, knowledgeable in the game, calm, reserved, and not a big winner or loser.

Several days later, Rome decided to make contact with Hargrove at the bar. He approached the bar for a drink, and she made sure she was there already. This time, she had a scotch, neat, just like Hargrove. She struck up a conversation, and he was willing to linger and talk. He came across as confident, soft-spoken, not at all brash, and still not at all cocky. Maybe that character trait went the way of the marriage. Hargrove openly told Rome that he was relatively new to the gambling world and newly divorced. After the divorce, he decided to hit his personal reset button and start over. Some of his "start-over" plan involved trying some things, like gambling, that he had never done before and could not have imagined doing

254 | MARK SHAIKEN

while married. His ex-wife simply wouldn't have tolerated such frivolous behavior, he grumbled.

Hargrove was the perfect gentleman, and after an hour of get-to-know-you talk, needed to get going because he had an early morning for work. Rome asked what he did, and he responded that he was in the tech world and worked for a London-based VPN company.

Bingo. Rome expressed interest and told Hargrove she also had a tech job and dealt with information systems. A partial truth, but enough for the mission.

§

Their rendezvous two nights later was similar. Rome and Hargrove met for a drink when he finished at the blackjack table. This time, she asked if he wanted to get a bite to eat, and shortly, they were sitting at a local brasserie waiting for pan-grilled Arctic char and lamb chops, respectively. As they sat at the table under flickering light, Rome decided it was time to start to lay the foundation.

"I was not entirely truthful in what I do for a living, Basil," she said. "I work for an international investigative firm, and I am on assignment, but I have run into a snag."

"What's that?" Hargrove asked.

"I need access to specific data in my current project. My employer is willing to pay a good price for access." She watched him carefully. "But I do not know how to make the data dump happen." Rome didn't let on that she knew Hargrove's company had the data.

He listened with interest and said, "It's all about the data in the current world we live in, isn't it? Take me. I work for a VPN company, and I'd venture that well more than half of our clients think that when they connect to the internet through one of our portals, they are anonymous, no one in the world will know their internet habits, and no one will have access to their data. But we both know that's not true. The data simply migrated to the VPN company."

"So true," said Rome, suggesting a working knowledge of the VPN world. "There are so many VPN companies in the world, and they seem to have quite a variety of business models, especially when it comes to data. It is fascinating."

Hargrove continued, "Some VPNs store their client's data; some don't. Some VPNs even sell the data, sometimes unbeknownst to the client. We don't sell data, at least not at this time, but we do store it. I assume that's to keep open the option of monetizing the data in the future." Rome rubbed her chin with her left thumb and pointer as Hargrove continued, "It's all about the data. People use VPNs because they think it safeguards their data. But the truth is, if you don't want people to know, it's better to stay off the internet completely, yes? Although that's definitely a tall order in the modern world."

"Oh, yes," Rome nodded her head in agreement. "Well, I have to complete some more legwork on this project; I need to figure out how the target accesses the internet. But I can see I am close to that information wall, and I am concerned that I will not be able to deliver the results my boss is hoping for. I only hope I don't fail. He is in New York, and he can be, well, mercurial, to say the least."

The food arrived and as they began to eat, Rome said, "Listen to us. Shop, shop, shop. I'm sure there must be other things you like. Do you fancy football?"

And, just like that, they changed topics and moved on from the world of VPNs and data to the world of the pitch and the Premier League and then onto Boris Johnson, the EU, and politics. As they ate, Rome rather enjoyed the discussion they had. It was free and easy, and Hargrove was interesting. But the man was nonetheless a target, so Rome had no interest in getting any closer than the conversation. No seduction. After dinner, they traded mobile numbers, he hailed her a taxi, and they said their goodbyes.

Rome returned to her flat and waited to see what happened next. To make this work, she felt Hargrove needed to make the next move.

§

Five days later, Hargrove contacted her for a drink after work. They met at a small pub near his workplace and again had a free and easy discussion. After about ten minutes, he asked how her project was coming along. Rome answered, "Well, at least I have figured out how my target gets to the internet. She uses a VPN service here in London."

"Oh? Interesting," he said. "Which one?"

"Sueden, I believe," Rome responded.

Rome hoped she had not pushed the discussion too fast or too far. But to get results for Milnes, she needed the conversation to move along so she could assess if Hargrove would be the weak link for which she hoped. Interestingly, when she said "Sueden," Hargrove didn't let on that he worked at the company. Instead, he asked what the going rate was for the purchase of VPN data in London these days.

She responded, "You know, I have not had a VPN project before, so I do not know, but my boss says it is twelve thousand quid. Have you ever conducted such a – shall we say, operation – before?"

"No. Not particularly ethical, but given the small amount of time that the delivery of data would take, that sounds like a princely sum."

Their conversation then turned to other topics, backgrounds, education, likes, dislikes, all as they consumed their dishes. Again, at the end of the evening, Hargrove hailed her a taxi, they said their goodbyes, and parted.

§

Several days later, Hargrove called again and asked if they could meet, this time for coffee over the lunch hour on December 14. They met at a coffee shop only a few blocks from Sueden's office, and he had undeniably been thinking about their last conversation. His demeanor had changed. There was nothing relaxed or casual about Hargrove's mannerisms. He seemed bothered, flustered, irritated, even agitated. Rome worried that this would be the end of the attempt to use Hargrove to get the data.

As they sat down in a corner of the small shop, Hargrove looked around the mostly empty establishment and then looked back at Rome blankly. "You know what I think? I think our first meeting wasn't a chance meeting at all, and I think you knew I worked for Sueden. And I think you've been trying to infiltrate my circle of habits, get to know me, and see if I might be willing to deliver the data you seek. I have to say, you're not exactly opaque; maybe I'd describe you as translucent. You might need to work on that if you're going to pursue a career as a spy." Rome didn't look away, but she said nothing. Hargrove had more to say, and he continued, as he scanned around the coffee shop, "What I don't know is this: is this data really for a project you're working on, or is there a greater purpose in your need for the data? I thought about that a lot last night instead of going off to sleep.

"But, then I thought to myself, *you know, Basil, you shouldn't be bothering with that question. You should want to figure out if there's any chance of overlooking the fraudulent pretense of an attractive woman who could be a spy out of an Ian Fleming novel, and take your fee for the data?* Y'know, would I secure the data for you, attractive spy woman, in exchange for that fee you dangled in front of me? That's what I thought last night and that's what I'm still asking myself today." He paused, returned his gaze to Rome, and looked directly into her chocolate brown eyes to see if he detected any discovery, or any reaction at all. What he saw were a pair of chocolate-brown eyes looking back at him and nothing else. No reaction. "Comments?"

Rome took her time in responding but took great care not to break eye contact with him. "I must admit that all you have deduced is correct. I must also confess that I am new to the infiltration game, so my lack of experience probably shows. I do not want to do anything to harm you, and of course, it would be up to you, and only you, to decide if you wanted to go down this path. If not, I understand, and we would both move on. If you need more time to consider the fee for the service, I would understand that as well."

Hargrove responded quickly, "Well, I've thought about it. Last night. A lot. Instead of sleeping. And I've now confirmed my suspicions. I'm no longer particularly bothered by the course of events. It is what it is, eh? Just business, right? You want a business transaction with me. I get it. And, at this point in my life, ethics need to take a back seat to personal economics. But, just so I'm sure I'm not leaving anything on the table here, nothing amorous, right?"

She raised her eyebrows in agreement, tilted her head left, and said with reluctant agreement, "Right on all counts."

"Right. Too bad on the last point, but I understand. Here's the thing: At this moment in my life, twelve grand would be, let's just say, most appreciated. What you're asking me to do can be done quite easily, and I can deliver flash drives to you when I get the money. I need a few days, starting from the moment I learn the target's name. I also need to know how much data you want."

Hargrove is in. Rome tried to hide her excitement. She said, "I use an app called *Flag* to transmit sensitive data, such as the name of Sueden's client and the information we seek. Can we use that to exchange information?"

"Absolutely. I know that app."

"Very well. I will get you the information about the target and let you know how we will exchange the fee for the data," Rome said.

"Sounds like a plan. So, that's it, eh?" Hargrove concluded with a wistful tone.

"That is it," Rome confirmed, relieved that the transaction was, in fact, *it*.

"Well then, I'll look for your message … and of course, ultimately, the money."

They stood, headed for the door, left the coffee shop, and this time, Rome was on her own for transportation. Hargrove hailed no taxi for her. He went his way, and she went hers.

CHAPTER 33

Thursday, December 27, 2018

"PLAN CONFIRMATION DAY, 3J. All packed and ready to roll?" Pascale asked.

"One hundred percent. Let's do this," 3J said as they headed down with their bags to walk to the courthouse. Once in the courtroom they organized their table and awaited Judge Robertson's entry.

"All rise," the clerk commanded as the Judge entered the courtroom, and as he made his way to the bench, the clerk said, "Everyone, please be seated."

Judge Robertson scanned the courtroom and asked the lawyers present to announce their appearance for the record. When Dennis Sample entered his appearance on behalf of StarBanc, Judge Robertson asked him, "Who do we have here today from StarBanc?"

Sample replied, "Brian Chimes, the bank's chief special assets officer."

Chimes stood, and the Judge said, "Welcome to Kansas City, Mr. Chimes."

"Thank you kindly, Judge," Chimes responded. Milnes was not present in the courtroom.

With the conclusion of the introductions, Judge Robertson looked to 3J and said, "Plan confirmation time, Ms. Jones. Are you ready to proceed?"

"Yes, Your Honor."

"Very well. The floor is yours."

"Thank you, Your Honor. As the Court is aware, these cases have fast-tracked to this confirmation hearing today. After the Court approved the disclosure statement, we served it on all creditors and parties-in-interest in these cases along with a ballot. If I might hand Your Honor a ballot report, you will see the votes tallied by class and creditor. More than ninety percent of the creditors who voted have accepted the plan. The report likewise shows that StarBanc submitted a ballot on behalf of the banks and, of course, the banks voted to accept the plan. Finally, no creditor filed an objection to court-approval of the plan. Unless the Court has any questions about the voting, we are ready to call Quincy Witherman to the stand to testify on behalf of the Debtors and in support of confirmation of the plan."

"Before Mr. Witherman takes the stand, Ms. Jones, does anyone else wish to be heard on the ballot summary?" The Judge paused and asked, "Mr. Sample?"

"We concur with Ms. Jones' comments."

"Very well. Thank you. Please proceed, Ms. Jones." Judge Robertson noted to himself that Dennis Sample was now able to give concise answers, since StarBanc became the Agent for the bank group.

"Your Honor, the Debtors call Quincy Witherman to the stand."

Quincy stood and approached the Court clerk, who already had her right hand raised as she looked at him. He raised his hand, and the clerk said, "Do you swear or affirm, to tell the truth, the whole truth, and nothing but the truth so help you, God?"

Quincy replied, "I do."

"Please state your name for the record, and be seated."

"Quincy Gunn Witherman."

Once seated, Judge Robertson said, "Welcome again, Mr. Witherman. Please speak into the microphone when you answer questions."

3J asked Quincy a series of background questions to identify him and his role with the Debtors. She then asked him if he was familiar with the various court filings made during the cases, and Quincy replied, "Yes." She asked him if he signed the Debtors' schedules and statements of affairs. Answer – yes. If he had signed the disclosure statement and plan. Answer – yes. If all the factual information about the entities and himself contained in those documents was complete, true, and correct. Answer – yes.

No deep breath. No pause. No change in verbal cadence. No flutter of the eyelids. No involuntary twitch. No increased blood pressure. No beads of sweat below his nose and above his lips.

Quincy looked over to Judge Robertson, made eye contact, smiled, and gave his answer firmly and unequivocally – yes – nodding his head up and down once for emphasis.

Through her questions, 3J had Quincy explain the companies' backgrounds, the economic developments, the bank payment demand, the need to file the bankruptcy cases, and the deal struck with the banks. Brian Chimes sat in the audience and listened with interest. 3J then asked a series of questions to meet the statutory requirements for confirmation of the plan. The questions were all simple and enabled Quincy to simply answer "yes" or "no" as appropriate.

Soon she was finished. "I have no further questions for this witness at this time," and she returned to her seat.

Judge Robertson asked the assembled lawyers if any of them had questions for the witness and when no one did, he looked at Quincy, nodded, and said, "Likewise, I have no questions for the witness. Thank you, Mr. Witherman. You may step down."

As Quincy returned to his seat, 3J said to the Court, "Your Honor, that concludes our testimony. If it pleases the Court, I would like to offer some closing remarks."

Judge Robertson said, "Certainly. Please proceed."

"Your Honor, with the deal we were able to strike with the banks, and Mr. Witherman's testimony today, as well as the results of the creditor vote, we submit that we have met all of the applicable requirements of the Bankruptcy Code. The Court should be in a position to confirm the plan. I would like to also personally thank Mr. Brian Chimes of StarBanc, who is here in the courtroom today, for his efforts and patience in negotiating with us and thereby clearing the path. We thank him for his professionalism. Your Honor, that is all we have today, and we request that the Court confirm the plan."

Chimes nodded his head and smiled at 3J. Judge Robertson smiled at Chimes. 3J nodded at Chimes but retained a poker face.

"Thank you, Ms. Jones. The Court will confirm the plan and finds and rules that it meets all of the requirements of the Bankruptcy Code and Chapter 11 for confirmation." Judge Robertson then went through each applicable Bankruptcy Code section and explained his ruling. Upon completion, he said, "Ms. Jones, can you and your team please submit a proposed confirmation order that the banks have approved as to form and substance? And congratulations to your team and to the Debtors. Good job. If there is nothing further, we are adjourned."

3J and Pascale packed up their bags while Quincy and Chimes shook hands. In the moment of camaraderie, one could imagine hearing an acappella group singing the folk song "Kumbaya" in beautiful four-part harmony with emotion: *Someone's praying Lord, Kumbaya, Oh Lord, Kumbaya.*

On the walk back, Quincy thanked the lawyers for all their help and hard work. "What comes next?" he asked.

Pascale answered, "The plan is effective in fifteen days. January 11, you're a free man. At least, free of us, and free of Stacy Milnes, and free of the bankruptcy process."

"That sounds great. No chance I wake up, and this has been a pleasant but unreal dream?"

"Not on our account," Pascale said. "In fifteen days, it's all in the record books, as they say."

"Then let's make a date to meet and celebrate. Hell, you might even convince me to celebrate at O'Brien's. I think it's time for me to appreciate some honky tonk with you guys."

"I'm down for that," 3J said.

"Me too," Pascale chimed in.

"Great. Let's just meet up at O'Brien's on day fifteen – January the eleventh of the new year, if that fits your schedules," Quincy said.

"It's a date," 3J confirmed.

As they left the courthouse, 3J's thoughts returned to one of her father's favorite phrases: *All's well that ends well.* But, like the Shakespeare play, 3J wondered if all really was well, and whether this did actually mark the end of the Quincy Witherman file.

Something inside of her continued to fight off the notion that she was done with Quincy Witherman.

CHAPTER 34

Saturday, December 29, 2018 to Saturday, January 5, 2019

Rome had already used *Flag* to message Hargrove with the information she sought and how they would exchange information for payment. Hargrove wrote back simply, "Got it."

She wanted to understand nothing about Sueden's security protocols, the level of Hargrove's security clearance, nor any details about how he would earn his fee. She just wanted the flash drives. From business articles she'd read, she learned that Sueden was a relatively new player in the VPN industry. It had sunk a substantial portion of its investors' cash into its infrastructure to get up and running as a VPN service provider. It had also launched a robust marketing effort, complete with a strategy to underprice its competitors to get a toe-hold in the market. Sueden had not, however, invested a great deal into internal layers of security, and in its five-year budget, its management had assumed it would get to those issues in due course … just *not now*.

§

Hargrove needed time to plan out his access to the servers, and to download the data for Rome. It was fortuitous that he could access the data over the New Year holiday. Not as many people hanging around the Sueden offices. Between the lax security and the holiday time, he should have little problem getting what was otherwise information to which he should not have easy access. His plan was to show up at the office late on Sunday, December 30, access the server room, locate the accounts, transfer the data to flash drives, and exit. Straightforward enough.

At 10 p.m., Hargrove showed up at the Sueden office building, signed into the building register, exchanged pleasantries with the night guard, and made his way upstairs to the sixth floor, which was dark except for auxiliary lighting. He made his way quickly to the server room, used his key card to gain access, turned on the lights, and made his way to the server interface. Using his laptop to access the servers, he quickly found the Huld and NOIRAM accounts, set the download for two years of data, inserted the flash drives into the server interface, and all that was left to do was wait.

He decided to return to his desk while the download proceeded and absentmindedly turned off the server room lights as he exited the room. Just as he got to his desk, Hargrove was surprised by the same building security guard who signed him into the building. The guard was now entering the Sueden office on a routine sweep of the building. Hargrove tried to control his anxiety. *Did the guard see me as I left the server room? Does he even know I'm not supposed to access the servers after hours?* His breathing quickened as he tried to control his mounting anxiety. Sitting at his desk, peering into his laptop screen would set off no alarm bells; hunching over the servers in a climate-controlled locked room could have been a red flag to the guard, though. He decided to wave at the guard, who waved back. He was beyond lucky that he had returned to his desk and that he had turned off the lights in the server room. No red-alert.

The guard apparently saw nothing suspicious, completed his rounds, and left to return to his desk in the lobby. It took minutes for Hargrove's breathing and heart rate to return to normal. *That was too damn close. I'm no good as a spy!*

Finally, the download finished. Hargrove retrieved the flash drives without turning on the lights. He grabbed his laptop, put the drives and the computer in his backpack, and left the offices. He signed out with sweaty hands, wished the guard Happy New Year, and exited the building to the misty London evening. Hargrove breathed deeply, held the breath, and exhaled slowly. *I'm not cut out for this intrigue and espionage shit. But I need the money. If I ever do this again ... no, wait, I'm never doing this again!*

When he returned to his small flat, he poured himself a scotch to slow his racing brain, and used *Flag* to message Rome.

Rome breathed a sigh of relief. The wait had been agonizing, and over the two weeks since they had met at the coffee shop, she had no way of knowing if Hargrove would perform or if he had gotten a case of the yips and backed out.

On New Year's Eve day, Hargrove and Rome made the exchange simply and without drama. They met again at his favored coffee shop. Rome asked if he had encountered any problems, and, trying to keep spy-like cool, he shrugged his shoulders and said, "All good." *No point sharing the gory details,* he thought. *Just give me the money, and let's move on.* He half-joked that he wouldn't access the internet in the coffee shop while Rome was there. Instead, he turned off his phone's Wi-Fi and used his carrier's 4G signal and his bank's app to confirm the deposit of £12,000 into an account he had established for this purpose. Upon confirmation, he looked up, smiled, and silently handed Rome the flash drives. They departed, one before the other; no hand shake. No words. No further inquiries about romance. Transaction completed: Book closed. James Bond plotline wrapped up.

§

Rome returned to her flat, cued a Spotify playlist of Scott Hamilton, her favorite jazz saxophonist who was a modern throwback to the post-bop heyday of saxophonists, and began the arduous task of sorting through the data to extract any information she could find about Quincy Gunn Witherman and his companies. She knew the extraction could be an arduous process, and Hamilton's breathy style would help her focus.

At first, she scanned the data manually to get a sense of what she'd received. Rome had developed an app to parse through the information automatically, not unlike how litigation lawyers search through endless reams of documents and emails. First, she had to import the data into her app before she could begin to search, in a time-consuming process of creating a dedicated searchable database. After two days, the app completed the creation of the database. She then began the process of developing search terms. Rome's searches generated several thousand hits of emails that she'd have to review. She quickly learned that Michaela and NOIRAM conducted substantial business in Switzerland for her many clients, and that Michaela Huld was extremely careful when she transacted business on behalf of Quincy Witherman. Her custom must have been to communicate with First Swiss Bank – Geneva by phone or secure text. Reviewing the emails was time-consuming.

Tellingly, even after a deep-dive, extended search, over several days, she found only a single email. This one email was an anomaly in Michaela's careful communication. But it took only one anomaly to make the operation a success.

It was time for a follow-up with Stacy Milnes.

CHAPTER 35

Monday, January 7 to Tuesday, January 8, 2019

"Ms. Milnes? This is Rome. I have an update for you."

"Good. What's the news, Rome?"

"I selected one of the targets and, over a few weeks, determined that he could be compromised. Compressing the interactions for this report, we met several times, and he agreed to perform the task at hand and harvest data for me. Several days ago, he delivered flash drives to me in exchange for his fee. A significant amount of data. I have been hard at work to comb through the data to identify relevant items." Rome paused. "I have found evidence of a single communication between NOIRAM and a Swiss bank discussing an account for which Michaela Huld acts as the financial advisor for her client, Quincy Gunn Witherman. I am organizing the information and will be in a position to send you the data I collated as well as the entire flash drives as soon as I receive the remaining payment from you for my services as we previously discussed."

"Wait! You are saying that the data reveals a Swiss account?"

"Yes. Only one email but quite clearly and unmistakably. I matched the account number to other source data and determined that the account has a value of approximately $25 million."

Milnes absorbed the message. "Message me the payment information when we finish this call, and I'll institute payment to you per your instructions, and then I'll look for the flash drives. Also, after you confirm receipt of your payment, forward that email to me. I'll need the flash drives delivered in the fastest international delivery service possible. Acceptable?"

"Acceptable, Ms. Milnes. Will you report these developments to Moses, or shall I?"

"I will. As soon as I've had a chance to see for myself what the data reveals."After a moment, Milnes asked, "Anything else I should know about all of this MI-5ish men in the middle?"

"'Man,' not men, to be precise. I would describe the fulfillment of the mission as complicated and multi-faceted. There is always risk associated with an intrusion such as this one. We were lucky both that Huld is a creature of habit and that she uses a VPN service. We were further fortunate to identify the VPN company through its IP address and select someone willing to compromise security for a fee. We were also lucky that the VPN company stores data on servers and is more focused on growing its customer base than implementing internal layers of security. Luck matters in missions of this nature, Ms. Milnes. Luck, and research and planning and skill. I provided research, planning, and skill. Providence provided the luck."

"Hmmm. Alright. Well, maybe we'll meet someday."

"I would not harbor any expectations that we will meet. Not advisable, in my opinion. Also, you will no longer be able to contact me once we exchange money for information. I will dispose of the burner phone I have used to communicate with you. I strongly suggest you do the same at your end. Have a good day, Ms. Milnes."

Click. The call ended. Milnes chuckled to herself. *Rome could have starred in* Mission Impossible. *That last message had an air of "this tape will self-destruct in five seconds" to it.* But she understood the message clearly: interactions with Rome were at an end except for the final exchange of money for information.

Milnes put down her burner phone. She needed to see what Rome had found, and she was trying not to get too far out ahead of herself, but she had begun to feel elated, almost euphoric. *Good is about to triumph over evil. It's hard to believe that I'm on the verge of having the information to show that Witherman is a felon. I've got him!*

She gave no thought to how the syndicate banks would react or to the consequences of her actions, that Moses had implored her to consider. She failed to appreciate that the syndicate banks just wanted to get paid. If she pursued the next logical course of action, Witherman might lose his discharge and go to jail. Then the banks might not be paid monthly loan payments from the Witherman entities as they were expecting – but instead, they might have the unenvious task of operating the buildings before they could sell them to repay the loans. Milnes was back to her old self – a loner on a mission. *Damn the fallout. Screw the syndicate banks,* she thought. *Complete the mission.*

§

The next morning, Milnes initiated the payment of Rome's fee, and Rome deposited the package of flash drives with an international delivery service; destination – Milnes' home address. Rome also forwarded the incriminating email, sent by Michaela Huld to FSBG.

CHAPTER 36

Friday, January 11, 2019

FIFTEEN DAYS AFTER CONFIRMATION, 3J found herself very unbusy. The Witherman cases had finished, and whatever bankruptcy cases came next had not arrived.

She had been through this part of the job many times before. At first, the end of the constant press of guiding companies through Chapter 11 was a welcome relief. But it was a false sense of relief. Quickly, the sudden lack of work played to the worse part of being an attorney: hard way to go when there is more work than there are hours in a day; even harder when there are suddenly many fewer hours of work and you worry when you will get the next case. Feast followed by famine. 3J had heard Pascale say to her many times, "You'd think we'd learn to enjoy the downtime after all these years, but during the downtime, all we do is worry that the case that just ended is the last case we'll ever work on. And then, when the new one shows up at our doorstep, all we can say is 'shit, look at all the work we'll have to do on this one.' Strange, manic way of going through life. Rough on the soul."

3J always responded the same way, "Amen to that, brother."

She looked forward to the get-together with Quincy at O'Brien's. It would be an excellent chance to thank a good, paying client for the business and talk about anything other than the just-completed bankruptcy cases and her fear of an extended work lull.

3J and Pascale headed down the elevator together at 6:15 p.m. to head over to O'Brien's. When they got there, Quincy was already in the back, sitting at their favorite table. He must have done some background checking with the bartender. They ordered drinks, and when the beer, the whiskey, and the wine arrived, the trio lifted their glasses for a congratulatory toast.

3J set the ground rules. "Some post-confirmation, drinkin' and talkin' ground rules we've developed over the years to help celebrate plan confirmation. One, no trashing the banks, bank counsel, the Judge, the creditors, or, of *course*, beloved debtors' counsel. Two, try to avoid lawyer shoptalk as much as possible. Recognize, however, that you're with lawyers here, and as a group, we generally have a limited ability to talk about much else besides lawyer shoptalk. But we'll try hard to adhere to the rule. And three, tell us what comes next for Quincy Witherman."

Quincy smiled at the rules and said, "Looks like rule number three belongs to me. Well, I don't have anything specific to report. I know it'll be a high-rise. I'm looking at a couple of new markets. Minneapolis and Salt Lake, to be specific. Both are interesting for different reasons. I'm leaning toward Salt Lake, so I can have a penthouse office suite that looks out over the Rockies, but I like Minneapolis as well. Super vibrant downtown and music scene there. I usually have a rule of only one high-rise office project at a time – you know the 'do one thing, do it right, then move on' maxim. But I like both markets, and maybe I can violate my rule this time to celebrate plan confirmation. If I go with two projects at once, I'll be busier than ever. I like being busy but, honestly, I'm not sure how I feel about that right now. Some down time would be nice so I'll be able to sort out my energy level. And I'll have to figure out how the capital markets feel about a former Chapter 11 debtor asking for money. Lots of hurdles. So, what's new?"

The evening progressed. More drinks, more talk about anything but the law, musicology lessons from Quincy about jazz, and, surprisingly, even about the 1950s and early 1960s rockabilly in America.

"Tell me, Quince, about your encyclopedic fascination with music," Pascale said.

"I guess it's just inside of me. I don't talk much about myself but music is my way of defining myself and relating to other people. I just find music to be one of the great creations of humankind. It breaks boundaries, it brings people together, and it seems to transcend differences. It bonds us to each other. It does all of that without regard for whether it's jazz, or rockabilly, or blues, or rock, or folk, or R&B, or soul, or gospel, or country, or classical, or whatever your genre of choice might be. It does all of that, whether it's Vivaldi's violins, or Paul Desmond's haunting alto sax, or James Burton's twangy guitar. It's important stuff to us humans, and it's important stuff to me."

"I can see that you're passionate about it," Pascale observed.

"What about you and music, 3J?" Quincy asked.

"We grew up on a pretty steady diet of New Orleans staples – Fats Domino, Earl King, Snooks Eaglin, Professor Longhair, Smiley Lewis, Marcia Ball, to name a few. Good ole New Orleans rhythm and blues, boogie, and swamp music. The feel-good music to play when you've got no good right or reason to feel good and every reason to feel hopeless. Oh, and Louie Armstrong and the Marsalis family as well. Mom loved them. I guess these days I would say I like my music with just a little touch of the blues . . . to make me feel good."

"Do you miss New Orleans?" Quincy asked.

"I don't know. I guess I do, and I don't. We lived in a push-pin neighborhood that no one going from point A to point B in the city ever notices. Stable but with its rough edges. Just a tiny hole in the map of New Orleans. But the city gets in your blood, and it stays with you no matter where life takes you. So, I'll always have in my mind and heart the food and the smells and the river and the nearby swamps. But mostly, I have the people. They're a special lot. You have to be to live in New Orleans. They have a collective ability to survive, renew, and even thrive. To be hopeful instead of hopeless. Uplifted rather than demoralized. Even after Katrina. That kinda stuff is good stuff. And, of course, I'll also always have the hurricanes, the floods, the heat and humidity, the airplane-sized insects, and the poverty. They tend to stay with you as well." Quincy smiled. 3J continued, "But I don't have family there anymore, and other than these eyes," she said, pointing to her hazel eyes, "I don't have, or need, a lot to remind me of my days in the Crescent City. What's your background, Quince? How did you come to build skyscrapers?"

After 3J's intimate discussion of New Orleans, Quincy felt he could open up and more fully answer the question. "I'm an only child. My parents died when I was a young teenager. I lived with an aunt and uncle until I turned eighteen. I had no idea what to do with my life. I drifted; no steady job; no stable place to live; and no college. If I'd gone to college, I would've just majored in indifference and flunked out. I had no purpose or direction.

"I was that scene from *The Graduate* where Dustin Hoffman graduates from college with no idea of what to do with his life, and at a backyard party, a neighbor implores him to pursue plastics. Plastics would give him a career and a sense of purpose and self-importance but he had neither, and had no interest in a life in the boring world of plastics. He wanted Mrs. Robinson. As I entered my twenties, I had neither purpose nor self-importance." And Quincy added, smiling, "And I had no Mrs. Robinson."

3J and Pascale listened carefully to Quincy's monologue. They hadn't probed quite this deep into his background before, and 3J found Quincy's self-analysis compelling, evidently something he had spent some time thinking about during his life. His openness struck them. He continued, "So, I drifted without a plan, and eventually fell into a job with my altruistic uncle who was in the real estate development business, and who was willing to teach me the ropes. I quickly learned I liked it. No, I loved it. It provided me with my first dose of success and self-worth. 'What I did' became my answer to the question, 'who am I?'"

As she watched Quincy delve more deeply into his background, 3J wondered if she identified herself too much as solely a bankruptcy lawyer. She tried to have interests outside the law, and strongly believed that such interests were essential to surviving a long legal career. But she always worried that, despite her best efforts, she had insufficient time set aside for anything other than her career and felt she regularly conceded defeat to the jealous mistress. *Maybe after the Witherman cases, I'll get more serious about having a life and doing some good in the world.*

Quincy had paused for a taste of his merlot. "I started out to make money, not out of greed, but to get a cushion, and when the cushion became big enough, I figured I'd pivot to what I really wanted to do. But I never made that pivot because I never seemed to figure out what else to do. Maybe there never was anything else besides real estate. Always a challenge to plan to do something else when you're young, and you don't have a clear idea of what that something else might be.

"So, I just kept on keeping on in the development world. I went from a nobody in my uncle's business to his partner, and then, when he died, owner of the company. I became important and well-known, but aside from building structures, I didn't much care for importance or notoriety, and in my middle age, I still don't exactly know who I am; I just know what I do.

"I moved to Kansas City for a bit of a reset, a fresh start, for some anonymity, and maybe to finally figure all of this out. So far, I think the preliminary answer to the question, 'who am I?' is, 'I'm a middle-aged guy who enjoys music, and people, and who enjoys building.' If that's where I end up in my analysis, I'm ok with that answer." Quincy smiled at both 3J and Pascale. "And if and when I suss out with some finality who I am, I will most assuredly let you know, but for now, I'm good with what I do, and I answer the question, 'who are you?' with the statement, 'why, sir or madam, I build skyscrapers.'"

Who am I? 3J wondered. *Why, sir or madam, I am a bankruptcy lawyer.* Aloud, she lifted her glass, and responded, "hear, hear."

A few moments passed at the table in reflective silence.

Pascale gulped his beer and said, "Well, I know who I am."

"Who's that, counselor?" Quincy asked.

"I'm a thirsty lawyer who's reached the bottom of his beer glass. So, I guess I'll answer the question 'who are you?' by saying, 'I'm a lawyer who needs another beer.'"

They all laughed as he moved the conversation to a lighter topic and away from Quincy's couch session. In doing so, Pascale avoided revisiting the story of his late wife and child and deferred on any revelations for Quincy at this point. Not a story Pascale shared with clients, or, for that matter, most anyone else.

The evening meandered on until Quincy looked at his watch. "Uh oh. Look at the time. I need to be up at 5 a.m. to catch a flight to Salt Lake. Let me pay for this and thank you both again for all the great work." He stood. "We may never know what was in Stacy Milnes' mind, and we may not even care, but whatever it was, it's behind me now, and that's a great place for it to be. Maybe I'll send her a holiday card this next

December and sign it, 'Quincy G. Witherman. Remember me? I'm the one who's not your fuckin' friend.'"

"Fun to think about," Pascale said, "but hopefully, you'll let it lie and just move on. Always best. Wait, this whole discussion violates Rule One!"

They all chuckled, shook hands and hugged, and left the bar. Quincy went one way, and 3J and Pascale turned to walk the other way to their cars. As they walked, 3J said, "I like this part of the representation. You know, where we get to see a relaxed client getting back to what he does best – in this case, building skyscrapers."

"Agreed," said Pascale. "Nice to see a case to a successful conclusion. But, lest we forget that we work in a big law firm with a set-in-stone business model, let's hope the phone rings tomorrow morning on one of our desks, and it's a potential client whose problems we can sink our teeth into."

"I call a Rule Two violation."

"Put it on my tab," Pascale said. "At least we had good compliance with rule number three."

"It must be nice to create beautiful things that last. I think Quincy knows who he is. Maybe Kansas City will help him become comfortable with his identity. And, by the way, I'm ok for the phone to wait a couple of days before it rings."

"Waiting a few is good. I'll accept that modification to my statement," Pascale conceded.

They walked in silence under black lamplights designed with a nod to the early 1900s, past local storefronts and bars. Then 3J observed softly, "The one sad part of the Chapter 11 bankruptcy lawyer's existence that I just never seem to get used to is that after confirmation, we see very little of the reorganized client."

Pascale looked at her and nodded in agreement. "Some clients come back for advice, but most sail into the night. My guess is that Quincy will sail off."

3J had no inkling of what was about to happen in the world of Quincy Witherman. They were not quite finished with each other just yet.

§

When Quincy got back from O'Brien's, he lounged around the apartment and read some demographic studies of Salt Lake and Minneapolis as he listened to Paul Desmond's *Bossa Antigua* on the turntable. Sweet, haunting, alto sax. He decided to get up early in the morning and call Michaela Huld and share the moment of confirmation, discharge, and fresh/head start.

CHAPTER 37

Saturday, January 12, 2019

BRIAN CHIMES FELT GOOD about the resolution of the
Witherman bankruptcy cases. Full payment in the not-too-
distant future; fair terms for all involved; good, solid collateral.
A win all the way around for all involved, perhaps with the
singular exception of Stacy Milnes. *Oh well,* he thought. *Her
bank also gets paid and will be happy, even if she's not.*

He picked up the phone and dialed Stephanie Bonde in
South Africa. She was at her desk working on a Saturday, just
like Chimes. She picked up the phone and answered with that
perfectly elegant, melodic South African accent. "Stephanie,
Brian Chimes here. Looks like we're both slaves to the profession on this Saturday morning for me and afternoon for you.
Never a shortage of folks in financial trouble. I just wanted to
dial you up and make sure you're as content with the Witherman outcome as I am."

"Completely content, Brian. I made my report to my upper
managers here at Silvermine, and they're pleased with the
outcome. Pleased they won't have to own office buildings in the
United States, pleased we voted First Commercial out of the
role of the agent, and quite displeased with First Commercial
for not reining in Stacy Milnes. I am not sure that our bank will
do syndicated bank loan deals with First Commercial again."

"I hear ya' Stephanie. My brass had the same reaction on all counts. StarBanc's done quite a bit of business with First Commercial over the years, and I wonder if that'll now end, at least for a while, courtesy of Stacy Milnes. If so, boy, she screwed the pooch on this one."

"Screwed the pooch?" Bonde repeated as she chuckled. "You Yankees have the most colorful ways of describing things."

"Yankee? Who y'all callin' a Yankee, m' friend? We don't call us down-South folks *Yankees*, Stephanie. Won't hold it against you ... this time," Chimes explained, smiling broadly the entire time. Bonde couldn't see the smile, but she knew it was there. "Now, as to the pooch. Wasn't me who invented the phrase. I think it came out of the early NASA space program. Something one of those Texas yahoos at NASA coined. I certainly didn't mean to offend."

"Fuckin' the dog. No offense whatsoever." Somehow, when Bonde used the word "fucking," it sounded so tasteful to Chimes, so perfectly, and inoffensively, appropriate.

"Indeed. Well, until the next deal, it was a pleasure working with y'all on this one. This'll be one to tell the grandkids about some day."

"Be well, Brian. Goodbye."

CHAPTER 38

I AWOKE AT 4 a.m. Saturday morning and used the burner phone to call Michaela. She answered quickly. "How goes the battle, Quince?" she asked.

"Just wanted to report in. The bankruptcy cases are over. The Court entered the discharge order. Looks like smooth sailing from here."

"That is wonderful news. Should we talk about your head start? Do you want to start thinking about moving the account from FSBG to a bank somewhere in the South Pacific?"

"Yes, and soon, but not just yet. I want to avoid doing anything out of the ordinary for a short while. I think all of the dust has settled, but just to be sure, let's give it another month. Will that work?"

"Whatever works for you certainly works for me. It's your call. Can anything happen in the bankruptcy cases to undo the finality of the process?"

"To my understanding, if someone found the FSBG account or the crypto within a certain period of time, they could ask Judge Robertson to set aside the confirmation order. So the risk is the same as I've always had: the risk that someone will discover the account or the currency."

"But the bankruptcy order doesn't eliminate that risk?"

"Unfortunately not for another hundred and eighty days after the Judge entered the confirmation order."

"I will circle that day on my calendar, my dear, as the day when we can put some measure of the risk behind us."

"As will I, Michaela."

"How do you feel, Quincy?" Michaela probed.

"I'm good."

"No, I mean how do you *really* feel about all of this?"

"I am trying very hard not to feel euphoric, Michaela. I don't want to have to deal with any emotional froth bubbling over and overtaking my life. So I'm just going with feeling good at this point. That more than suffices, and is safer than euphoria!"

"Ahhh. I understand. Quincy Witherman sets a cap on how good he will allow himself to feel," Michaela teased him.

"Exactly. My own little emotional stop order, if you will," I elaborated. "I'm spinning Miles Davis' *Kind of Blue* to keep me grounded."

Our conversation drifted away from my emotions to a discussion of potential next projects, possible lenders to approach for a construction loan, when we could see each other again, and whether I thought the bankruptcy cases would make it impossible for me to secure a new construction loan. As I thought about that difficulty, I said, "The bankruptcy filings certainly aren't going be a positive when I go out to the market for new financing. I can't go back to any of the banks in the First Commercial bank group, and my relationship with First Commercial itself is at an end. But I'm optimistic that I can get a new group of lenders to partner with to construct a new high-rise in either Salt Lake or Minneapolis. There's always too much money ready and waiting to be lent in America. My job is just to find it, and I believe I will." Our conversation drew to a close as Michaela told me she had a Saturday meeting to attend. We promised to talk again shortly, said our obligatory "I love yous," and the call ended.

As I replaced the burner phone in my desk drawer, I felt good about my prospects of future construction lending, and even better about the expiration of the hundred and eighty-day bankruptcy waiting period. *No one knows about the FSBG account and crypto, and no one will ever know.*

CHAPTER 39

Saturday, January 12 to Tuesday, January 15, 2019

A DHL PACKAGE ARRIVED at Stacy Milnes' house on Saturday, January 12, 2019 at 10 a.m. She signed for it, tore open the package, and inside was the damning email printed out as well as three flash drives. She had read an electronic version of the email several days ago as she waited for the package. It seemed even better in hard copy. She already had read and re-read it numerous times, but another read seemed in order.

FROM: Michaela Huld – NOIRAM Advisors
TO: Frederick Schultz, FSBG
Re: Account # 7364
Date: October 12, 2018.
Mr. Schultz, I write to discuss Account #7364. This is an investment account for which I have a power of attorney to manage, which POA you have on file. I write to ask you to educate me on the process for liquidation of the account in the event same becomes necessary. Please advise as to lead time and steps. In the meantime, please confirm that the account balance is invested 100% in ten-year United States Treasury Bills, and if not, please take steps to so invest as soon as possible. Please know

that in addition to my general power of attorney, I
have the written authorization of the account owner,
Quincy G. Witherman, to send this email, as you
can see from the attachment to this email. Please
advise.

Yours faithfully,
Michaela.

Milnes read the email, reread it, paused, and then read
it again. As she continued to review the culled information,
nothing was as clear as that email. *One email*, she thought. *One
email, to bring down Witherman.*

Milnes knew that as a part of the Bank Secrecy Act, Americans filing federal tax returns had to disclose foreign financial
accounts that exceeded $10,000 each year on a Form 114. She
also knew that the Bank Secrecy Act had been on the books
since 1970, that First Commercial had copies of all of Quincy
Witherman's state and federal tax returns for the past six years,
and that Witherman had never filed a Form 114 with the IRS
to disclose his interest in Account #7364 held in First Switzerland Bank, Geneva. Based on account data that Rome culled,
it was an account worth $25 million.

So there it was, in black and white, but it may as well have
been in gold, gilt typeface. *And just like that, I've got him!* She
had seen her share of Hollywood movies where the private
investigator makes a breakthrough, and on hearing the news,
the heroine client's heart skips a beat. She was not usually one
to believe in hearts skipping beats outside of the Hollywood
set, but she was about to rethink that view because not only
did her heart skip a beat – or three – but she missed several
breaths, and ended up gasping for air. The air that finally
filled her lungs was sweet, cool, satisfying and life-affirming.

That's how Milnes felt – affirmed by a successful mission, the beginning of the end for Quincy G. Witherman.

She needed to hire a criminal attorney fast, preferably in Kansas City, to help get the information to those in the U.S. Attorney's office in Kansas City who handled white-collar crime, such as bankruptcy crimes and the Bank Secrecy Act's violations. Could the U. S. Attorneys even use the information she had gathered from Rome, given how she had acquired it? In a case she had handled many years ago, Milnes remembered a criminal matter where the prosecutors could bring no charges against the debtor because the Government obtained information illegally. She recalled an illegal wiretap, obtained without probable cause, and from the wiretap, the Marshals had gleaned information that led to incriminating evidence. But at the hearing to suppress the evidence, the defense attorney had eloquently argued that the evidence was the "fruit of the poisonous tree" and since the tree – the illegal wiretap – was poisonous, the fruit – the incriminating evidence – couldn't be used.

Milnes was concerned that the man-in-the-middle attack on Michaela's computer and the illicit transfer of the actual data from the Sueden servers to the flash drive were all poisonous trees. Perhaps the email she now held in her hands couldn't be used as a result. She needed to get to the bottom of this, and needed some succinct criminal law advice quickly. She would also need help reaching out to the federal prosecutors in the United States Attorney's office in Kansas City.

She knew of two criminal attorneys in Kansas City whose reputations were squeaky clean and who were well known to the federal prosecutors. One was a partner in the Greene Madison firm, who she assumed would represent Witherman when the news of the secret Swiss account started to break. *Well, he's out*, she thought. The other was an attorney in a small law shop specializing in criminal law – Martin Andrews at the Andrews and Cardison law firm. She did some research on Andrews and liked what she read about him.

For more than three decades, Andrews had been a criminal attorney, starting his career in the Kansas City U.S. Attorney's office as a criminal prosecutor and then leaving the office after a fifteen-year career to form Andrews and Cardison. Therefore, he had many years of experience both prosecuting criminals and defending them. In particular, his résumé indicated he had significant experience with white-collar crime. On the firm's web page, he listed several cases he handled that appeared to involve banks. He had spoken and written articles on the inter-section of criminal law and a bank's duties when its customer appeared to have committed a crime. He was the one to hire if he could take the case.

Although it was Saturday, Milnes figured that Andrews could be working at his desk. She called the main phone line at Andrews and Cardison, asked to speak to Martin Andrews, and on the second ring, Andrews answered.

"Martin Andrews."

"Mr. Andrews, this is Stacy Milnes. I'm an officer at First Commercial Bank in St. Louis. We're working on a bank-ruptcy case pending in the Western District of Missouri. We believe we've uncovered evidence of one or more bankruptcy crimes and evidence the debtor lied to federally insured bank-ing institutions including my bank. We need help in making the criminal referral and to represent my bank in the criminal process. I'd also like to get some advice on a criminal law question or two. I'd be your main point of bank contact. Is that something you'd be able to handle for us?"

"Certainly, Ms. Milnes. Give me the pertinent names so I can make sure we have no conflicts of interest, but assuming none, I'd be happy to represent the bank. When could we have a longer meeting to discuss all the background, and how time-sensitive is this matter?"

"I can email all the names when we finish the call. The matter is *very* time-sensitive. It involves a secret bank account in Switzerland, and our former bankruptcy attorney has advised me that the Bankruptcy Code has a relatively short window to take bankruptcy action. That wouldn't be a criminal proceeding, to be sure, but if at all feasible, I'd like to see the bankruptcy issues and the criminal issues play out at the same time."

"Ok. Understood. Email the names for our conflicts-of-interest analysis, and can we do a video conference Monday morning, first thing?"

"Yes, that would work well. What other information should I email to you?"

"Send me the bankruptcy filings; samples of any documents in which the Debtor has made a false statement to the bank; and the evidence you have to show the Swiss bank account. Who represents the Debtor in the bankruptcy case?"

"There are seven related bankruptcy cases, and the firm is Greene Madison."

"Excellent firm. Assuming no conflicts, I look forward to working with you."

After the call ended, Milnes emailed Andrews the information he requested. Within two hours, he emailed her and reported no conflicts.

Andrews reviewed the information provided by Milnes with great interest. One email clearly seemed to show that Witherman owned a Swiss bank account. From his call with Milnes, he understood that Witherman had disclosed the Swiss bank account in neither the financial statements he had provided to the bank, nor in the bankruptcy papers he filed when his bankruptcy cases began. One curiosity had Andrews' attention.

How did Milnes come into possession of the email?

§

On Monday, January 14, Andrews and Milnes logged on to a videoconference to discuss the new matter. Milnes gave the attorney the background, filling in the details that weren't apparent merely from the documents she emailed to him the day before.

"Mr. Andrews, go over the criminal referral process for me."

"Please, call me Martin. Certainly: You may be familiar with a bank's duty to file a Suspicious Activity Report. A financial institution must file a SAR no later than thirty calendar days after the bank detects any activity that's out of the ordinary. For example, the SAR may include an activity that gives rise to a suspicion that the account holder is attempting to hide something or make an illegal transaction. What you appear to have uncovered here would fall squarely within the purview of suspicious activity and give rise to the requirement that First Commercial must file the report. The bank files the SAR with the Financial Crimes Enforcement Network, or FinCEN for short, an agency in the U.S. Treasury. FinCEN then investigates the incident. It's not necessary that you have proof of the commission of an actual crime, although here, you seem to have the evidence of it. No one will notify Witherman that the bank filed the SAR."

"How about the other banks? Will they be notified?"

"No. And you're obligated to tell no one that your bank filed the SAR. Neither confirm nor deny. In my practice, I go further in my advice and tell my clients they should have no discussions whatsoever about the SAR with anyone other than in-house counsel and me."

"Mr. Andrews, if we file the SAR …"

"Excuse me for interrupting. Not 'if.' Rather, *when* you file the SAR. Based on the information you've uncovered, it's required."

"Right. Sorry. When we file the SAR, is the bank still free to pursue its bankruptcy remedies against Witherman?"

"I believe so. The bankruptcy remedy and the SAR will proceed independently of each other." Andrews paused to let his advice sink in.

Milnes then asked, "What can you tell me about Swiss bank secrecy?"

"I know a little bit about the topic, but I don't count myself an expert, I'm afraid. I figured the subject might come up based on the Huld email you sent me, so last night, I called in a favor or two, and I talked to a law school professor friend of mine who is an expert on the topic to give me a crash course on Swiss bank secrecy. Here is what I know. Before October 2018, the Swiss banks viewed their role in protecting their depositor's information from prying eyes as akin to a doctor-patient or lawyer-client privilege. Like a doctor or a lawyer, the Swiss banks held information about their clients' banking habits in the strictest of confidence. The Swiss banking laws went even further and *imposed* a duty of confidentiality on the banks.

"Then effective in October, 2018, the International Convention on the Automatic Exchange of Banking Information (AEBI) drew Switzerland in line with international standards on taxation. The convention, developed by the Organization for Economic Cooperation and Development and the global financial industry, provides that Swiss banks must share bank account information about citizens of certain countries annually and automatically. Since it went into effect just recently, I would assume that the first automatic information dump from Witherman's Swiss bank to the Internal Revenue Service would not occur immediately, maybe the end of the year or beginning of next. If I were Witherman, I would plan to finish the bankruptcy case as expeditiously as possible, and then perhaps, even faster, move the Swiss account somewhere else. There are other international havens for this kind of thing besides Switzerland."

Milnes listened intently. Andrews was thorough and he drew the information together in an organized and cogent fashion in a mere twenty-four-hour period.

"We haven't discussed the element of the bankruptcy crimes involved here," she noted.

"Yes, I took a quick look last night at the bankruptcy crimes statutes, and they're straightforward enough. Failing to disclose assets on the bankruptcy schedules is a crime. A federal felony."

"Next steps?" asked Milnes.

"Well, before we get to that. Are you comfortable sharing with me how you obtained the information about the Swiss account? I'm sure that will come up in my discussions with the prosecutor and the FBI."

Milnes had a long career interacting with lawyers, and her suspicious nature long ago dictated that she should always make sure that her conversations with counsel were privileged. "Comfortable? Nothing about this case makes me feel real comfortable. But before we talk about it, I guess I need to know whether the ensuing discussion is privileged."

"I'll treat it as such, but as soon as you start to float the email and the other information you sent me, the Government is inevitably going to ask how you obtained it. So you might as well get used to answering the question."

Milnes took a deep breath and, leaving out her own caustic approach to the collection of the Witherman loans and her actions that led to the removal of First Commercial as Agent, started to explain the process, "At some point after I met Witherman, I had a gut reaction that he wasn't completely truthful." She omitted that she had that same gut reaction to almost all borrowers for whom the special assets group had responsibility. She continued, "The other banks in the bank group had little interest in pursuing Witherman. They only focused on repayment of the loans. Repayment is, of course, important to First Commercial as well, but I wanted to know the truth. I hired an investigator of sorts I've used before in New York City – Moses Aaronson. Moses has a network of what I'd call operatives nationwide and, to some extent, as needed, worldwide. That network included a woman, code name Rome – I don't know her real name – who was able to access the laptop of Witherman's financial advisor in a coffee shop in something called a 'man-in-the-middle-attack' and was able to determine the advisor used a particular VPN. Then Rome bribed an employee of the VPN company to deliver the data, a portion of which I culled for you."

Milnes' explanation was more involved than Andrews expected, and he said, "Fascinating," followed by a pause as he processed what he heard. "We should hone down the nature of my firm's representation a bit in light of that story. My firm can represent the bank in its interactions with the Government to try to steer the Government to bring charges against Witherman. If the Government, however, turns its attention to an examination of whether your conduct on behalf of the bank, and the bank's conduct as an institution as a result of your actions, merits a criminal investigation, we'll need separate counsel for you."

"I think I understand."

"I have to say, at this point, Ms. Milnes, there is risk in the actions you took to get the information. You may have committed a crime. Did you realize that when you went down the path you chose to obtain the information?"

"What I did was catch a bad guy. A felon. I protected my bank and the other banks in the bank group. I did what I needed to do."

"The more I think about this, I don't think there's any question you'll need your own separate counsel who will have to advise you about explaining how you got the Huld email."

Milnes sighed as she absorbed Andrews' suggestion of the need to hire her own lawyer, "Another lawyer? Is that really necessary?"

"It is, Ms. Milnes. You need to make sure you are protecting yourself as you pursue Quincy Witherman."

"Alright. This discussion reminds me of a question I had. Many years ago, I worked on a file involving a borrower who had committed a crime. The Government obtained evidence about the borrower without a proper warrant and, in that process, discovered damning evidence. At a hearing, the judge suppressed the evidence. Will that come up in this case?"

"Good question. I don't think so. Your question raises the Fruit of the Poisonous Tree doctrine which stems from a concern in the courts that in a criminal case, the ends shouldn't justify the means. The Government shouldn't be able to use evidence it wouldn't have obtained if not for something illegal it did, such as an illegal search and seizure. But the entire doctrine solely applies to the *Government*, and how *it* acquires evidence in a criminal case. As long as the Government wasn't in cahoots with you and your operatives as you, shall we say, acquired this damning information, it can be used in the bankruptcy case against Witherman and by the Government to bring criminal charges against him as well. There'll be some other hurdles to clear, such as authentication and the hearsay rule of evidence, because certain players in the process might not appear in court here in the states. Still, the Fruit of the Poisonous Tree doctrine shouldn't be a hurdle."

"Ok. Then what are the next steps?"

"Prepare and submit the SAR and then let me have a conversation with one or more of my contacts at the FBI and the U.S.

Attorney's office, both of whom will have access to the SAR.
I can certainly alert both the prosecutor and the investigators
at the FBI of our concerns about Witherman and broach the
topic of bankruptcy crimes with them. They'll know to look
for the SAR and see what the bank reported."

"I think we'll need to have you coordinate with our bankruptcy counsel. I'd imagine bankruptcy counsel wouldn't be
comfortable with the criminal parts of what we've discussed,"
Milnes said.

"That won't be a problem. Who is the bank's bankruptcy
counsel?"

"Unclear," Milnes said. "I need to hire a new bankruptcy
attorney. I should be able to do that today and then introduce
the two of you."

"Very well, Ms. Milnes. Let's stay in touch by email as this
all starts to play out."

"Agreed. I'll send you a draft of the SAR for you to review
and comment on as soon as I have it ready for your eyes."

"I'll look for it. Thank you," Andrews said, and they terminated the video conference.

§

After Milnes completed her discussion with Andrews, she dialed
Moses Aaronson. Usually, she'd send an email first to make sure
he had time to talk with her. But this time, she just called him.
He answered, and she could hear New York City background
noise, so she assumed he was in Madison Park on his favorite
bench, with Emily curled up next to him.

"Why, good day, Ms. Milnes. This is a pleasant surprise."

"I hope this call finds you well, Moses. I wanted to report to
you how the project is resolving."

"I'm all ears."

"I won't bore you with all the details, and to be truthful, I'm not tech-savvy enough to give you *all* the details. Suffice it to say that Rome did her thing, and as a result, I'm in possession of written evidence of Witherman's substantial secret Swiss bank account. The next steps are to interest the authorities to prosecute Witherman for a bankruptcy crime and reverse the Chapter 11 plan's confirmation in his bankruptcy case. So I'm happy to report that the operation was quite successful. When you are involved, that always seems to be the case."

"I am pleased to learn of this news," Moses said. "Yes, pleased indeed. Am I correct in assuming that this ends our intriguing project together?"

"Yes, it does. We still have some hurdles, I understand, and while I don't foresee your involvement in getting over the hurdles, if I need you, I have your contact info."

"Indeed you do, Ms. Milnes. Call or write anytime, and until our next engagement, *au revoir.*"

"Thank you, Moses," Milnes said, violating her rule of terminating a call without closing pleasantries.

§

After the call ended, Milnes researched new bankruptcy counsel she could hire and settled in on one Jacob Steinert. He was a solo practitioner in Kansas City, sixty-four years old, a lifetime bankruptcy attorney, and certainly seemed to know his way around the courthouse. A special assets colleague in a large bank in Kansas City gave her Steinert's name and spoke highly of him. The case didn't seem like rocket science to her, so she placed a call to his number, left a voice mail, and waited for his response.

Steinert called back in twenty minutes. There was a considerable amount of background to share, including that the email was from the server of the VPN company, Sueden. He listened, and at the conclusion of the story, he said, "And what's your goal, here, Ms. Milnes?"

"I want to undo the discharge and the plan confirmation order."

"Then what happens?"

"I assume Witherman loses his companies, and someone will sell the buildings to pay off the banks."

"Is there a risk that the sale of the buildings won't bring sufficient proceeds to pay the banks in full?"

Another damn lawyer trying to make business decisions, Milnes thought. *Stay civil, Stacy. You need him.* "I've been at this my entire adult life. My assessment is that we'll be fine, and the sale of the buildings will generate enough."

"Do the other banks in the group know about these developments?"

"Not yet. We won't be handling this issue as a group. This will be solely First Commercial's row to hoe."

"Very well. Subject to reviewing the documents and giving this a little more thought, my initial reaction is that it sounds like you have a strong case to set aside the discharge and plan confirmation orders. Except for one thing: We won't be able to just waltz into bankruptcy court and show the Judge the email. The email is hearsay, and not admissible in a court trial, not to mention that it also has to be authenticated. How would we do that?"

Andrews alluded to a similar problem but Milnes hadn't probed further. Now she needed to understand the problem, and said, "English, please, counselor. What are hearsay and authentication in this situation?"

"Hearsay is an out-of-court statement that we would offer into evidence for the truth of the matter asserted in the statement. Here, the statement is the text of the email which wasn't made by the author in court. In other words, Michaela Huld is not in court testifying to the content of her email. But we would still offer the email into evidence to prove that the text of the email is true – that Witherman has a secret Swiss bank account."

"And authentication?"

"Authentication is proof that the email is genuine; that it came from Sueden's business records, and it's something that Sueden keeps in the ordinary course of its business, and that Michaela Huld sent the email."

Milnes thought for a moment and realized that the process might very well be much more complicated than she expected. She was wrong – definitely rocket science. From her point of view, nothing about bankruptcy law seemed to go simply or smoothly. Thinking out loud, she said, "Michaela Huld wrote the email, and she lives in London as far as I know. Huld sent the email to a bank in Switzerland named FSB-Geneva. The documents came from one of Sueden's employees; Sueden may or may not have some kind of office here in the United States."

"We can start with Sueden. We should figure out if it has an office stateside, and if so, we can probably use that hook to authenticate the record we want to use. That won't solve the hearsay problem, however. Let's do this. Yes, I can represent the bank in this matter. Send me the Huld email to start with and let me have some quiet time to think about this a little. Then maybe we can talk tomorrow, end of day. In the meantime, can I ask you to figure out if Sueden has an office in the United States?"

"That'll be fine. I can have my investigator do that," Milnes agreed.

They ended their call, and Steinert sat at his desk and considered how he could make his case and get the evidence admitted into the record. He wanted to read the email and make sure he had all the facts and nuances as he tried to figure out a way. There were exceptions to the hearsay rule. He just had to hope one of them would apply.

Before long, he received an email with the Huld email attached. He printed it out and read it. It certainly said what Milnes had represented that it did, but there was more that she would not have known was relevant to the hearsay issue. Steinert noted that the email was sent by Michaela Huld in a *representative* capacity – as the financial advisor for Witherman and as the holder of a power of attorney from Witherman. And Huld expressly noted in the email that she was acting with Witherman's authority. Her email gave authorized instructions to the Swiss bank and sought information. Steinert pulled out his battered copy of *Federal Rules of Evidence* and smiled to himself as he read:

> A statement ... is not hearsay [if] [t]he statement is offered against an opposing party and: ... (C) was made by a person whom the party authorized to make a statement on the subject; [or] (D) was made by the party's agent ... on a matter within the scope of that relationship ... .

The rule would allow the email into evidence because it was sent by Witherman's authorized agent. *Subsection (C) looks like a winner, and (D) might work to permit Judge Robertson to admit the email into evidence. This is going to work!*

CHAPTER 40

Tuesday, January 15, 2019

MARTIN ANDREWS REACHED OUT to his contact at the FBI's office in Kansas City, Missouri. The office was just west of downtown on a bluff overlooking the convergence of I-29 and I-35, with Kansas City's skyline beyond – a prized view in the early evening as the downtown lights came on against the backdrop of a dusky blue Midwestern sky. Prominent on the skyline was the Witherman high-rise building.

Andrews and his contact had a good discussion, and it sounded like the FBI and the U.S. Attorney's office had already reviewed and talked about First Commercial's SAR. It was a straightforward report that attached the email and account value data and Andrews felt that the SAR made a succinct and direct, open-and-shut case for a bankruptcy crime against Quincy Witherman.

Andrews called his favorite Assistant United States Attorney, AUSA Robert Hickman. When Hickman started out as a prosecutor, he worked with Andrews in the Kansas City U.S. Attorney's office in the criminal division and learned the ropes from Andrews before he left to set up his own firm and started representing criminal defendants. Hickman had called it a defection of the highest order, and never missed a chance to ask Andrews about his new life on the dark side. For years,

Andrews had asked Hickman to join the Andrews and Cardison law firm, but Hickman always declined, saying he enjoyed putting the bad guys away and didn't think he would enjoy helping to set them free.

When the phone rang, Hickman picked it up and grumbled, "Hickman here."

"Robert Hickman, is that really you?" Andrews asked with feigned astonishment.

Recognizing Andrews' voice immediately, Hickman shot back, "Jesus. I gotta talk to our IT folks here, 'cause we gotta do a better job of screening calls from the dark side. I mean, if *you* can get through to a federal prosecutor on his private line just that easily, who knows what kind of bad guys can just dial me up any damn time they want."

Andrews laughed, and now that their regular lunge and parry had concluded, Hickman asked, "Ok, counselor. To what do I owe the honor?"

Andrews explained that First Commercial hired him, and he told Hickman about the Witherman bankruptcy cases and the failure to list the Swiss bank account on the schedules and statement of affairs. Hickman listened closely as Andrews described the email that proved the existence of the secret account and concluded by asking, "I assume it's still a priority in the Department of Justice to prosecute bankruptcy crimes, to send the message that debtors can't use the bankruptcy system while they hide assets?"

"Most assuredly it is, counselor. One hundred percent. That's a fascinating story, Martin. You know that the Swiss just finally agreed to dispense with their veil of bank secrecy, but that process of sharing has barely begun. So, I'm more than a little curious – how would you and your bank client have come upon the email that discloses the hidden account?" Martin asked slowly.

302 | MARK SHAIKEN

"How *I* came upon the email is an easy one, Robert. My client representative sent it to me. How my client rep. came upon the email is a bit of a more complicated matter. I'll let the bank officer's lawyer explain that part of the story when the time is right. Suffice it to say, it's all high-tech stuff."

"High-tech intrigue. How enticing. A welcomed respite from my day-to-day crooked doctor trying to defraud the Medicare system. And shall I assume that the author of the email *consented* to all of this, counselor?" Hickman asked, fully believing the answer would not be "yes."

"I'll let the bank officer's lawyer explain that as well."

Hickman thought for a moment and then said, "I have some legwork I need to do at my end, but you have certainly piqued my interest, and I'll get back to you in a few days. In the meantime, you might alert your client rep. that I'm going to want to meet and talk with him here at my offices. You know the drill."

"'He' is a she. I've alerted her to the likely course of events, including your request for a meeting. Technically, the bank, not the banker, is my client. I'll need to find her an attorney before the meeting with you and you'll have to work out the requested meeting with the new lawyer."

"I see. Well, no worries. Still need to meet with the banker," Hickman said as the conversation wound down. "We need to catch up over lunch or a drink, my friend. It would have to be in a particularly dark place, so no one sees me there with you. Bad for my stellar reputation and all to be seen with such a prominent defender of all that's evil. Of course, I'd want to take all reasonable steps to avoid a headline the next day that read 'good and evil meet for barbecue.' But we *should* get together."

"Not too great for my rep either, my friend. I usually try to avoid hangin' with the big, bad prosecutor. But I agree. We ought to be able to find an out-of-the-way venue where no one will recognize us in each other's company. How about next week for lunch?"

"Works for me. I'll shoot you an email with the name of the venue."

"Great to catch up with you, Robert."

"You too, Martin."

§

At 4 p.m., Milnes called Jacob Steinert to exchange information. She went first, telling Steinert that Moses had found out for her that Sueden raised venture capital money from an Angel fund as seed money to get started. The Angel fund had an office in Manhattan, and it leased one of its small offices to Sueden to use when their founder came to the States. So, she reported, Sueden had an address and an office in New York City.

Steinert was pleased. "That should solve my authentication problem if I can't get Witherman to authenticate the documents himself in his deposition. And I think I've solved my hearsay problem as well. Huld acted as Witherman's agent when she sent FSBG the email, and the email expressly says that Witherman himself authorized the email inquiry and directive. In that context, the email wouldn't be treated as hearsay in Federal Court and should be admissible."

He let that sink in, and Milnes said nothing.

Steinert continued, "I have what I need to draft a motion to set aside the confirmation order, if that's what you'd like me to do.

"Yes, please proceed."

"Very well. Should be able to get you a draft by close of business tomorrow."

"Excellent," Stacy Milnes said. As the call ended, she gloated, *this is more than excellent. Can't wait to see what Witherman and the syndicate banks think when they read this.*

§

Milnes kicked back at her desk and called Martin Andrews for a report. He told her about his conversations with the FBI and Robert Hickman and Milnes again said she wanted to coordinate the bankruptcy motion to set aside the confirmation order and discharge with the criminal proceeding.

"I don't see how we'll be able to coordinate the two, Stacy. We aren't the puppet master in the criminal process, pulling the Justice Department's marionette strings. We can try to stay informed, and we can informally cajole the Government players to action, but there's no agreement we'll reach with them as to a timeline, or indeed if the DOJ will even bring charges against Witherman."

"So, we'll have no influence whatsoever?" Milnes asked, with disappointment in her voice.

"I didn't say that, Stacy. It'll be subtle and hard to measure the degree of influence. My thought was that you'd proceed expeditiously to file your bankruptcy papers where you'll lay out the entire story and include the supporting email. I'll send that filing to my prosecutor contact, who'll read the papers, and undoubtedly feel a gravitational pull to begin to act to bring corresponding charges against Witherman. In following this course of action, the Government and we will also get a free preview of the Witherman response."

"That sounds reasonable. What kind of response could Witherman offer?"

"That's a *very* interesting question. Witherman will need to be extremely careful not to waive his Fifth Amendment right against self-incrimination. In the bankruptcy case, if he testifies or offers an affidavit on the topic of the FSBG account, he'd likely waive any privilege not to testify in the criminal matter."

"If he doesn't testify, how would he be able to contest the

motion?" Milnes asked, intrigued by the topic.

"He very well may not be able to. He wouldn't be the first person to find himself hampered and muzzled in a civil proceeding with the threat of criminal charges looming."

"Fascinating," Milnes said. "I like your idea to proceed forward in the bankruptcy case. Our new bankruptcy counsel is drafting papers for my review. When I get them, I'll shoot you a copy, and I'd love your input."

"Not a bankruptcy expert at all, but I can give you the criminal side of it, and with the papers in front of me, maybe I can expand my thinking on how Witherman would contest the bankruptcy motion," Andrews said. "One other matter, Stacy. My contact at the U.S. Attorney's office wants to interview you. This isn't surprising; but you'll need your own counsel present to represent you, due to the method by which you acquired the documents. So finding this attorney is now urgent. Do you understand?"

"I understand, Martin. Can you recommend someone to represent me, please?"

"I'll email you some names."

"Just email me *the* name of the person you'd use if you required criminal counsel."

"Ok, will do."

I like where we are in this one, Milnes thought. *Witherman's going to feel some significant pain shortly. Good. And the bank group's reaction? Pain for them as well: The pain of conceding I was right all along. Can't wait to talk to those pricks from Houston and South Africa. I'll remind Ms. Bonde that this all happened at her suggestion that I could go after Witherman on my own nickel.*

CHAPTER 41

STEINERT DELIVERED TO MILNES a draft of the *Motion
to Set Aside Confirmation Order and Discharge.* She immediately
reviewed it and noted that Steinert attached the relevant email
as an exhibit to the motion. The motion did an excellent job of
tracing both Witherman's failure to reveal the FSBG account
for years in reports submitted to the banks and that he continued the subterfuge in the bankruptcy filing papers. She
felt confident that the motion would catch Judge Robertson's
attention, hopefully in a positive way, and would catch the
syndicate bank group members' attention, hopefully in a way
that would feel like they had just jammed their thumbs into
an electrical socket.

She forwarded the motion to Martin Andrews to see if he
had any comments from the criminal law perspective and then
called Jacob Steinert to discuss the motion and next steps.

"Steinert here."

"Jacob, this is Stacy Milnes. Thanks for the quick turnaround
on the motion. I read it, and I like it. I don't have any edits
or comments."

"Thanks. It was an easy one to write. Kinda wrote itself, to
be honest. This type of motion is very serious and the facts
alleged are usually involved. Despite the gravity of the allega-

tions in our motion, the facts in this one aren't involved, and the attachment pretty much tells the story."

"I asked the bank's criminal attorney, Martin Andrews, to take a quick look at it and let me know if he has any questions or concerns from the criminal law side of this. Once we get Martin's comments, what happens next?"

"We file the motion, ask for a hearing date, and set up Witherman's deposition. If I can get Witherman to admit the authenticity of the email, we're ready for trial. If I can't, then we turn to Plan B. Then I'll need to hire a lawyer in New York City and serve Sueden with a deposition subpoena to produce a witness to identify and authenticate the documents. Sounds complicated, but it isn't. It's called a Rule 30(b)(6) deposition. I should be able to get Sueden on the record in two to three weeks, max. Once Sueden identifies the documents as its business records, and once we have that transcript, we're pretty much ready for our hearing."

"That all sounds good. So, outside timeline, we're looking at a hearing in about a month?"

"That would be a good target. One thing I wanted to circle back to discuss with you. You'll note that the motion focuses on Quincy Witherman. Not his companies. It's *his* SBG account. It's *his* personal failure to report the FSBG account to the banks over the years. When we first talked, I asked you what your goal was. You said the goal was to get the buildings and sell them. Now that I've thought this through, I don't see that happening. Four of the LLC entities are debtors that own the building. A holding company owns the LLC entities, and Witherman owns the holding company. The LLCs don't have an interest in the FSBG account, and therefore, in their bankruptcy cases, they committed no fraud. What I'm saying – and sorry to be so long-winded – we can try to achieve your goal of setting aside the Witherman discharge and set the stage for a federal criminal proceeding against him personally. But the entities will continue to own the buildings, and as long as they perform under the plan, no one will sell the buildings."

"I missed those nuances in the motion. I guess I got caught up in how well it read and how close I am to reversing Witherman's 'win' in bankruptcy court," Milnes replied. In an uncharacteristically conciliatory moment, she murmured, "To be truthful, when I said I wanted the buildings sold, I was puffing; a little too much bravado. If we did something to trigger the sale of the buildings, the syndicate banks would have a collective shit fit of epic proportions. As it stands now, they're going to be plenty pissed off. Not that I care what they think, and the shit fit would be most satisfying to see. But I don't want them doing anything in court that would distract from what we're trying to do. So focusing just on Witherman will work. It'll send the message that our borrowers can't lie to us and get away with it. It'll seal Witherman's fate. And it navigates the tightrope of going after Witherman while not disturbing the LLC payment plan. So, I'm good with the way this came out," Milnes concluded.

She was impressed that Steinert had absorbed all the facts in the bankruptcy cases and so quickly drafted the motion. Especially given Judge Robertson's reaction to the discovery motion, and his anger over the banks' initial approach, honing in on just Witherman would hopefully appease the Judge this time around and return him to a neutral corner. All she needed him to be was neutral. The Huld email would do the rest.

"One other thing," Steinert added. "Robertson likes to have chambers conferences in complicated cases after a party files a motion like this to make sure the suggested timeline works for all involved and to get a flavor of how to handle the motion. I'd expect him to call a quick meeting in chambers on short notice to discuss this motion. Sometimes clients are permitted to attend, and sometimes not. If he allows clients to be present, do you want to come?"

"I don't need to attend. I wonder if Witherman will come?" Milnes mused.

"Good question. I'd think he'd avoid such a get-together at all costs. It would be hard for him to avoid the good Judge's ire if we're all sitting in a small conference room within spitting distance of each other. He's already lied to the bankruptcy system and the Judge, and I'd expect that he'd want to avoid any chance of having to lie to the Judge's face again, this time with a criminal lawyer at his side," Steinert offered. "I'm sure I'll get a call from Ms. Jones or Mr. Pascale after they read this. Am I clear to talk with them?"

While Milnes had muzzled Dennis Sample, not allowing him to talk with debtors' counsel, she felt more comfortable with Steinert, and decided to free him up to talk: "Do whatever is customary in these types of situations."

"Will do," Steinert acknowledged.

§

Later in the day, Steinert received the email from Milnes that Andrews had no comments and that he should file the motion, which he did immediately. He then sent a file-stamped copy of the motion and attachments to Milnes. Steinert's phone lit up within five minutes, but it was neither Josephina Jones nor William Pascale calling.

"Steinert here."

"Holy shit, Jacob!" Sample exclaimed without introducing himself.

Steinert didn't recognize the caller ID phone number on his screen and said, "Who is speaking, please?"

"Sorry. This is Dennis Sample. I represent StarBanc, the agent bank in the Witherman bankruptcy cases." Steinert and Sample knew each other in passing from various bankruptcy conferences over the years, and a handful of cases in which they had both represented clients. Steinert found Sample to be the nervous sort.

"Ahhh, Dennis. How's it going?"

"It's going. I just read the motion you filed on behalf of First Commercial."

"Hopefully you read and absorbed the Huld email as well. It's kinda pivotal in the story set out in the motion."

"I read it. How did you get it?"

"Not sure that's pertinent at this stage."

"Is it real?"

"Not sure I follow."

"Is it authentic?"

"It's my understanding and belief that it is."

"StarBanc is going to shit a brick when this hits Brian Chimes' desktop."

"Oh, Milnes tells me that Chimes is a stout Texas boy from Houston, so I'm sure he'll recover. I doubt he'll pass any bricks through his gastro system. Dennis, is there something I can specifically help you with?" Steinert asked, hoping to end the call and get back to other things demanding his time.

"Not right now. I'm sure there will be shortly."

"Very well. Have a good rest of your day and week, Dennis."

When the call ended, Steinert thought, *Well, that was a total waste of time. Sample's nervous tendency has certainly bubbled to the surface in this case.*

§

Brian Chimes sat at his desk, reading financial statements provided by one of his borrowers. It was a typical special assets,

StarBanc day in a welcomed return to normality now that the Witherman mess was behind him. He looked up from the papers and saw an email come through from Dennis Sample with a motion attached to it. The email simply said, "Please review and call me. Dennis."

Chimes opened the attachment and, as he read the motion and the attached email, murmured softly several times to himself, "What the fuck?" Just as he finished reading the motion, his phone rang: Stephanie Bonde. He put Bonde on his desk speaker phone.

"Brian, have you read this?" she asked, her voice not hiding just how perplexed she was.

"Yes, indeed. Milnes strikes again. She's like a bad arch-villain in some comic book story who just won't fade away. Just when everyone thought it was safe to come out, she reappears."

"I have no idea how she got her hands on the email, but it is pretty damaging," Bonde observed.

Chimes agreed. "Yup. I guess she took it to heart when you told her that she could go after Witherman if she wanted − I guess she wanted. The way I read this, she's going after only Witherman. Not the LLCs that own the buildings or the management company that run them. Is that your read?"

"Yes, but that draws a pretty fine line and I think we need to make it clear that the heavens will rain down on Stacy Milnes if she does *anything* to put at risk the payments to the banks. And I mean *anything*," Bonde said sternly.

"I hear ya'. What a total cluster fuck this is about to become," Chimes added.

"Cluster fucks seem to follow Witherman and Milnes wherever they go," Bonde agreed with Chimes. "Brian, there can be no prospect that First Commercial will imperil steady payments to the banks under the plan," Bonde stated, to reemphasize how vital the payments were to her bank. "The whole premise of the negotiations was to avoid the possibility of owning the buildings, that's why we decided against any attempt to bring the entire Witherman empire down."

"Agreed. We'll need to gather up the banks and have a meeting to deliver that message and ask Milnes and her new attorney any questions the group may have. I'll get that set up for us, pronto."

The two paused in silence for a moment, and then Bonde sighed. "Never a dull moment on this one."

Chimes agreed vehemently, "You took the words right out of my mouth. Not with Stacy Fuckin' Milnes circling." He took a deep breath and as he slowly exhaled he said again much more quietly, "Not with Stacy Milnes." He concluded, "I'll set up our meeting and talk to you soon."

After the call, Chimes leaned back in his chair, harkened back to his thoughts about Witherman's integrity, and thought, *well if this don't just beat all!*

§

Jamie Li read the *Motion to Set Aside Confirmation Order and Discharge* and the attached email before bringing it into Judge Robertson's office to review and discuss. He again found himself in uncharted territory. When he had signed on as Judge Robertson's law clerk, a coveted position among graduating law students, he had taken the bankruptcy overview class in law school, which included only an introduction to Chapter 11 and didn't delve into the reorganization topic in any detail. So most of what Jamie had learned so far about Chapter 11 came from sitting in the courtroom with Judge Robertson as he presided over cases, from articles he read, from briefs and pleadings filed by the lawyers, from his research for the Judge, and from discussions with Judge Robertson in chambers and over lunch. He was a quick study, but he hadn't yet encountered a motion to set aside plan confirmation or Chapter 11 discharge based on fraud.

He made his way down the hallway to Judge Robertson's office and knocked on the door, which was half-open. Judge Robertson already had a copy of the motion brought to him by one of the court clerks, and was mostly through the motion as he waived Jamie in.

He took his usual seat in a dark, soft, tufted, high-backed club chair that faced the desk, the picture windows behind the Judge, and the metropolitan area beyond. He waited for the Judge to finish and look up. After about a minute, Judge Robertson looked up, shook his head slowly east and west, raised his eyebrows, and said one word, "Lordy!"

Jamie still said nothing, as he assumed Judge Robertson had more to say. After a few moments of silence, however, he began to doubt that the Judge had any further comments to offer on the motion, but he was wrong.

"Did you read the email attached to the motion?" Judge Robertson finally asked.

"Yes, Judge."

"I have no idea how First Commercial got its hands on the email, but here is what I know. Witherman looked right into my eyes at the confirmation hearing and, under oath, told me that the papers he filed to start these cases were all true and correct. Right into my eyes."

"Yes, Judge."

"Takes a lot of moxie to lie under oath to a federal judge," Judge Robertson said as he clasped his hands behind his head and leaned back in his chair.

Jamie said nothing in response.

Judge Robertson took a deep breath, and as he exhaled and continued to shake his head slowly left to right and back again with a disbelieving look on his face, said, "Alright, Jamie. Call counsel and get them in here for a chambers conference … again. And let's hear what they have to say as to process and timing."

"Judge, is this a normal part of the Chapter 11 process?"

"Normal? Well, to the extent anything in bankruptcy is normal, I'd say not. I don't have stats, but a debtor who procures confirmation by fraud has to be a pretty rare debtor. As I think about this, I suppose that if he lied to the banks for years, he must have thought he had no choice but to lie on the bankruptcy papers as well. Not much of a defense, however. And, lying on the papers is a felony under Title 18 of the United States Code. My guess is an order setting aside confirmation and discharge will be the least of his worries when all is said and done. Let's get the conference scheduled. Thanks, Jamie."

As Jamie rose to leave Judge Robertson's office, the Judge said, "Oh, one other thing comes to mind. Could you please take a look at the email attached to the motion and give me some analysis of whether it's admissible as evidence in a trial? If not, what will the bank have to prove to admit the email into evidence? Without the email, the motion is just another fairy tale filed by this bank. It looks like the new First Commercial counsel is Jacob Steinert. He's good. Pretty conservative and knows his way around the courtroom, so I'm going to assume he already has a plan baked into his analysis of how to get the documents admitted into evidence."

"Absolutely, Judge," Jamie said as he turned to exit the Judge's office.

§

No new prospective client had phoned 3J and Pascale since their get-together with Quincy at O'Brien's, so they were still in a mode of trying to relax – catching their breath while they did clean-up work on the Witherman cases. Then, without fanfare, each received an email notifying them of a new ECF filing in the Witherman case. 3J clicked on the link in the notice, and the First Commercial motion instantly appeared on her screen for her to read. She leaned forward closer to her computer screen as she read the motion, and all of a sudden, she was busy again, not with a new client, but with an old one whose case just didn't seem willing to close.

She could feel her blood pressure rise and her eyes go slightly out of focus as she re-read the motion and the email attachment. *He's been lying to me all along! Shit, he's been lying to everyone!* She immediately thought back to her first encounter with Quincy Witherman and all of her meetings and interactions with him since. Those encounters ran through her mind with the speed that a dying man sees his entire life flash before his eyes, just before his last breath. 3J wasn't dying, but she had momentarily stopped taking any breaths. As she started to breathe again, her mental picture of her meetings with Quincy turned to a strong sense that, as a member of the bankruptcy debtor's club, Quincy had committed treason. A high crime and misdemeanor. He had lied to her, to the Judge, to the banks, to the IRS, to the entire bankruptcy system. And he did it without so much as a flutter of the eyelids that protected his bi-colored eyes.

Seeing into Heaven and Earth, my ass! He saw into my thoughts and lied right to my face. All at once, she felt double-crossed and deceived, metaphorically kissed by a bankruptcy Judas.

Seething, 3J hustled down the hallway to Pascale's office. He subscribed neither to the theory that a clean desk was the sign of an organized mind nor that a cluttered desk was the sign of a muddled mind. As he liked to say, it's just a desk, not a path to a Freudian analysis. His desk was stacked with piles of papers, at times so high that the two chairs facing the desk, originally designated for anyone brave enough to meet with Pascale in his office, served as makeshift desk annexes for the storage of additional papers.

When 3J arrived at Pascale's office, she entered, closed the door loudly behind her, removed a stack of files and papers from one of the chairs, dropped them on the floor with a thud, and sat down in what was normally a remarkably comfortable chair, that, in peaceful times, served as an island refuge in an otherwise sea of uncomfortable clutter.

Pascale looked concerned as she dropped his files to the floor, as if she had altered his carefully balanced filing system. She ignored his concern as she sat in the now-cleared chair. She didn't blink and she said nothing. Pascale said nothing. Maybe nothing needed to be said, at least at this stage when they both were still processing First Commercial's filing and the implications of the allegations.

Finally, Pascale pursed his lips, raised his eyebrows, and drew on a quote he had used in the past to minimize the impact of negative news. "To quote Oliver Hardy, 'Well, here's another nice mess you've gotten me into.'"

Normally, 3J would respond and say, "To quote Stan Laurel, 'Here's another nice mess I got you into.'" Pascale would conclude with, "Well, I think that completes our analysis, eh?"

Not this time. 3J was having none of their traditional Laurel and Hardy interchange used to diffuse a difficult situation. She was angry and she wasn't ready for that moment to pass.

3J looked at Pascale, and wagged her pointer finger left and right as she tersely said, "Not this time, Pascale. This is too serious."

She was about to vent at a high decibel and Pascale was about to catch her ire. He waited for the 3J eruption and it began almost immediately. "Quincy fuckin' Witherman just got caught in a long-standing commission of a felony. All of our hard work just got flushed down the god damn porcelain commode. He obviously gives a shit about no one but himself, because surely he knows we're going to get flushed as well! What the hell did he think was going to happen?" As she ranted, she stood and jammed her hands into the pockets of her suit jacket, almost ripping them from the coat.

She stopped to catch her breath. Rather than lowering her blood pressure, as a visit to Pascale's office typically did, 3J's blood pressure seemed to be on a steady upward trajectory, and as she started to be able to hear her heart beating in her ears, she realized that she had been ranting and decided to sit down and take control of her anger. She sat back in the chair, kicked off her high heels, and folded her legs under her body as she stared out of Pascale's window into the heart of Kansas City's downtown.

After a few moments, 3J said, "I'm having several reactions to this. On a personal level, if this is true, Witherman lied to us, repeatedly. How many damn times did I tell him that everything we said and filed had to be true and correct? How many freakin' times, dammit? I knew from the start that he held something important back. I knew it! On a case level, we've gone from the peaceful breeze of confirmation to the galestorm of Defcon 5. The Judge, the banks, everyone is going to freak. On a professional level, if this is true, I'm just embarrassed."

Pascale had seen 3J explode before. Emotion and passion in a lawyer were good traits to have, although it was always best to let this level of emotion play out behind closed doors. So he let her rant run its course, added a few seconds of silence to the end of her comments, and then said, "Here's what I think, 3J. Clients lie to lawyers. We hope it's a rare occasion, and I believe it is, but they do lie, and we both know that. Old Quincy has bigger problems than us – he lied to the *Judge*. On a case level, freakin' Defcon 5 it is, indeed. On a professional level, it is what it is, but there's nothing for us to be embarrassed about. Judge Robertson will know this isn't our doing. Some judges imprint the lawyers with the misdeeds of their clients but Robertson won't. I suspect that our favorite real estate developer is going to end up in a federal prison somewhere. I mean, I want to wait to hear his story, but my gut tells me his story won't much matter. He's been at this asset-hiding deception for years. In a word, he's fucked."

3J felt drained as her brain took its usual involuntary steps to calm her down. As she came down, she absent-mindedly rubbed her forehead and her right temple with her thumb, pointer and middle finger, said softly as if she had not heard Pascale's comments about prison, "Pascale, the bank is accusing Quincy of a crime. It doesn't say that in the motion, but we both know the Bankruptcy Crimes Act, and the conduct described in the motion is a felony. We're going to have to get Quincy in here and get our criminal law partner, David Atwell, to dive in, if he has the time."

"Agreed. Let's set up a meeting first thing in the morning if Atwell and Quincy can make it."

"I can do that, Pascale. Any other words of wisdom?" 3J asked.

"'Fraid not, 3J. This is just a hot mess, so no real words of wisdom," Pascale confessed. "Just another one of those bankruptcy case 'it-is-what-it-is' moments."

As she rose to leave Pascale's office, she said dejectedly, "Yeah. On this one, I'm not there yet. It ain't what it is, Pascale. It's Quincy Witherman, and the jig is up for him."

On returning to her office, she emailed the motion to Quincy and asked him if he could be at a meeting first thing in the morning. As she wrote the short, curt message, 3J felt her anger bubbling up to the surface again and she wanted to *order* him to be at her office in the morning. But he was still the client, so she asked rather than directed. She then reached out to David Atwell, who said he had time to work on the matter and could attend the meeting. 3J and Atwell talked to bring him up to speed for the morning. She didn't envy his role, but she could tell already the Witherman file was about to change from a bankruptcy matter to a criminal defense case.

CHAPTER 42

Thursday, January 24, 2019

PROMPTLY AT 8:15 A.M., Quincy arrived at the Greene
Madison offices. The receptionist took him to Conference
Room 27A to await his legal team's arrival, including his new
criminal attorney, David Atwell. Within moments, 3J, Pascale,
and Atwell entered the room and sat down across from Quincy,
who sat at the table with his hands clasped together loosely on
the tabletop. Quincy brought no papers to the meeting. Atwell
introduced himself and handed Quincy his card.

Atwell looked middle-aged, trustworthy, and distinguished.
Criminal juries liked that. He was Yale-educated, and well-
respected in the criminal defense lawyer community. Quincy sat
in silence as he waited for one of the attorneys to break the ice.

3J spoke first. "Have you had a chance to read the motion
I emailed to you yesterday afternoon, Quince?"

"Yes."

"Thoughts?"

"Such as?" Quincy asked.

3J was instantly irritated by Quincy's question and blurted
out forcefully, "Thoughts such as, '3J, it's all bullshit,' or, '3J,
those are doctored email attachments,' or, '3J, I haven't been
truthful with you,' or, '3J, I'm sorry I let you down.'"

"I don't have any of those thoughts."

3J glared at Quincy, who made eye contact – her hazel eyes piercing through his blue eye and brown eye; his ghost eyes devoid of emotion. If he was gazing into both Heaven and Earth, she couldn't tell. He gazed back at her, but without any apparent expression and without any access to Heaven. His eyes looked empty and dull as if he was gazing into Hell.

Pascale jumped in and said, "Quince, this is Greene Madison's lead criminal attorney, David Atwell. We three believe you'll need to get criminal law advice. 3J and I aren't competent to give you that kind of advice. You don't have to use Greene Madison, but if you decide to, we think David is the person to help you. He has expertise in white-collar and bank-related criminal matters and has handled several bankruptcy crime defenses over his career. Do you appreciate why we're recommending criminal counsel to assist and advise you?"

"Yes."

"Good. Then I think the thing to do is let David take the lead in this discussion, if that's ok with you."

"Sure."

Atwell had been watching Quincy during his exchange with 3J and Pascale – if one could call Quincy's one-word non-answers an exchange. Atwell had seen this type of conduct before from clients at the beginning of their first brush with criminal law. They didn't know what to say, so they said as little as possible. At this stage, they were usually full bore into the "anything you say can and will be used against you in a court of law" mode. Atwell decided to ignore the uncomfortable one-word atmosphere Quincy had created, and just dive in.

"Quincy, it's a felony under federal law to fail to disclose all of your assets on the bankruptcy papers filed to commence your bankruptcy case. Likewise, it's a felony to testify falsely in court and a felony when you fail to disclose assets to your lenders on financial statements you submit to them. The Bankruptcy

Court isn't a criminal court, but if the allegations contained in the First Commercial motion are true, they could very well lead the Government to bring felony criminal charges against you. Do you understand so far, and do you have any questions?"

"Understood, and no questions."

"Very well. Here's the immediate problem. In all proceedings, criminal and civil, you have the right against self-incrimination. Meaning, when called upon to testify, you would respond to questions by saying that you decline to answer based on your Fifth Amendment right against self-incrimination. In a civil proceeding, when you do so, no one can make you answer the questions, but the Judge is permitted to, and undoubtedly will, draw an inference that you admitted whatever the question asked. So, if the question asks 'is the sky blue?' and if you invoke the Fifth Amendment, the Judge will determine you've admitted the sky is blue. If the question asks, 'isn't it true that you have a secret account at FSBG?' and you invoke the Fifth Amendment, the Judge will conclude that you have a secret account at FSBG."

"I understand."

"Very well. A criminal prosecutor couldn't use your decision to invoke the Fifth Amendment in the bankruptcy cases to show you admitted anything. In a criminal proceeding, the Government would have to prove its charges against you beyond a reasonable doubt. But if you waive the Fifth Amendment privilege in any testimony you give in bankruptcy, whether in court, a deposition, or an affidavit, you can't go back to asserting it in a criminal case, and you must then answer any questions on the topic for which you waived the privilege."

"So, if you advise me not to answer questions in the bankruptcy case and I assert the Fifth Amendment, how could we effectively respond to the motion?" Quincy asked.

"Let me preface my answer to that question with some questions. Do you have any reason to believe that the email attached to the motion is not genuine?"

"No reason."

"Did you instruct Michaela Huld to send that communication to the FSBG bank officer as the email states?"

"I believe so."

"At or near the time of the date of email?"

"I believe so."

"Do you own an interest in any other assets besides the FSBG account that you failed to disclose to banks, to the IRS, or in your bankruptcy papers?"

Quincy sat on the question for a moment.

Quincy's silence made 3J and Pascale increasingly uncomfortable. As the seconds ticked off, their feeling grew into distress. Quincy then looked down to his folded hands on the conference table, looked up, made eye contact with Atwell, and replied softly, "Yes."

Pascale just stared at him. 3J felt her chin twitch to the right ever so slightly as her forehead titled to the left. She felt that anger welling up inside of her again.

"What are those assets, Quincy?" Atwell quizzed.

"Cryptocurrency held in a dark web crypto wallet. Not traceable, at least not at this time."

"Value?" Atwell probed.

"Crypto fluctuates wildly at times; my best guess of the current value is about $3 million," Quincy responded.

"Does Michaela Huld have anything to do with the crypto?"

"No."

"Who knows about the crypto?"

"Michaela and me. And, I suppose, the crypto wallet company."

"Any other hidden assets?"

"No."

The three lawyers in the room said nothing. Quincy said nothing. Just silence, which seemed to drag on for minutes, though it was only seconds. Quincy gave the impression that he had nothing more to say, and 3J broke the silence, stared at him and said, with more than just a hint of unhappiness, "Look, Quince. I appreciate how hard this must be for you to share with us, but you're clipping your answers, and I'm left wondering if we're asking *all* of the right questions. I'm not sure we are. You know everything, and we only know the answers you give us to the questions we can think of to pose, but we need to know everything. It would be better to just explain this in as complete a fashion as you can, leaving nothing out." 3J paused, and then added, with annoyance bubbling out, "'Cause I gotta tell you, the one-word answers aren't doing it for me at this point."

Quincy didn't respond immediately. 3J assumed that his silence was his way of saying he had no intention of giving complete, narrative answers. She continued, "You know, a wise elder partner here at the firm once told me that there are times when a lawyer shouldn't work harder at solving a client's problem than the client is willing to work. We're here to try to help. And Lord knows, all of a sudden you need lots of help, but we can't make you take the help. If you want the help, great. If you don't, we can end the meeting, and all get back to other business."

Quincy scanned each of the lawyers' somber faces, decided to dispense with his one-word answer methodology, and broke the silence. "Look, folks," he said. "The money in the account is an inheritance. Traceable back to Gunnie Witherman in the 1800s. Another reason I'm so interested in the Witherman clan history, I suppose. The money has always been held in a Swiss account since Gunnie died. When my parents died, it passed to me. To my knowledge, it's never been reported

by any Witherman, and since it's been in Switzerland for so
many years, there's really no way that the banks could know
about it. At least until now." He took a slow drink of water, his
hands completely steady. "Many years ago, when my companies began to borrow significant money from lenders all over
the world, I had to fill out financial statements periodically. I
didn't guarantee the bank debt in those days, but the banks
still wanted my personal financial statements. I never listed
the FSBG account. Back then, I didn't own the crypto. Each
time I omitted the account from my financial statements, I
committed a felony. I knew that." 3J exhaled audibly through
her taut lips which Quincy ignored. "At first, I rationalized that
it wasn't much of a felony, because I didn't guarantee the bank
debt. But later, as new banks came on the lending scene and
demanded a guarantee from me, I could no longer rationalize
my conduct. Still, on the other hand, I had no motivation to
alter my behavior either. Banks killed Gunnther Witherman.
My view was that they already took a Witherman life and
that was all they were going to get from the Withermans. In
the beginning, I was nervous about what I failed to disclose.
But over time, I became calm, almost fatalistic about it." He
paused for another drink of water, then continued: "Later
on, I acquired the crypto and took the same approach – no
disclosure."

Quincy stopped to gather himself. The lawyers focused on
his every word. He continued, "When the row began with First
Commercial, my choices, if you want to call them that, were
first, I could let the banks take down my little empire. Second,
I could pay the banks with the money in the FSBG account
even though I well knew the account wouldn't satisfy Stacy
Milnes' desire for payment in full of $520 million. Or third, I
could file for bankruptcy protection. What I wasn't going to
do was just let Stacy God-Damn-Milnes just have my build-

ings," Quincy said with his voice rising in volume. Lowering his voice again, he continued, "So, I chose bankruptcy. In my estimation, it was the only rational decision to make. Then, I had to decide if I would list the FSBG account and the crypto on my bankruptcy papers. If I did, true, I'd avoid the commission of a bankruptcy crime. But also true, the disclosure would admit I had repeatedly committed a felony over the years in the omission of the account on financial statements submitted to banks, not to mention the problem I created when I failed to disclose the assets on my tax returns."

Again he paused. During the silence, the lawyers continued to observe his demeanor as he revealed his thought process. What they saw was a poised, articulate man, who, except when mentioning Stacy Milnes, made an emotionless report to them, of a carefully planned course of dealing over a long period of time with which he appeared to be comfortable, relaxed, and almost at peace. Quincy wasn't offering an excuse. He was just telling his story. Still hearing no comments or questions from his lawyers, Quincy continued, "I didn't think I had any choice when it came time to sign the bankruptcy papers. What's the difference, whether I committed ten felonies over ten years when I submitted ten false financial statements to the banks, or eleven when I signed false bankruptcy papers, or twelve when I offered false testimony in court? It wasn't multiple lies; it was one lie repeated over and over. That's all. And 'lie' may be the wrong word. I left stuff out. What I said was the truth; just not the whole truth."

In this explanation, the lawyers now heard a cold, calculated, almost mathematical rationalization for the commission of a series of felonies for years. 3J was surprised by the lack of emotion in Quincy's explanation and rationalization. He seemed to try to draw a distinction between a misstatement and the omission of critical information. The lawyers didn't buy it.

There was no distinction. Not in the law. Not in the Greene Madison offices. And not in the Daniel Robertson courtroom.

3J had heard enough and at the moment, she needed no more personal time with Quincy. Her disappointment was exceeded only by her feeling that she knew all along something was up with Quincy Witherman. Pascale sighed audibly and deeply. "What about Huld?"

"Michaela is my financial advisor and has been for years. She also has a power of attorney from me to manage my assets, including the FSBG account. As I said, the FSBG account has its inception in a trust established by a dying Gunnie Witherman in the 1800s. The original trustee was Francis Marion Roston, Michaela's great-great-grandfather."

3J had been looking down at her yellow pad during Quincy's explanations but looked up abruptly when Quincy revealed the connection between Huld's and Quincy's ancestors. She was surprised. *My Lord, what are the odds?* But she decided that nothing at this point should surprise her, especially given Quincy's obsession with history in general, and his family's history in particular.

Pascale brought 3J's focus back to the conversation. "Where is Huld?"

"She lives in London."

"Does she know about these developments?"

"Not yet."

"We need to be careful about how we communicate this to her."

"We always use burner phones."

"Really?" 3J exclaimed. "Why?"

"Can't be too careful?" Quincy responded with raised eyebrows, a slight head tilt, and a small smile as the inflection in his voice framed his answer as a question. It came off as insincere and shifty.

To 3J, the use of the burner phones was evidence that Quincy had planned for the day when his hidden assets would come to light. She wondered if there was more to the plan.

"What would you guess is the value of the FSBG account right now?" Atwell asked.

"$25 million, more or less. Probably a bit more."

Atwell thought for a minute. "Quincy, how do you think the bank got the email?"

"You know, David, I thought about that all night," Quincy said, shaking his head. "I truly have no idea. Michaela and I are pretty careful. More than pretty careful: very careful. We use VPNs as a matter of course. Someone must have hacked into Michaela's records in some manner. Is there any way to find out?"

"There may be," Atwell acknowledged. "Maybe our best bet here is to keep the Fifth Amendment intact and to challenge the email attachment. Hearsay, authenticity, and also challenge the methodology used to acquire the documents. That would require a deposition of someone at First Commercial."

"Not someone. Stacy Milnes," 3J said. "She's the bank officer, and if anyone has the stones to orchestrate a hack, she'd be the one."

Pascale rubbed his chin unconsciously and asked, "Quince, at O'Brien's, you told us about your uncle who provided your passage into the real estate business. Is there any more to that story?"

"He had nothing to do with the FSBG account. Uncle was in Philadelphia and built commercial properties, although not high-rises. At some point, his bank group made a demand on him to repay some $50 million based on a bullshit default. It was so very stressful for him. Ultimately, he worked out a deal with the banks, but it meant he had to liquidate a bunch of properties, and he couldn't borrow from those banks anymore. He needed to find different banks to supply him with construction capital. It unquestionably adversely affected his health, and he keeled over at his desk and died one day from a massive heart attack. I'm the one who found him face down at his desk. I called 911. I tried to revive him before the medical team arrived, and neither I nor the medical team could bring him back. The doctors said it was a congenital heart defect; I said the real defect was the business he did with the banks. Another Witherman death at the hands of the financial bloodsuckers.

"I took over the company, and I had great difficulty in finding any bank willing to loan me money to keep the company going. I was young, and it was at that point that I formed my lasting view of lenders, I suppose, and it was at that point that I decided not to report the FSBG account to – well, to anyone. The rest is history."

Pascale nodded his head, not in agreement, but to signify he understood. "Alright, I think that's all we can accomplish at this meeting. Quince, talk to no one about this. Do you understand me? *No one.*"

"I understand you, but I need to tell Michaela. I just have to, counselor. Sorry. What I know, she knows. Burner phones."

"Burner phones are fine to leave no trail of the call, but that won't protect Michaela if she's called upon to testify," Pascale admonished.

Quincy said softly, "Pascale, I have to tell her. Keeping Michaela in the dark isn't an option." He paused then added, "She means too much to me."

Pascale raised his eyebrows, widened his eyes, and bit his upper lip. *You've been advised.* But he said nothing aloud; Quincy knew what he meant.

And with that, the meeting ended. Quincy rose, shook Atwell's hand, told the three attorneys he was comfortable

330 | MARK SHAIKEN

with Atwell serving as his criminal counsel, and exited the conference room. 3J and Pascale walked Quincy out to the elevators and said nothing. When an elevator arrived, 3J said, "We'll be in touch."

Quincy nodded and entered the elevator cab without saying anything else.

3J and Pascale returned to the conference room, and the three tried to formulate their opposition. In light of Quincy's comments, the three attorneys decided to challenge the evidence that served as the basis for the motion. As attorneys, there was little more they could do; they had a tight-wire to navigate, as their client's answers left them scant wiggle room to deny things they knew were true.

Based on the revelation of the hidden cryptocurrency and the FSBG account, Atwell recommended that they formally advise Quincy to assert his Fifth Amendment privilege against self-incrimination and refrain from answering questions, certainly at the deposition they expected First Commercial to take of Quincy, and also at the bankruptcy hearing. 3J and Pascale had no choice but to agree. It was sound advice. Sound, yet painful for the bankruptcy team. The assertion of the Fifth Amendment would likely doom any bankruptcy defense they could conjure up, but 3J and Pascale knew they had to at least try to come up with something to say in response to the First Commercial motion. So far, all they had in their bag of tricks was to demand that the bank prove the allegations with admissible evidence. In other words, without necessarily denying the allegations, the team would demand that the bank "prove it." In bankruptcy, that meant the bank would have to prove the allegations were more likely than not true. No "beyond a reasonable doubt proof" requirements in bankruptcy court.

But with the assertion of the Fifth Amendment on the horizon, even a defense of "prove it" would be toothless and would be brushed aside by competent bankruptcy counsel. And they knew that Jacob Steinert certainly was more than just competent.

Atwell returned to his office, and 3J followed Pascale back to his office. 3J took her place in that same cozy chair she cleared and just sat there, thinking over what she had learned. As she rewound in her mind the discussion with Quincy, she shook her head slowly for each fact Quincy revealed, simultaneously reflecting disbelief and recognition that all along, she had a concern about whether Quincy had been truthful. A concern she probed with Quincy, that she conveyed to Pascale, and about which, in the end, she could do nothing.

This was not 3J's "I told you so" moment. It was merely another example in her career that the stress of owing money can do strange and unpredictable things to debtors.

Pascale silently watched 3J try to process all of this. Finally, he had seen enough and said, "3J, the good Lord giveth and taketh away. You and me just got the shit taken away from us, although it was certainly not the good Lord who did so. Just Quincy G. Witherman. I'm thinking that we may need to move this one from the W column to the outcome-pending column briefly and then, pretty darn quickly, it moves to the L column. 'Cause, that's where this one's heading. Right?"

3J looked up at him, stretched her neck from side to side, and said, "Right. What you're saying is that we're fucked. I get that. I'm just so deeply disappointed in Quincy Witherman. He's gonna go to jail over this. The sins of the past revisited over and over. The man's obsession with history and his use of it to justify his decisions made in the present – geez. It'll bring him down. He told us that you need to know where you've been to appreciate where you're going. But he never fully told us where he'd been and now he's going nowhere good, and real fast. I thought he was smart. Turns out, he's a damn fool."

Pascale listened patiently. "He's certainly a fool and he may very well go to jail. Or he and Atwell may come up with some kind of defense or plea bargain. First offense and all. But Quincy's life of borrowing money to build magnificent buildings may be drawing to a close. He may not drop dead at his desk like his uncle, and he won't end up in a debtors' prison like his ancestor, but he won't be in the real estate business for long either. Another Witherman real estate tycoon who'll go down in flames. Once he crashes, I don't see him rising from the ashes and he certainly won't need to decide whether to build the next edifice in Salt Lake or Minneapolis so soon. No penthouse office overlooking the Rocky Mountains. That's for sure."

3J inhaled deeply and let the breath hiss out slowly between her clenched teeth. "Alright. No more anger, no more outrage, and enough of me feeling sorry for myself … and of course, for Quincy. Back to work, as that's all I can think of to do at this point. We have some work to do. I can go ahead and draft a response to the motion. I suppose to add insult to injury, we should expect a chambers conference with Judge Robertson on this one. That'll be uncomfortable."

"Yes, to conference. Yes, to uncomfortable. I'll get a notice of deposition out to Mr. Steinert to depose Ms. Milnes. That should be fun."

"Yep. As much fun as a molar extraction without novocain."

When 3J returned to her desk, she had a voice mail from Judge Robertson's administrative assistant asking if 3J's schedule would permit a chambers conference on January 30. The message didn't ask if 3J *wanted* to attend such a conference. *Oh well*, 3J thought as she sighed, *a girl can dream.* She looked at the calendar to confirm what she already knew: she could attend. She called Judge Robertson's admin to confirm. The admin told her that the Judge would like the response to First

Commercial's motion filed before the chambers conference if at all possible, and 3J said she could. The admin told her Judge Robertson would like to know if Mr. Witherman would also attend. "Please let the Judge know it will just be Mr. Pascale and me, if that is ok." *It'll be uncomfortable enough, without having Quincy at the conference. At least the Judge didn't order Quincy to appear.*

CHAPTER 43

The Debtor recalls Thursday, January 24, 2019

As soon as I returned to my apartment, I called Michaela on my burner phone; a call full of tension and worry. Early on in our relationship, we both suspected such a call might come one day. Back then, we thought we were living on borrowed time. But as the years passed and no one discovered the FSBG account or the crypto, our attitude changed from one of living in the moment to one of thinking about the future. Turns out, continuing to live in the moment would have been better for us, now that the situation called into doubt the prospect of any meaningful future.

Neither of us shed tears. Neither of us expressed remorse. Maybe we should have. I read Michaela the motion, and she said nothing. I asked about the email, and she said it was real. She wondered if the bank knew about the crypto; it was unlikely.

At one point in the call, I found myself in the middle of a disjointed, philosophical soliloquy. It went like this: "I live in an 'us and them' world and I hate it. I'm obsessed with it. I file bankruptcy, and they contest. I can't pay them back, and they want to force me to. I pay them, and they want more. They want to know my assets for future reference, and I don't want to tell them. I hate them, but I need them. They despise me, but their success depends on me. And now, they have me, and I'll end up paying with money and freedom. I'll be the second Witherman to end up broke and in jail."

I'm sure it was too much for Michaela to process. She said, "Quincy, history brought us together. But will it pull us apart? We can't let it."

"I can't undo what I've done, Michaela, any more than old Gunn could."

Michaela let that sink in and said nothing.

"Michaela, I'm so sorry you're involved in this. So sorry." Still no tears and no remorse for what I had done.

"Quincy, how does this end?" Michaela asked.

"It just ends. The curtain goes down. They win. It was a good run, but there's always a finish line, and I'm about to cross mine right into the waiting arms of no future and nothing good."

As Michaela listened, I was sure her mind raced, and her blood pressure rose. "Quincy, once when we were sitting in front of the fireplace in our bed and breakfast room, you joked that you would need to make sure you had your escape plan ready to hatch if you ever got caught."

"Yes, I remember the discussion."

"Do you have an escape plan?"

"You mean, do I have a way to run and avoid all of these unpleasantries? Sorta yes, and sorta no."

"Tell me about the sorta yes part."

"I have a way to leave the country if I have to. I have a vague idea of where to go. I have no idea how you fit into the plan, if at all, and I have no idea what comes after I run. I have no belief that the Feds would just let me go, and these days, they can and would find me, I'm afraid. I can't begin to understand how a failed plan to run would affect my sentencing, but I'm sure it would eliminate minimum security prisons and first-time-offender sentences." I paused and then continued, "Truth is, Michaela, I have the account, and I have the crypto, but I've never used them – just counted on them for my rainy day. Knowing they were there made me feel good. That's what I'll lose – the right to feel good. Though maybe it's not a right, after all. Now it's starting to rain on me but the account may not be there to protect me. All I know is I'm going down without reaping the benefits of the money Gunnie Witherman set aside for my ancestors and me."

Michaela said nothing. What could she say? What could anyone say?

We finished the call, just listening to each other breathe on the line. In. Out. In. Out. Not a bad way at all to finish a call with Michaela. And it had a soothing effect on me. I needed that. When the call ended, I had no music for my turntable. Nothing in my collection would be able to capture this moment, and no amount of jazz would be able to help me focus my way through the unfolding events. Music would not be my partner on this one and could offer no more insight into my inner workings. For the first time, I was on my own in silence.

CHAPTER 44

HICKMAN AND ANDREWS AGREED to a Friday lunch at R.J.'s Barbecue Shack on Johnson Drive in Mission, Kansas, about twenty minutes south of downtown Kansas City.

Before the lunch, Hickman had a moment to read First Commercial's *Motion to Set Aside the Confirmation Order and Discharge* that Martin Andrews had emailed to him. He found it a fascinating read. Typically, when he worked on a SAR, there were significant amounts of investigative work the FBI needed to do to fill in blanks before he could begin to decide if he had enough information to convene a grand jury and seek an indictment. Financial crimes were usually quite involved and frequently required detailed and lengthy forensic accounting work. With the Witherman course of dealing over an extended period, however, he didn't foresee much leg work in the offing.

Instead, he saw lots of indisputable facts presented in a clear, straightforward fashion. There was clearly an account; Witherman certainly kept it hidden. It had significant value. Witherman plainly didn't report the account to the taxing authorities or his banks. Witherman undeniably failed to disclose the account in his bankruptcy papers. *Felony upon felony upon felony for years upon years,* Hickman thought.

338 | MARK SHAIKEN

It had been a while since he had an easy case to prosecute. *This one will go down quickly.*

R.J.'s wasn't exactly the dimly lit venue they had laughed about on the phone, but it was out-of-the-way, mostly low-keyed at lunchtime, easy to get to, and the food was outstanding.

They met outside the restaurant where patrons and sweet hickory smoke converged. They entered, each ordered, and sat down to await the delivery of the smoky barbecue that made R.J.'s renowned.

As the food arrived, the conversation turned to the business at hand – bankruptcy crimes. Hickman had done some quick background research on Witherman before leaving for lunch. "This guy Witherman's an interesting bloke," he began. "He certainly isn't a characteristically criminal person. No record. Anywhere. Not even a speeding ticket. No brushes with law enforcement in his life at all. And yet, for decades, he seems to've successfully misreported his assets to federally insured banks with impunity. Or should I say, under-reported his assets. It's not surprising that when the banks squeezed him, and he filed for bankruptcy protection, he continued the practice of excluding any mention of the FSBG account in the bankruptcy papers. He must've thought, 'in for a penny, in for a pound.' He had no choice. He couldn't report the account in the bankruptcy papers. If he did, he'd admit to the felony of lying to numerous federally insured banks for years and years. Do you see this any differently?"

"I agree. It's remarkably straightforward," said Andrews. "Now that the bank has filed its motion, Witherman will have to respond. But when Witherman sits down to strategize, he'll have to face up to his right not to testify to avoid self-incrimination under the Fifth Amendment. The way I see this, he'll have no good way around the problem, and he may be very limited in his response options. No self-respecting criminal attorney will let him testify."

"Any idea who'll represent Witherman?" Hickman asked.

"I assume his counsel will be David Atwell at Greene Madison, since the firm represents Witherman and his companies in the bankruptcy cases. Atwell is good."

"Yes he is," Hickman agreed. "A little too silk stocking and attitudinal for my taste, but unquestionably, very good at his trade."

They each paused and turned their attention to the melt-in-the-mouth hickory-smoked brisket smothered in R.J.'s amazing sauce, spicy, smoky, sweet, tangy, and thick, with hints of heat from cayenne pepper and intrigue from paprika and cloves. They also shared orders of baked beans, and BBQ shrimp in wine sauce and barbecue butter. As he savored his dish, Hickman said, "Mmmm. Whoever invented barbecue must be looking down from Heaven above and nodding his approval over the entire Kansas City metropolitan area each day at lunchtime."

Andrews shook his head in agreement and said, "Low and slow, my friend. Cook it low and slow, and this is what you get. And keep that smoker lid down 'cause if you're lookin', it ain't cookin'."

"Here's my barbecue question. How can it be sweet and spicy and tangy and smoky all at the same time?"

"Don't know, but it is. And thank the Lord that it is, right?"

They attended to their food, and the only sound was lip-smacking and chewing. As they neared completion of their lunch, Andrews asked, "What happens next, my friend, with Witherman?"

"I still want to set up a meeting with the banker. What's her name again?"

"Stacy Milnes. She's in St. Louis."

"Get me her lawyer's name so I can work out that meeting."

"Will do. Robert, time for my usual lunch pitch."

"Oh great, here we go."

"You know it. Leave the Justice Department. Join Andrews and Cardison."

"Standard pitch begets my standard answer. I'm honored, and I'm staying. I enjoy what I do."

"Robert, will there ever be a time when I ask and you say 'maybe' or even 'yes'?" Andrews asked.

"Well, I'm touched, and if I ever left the DOJ, it'd be to join your firm. But I'm staying because I'm happy, and since I'm such a self-centered son-of-a-bitch, my happiness is paramount," Hickman said as he smiled.

"Can't fault a guy for trying," Andrews countered.

Hickman smiled. "Pending a meeting with Milnes, can you send me Witherman's bankruptcy filing when it happens? Since I'm not in the bankruptcy cases, I don't get notice of the filings."

"Will do."

They wiped off the sauce from their hands and mouths with the traditional, standard-issue, wet wipes, bussed their trays, and headed out to the parking lot to resume their days. They both inhaled with satisfaction the wisps of sweet hickory smoke that gently engulfed the corner where R.J.'s resided, caressing the air they breathed. The smoke was R.J.'s way of welcoming patrons upon arrival, and shaking the patrons' hands to thank them as they departed. One more deep breath before they entered their cars and headed to I-35 and back to downtown Kansas City.

§

"Quince, this is 3J. Judge Robertson wants to have a chambers conference with the lawyers on January 30. He asked if you were coming, and I said you were not."

"That's fine. I'd prefer not to attend."

"Did you talk with Michaela?"

"Yes."

"Is the email authentic?"

"Yes. She sent it."

"I hope you didn't email Michaela the motion."

"I didn't. I read it to her."

The conversation paused while Quincy thought, and then he asked, "What if I don't go to the hearing?"

"They'll subpoena you to go, so you'll have to. If you don't after you get the subpoena, the Judge will issue a bench warrant and send the U.S. Marshals after you. The bank will also depose you to get you on the record."

"You mean, to document that I took the Fifth."

"Yes. They'll have you under oath on the record invoking the Fifth Amendment. When you refuse to answer, you'll thereby admit the existence of the account, and perhaps the authenticity of the email as well."

"I understand. I probably need to talk to Atwell."

"You do. You or David can let me know if questions arise."

"3J, I'm truly grateful for all you and Pascale have done."

"I know that, Quincy. I know that." And the call ended. 3J noted that Quincy was grateful, but not sorry. Maybe he'd never be sorry. Perhaps sorry wasn't part of his composition.

§

Quincy called David Atwell to discuss and finalize the tactics. As expected, Atwell strongly recommended against Quincy providing any answers at a deposition or the hearing on the motion and admonished him to state for each question that, based on advice of counsel, he invoked his Fifth Amendment right against self-incrimination and declined to answer the question. Quincy listened and told his attorney that he would follow the advice.

"If the bank takes my deposition, and I invoke the Fifth Amendment, does that mean they'll leave Michaela alone?"

Atwell responded, "I can't say for certain, but she's in London, so while they can eventually compel her to appear in London for a deposition, it'll be a time-consuming process and expensive. If you invoke the Fifth Amendment, they should have all they need and, therefore, not pursue her for the time being."

"Assuming the bank hired someone to hack into Michaela's computer or her business' technology, is that a crime?"

"It would be here in the States. My guess is that it would be in Britain as well, but I frankly don't know for sure. I have a criminal law friend in London who I can ask if you'd like."

"Yes, I'd like to know what Milnes was willing to do to have the last word. My assumption has always been that she's a 'whatever-it-takes' banker, the worst kind, but I'd like to know with certainty."

"Ok. Will do. Anything else, Quincy?"

"No. That covers it. At some point, I'd like to have you give me a primer on what to expect from the federal prosecutors if you don't mind. Not today. I'm maxed out. But in the next couple of days if you have time."

"I have time, and I'm happy to talk when you're ready. You pick the time and let me know what works for you."

"Thanks, David."

§

Atwell called his barrister contact in London, explained the situation, and asked if a hack into Michaela Huld's computer was a crime in Britain. The answer was straightforward: Yes. Britain's Computer Misuse Act was enacted in 1990, under which unauthorized access to a computer was a crime. Atwell called Quincy back and left him a voicemail explaining British law. He also called 3J and suggested that Pascale should question Milnes at her deposition about her role in the commission of the crime in Britain. 3J agreed.

§

3J and Pascale completed their draft response to the *Motion to Set Aside Confirmation Order and Discharge*. Without necessarily denying the pertinent allegations directly, the response "held the Bank to strict proof," and called into question the methodology the bank used to obtain the Huld email. In particular, in the response, they asserted that it was a crime in both the United States and Britain for anyone to hack into a computer, arguing that if the bank hacked or commissioned a hack, none of the evidence gathered from that hack should be used in a bankruptcy hearing. They had little faith in the defenses they raised, but it was all they had to offer to try to avoid the consequences of the allegations contained in the motion.

They filed the response and prepared for the conference with Judge Robertson.

CHAPTER 45

Monday, January 28, 2019

As the bank group's new agent, Brian Chimes set up a short-notice bank group meeting to discuss First Commercial's motion. He debated whether to separately call Stacy Milnes to tell her that her attendance was mandatory. Still, he knew full well that he had no power to compel her attendance, and he also had no patience to be alone on a call with Milnes at this point. *It would be just fine if I never talk to Milnes again.*

Instead, he emailed her the video conference invite and set up the email so he would know that she received and opened it. Moments later, Milnes received it, opened it, and accepted the invite, surprising Chimes; he didn't yet fully appreciate the extent to which Milnes believed with conviction that she had done nothing wrong, and even expected a thank you.

At the appointed time, the bank group members logged on to the video conference, and both Milnes and Jacob Steinert joined. Chimes said to all present, "By now, we've all read the *Motion to Set Aside Confirmation and Discharge*, and we have a few comments to deliver to First Commercial as a member of the bank group. First, we understand that First Commercial filed this as a solo mission. First Commercial is still a member of the bank group, however, and Stacy, I remind you, your new lawyer, and your bank that you still have duties to the bank group. You violate those duties, and there will be hell to pay. I'm deadly serious when I say that." Milnes said nothing but stared back stony-faced. "Second, you've gone after only Quincy Witherman. But he still guarantees a significant portion of the bank group debt, and he still owns the holding company which owns the building companies, and he still owns the management company that runs the buildings on a day-to-day basis. If any of your actions endanger the continued operation of the buildings and in any way places at risk the payment of all of our respective debts each month, and I mean in *any* way, you'll have us to answer to, and you won't like it. Last, since you have no problem dispensing with the niceties of human interactions, let me personally tell you how hard it is to talk to you in a civil tone right now."

Milnes responded, visibly struggling to control her tone, "I did what I had to do once I had the information proving what I've been telling all of you good folks from the beginning. You oughta be thanking me, but I know that *this* group won't. That's really all I have to say to any of you."

Stephanie Bonde asked, "How did you get the email? Is there other information you have in your possession?"

"Not any of your business, and yes, would be my answers to your questions, Stephanie," Milnes responded, quickly becoming defensive.

"You do realize that the Debtors' lawyers will depose you and are gonna be all over you to get to the bottom of what you did?" Chimes asked.

"If I get deposed, you can attend the deposition if you'd like, and if they ask those questions, you'll hear my answers," Milnes shot back.

Steinert broke in to prevent his client from saying anything further about what she might and might not say under oath. "Mr. Chimes, we've heard your warnings, and I wrote them down here accurately in my notes. Are there any other issues you wish to tackle on this video conference? If not, can we conclude, please?"

"We're done with you for now," Chimes said. "Why don't you and your client just drop off the conference, and the rest of us can stay on and talk about what we've heard here from your client?"

The banks had a brief discussion about possible management options and then took a few minutes to vent, including the hope that Milnes would eventually have a lengthy and unpleasant stay in Hell. Chimes ended the call by saying, "I don't know how this motion is gonna affect payments under the plan, but I have to believe it's not a positive development, to say the least. We need to be prepared with a contingency plan if this First Commercial tactic succeeds, and we have to figure out another way to run the buildings other than by the Witherman management team."

After the call, Chimes decided to escalate the problem now to his senior management. *Time to have our chairman reach out to First Commercial's chair and discuss Milnes' future in the banking industry.* Stephanie Bonde was in the process of doing the same at her bank. There were some tense conversations on the horizon between First Commerical's senior management and Star-Banc's and Silvermine's presidents.

CHAPTER 46

Wednesday, January 30, 2019

ONCE AGAIN, 3J AND Pascale found themselves seated at Judge Robertson's conference room table along with Jacob Steinert and Dennis Sample. Judge Robertson and Jamie Li entered the small conference room and took their seats.

Judge Robertson said, "I have reviewed the motion and the Witherman response. Thank you, Ms. Jones, for filing the response quickly. Is any discovery contemplated?"

"We want to take Mr. Witherman's deposition, Your Honor," Steinert said. "We don't anticipate it will be a long one. Maybe 2-3 hours at most. Maybe even less. Depending on his responses, we may also need a quick records deposition in New York City."

"Thank you, Mr. Steinert, and welcome to these cases. Am I correct that you represent First Commercial Bank, and not the bank group?"

"That is correct, Your Honor. I believe Mr. Sample now represents StarBanc, the Agent for the bank group."

"That is correct, Your Honor," Sample stated.

"Very well," the Judge said. Then, looking at 3J, "And does Mr. Witherman need discovery?"

"We will depose Ms. Milnes, Your Honor. I am not sure, but that may take longer."

"Very well. Ms. Jones. I am curious to know if your client, Mr. Witherman, will answer questions at the deposition, or will he invoke the Fifth Amendment?" Judge Robertson hadn't thought to ask the same question of the bank's attorney.

"Your Honor, things are moving very quickly at our end as we try to get up to speed on these developments and determine how the bank acquired its alleged evidence. We don't have an answer to Your Honor's question at this point," 3J said. She then took a deep breath. "We will know of course soon, but we don't know as we sit here today."

"That's fine. I just thought I would get an obvious issue out on the table. Can the depositions take place in the next seven days, counsel?"

"I believe we can make that work, Your Honor," 3J said.

Steinert responded. "Your Honor, if we need the New York business records deposition, we'll need more than seven days. If we don't need the extra deposition, seven days works fine."

"Ok, I understand. Let my law clerk know after you complete Mr. Witherman's deposition and we can set the hearing to conform to the discovery timetable. Once we know, the Court will send out a notice of hearing. Anything else on behalf of your clients?"

"Nothing from the bank, Your Honor," Steinert said.

"Nothing on behalf of Mr. Witherman," 3J confirmed.

"Good. See everyone in the very near future," the Judge said.

After the lawyers cleared out of the conference room, Jamie said, "That didn't take very long at all. I thought there would be more fireworks."

Judge Robertson responded, "I don't think either side is lighting the fireworks to go off here in chambers. There may not be any fireworks at all in Witherman's deposition. My best guess is that he'll be instructed not to answer any questions under the Fifth Amendment, and assuming he takes the advice, he'll thereby admit everything – or at least permit me to draw an inference that he admits everything. I am most curious, however, about the Milnes deposition. That one should be fascinating."

"I'm almost done with the memos you asked for, Judge. The research is going pretty well. I haven't run into any roadblocks, so – no questions. Hopefully, the memos address the issues."

"Great, Jamie. I'm sure they will be your usual stellar work product. Drop them by when you finish so we can discuss what you learned."

CHAPTER 47

Friday, February 1, 2019

MARTIN ANDREWS CALLED GABBY Price to discuss the separate representation of Stacy Milnes. Gabby had worked for Andrews at the U.S. Attorney's office, and later for Robert Hickman, before venturing out on her own last year to set up her office, providing white-collar crime legal services. Andrews thought Gabby would be a good fit for Milnes and would provide solid advice. Gabby was hungry for clients and trusted Andrews when he told her the engagement would be intriguing and challenging. He put Milnes and Price together on a call, and Milnes agreed to hire Price to provide advice and represent her in the upcoming deposition and any other matters resulting from her actions in commissioning the hack.

After Milnes dropped off the call, Andrews and Price talked at length to get her up to speed.

"Lots going on here," Price said.

"Indeed, Gabby. Between you and me, your new client Stacy Milnes is sometimes something of a loose cannon. It sounds to me that she decided to cross over the line and commit a crime or two in order to catch a real estate developer who himself had no problem crossing that line. I would bet that when the dust settles on this one, both of them will be in the market for new careers, and at least the developer may be searching for his from prison. Not sure about the deal you might be able to cut for Milnes. Oh, and your former mentor, Mr. Hickman, wants to interview Milnes. You may need to work through with Hickman some kind of trade – information and cooperation for immunity from prosecution – if he's willing."

Gabby responded, "True enough, Martin. Right now, the upcoming deposition and court testimony loom pretty large. Standard advice would be that Milnes should invoke the Fifth Amendment for both and offer no substantive answers to any questions."

"She's your client, Gabby, but I concur with the notion that application of the standard advice is the way to go on this one. Then you'll have to see if Ms. Milnes is inclined to accept your advice. She seems pretty proud of what she did and adamant that her conduct helped the greater good. She's an interesting character."

§

Milnes scheduled a call with Gabby Price to discuss her upcoming deposition.

"Stacy," Price began, "Martin and I have talked, and I'm mostly up to speed. The thing is, it's a crime in both the United States and Britain to hack into another person's computer. You hired this Rome person in London to do just that, and she did. If you're deposed, they'll ask you about it. My guess is that's the sole purpose of the deposition. If you testify about any part of the computer operation, you'll be obligated to testify about the entire operation in all proceedings, civil and criminal. In other words, you'll have waived your right against self-incrimination."

Price continued, "Stacy, I just don't think it would be in your best interest to answer questions under oath. I think you have no choice but to invoke the Fifth Amendment privilege against self-incrimination as well as the British version of the the privilege. That's my strong recommendation."

"What I did was bring down a felon. That's a *good* thing. Is anyone listening to me? I feel like I'm speaking from a sound proof room. People seem to be able to see my mouth moving, but no one is hearing me. Geez. What's my risk if I answer fully?"

"Frankly, Stacy, your risk is prosecution for a crime in either or both of the United States and Britain," Price said as she attempted to be unsparing in her analysis and advice.

Moses had warned her about the risks of hiring Rome, and she had decided to ignore his clear warning about potential dangers in a computer intrusion. *Whatever it takes*, she had decided. Now, she found herself being chased into a corner wearing a Fifth Amendment muzzle over her mouth to fend off incoming prosecutorial fire. She hated the thought that she might have to remain silent and not tell her story. Perhaps that prospect was part of the risk about which Moses had warned her.

She ended the call as she told Price she needed to think about the Fifth Amendment advice. Next, she called Jacob Steinert.

"Jacob, I just got off a call with my new criminal lawyer. If Witherman takes the Fifth and I take the Fifth, what happens at the bankruptcy hearing?"

"I gotta tell ya', Stacy, I have no idea. Do I see debtors in isolated cases assert the Fifth Amendment? Sure. Have I seen a banker do it? I suppose once or twice, years ago. Have I seen both the banker and the debtor assert the Fifth Amendment in the same trial? Absolutely not. Never. I bet neither has Judge Robertson."

Milnes called Martin Andrews, explained Price's advice and asked, "Martin, do you agree that I should invoke the Fifth Amendment?"

Andrews responded, "Gabby's your lawyer on this one, Stacy, but I do. I see no reason to play around at this point with your freedom. Jacob should be able to navigate the motion through the hearing without your testimony."

All the lawyers were in agreement. She sighed, exasperated. "Alright. I understand the advice. I need to think."

§

Milnes sat in her office with the door closed and tried to focus. She had no regrets for the man-in-the-middle attack on Huld's computer that she authorized in London. "Whatever it takes," had worked. Plain and simple. People should thank her. But instead, she felt a growing concern in her gut that maybe she should have given more thought and consideration to the personal consequences of the attack. Just as Moses Aaronson had advised her. *Listen to Moses. Listen to the old man!* She still would have authorized the attack, though. So at this point, all she could do was sigh, try to control her annoyance with the system, and take the advice of her lawyers.

She was amazed that the count was now at three lawyers that it would take to finish the job and nail Witherman. "Three lawyers! And I thought the process wasn't rocket science," she muttered softly to herself.

She sighed again. She saw no choice but to accept their advice and refrain from answering questions at the deposition and the Court hearing. She could only hope that the prosecutorial focus would be on Witherman and not her. Even in her private thoughts, she was completely intransigent in her view. *Witherman, after all, was the real bad guy here.*

§

Following her call with Milnes, Gabby Price called Robert Hickman.

"Robert, this is Gabby Price. How are you?"

"I'm good. How goes the launch of your private, boutique, white-collar practice, my friend?"

"I haven't starved just yet. But this whole business of hustling for clients is a new one for me."

"You'll be great at it, Gabby. I have absolutely no doubt."

"Robert, I'm calling to discuss my new client, Stacy Milnes."

"Martin told me you might take the Milnes case, and I figured if you did, I'd hear from you," Hickman said.

"Here's the thing. You want to talk with my client, but as you might imagine, I have a bit of heartburn, but not because Stacy Milnes doesn't want to cooperate in any investigation and prosecution of Quincy Witherman. Just the opposite. She wants to help. She believes she's helped bring down a bad guy. But, as you may have guessed, she has a couple of her own – I'll call them *issues*, to wrestle with. I don't want her admitting to anything in her talks with you only to then find herself on the wrong end of the Government's prosecution stick."

"Go on."

"Well, when you were in the business of mentoring me, you said that as a prosecutor, you had to keep your eyes on the bigger prize, and if that meant cutting immunity deals to get information, it was just part of the game."

"Gabby, the thing of it is, I'm still unclear who's the bigger prize here. I have a pretty good idea what Milnes did, although I don't know precisely the particulars of how she pulled it off. I think I generally know that she infiltrated a computer to get the goods on Witherman. Joe Blow doing that isn't front page news. A member of the senior management team of a large banking institution – well, that may be a very different story. This is America. We can't have banking officials, senior officers at that, regulated by the U.S. Government, doing these kinds of things. Right, Gabby?"

"I understand, Robert. But we'll need to reach an understanding on this matter before I can, in good conscience, tell Stacy Milnes to sit down with you and talk voluntarily, without asserting her right against self-incrimination. I think that's the right play from our side of the problem. I think when we leave this call, you'll find yourself concurring with my strategy and acknowledging that you taught me this fine point well."

"Alright, Gabby." Hickman chuckled and said, "Damn students of mine. They never let me forget. Thanks for the call, and let me give this a little bit of thought."

"Thanks, Robert," Price said.

CHAPTER 48

Monday, February 4, 2019

QUINCY RAISED HIS RIGHT hand for the court reporter and affirmed to tell the truth, the whole truth and nothing but the truth. *There's that damn middle phrase again*, he thought.

The Andrews and Cardison conference room was crowded. Sitting to his left was David Atwell. To his right were 3J and Pascale. Jacob Steinert, Gabby Price, Martin Andrews, and Dennis Sample sat across the table from him, and the court reporter sat at the head of the table to transcribe everything the witness and the lawyers said.

Pascale and 3J had told Quincy that Steinert would ask the questions. Under questioning from Steinert, Quincy explained who he was, where he lived, how he made a living, and his relationship to the companies in the bankruptcy cases.

With the preliminary questions behind him, Steinert asked, "At the time you filed these bankruptcy cases, you owned an interest in an account maintained at First Switzerland Bank, Geneva?"

"On advice of counsel, I invoke my Fifth Amendment right against self-incrimination and decline to answer that question."

"At the time you filed these bankruptcy cases, your account at FSBG had a value of approximately $25 million, didn't it?"

Quincy declined to answer.

"Isn't it true you have owned your interest in the FSBG account for more than fifteen years?"

Quincy declined to answer.

"Isn't it true you never disclosed your interest in the FSBG account to any lender from whom you or your companies borrowed money over the last fifteen years?"

Quincy declined to answer.

"Isn't it true you never disclosed your interest in the FSBG account to your current group of bank lenders?"

Quincy declined to answer.

"Isn't it true you never disclosed your interest in the FSBG account on any state or federal tax returns you filed over the last fifteen years?

Quincy declined to answer.

"Isn't it true that you failed to disclose your interest in the FSBG account in your Chapter 11 bankruptcy schedules and statements of affairs that you signed under oath and swore the information contained therein was true, complete, and correct?"

Quincy declined to answer.

"Isn't it true that the email, a copy of which I am handing you, that was attached to the bank's *Motion to Set Aside Plan Confirmation and Discharge* is a true and correct copy of an email sent by one Michaela Roston Huld to FSBG?"

Quincy declined to answer.

"Isn't it true that Ms. Huld sent the email you have in front of you in her capacity as your agent and on your behalf?"

Quincy declined to answer.

"Isn't it true that you authorized Ms. Huld to send that email to FSBG?"

Quincy declined to answer.

"Isn't it true that the email is a true and correct copy of a business record, kept and maintained by Ms. Huld in her capacity as owner and chairperson of the company, NOIRAM Advisors in London, England?"

Quincy declined to answer.

"Isn't it true that the email is a true and correct copy of a business record kept and maintained by Sueden, plc, a British company in London, England?"

Quincy declined to answer.

The deposition from start to finish took all of forty-five minutes. And in those forty-five minutes, Steinert created a record from which Judge Robertson could infer the truth of everything that Quincy declined to answer. The entire predicate to support the motion was now in the record books and things boded poorly for Quincy.

3J knew it. Pascale knew it. Atwell knew it. Most importantly, Quincy now knew it. As he himself said, once you do it, you can't undo it. And once you know something, you can't unknow it. The two truisms working hand in hand would spell the beginning of the end of his current life as he had come to know it.

§

At the conclusion of the Witherman deposition, the parties took a short break. When they returned to the conference room, Stacy Milnes entered the conference room and the court reporter swore her in. In response to questions from Pascale, she duplicated Quincy Witherman's performance. She explained who she was and where she worked but declined to answer any other questions.

"You caused someone to hack into the computer owned by Michaela Huld without Ms. Huld's permission?"

She asserted the Fifth Amendment just as Quincy did and declined to answer the question. In addition she asserted the similar rule of evidence in Britain.

"That is how you obtained the email attached to the motion your bank filed in the bankruptcy case?"

Declined to answer.

And so on. No answers, based on the right against self-incrimination on two continents.

§

Hickman turned his thoughts to Milnes. The motion skillfully avoided any discussion of how the bank acquired the Witherman account information, but as he suspected when he talked with Gabby Price, it seemed pretty clear that Milnes hired an operative who violated one law or another to invade someone's computer to gather the damning information.

Hickman decided to attend the bankruptcy hearing and observe the trial of the bank's motion. It would be a prime opportunity to see Witherman in action and get a flavor for any other evidence the bank might present. It would also give him the chance to see Stacy Milnes and start to decide what he should do to further a meeting with her.

He phoned Andrews to confirm the hearing's time and date and said he might wander up from his office to see the matter play out. He wondered if Andrews thought it would be an all-day hearing.

Andrews responded, "Robert, I don't know, but something tells me this is going to be an unusual one. I'm not sure any of the witnesses will offer any factual testimony."

"I can see that. Then I think I'll invest a little time to get the lay of the land," Hickman mused.

CHAPTER 49

Friday, February 8 to Thursday, February 14, 2019

JUDGE ROBERTSON ENTERED THE courtroom, and after the parties introduced themselves for the record, the Court invited Jacob Steinert to begin the bank's presentation. "Your Honor, the Bank calls Quincy Witherman to the stand as an adverse witness."

Present in the courtroom, sitting in the back, was AUSA Robert Hickman. In the courtroom pews near the front of the courtroom sat Gabby Price and her client, Stacy Milnes. Brian Chimes flew to Kansas City that morning for the hearing and sat in the middle area of the courtroom pews next to Dennis Sample.

Quincy approached the courtroom deputy, raised his right hand, and once again swore "to tell the truth, the whole truth, and nothing but the truth, so help me God." This time Quincy felt he might actually need God's help, but he once again knew he was on his own.

Once on the witness stand, Steinert proceeded to ask the same questions he did in the deposition. Once again, on the advice of counsel, Quincy invoked his Fifth Amendment right against self-incrimination, exactly as he had done in the deposition. Based on Witherman's testimony, Steinert offered the email into evidence and 3J stood and objected to the use of the email. Steinert argued that the Court could and should draw an inference from Witherman's testimony that the email was authentic. Steinert further contended that the communication was one made by Witherman's agent, sent with his authority and approval and, therefore, wasn't hearsay.

3J asked Judge Robertson to delay deciding whether to admit the evidence until the hearing's end because she had an argument she wished the Court to consider. Judge Robertson agreed to postpone the evidence decision as requested.

The entire process took twenty minutes. Upon completion, Judge Robertson asked if the Greene Madison team had questions for Quincy, and they declined to examine him. With that, the Judge told Witherman to step down from the witness stand without making eye contact and without thanking him for his testimony. Steinert advised the Court that he had no further witnesses to call to the stand.

Next up, the Greene Madison team called Stacy Milnes to the stand. Like Witherman before her, she swore to tell the truth, but on the stand, she declined to answer questions based on both the Fifth Amendment right against self-incrimination and the similar rule of evidence in Britain. Milnes' examination took even less time, and the Greene Madison team rested. She stepped down from the stand without any prompt from the Judge. The Judge didn't look at her as she left the witness stand either. When Witherman finished invoking the Fifth Amendment, the Judge looked stern. When Milnes finished, the Judge looked perplexed. His body language communicated to everyone in the courtroom that he wasn't happy with either Quincy Witherman or Stacy Milnes. No judge would be.

The courtroom was peppered with criminal lawyers. In addition to Hickman and Price, Martin Andrews, criminal attorney for First Commercial, sat anonymously in the audience and took in the proceedings from that vantage point. David Atwell, criminal counsel for Quincy Witherman, sat next to Pascale at counsel's table and did the same. Judge Robertson knew none of the criminal lawyers. Since they didn't introduce themselves at the beginning of the hearing, the Judge had no idea that criminal lawyers, including a federal prosecutor, made up a significant portion of the population of observers. All of the criminal lawyers watched the unusual hearing unfold with interest, of course, but none of the events that had yet transpired were at all a surprise to any of them.

All told, the parties and the Judge had been in court for less than an hour, and the evidentiary portion of the hearing was over. Judge Robertson asked to hear argument from 3J first on the issue of the admissibility of the email. She rose and addressed the Court. As was her custom, she spoke from no prepared notes, just an outline. She had to work much harder this time, however, to maintain eye contact with Judge Robertson. This wasn't the first day of a new bankruptcy case and the Judge was visibly more uncomfortable with the proceedings.

"Your Honor, when a witness invokes the privilege against self-incrimination in a civil case like this, the trier of fact – you, Your Honor – can draw an inference the witness admitted the matters about which she declined to testify. Here, that means that the email offered into evidence by Mr. Steinert was obtained through the commission of a serious crime by a bank officer. A crime, I might add, both here in the United States and in Britain."

Judge Robertson surveyed the courtroom, wondering who all the observers were sitting in his pews. 3J saw the Judge look away from her, and knew that was always a bad sign. There was nothing she could do about it and she knew it. All an attorney could do was to play the hand dealt to her by her client. She continued, "The Court should not sanction that kind of behavior by a bank – and its senior officer, no less – by admitting the email into evidence. We just can't have federally regulated bankers committing felonies. If you let the email into evidence, you will only be rewarding the commission of a serious crime."

Judge Robertson returned to looking directly at 3J, and broke in: "But, counselor, if I don't let the email into evidence, your client will keep his discharge even after he lied to this Court and on his bankruptcy filings. So if I don't let it in, won't I be sanctioning conduct that the bankruptcy system in the United States takes great pains to prohibit?" He did not pose the question with anger. Rather, his tone was conciliatory, sympathetic to her plight, almost apologetic, and the question was rhetorical, not designed to engender any dialogue. Before 3J could formulate a response, the Judge looked away and said, "Ok. Let me hear from Mr. Steinert, now, please."

She took her notepad and returned to her seat as Jacob Steinert rose to address the Court. Steinert and 3J passed each other without making eye contact. As she took her seat, 3J watched the Judge. She made no eye contact with either Quincy or Pascale. She sighed deeply at counsel's table and Quincy heard her exhale. He said nothing.

As Steinert reached the podium, Judge Robertson began by saying: "To pick up where I left off with Ms. Jones, Mr. Steinert, I want you and Ms. Milnes to know in no uncertain terms that I am frankly shocked that a senior bank officer would somehow feel it was acceptable conduct to violate the law in not one but two countries."

Steinert expected the question and responded with his practiced response, "Your Honor, as you are aware, I represent the bank, not Ms. Milnes. As is evident, these are unique circumstances that are before the Court today. The Court's comment delves into a criminal law matter, and I am far from a criminal law expert. Nor, with all due respect, Your Honor, is this a court of criminal law. We think the Court should simply decide the civil evidentiary matter presented by the testimony. In doing so, the email is most certainly admissible into evidence. Mr. Witherman admitted that his agent wrote the email. Mr. Witherman admitted he authorized the transmission of the email and the message contained therein. Therefore, the email isn't hearsay. Mr. Witherman admitted the email is genuine. So, there are no authentication issues.

"Your Honor, the email is absolutely admissible. Upon admitting it into evidence, the Bank has proven that Mr. Witherman lied on his bankruptcy filing papers and to this Court in testimony given to support confirmation of his plan and his discharge. That lie does not encompass an insignificant asset. Rather, based on the implicit admission made by Mr. Witherman when he asserted his Fifth Amendment privilege, the asset is worth $25 million. As such, the Court must set aside the order confirming the plan, and upon doing so, the Bankruptcy Code mandates that the Court must revoke Mr. Witherman's discharge."

Judge Robertson gazed at both lawyers. 3J saw in the Judge's eyes that he harbored a melting pot sense of discouragement, frustration, anger, resignation, and even bemusement – all of the witnesses in his courtroom just showed a justified concern that they had committed serious crimes, with one witness potentially committing crimes on two continents.

He prided himself on his rule that he would never reprimand attorneys for their clients' sometimes remarkably foolish actions. Usually, it was an easy rule to employ. In this case, however, he found himself irritated with the situation and almost everyone in the courtroom – Milnes, Witherman, and their respective lawyers. But instead of displaying any ire, he said, "The Court will take a forty-five-minute recess, after which I will come back into the courtroom and give you my ruling."

He and Jamie left the courtroom and headed for his office. The law clerk took up his usual position in the club chair, and Judge Robertson sat down behind his desk. They sat in silence as Jamie waited for the Judge to start to disclose his thought process.

§

Quincy, Atwell, 3J, and Pascale left the courtroom and met in a small room just beyond the courtroom's doors. Quincy said behind closed doors, looking at 3J, "The Judge seemed more upset with the bank than with me."

She showed no interest in responding. No one said anything for a moment and then Pascale said, "I wouldn't bet on that." Another pause, and Pascale continued. "Always watch the eyes. He was pretty exacerbated with you. How could he not be? It's *you* that has taken up residence in his Court, so to speak, and sought protection, which he afforded to you. Plenty of cause in this one to be fed up with both sides. But make no mistake: He's focused on you."

"So, does that mean we have *any* chance?"

For the first time in an hour, 3J looked squarely at Quincy and said flat and emotionless, "Negative. Not a chance. This doesn't end well at all. He's going to process his ire and come out and rule against you. If he says anything about the bank, it'll be editorial comment. It's called *dicta*. It won't matter."

Quincy understood the prediction, even as he showed dismay for being chastised by 3J. She hadn't been wrong yet, but this time, of course, he hoped she was.

§

Steinert and Milnes walked down the hallway to the end. Gabby Price and Martin Andrews joined them. No one was

366 | MARK SHAIKEN

there besides them, and Steinert said: "Oh, he's plenty pissed at both sides. Not sure what to expect when he comes back with his ruling."

"I did what I had to do, Jacob. I protected the banks and the bankruptcy system," Milnes asserted, adamant. "The Judge has no right to be mad at me."

The lawyers were surprised by Milnes' verve in her continued attempt to justify that she took her actions for the greater good. She seemed to have convinced herself that she was a modern-day Mr. Spock from *Star Trek* and that in true Spockian fashion, the needs of the many – the bankruptcy system – outweighed the needs of the few.

As a bankruptcy lawyer, Steinert fully understood the importance of the integrity of the system, but he didn't for a minute believe that Milnes really thought she was protecting the system. She was laser-focused on bringing down Witherman, in Steinert's assessment. He also thought that Stacy Milnes was used to always getting her way, and often unwilling to admit she was wrong. Steinert felt he couldn't let her comment go without a reality-check response. "Stacy, the syndicate banks aren't going to thank you. They're all pissed at you and the situation. Don't for a minute think that the good Judge Robertson is going to thank you for protecting the bankruptcy system's integrity either. That ain't how any federal judge will roll on this one," he said, reverting to his ancient Queens, New York roots. Not trying to hide his disappointment in her, he adjusted his tie and said as he sighed, "Let's just go back in and wait for the Judge and his ruling. All right?" Steinert walked away from the group and headed back to the courtroom before Milnes could say another word to him.

§

"One for the record books, Jamie. One for the freakin' record books," Judge Robertson said softly to his law clerk after a few minutes of silent contemplation. "Freakin'" was about as close to profanity as Jamie had ever heard Judge Robertson stray. "Two witnesses. No direct testimony. No direct facts. Just permitted inferences. Two crimes." He paused to gather himself. He felt tired. Bone weary. Something about this case took the wind out of his sails. "You know what Albert Einstein said? 'Only two things are infinite, the universe and human stupidity, and I'm not sure about the former.' Well, me neither. Two of the most half-witted, short-sighted folks I've bumped into in some time, and just my luck, they're both in my courtroom – *not* testifying – and they're my only two witnesses."

Jamie enjoyed sitting with the Judge as he sorted out a case over which he presided. But this was the Judge's first complex chapter 11 case and never before had he sorted out disputes quite like this. Jamie's job was to help, but the only way he knew to help was to drift back to the law. After all, he was the *law* clerk. "According to my research, Judge, the operation of the Fifth Amendment in a civil proceeding like this one is not controversial – as the finder of fact, you infer that the witness admitted the matters that were the subject of the questions. I found no cases where there were two witnesses, one for each side, and they both invoked the Fifth Amendment."

The Judge appreciated the subtle shift back to the law and thought about Jamie's conclusion. "Not surprised, Jamie. I'm just very bothered by the way the bank obtained the damaging information about Witherman. Milnes seems like a solid ends-justify-the-means person. She's bad news."

The Judge was silent for a few minutes as he rotated his chair so he could gaze out his windows and watch the Missouri River flow to the east. Even in the winter, when small icebergs developed in its meandering river waters, the mighty river flowed to the east. He found something comforting about the Missouri River's unrelenting reliability as its waters headed each morning toward the rising sun. It was the way things were supposed to be. No surprises, and it always seemed to help him find the right answer to a looming problem. *The bankruptcy system needs to be reliable, like the river,* he thought. *Or else it doesn't work. It has to work for all the honest people and businesses who need its protection and the second chance it affords.* He needed to fashion a ruling that was as reliable as the river.

He turned back around to face Jamie and said, "My job is to rule, and that's what I intend to do here today. As Teddy Roosevelt observed, 'In any moment of decision, the best thing you can do is the right thing. The worst thing you can do is nothing.' So, here's how I see the right thing in this case. I am a bankruptcy judge. I don't hear criminal matters. Only the District Court Judges preside over criminal proceedings. As a bankruptcy judge, I can't allow a debtor to violate one of the four sacred cornerstones of bankruptcy law: full, transparent disclosure. Without it, the other tenets – automatic stay, discharge, and equal distribution – lose their efficacy. Despite how Milnes obtained it, I will allow the email into evidence as the consequence of Witherman's invocation of his right against self-incrimination. As your research reveals, once Witherman invoked the Fifth Amendment, he admitted the email is genuine and that it's not hearsay. So it's admissible, and I'll allow it into evidence. Once I do that, it's all-she-wrote for Witherman: Plan confirmation revoked. Discharge revoked. End of story. Matter turned over to one prosecutor or another. Bankruptcy system protected for the honest citizens."

"That is completely consistent with my research, Judge," Jamie concurred.

"Thanks, Jamie. But before these two folks leave my courtroom, I'll let them know what I really think. After that, I'll leave it to the United States Attorney's Office and the FBI to sort out if one or both of these folks should go through the criminal system. Not my job. Maybe they both get prosecuted, and maybe they both end up in a minimum-security prison somewhere together. That would certainly be fitting. A 'pox on both of them' might be the best sentence the law could impose."

"Understood," Jamie said in agreement.

"One other thing. I don't think I should revoke the companies' plan confirmation or discharges. My ruling will affect only Witherman personally. Not sure how that will play out, but when we go back into the courtroom, I'll get the lawyers to give me their thoughts."

"That seems logical, Judge, although the future of the companies may be quite complicated since, ultimately, Witherman owns and runs all of them."

"Correct, Jamie. Well, maybe we appoint someone to run all of them for a while, but that's something to address later. For now, please peek out there and, assuming they aren't yelling at each other, go ahead and let the attorneys know I'll come back into the courtroom and rule in five minutes."

§

The litigants, the bankruptcy lawyers, the observers, the criminal attorneys, the Judge, and his staff all gathered back in the courtroom. AUSA Hickman resumed his place in the back of the courtroom. From the bench, Judge Robertson said, "Ok, I want to thank you, counsel, for your work on this matter and your arguments here today. This has been an unusual hearing, to say the least – an extraordinary hearing in complicated and unique cases.

"Here is what I see. I have the unusual situation of wrongs alleged by the litigants against each other. The bank accuses the Debtor of lying on his bankruptcy filing papers and to me in open court, not to mention to taxing authorities and federally insured banking institutions. And, the Debtor accuses the banker of the commission of a form of hacking crime, perpetrated in a quest to prove the Debtor committed a crime. The conduct of both Mr. Witherman and Ms. Milnes is nothing short of shocking and reprehensible."

Quincy sat stone-faced as the Judge began to explain his ruling. He expected a tongue-lashing and wasn't surprised by the Judge's comments. Milnes, on the other hand, felt her level of anger rise as the Judge called out her crime. She expected the Judge to express an understanding of why she did what she did, an appreciation for her actions. He did not, and she felt betrayed, and unappreciated, and struggled to contain her anger.

Judge Robertson continued: "My job, however, is to handle the issues raised in this hearing that are before me today. Those issues are evidentiary, not criminal. To handle those evidentiary issues, I must focus on the email. To address Ms. Jones' argument, I can assume Ms. Milnes acquired the email, shall I say, improperly, and for my discussion, potentially in the commission of a crime. Nevertheless, as I said, this is not a criminal proceeding. And Ms. Milnes appears in this Court only as a witness, not as a defendant.

"There is no 'fruit of the poisonous tree' doctrine in civil law or evidence and it only applies to use of evidence by the government, not a private party like First Commercial. So the method by which the bank obtained the email is not relevant to me. Rather, because the Debtor invoked the Fifth Amendment, I draw the inference that the Debtor admitted that the email is genuine and not hearsay. With those two evidentiary predicates resolved by the inference I draw, the email is admissible under the rules of evidence, and I have no alternative but to admit it into the record. Therefore, I overrule the Debtor's objection to the email, and I hereby admit the email into evidence.

"With that, I have no other evidence offered from the Debtor to counter the text of the email. Therefore, I must conclude that the Debtor intentionally omitted disclosure of a Swiss bank account valued at $25 million in his schedules, statement of affairs, tax filings, and prior testimony. Simply stated, the Debtor lied repeatedly. Based on that fact, I am duty-bound to revoke the Debtor's plan confirmation. Upon doing so, I am mandated by the applicable bankruptcy statute likewise to revoke his discharge." Judge Robertson looked directly at Quincy and said, "Mr. Witherman, it seems to me that the bankruptcy fresh start was not good enough for you, and you tried for a head start as well. It didn't work. So, with the loss of your discharge, you have not only lost that head start you appear to have coveted, but you have also lost the fresh start afforded to honest debtors under the Bankruptcy Code. I must wonder – was it even worth it?"

He continued, his voice remaining calm but his tone taking on more gravity, "More than that, you took oaths to tell the truth. All oaths in this Court are solemn. Our society has become all too willing to look past the meaning of truth and with that we have often lost sight of what is important. I don't look past the meaning of truth nor should anyone who appears before me in this courtroom. Not in the least. Not in my Court; not in any court. You violated a trust. The trust we place in our debtors to do just one thing – tell the truth, a trust you breached. You have now lost your discharge, and your fresh start, and I suspect that is just the beginning of your problems. Just the beginning, sir."

Quincy said nothing. He had no interest in a dialogue with the Judge. He was pretty sure the Judge didn't have an interest in a dialogue either.

Stacy Milnes was delighted with the Judge's comments. *Quincy Witherman – you've just begun to get what you have coming.*

While Stacy Milnes privately celebrated in silence, Judge Robertson looked directly at her and said, "Ms. Milnes. That a senior officer at a federally chartered bank would go as far as the commission of a felony for any purpose to achieve any end should be unthinkable. But here we are – talking about it in open court because of your completely unlawful actions. I don't have the words to tell you just how offended I am by your conduct, Ms. Milnes, but I am hopeful that our system of justice will adequately deal with you as well in due course."

Judge Robertson looked away from a seething Stacy Milnes and began to address the lawyers. As he looked away, she was no longer able to control her swelling resentment for the Judge, the syndicate bankers, and all of the lawyers she felt had turned against her. As her anger festered, she rose and, with a bitter look in her eyes, pointed at the Judge and bellowed, "And *I* am *offended* no one has recognized that I'm the reason a felon will be brought to justice!" Gabby Price, sitting next to Milnes, was momentarily stunned by the outburst and tried to pull her client back down to the pews. But, Milnes would not be denied her moment.

Judge Robertson quickly pivoted from the lawyers he was about to address, returned his gaze to Stacy Milnes, and as he stared at her, said to his courtroom clerk resolutely and without raising his voice, "Clerk, please have the marshals come into the courtroom and escort Ms. Milnes away." Moments later, a U.S. Marshal complied and cleared Stacy Milnes from the courtroom.

Judge Robertson took a moment to recompose himself, shook his head almost imperceptibly from side to side and said, "Mr. Steinert, before that interruption, I gave the parties my ruling. Will you please submit to me an order reflecting my ruling?

Before we leave the courtroom today, I want to hear from the syndicate banks. What happens next? Mr. Sample, I understand you are now StarBanc's counsel, and Star is the agent for the group?"

As Dennis Sample walked to the podium, Brian Chimes felt his level of shock begin to subside. *This case is completely chaotic*, he thought.

Sample walked to the podium and said, "That is correct, Your Honor. The bank group's view, *sans* the views of First Commercial, is that they cut a deal with the debtor entities who generate the cash flow used to pay the banks. The plan accurately sets out that deal. Those other entities did nothing wrong, and in fact, are not involved in First Commercial's motion here today. The banks want to receive payments in full over time as we negotiated. We don't want the buildings back, we don't want to foreclose our mortgages and deeds of trust, and we don't want to run the buildings on a day-to-day basis. We're banks, not property management companies."

"Mr. Sample, thank you. I understand the banks' position. I think I know the answer to this question but here goes. Did First Commercial run any of this by the syndicate banks before filing the motion?" Judge Robertson queried.

"It did not," Sample answered quickly.

"So the syndicate banks had no idea what Ms. Milnes was up to?"

"None. That is correct, Your Honor," Sample confirmed for the Judge.

"Hmmm. As I figured. Ok. Well, the matters you raise are serious and have my attention, but they are not pending before me right now. I acknowledge that the parties and the Court need to quickly address the issues and resolve them. I suggest the parties meet, and in light of my ruling, figure out what should happen. How will the buildings continue to operate and for how long? You can then call my chambers, and we can figure out what to do next."

Sample nodded his head in agreement, and with that, the hearing adjourned.

§

3J, Pascale, Atwell, and Quincy returned to the small room outside the courtroom, closed the door, and sat down around the table that took up most of the space in the room. Quincy said, "I feel like the Judge has not only taken away my discharge, he's taking away my buildings – my creations."

3J privately thought, *what the hell did you expect?* but she and her collegaues offered no response. Quincy surveyed the lawyers and resigned himself that he would not hear a response to his comment. He took a breath and asked, "Alright, what happens next?"

Pascale and 3J looked at each other. 3J really didn't want to have a conversation with Quincy at this moment and she looked away, so Pascale said, "I'll field that question, Quince. 3J and I need to give you some advice on the last bankruptcy issue raised in Court – how the companies will run going forward. Give us until tomorrow to develop some options for you that we can then discuss. For the immediate period, I think you and David need to spend some time together. 3J and I have talked, and we're beyond uncomfortable with the notion that you've hidden crypto assets that you haven't disclosed. All three of us are advising you in the strongest terms to come clean about the crypto. While that will cause a shitstorm in the bankruptcy cases, it'll pass and it's more important that you and David come up with an overall plan for dealing with the Justice Department. Our bankruptcy advice is simple – you must disclose the crypto. No ifs, ands, or buts."

Atwell and Quincy agreed to meet in the morning to discuss the criminal options. Quincy stood to leave, shook everyone's hand, and silently exited the room. If he felt bothered or concerned about the hearing, he hid it well. His eyes were blank and emotionless, like a football player's eyes after a helmet to helmet hit. In the dimmer light, his pupils dilated and for a moment, it seemed that his brown and blue eyes were mostly black.

The lawyers remained behind. Atwell spoke first. "If Quincy has any chance of cutting a deal with the DOJ, he's going to have to come clean about the crypto. I don't see that he has any choice. If we're to try to cut a plea deal with the Feds, they'll require him to disclose any other hidden assets. It would be a terrible idea to cut a deal, then lie to the Feds and continue to hide the crypto."

"I agree, David," 3J said. "I truly have no idea if Quincy will agree. I don't know what he's thinking. All we can do is advise."

"I took a look at the federal sentencing guidelines. If we go to trial and the jury finds Quincy guilty, then generously applying the factors of which I'm aware, if we get lucky, I see a sentence on the low end of maybe six to eight years, plus fines and forfeiture of the hidden assets. There's also some potential for sentencing enhancers, which could increase the possible sentence. So, he's looking at doing time, in my estimation. If we cut a deal, maybe we can shave a few years off that sentence, especially if the money is paid over and used to pay creditors and the IRS. That's going to be tough, though. Quincy is a first-timer, but make no mistake about it: He tried to gig the bankruptcy system, banks, and the taxing authorities, and he lied to the Judge from the witness stand. Looked the Judge right in the eye and lied. That never plays well. Never. I know Quincy likes to call this 'only one lie.' But it's a lie he told over and over and over again. District Court judges and the DOJ take a dim view of all of that."

"We figured as much," Pascale said. "I think we need to lay all of this out for Quincy with some recommendations, and then we can see how he reacts."

"He doesn't look like he reacts to much of anything," Atwell observed raising his eyebrows. "Those are the ones to worry about." 3J and Pascale nodded their heads in agreement. Atwell continued, "I'll try to get Quincy into the office tomorrow afternoon for a couple of hours to discuss. My recommendation would be that he comes clean and tries to cut the best plea bargain that he can. What about the companies and the issue the banks and the Judge addressed?"

Pascale observed, "The Bankruptcy Code permits a plan to change management, so perhaps the fix is to replace the board and the management company's officers in a plan amendment and allow the management company to continue to run the buildings. We need to figure that one out and talk with Dennis Sample after we speak to Quincy. Whatever we do, there's no way the Judge lets Quincy run the companies from prison. That only happens in the movies and even in the movies, the prisoner runs the business surreptitiously without the sanction of a federal judge."

"No end of cutting edge issues presented when a client goes off the rails," Atwell mused, looking down and shaking his head.

"Correction. Quincy didn't just go off the rails," 3J observed with a tone of bitterness in her voice. "As far as I can piece this story together, the Witherman Express may never have been on the rails."

On the walk back to the Greene Madison office, 3J thought about Stacy Milnes' outburst in court. A rare occurence in any courtroom. Even rarer in a bankruptcy courtroom. Indeed, in her career, she had never seen such an outburst or the removal of anyone from a bankruptcy courtroom. She thought of something her mother would say to her: "Josephina, every human being deserves respect regardless of their life choices." Words to live by, but 3J was having difficulty living up to them as she thought of Quincy Witherman and Stacy Milnes. All she could think was, *neither had any respect coming for them.*

§

After the hearing concluded, Jacob Steinert, Martin Andrews, and Gabby Price, found Stacy Milnes in the Marshal's office and asked if they could use a room to talk. By then, Milnes had calmed down and the Marshal gave them access to a small room. Gabby Price delivered the simple message: "Stacy, before your outburst, you had some significant criminal issues to address and now you have one more – the Judge."

Milnes responded softly, but petulantly, "No one seems to appreciate what I did here for the banks and the Judge."

"Stacy, please listen to what I'm saying. We're going to have to deal with the prosecutor in this case, and now we're also going to deal with the Judge and figure out how to address your courtroom outburst."

§

When Hickman returned to his desk, he thought to himself, *Hell of a hearing.* He called his liaison at the FBI's Kansas City branch, explained what had just transpired in Bankruptcy Court, and expressed concern that Witherman would flee. Hickman knew he had no hard facts to support his concern, but given the magnitude of the amount involved, he was concerned that Witherman could be a flight risk. The FBI agreed to "keep an eye" on private plane travel and flight plans lodged with the FAA that involved Witherman, and any tickets he might buy to fly commercial. The FBI didn't have the manpower to simply tail a man 24/7 in a case that wasn't even a case yet. Yes, the FBI was aware of First Commercial's SAR, but at this point, Witherman had simply refused to testify in a civil case. Nothing else. Hickman would need to move the Witherman matter much closer to the top of the pile to protect against Witherman exiting the confines of the United States.

§

Hickman went out for a brisk walk along his typical thinking route: from the Federal Courthouse at the northern edge of downtown Kansas City, across I-70, to the River Market area of Kansas City, down to the Missouri River, and then back to his office. He needed the walk to try to help focus his thoughts.

Judge Robertson called the bankruptcy hearing "unusual." Hickman didn't know much about bankruptcy law, but it sure seemed unusual to him that no one offered any actual testimony. *Did anyone ever actually offer testimony at bankruptcy hearings?* Hickman had seen outbursts in court before but this one was a doozy. *Chaos in bankruptcy! Judge Robertson handled it well.*

He tried to organize his thoughts, and he started his analysis with Stacy Milnes, trying to ignore the outburst. He assumed she lacked the technical skill to hack. *Pretty clearly, she hired someone to illegally infiltrate a computer.* As he walked across the bridge over the interstate, he considered the important questions: who hacked; what computer was the target; where the hack occurred; when it happened; and how it happened.

On the other side of the interstate, he entered River Market, Kansas City's oldest incorporated district. Hickman knew River Market well; it was his go-to destination when he needed a walk. He liked its old two-story and three-story brick façade buildings that housed restaurants, bars, stores, businesses, and residential lofts. The Market had a laid-back vibe, except on Saturday when its farmer's market was in full swing. Its history spanned French fur traders in the early 1800s to a mob war in the 1970s, during which mob factions blew up several buildings and killed each other as they vied for control. *The Market cleaned up nicely after the war, and now it's the perfect neighborhood for me to sort out criminal matters*, Hickman thought.

He had a visceral reaction to cutting a quick deal with Milnes and getting answers to all of the questions quickly, easily, and inexpensively. He also considered that if he held fast and opened an investigation in lieu of dealing with Milnes, the investigation would take resources and potentially significant time, during which Witherman remained free. Finally, he considered that if the investigation led to charges against Milnes, she would be a first time offender and would get off lightly. Likely, the only lasting penalty she would suffer would be a loss of employment in the banking industry, probably forever.

He arrived at the small, concrete deck overlooking the river. He hung his arms over the deck's wrought-iron fence, and as the river flowed by, watched steam drift out of his mouth. As he watched, he continued thinking. He sighed to himself. Given the analysis, Hickman concluded that he could have his answers if he cut a quick deal with Milnes. He could structure the agreement so that she would cooperate in exchange for prosecution immunity and an understanding that she would never again seek employment in the banking industry.

Would Milnes agree to such a deal? he wondered. *How could she not? Maybe because she's a hot-head.* Her tenure in the banking industry was quickly coming to a close, so that component of the deal would play out the same whether she agreed to a deal or not. *Should the Government agree to such a deal?* he considered. *Why not?* he thought. *She would get little to no jail time on this one anyway,* he concluded. So, he wasn't trading any significant penalty away.

He left the river deck and headed back to the U.S. Attorney's office at the courthouse.

By the time he finished his walk and arrived at the Federal Courthouse, Hickman had made up his mind. Once back inside the courthouse, he flashed his government credentials to the marshals on the main floor and walked up the stairs to his office.

He placed his call to Gabby Price and proposed the trade: information and a promise to exit the banking industry in exchange for immunity, with Hickman's express caveat that Milnes would fully and completely disclose each of the whos, whats, whens, wheres, and hows, and that she would fully cooperate in the apprehension and prosecution of Witherman. He made it clear that any deal would exclude a resolution of the consequences of Milnes' courtroom outburst. He wouldn't presume to settle that issue; it was between Judge Robertson and Stacy Milnes. Price expressed interest and said she needed to talk with her client, of course.

§

Gabby Price called Stacy Milnes immediately. She explained the straightforward arrangement proposed by Hickman. Milnes was on board with all terms except the required promise to exit the banking industry.

"What the fuck will I do with my life if the Government bans me from banking? And what does it mean 'between the Judge and me'?"

"Look, Stacy, I understand your concern but here's the reality. Without a deal, the Government may very well prosecute you. It could take a while, but with bank records of payments you directed to the hacker and Aaronson and the payment you indirectly made to the Sueden employee, it'd only be a matter of time until they had you dead to rights. At which point you'd be out of banking anyway." Price stopped there to let the reality of the situation set in. Hearing nothing, she continued, "And once your bank gets its arms around this, they'll terminate your employment. There are so many other substantial banks in this deal that word will be on the street that you did what you did. The banking industry may very well blackball you. Probably, *likely* will. Also, you don't just want to be in the banking industry. You want to be in special assets, at a big bank. When all of the dust settles here, as my Dad used to say, 'that dream ain't gonna come true.'" Still hearing nothing from Milnes, she finished by saying, "I hope you hear what I'm saying. I'm sorry to be the bearer of such bad news, but your days in the banking industry are over anyway, Stacy."

She paused to let Milnes' new normal sink in. "Hickman isn't going to presume what Judge Robertson might do in response to your outburst. What he's saying is simple − if Judge Robertson takes steps to find you in civil or criminal contempt of court, Hickman isn't in a position to settle that issue. So your problems with the Judge will persist even if you settle with the Government on the hacking crimes."

Milnes growled into the phone, "I hear you. I need time to think. What's the time frame?"

"Hickman's proposal is a good one for you. We need to get back to him quickly, Stacy."

"I'll let you know tonight," Milnes said and then hung up with no further comments. It was the first time a client had hung up on Gabby Price. *So this is the private practice of law?* Price thought.

Later that Friday night, Stacy Milnes called back and said, "Cut the damn deal." She then hung up, again. *Twice in one day. Well, ok, then,* Price thought sarcastically to herself.

§

Monday morning, Price conveyed Milnes' acceptance of the deal to Robert Hickman. Two days later, Milnes sat in a conference room in the U.S. Attorney's office with a government-brewed coffee in her hand across from Hickman and his government recording device as she revealed and confessed to all of the facts. Milnes left nothing out. She protected no one. She made it clear that while Moses Aaronson gave her Rome's contact information, he had cautioned Milnes against going down the computer infiltration path, and he didn't hire Rome for her.

Hickman reduced everything to a written witness statement, presented it to Price and Milnes for review, and Milnes signed it. He was now ready for Witherman and his button-down-starched-shirt criminal attorney, David Atwell.

§

After Milnes and Price departed, Hickman sat at his desk plotting how he would deal with David Atwell, and his thoughts turned back to Milnes' description of the infiltration operation. A *"man-in-the-middle" attack*, he thought. *Digital and analog all in one case:* Bivouac, *followed by a good old fashioned bribe. Fascinating.* He was sure the details would be a revelation to Atwell. Hickman wondered what revelations Atwell and his client would have.

§

Hickman and Atwell talked Thursday morning, and Hickman made it clear that he wanted to meet with Atwell and his client promptly. They made an appointment for Friday, February 15 at 8 a.m. Atwell called Quincy and informed him of the meeting. He made it clear that he expected the meeting to be a chance for Hickman to begin laying out what he knew. Quincy said he would be there.

CHAPTER 50

Friday, February 15, 2019

FRIDAY MORNING, THE *KANSAS City Star* ran an article reporting about Quincy Witherman, his life, his legacy, and his crime. The article reflected the *Star's* usual comprehensive treatment of a topic. On the way to work, Hickman stopped for a cup of coffee at his favorite coffee dive on the Country Club Plaza. He read the article in the paper with interest as he sat at a small table at the back of the coffee shop and drank his dark roast. He drove to the courthouse and awaited the arrival of his guests for what he hoped would be an interesting and fruitful discussion.

Just before 8 a.m., Atwell arrived at the U.S. Attorney's office, and a receptionist escorted him to a conference room. Moments later, Hickman arrived, and they shook hands and awaited the arrival of Quincy Witherman. By 8:15, however, Quincy had not appeared, and Hickman was both agitated and peeved. Atwell stepped out of the conference room to call him, and to his surprise, his client answered on the second ring. Atwell was startled and said, "Quincy, where are you? Hickman is here at his office, and he's agitated. Not how we want to start our communications with the AUSA in charge of your matter."

"I'm not coming," Quincy said.

"Why not?" Atwell asked, his voice rising in tone.

"Just … not," Quincy said, repeating himself but offering no explanation.

"Quincy, where are you?"

"Better if you don't know."

"Quincy, are you in Kansas or Missouri?" Atwell probed, ignoring Quincy's admonition.

"No," Quincy replied.

"Are you in the United States?"

"For now, anyway."

"Quincy, this isn't a plan. Not a plan at all. You can't run from the Feds. We have a chance here to come clean and cut a deal before indictment. This is the best chance you have to cut a deal. There won't be a deal if you're on the run. And the Government catches the overwhelming number of the folks in your position who bolt. Once they catch you, it'll add to the length of your sentence, not detract."

Quincy remained silent. Atwell had little left to say but mustered a plea, "Quincy, please, come back."

"Look, David. I need time to think. I haven't left the country. Tell the prosecutor I'm sick, and reschedule for a couple of days from now."

"Quincy, if I tell AUSA Hickman that, he may send a Marshal or an FBI agent to your apartment to find you. They won't find you in the apartment, sick. Not a good plan at all."

"David, it's all I have right now."

"Jesus, Quincy," Atwell exclaimed. "Jesus."

"Just a couple of days, David. Just tell him."

"Quincy, I can't be involved in helping you run from the Feds. Why do I feel like a couple of days will help you to execute some kind of plan to flee?"

"Because I'm telling you that I am in the States, and I need to think."

"If I go back in and tell Hickman what you want me to say, I want to talk to you at the end of today. Understood?"

Silence.

"Quincy, are you listening to me?"

"Truthfully, David, I'm trying very hard not to at this particular moment. I know you mean well, but I can't think while you're talking and barking at me."

"Quincy, I'm not here to judge you. I'm here to give you the best advice and defense I can give to you. What you do with that is up to you. So far, you aren't doing much with the advice at all. Why?"

More silence. Quincy broke the silence with a sigh and said, "Alright, David. Alright. I'll call you at 5 p.m. Central time." As things turned out, Quincy would not need to make that call.

§

Atwell took a moment to gather himself before heading back into the conference room. Hickman was still in the room and appeared to be deep in the process of reading papers. He couldn't tell if he was really reading or feigning activity to try to make him even more uncomfortable. He sat down at the conference room table, and before he could utter a word, Hickman looked up and said, "Just you? He's on the move, isn't he, counselor?"

Atwell responded, "Say what?"

"Your client, Witherman. He isn't here because he's decided to run for it, hasn't he?"

"Robert ... look. I talked to Witherman just now and he asked me to tell you he needs to reschedule. He said he was sick and needs a couple of days to think."

"Counselor, let's cut to the chase. We've both been at this too long for this type of back and forth nonsense. When I saw

Witherman in court the other day, that little prosecutor voice in my head said to me to be careful with this one. I asked the FBI to devote some resources to Witherman to track his whereabouts. And guess what? He's not sick. He's not here. He chartered a flight to Houston last night and then a car to Laredo. If he tries to get to the border, he won't get across. Witherman doesn't need time to think. And I'm not offering time. Not at all. So, do me a solid, goddammit, and go back out to the hallway, get your idiot client on the phone again, and tell him to get his developer ass on a plane back to Kansas City now. Otherwise, I'll have him picked up and returned to this fair city with the information I have. Do we understand each other?"

Atwell understood fully. He excused himself and went back to the hallway and called Witherman, who took his call. He explained the situation and told Witherman he had no choice and had to return. "Quincy, where exactly in Texas are you?"

"Who said I'm in Texas, David?"

"Hickman knows you're in Texas."

"Laredo," Quincy replied. "Looking at the gateway to Nuevo Laredo and Mexico."

"Won't work, Quincy. The FBI is about to pick you up. Don't head south. Head for the airport, get back on a plane to Kansas City, now, and return."

"Schedule a meeting with Hickman for tomorrow morning, David," and Quincy hung up.

Atwell went back into the room where Hickman had taken up residence. "Meeting tomorrow, please, Robert."

That was all Hickman could take and he transitioned to sarcastic mode. "Sure thing. I have plenty of time to drop everything I'm doing and schedule multiple meetings with a felon who has left the state but says he may or may not be back for a meeting sometime tomorrow. I can meet on a weekend.

No problem at all. I'll just hold my very empty calendar open for this guy." He gulped his coffee and continued, "These rookie, corporate white-collar crime guys. They're just so used to thinking they can give me orders. They sit in their corporate lairs and say to me: 'Do this, Mr. Prosecutor. Meet later, Mr. Prosecutor. Accommodate my needs, Mr. Prosecutor. I'm very important and very busy, Mr. Prosecutor.'" As Hickman talked, his voice steadily rose in volume. "I've seen this so many times in my life. Quincy Witherman may be the best guy to work with on Planet Earth, but he doesn't cancel meetings in here. He doesn't give orders. So while you were out there talking with him, I got me a warrant, and in a moment, my guy on the ground in Texas will pick up Mr. Quincy G. Fuckin' Witherman and bring him back here to me. Shouldn't be hard. Witherman is sitting in a coffee shop in Laredo, looking out of a south-facing window to Nuevo Laredo, Mexico. He keeps looking south and seems to be doing some kind of deep thinking exercises. Well, he can do his damn thinking back here in the good old Western District of Missouri."

Atwell said nothing. His worst fears were coming true.

Hickman continued sternly, "Oh, and then we can meet. You, me and him, as we used to say back in the neighborhood. I'll let you both know when that meeting will be."

"What do you have, Robert? What's the preview?"

Hickman smiled a prosecutor's "gotcha" smile and said, "Why, David. I have flash drives with all of the communications between one Michaela Huld and First Switzerland Bank, Geneva. I have the email you already saw in the bankruptcy case. I have the data showing $25 million in the account. I have the operative here in the U.S. that Ms. Stacy Milnes hired to look into Mr. Witherman's affairs. I have the operative in London that Ms. Stacy Milnes hired to perform something called a "man-in-the-fuckin'-middle" attack on Ms. Huld's computer to determine the VPN company Ms. Huld used. I have one Basil Hargrove in London who the London operative bribed to download Ms. Huld's data, stored by the VPN company on its servers, onto said flash drives. So, what I have, to answer your spot-on question, is one sentence enhancer after another. And what Mr. Witherman has is … well … pardon my lack of class here, but he has shit. Diddly shit. Nothing to trade with me at all."

Hickman paused to let the facts sink in and after another gulp of coffee, said, "See ya' tomorrow, David. Saturday, goddammit. 9 a.m. You know the 'where.' Your boy better show."

Atwell headed for the door. Non-meeting over.

CHAPTER 51

I SAT DRINKING BLACK coffee at Laredo's Do Drop In coffee shop, just blocks away from the entrance to Nuevo Laredo, Mexico, in what I thought could be step one on my way to a new life. Could've been, but yet, I didn't move. I just sat. No movement except to bring the coffee mug to my lips, blow away a wisp of steam, and sip. I told Atwell that I needed time to think, and as I sat at the table, I tried. But I was without thoughts – a complete blank. I could stand up and flee. But I didn't take off. Why not?

I could make it to Mexico, I figured. But what next? I alluded to a rough plan when I talked with Michaela, but, sadly, I had never fleshed out the answer to the "what next" question. It would've cost some significant money to plan for the next steps to escape from the United States authorities. Lots of unanswered questions – how to run: charter a plane or a boat? Where to go? Which countries had no extradition agreements with the United States? All excellent questions that were way over my pay grade.

Oh, about five years ago, I met with a guy who claimed to be an escape "travel agent" to the rich and infamous, "on-the-run" population. We met at a nondescript, dark bar just west of Denver International Airport. He wanted lots of money, and he offered no papers to sign. I just had a bad feeling about him that I never resolved. So I never paid, and he never planned for me. I don't even know if his plan would've involved Laredo and Nuevo Laredo.

I still don't know why, but as I sat at my Do Drop In table for two – one of those diner type of tables, covered with a plastic, red-checkered table cloth that cleaned up easily with a wet rag that sat in a bucket of luke warm, cloudy water – I called 3J using my burner phone, and she picked up. She shouldn't have been able to identify the number. As I established the connection, I said nothing. I called her impulsively and had nothing in mind to say.

3J spoke first: "Quince, is that you?" I didn't answer. She continued, "Quince, if that's you, please say something."

"It's me, 3J," I said.

"Where are you?" she asked.

"I'm in Laredo."

"Laredo? Jesus. What the hell are you doing there?"

"Sitting at the Do Drop In coffee shop, drinking my third cup of black coffee."

"Why are you there, Quince?"

"I'm thinking about Nuevo Laredo, and points beyond."

"What points?" 3J asked.

"Just points, 3J. Just … points," I sighed, as I responded with a non-answer and a tone of tired resignation.

"Quince, please. Listen to me. Come back to Kansas City so we can help you sort out all of this."

"I think we're well past the sorting stage, 3J." I was well beyond sanguine at this point. I saw nothing to sort.

"Maybe so. But I can't help you on a burner phone call."

"I don't know that I called for your help, 3J. I just called."

"Quince, look. You made a mistake. Come home so we can try to fix it."

"3J, sometimes we can fix mistakes. But this isn't a mistake. A mistake is something you didn't mean to do. You know, a blunder or a misstep," I said, speaking slowly. "I didn't make a mistake. I made a plan. An intentional plan. A plan that met my needs and furthered my goals. The plan worked perfectly for many years. Then, one day, the plan failed. The choice I have to make is: should I run or not? Both options lead to the same quandary: Then what?" Before 3J could answer, I heard myself say, "I suppose I have a third choice. I could leave the Do Drop In and walk in front of a speeding eighteen-wheeler or city bus. That wouldn't be a fix, but it would add some finality to the problem."

I knew that 3J was nearly a thousand miles away. I heard myself suggest that I might take my life. It didn't feel right, but on the other hand, I was surprised that it didn't feel wrong either. It took no guts at all to consider such an end, though I suspected it would take quite a bit more resolve to take that first step off of the curb. At the time, I didn't know if I had it in me. Maybe no one knows if they have it in them until they get to the curb and then … beyond. Gunn must've thought about ending his life in Prune Street before the Yellow Fever did it for him. Maybe I should've been wishing for a disease to put an end to my problems.

"Quincy," 3J said slowly and softly. "Please don't. For me. Please don't."

I responded, "Thank you for saying that."

"I mean it. In my life, I've met a lot of people who owe money. Debt is bad. It messes with us. It messes us up. It makes us do things we'd never otherwise do. But, if I can just please, please convince you to come back to KC, you and I will figure this out together. I can help."

I said nothing for a moment. 3J couldn't help. I knew no one could. How could they? Unless they had a time machine handy. Even then, I doubt I'd do anything differently.

As I sat at the Do Drop In, I wished I'd gone further to plan an escape, but I hadn't. If I only had done so. That was my mindset. A review of my past actions resulting in "ifs." Remorse finally, but not for hiding the assets, for not finishing off the plan. My mistake wasn't that I hid the account. My main mistake was that I got caught without a plan to deal with the moments after I got caught. But that wasn't everything. Over the years, I assumed the Swiss would be stout enough always to rebuff attempts by the rest of the world to bring transparency to the Swiss banking system. Mistake. I assumed that no banker would break the law to prove I'd broken the law. Mistake. I assumed things would never change. Mistake. The one constant was that things always change.

I sat there with my coffee at my table covered with synthetic red checked fabric cleaned with cloudy water and wallowed in my foolishness. Stuck on my "ifs." "Ifs" are fine when reviewing and analyzing history. They were not helpful in the moment of truth.

My call with 3J. I had almost forgot she was still on the line. "Look, 3J. I gotta go. Thanks for everything."

"Please stay on the line, Quince," she said to me, her voice taking on an air of desperation.

I saw another eighteen-wheeler pass by, followed by a bus. Either would work well. And I realized I had made my decision. It would be quick. I wasn't so sure about painless, but quick would have to suffice. I would stroll to the curb and venture forward. Life is a valuable resource, but I realized that I no longer respected and valued that resource. *It was time*, I thought.

I hung up, dropped a ten-dollar bill on the table, and just as I rose to exit the coffee shop, a large man with a large mustache dressed in an appropriately large three-piece brown suit rose from his nearby table and came toward me. As he approached, he showed me a United States Marshal's badge and credentials, and explained that he was my federal escort back to Kansas City.

He undoubtedly thought I stood up to flee and decided it was time to intervene.

He had no idea.

I looked up at him as he flashed his badge. Saved from myself and my thoughts by my very own large United States Marshal, who probably thought he'd apprehended a fugitive attempting his escape. That's what my Marshal would probably tell the other Marshals back in Kansas City. He wouldn't tell the Marshals that he stopped a real estate developer from ending his life, because my Marshal had no idea he had saved me from a messy ending – the musical coda of my life, like the final piano chord in the Beatles' "A Day In The Life." My Marshal thought he'd prevented an escape. He had no idea that he had prevented the sudden meeting of vehicle and man. He grabbed my elbow forcefully to guide me to the door, and I went with him, out the door, into his car, back to the airport, and the two of us headed to Kansas City. No eighteen-wheeler. No bus. No resistance.

The moment had passed. Only 3J would know the details of the moment. And she couldn't tell anyone except Pascale and Atwell. Client confidences.

Turns out, these types of sordid affairs don't go down like in the movies.

CHAPTER 52

Friday, February 15, 2019

3J WALKED INTO PASCALE'S office after her call with Quincy ended. She stood just inside the door frame with her hands in her suit jacket pockets. David Atwell had just returned from his meeting with Robert Hickman and was already in Pascale's office. 3J reported, "Quincy's in Texas at the border. He's talking about suicide, Bill." Pascale shook his head in disbelief.

"Frankly, I'm surprised that Quincy didn't cross over to Mexico and points beyond. Why would he have stopped in Laredo, Texas?" 3J asked.

"Cold feet, I would expect. Or no good plan of what came after Nuevo Laredo. Who knows?" Atwell said.

"Maybe he was just scared and wasn't planning … or thinking," Pascale offered. "Maybe he doesn't want a life of running from the law. That life didn't work out all that well for Jesse James or Billy The Kid." He had no additional pithy observations to offer, so all he said was, "Jesus. For fuck's sake." As apropos a comment as it was useless.

3J and her two colleagues remained in Pascale's office, stone-faced, distraught, each with their arms folded across their chests, and said nothing. *Lawyers solve problems*, but 3J saw no solution to the problem that was Quincy Witherman.

More silence. After five minutes of silence, 3J said to Pascale, "I'm sitting here thinking back to Judge Robertson's comments about the sanctity of truth and the oath. From the first time I met Quincy Witherman, he seemed hell-bent on righting a wrong occasioned by bankers on his ancestor. His methodology to right the wrong? He wronged what was right. And the sacred oath? He lived a lie. I'm not so naïve to think that law enforcement catches every criminal. But I feel good that Quincy was caught, and I feel guilty for feeling good. My feeling betrays my obligations to Quincy as his lawyer."

Pascale rejected 3J's feelings and countered, "You've got no obligation to assist him in the commission of a crime. You've more than fulfilled all your obligations to Mr. Witherman. We move on. That's what we do."

"Maybe so … maybe so. You know, Pascale, Quincy lives in the Crossroads, right?"

"I do," Pascale said, wondering about the tangent 3J was starting down.

"In Black folklore, the Crossroads is a location between two worlds – where Earth and the supernatural world meet. Kind of like Quincy's ghost eyes seeing into Heaven and Earth. My dad used to tell me about the Crossroads when he wanted to scare me. He told me it's the place you go to meet the devil who'll grant you magical skills, of course in exchange for your soul." She stopped to gather her thoughts. "I think the point of the story and the folklore is that nothing's without a price. Well, I wonder if our friend Mr. Witherman moved to the Crossroads here and thought his deal with the devil to continue to hide assets would hold up forever, only to learn that the devil sent Stacy Milnes after him."

"So you think Stacy Milnes was working for the devil?"

"Just saying. If anyone would be working for the devil, wouldn't you think it'd be her?"

"Can't argue with that," Pascale said, only half-jokingly.

"Milnes was the price. And, now, Quincy has paid up." 3J sighed. "Well, not much room for folklore in the bankruptcy world. Not much room at all." She lost her focus and watched out of the window as a jet flew by on the way to or from one destination or another, silently glad she wasn't on it.

3J stayed in Pascale's office for ten more minutes, but no one uttered a word. She quietly hoped that her mobile phone would ring. It did not. Quincy didn't call. He had finished with bankruptcy, had started to pay the price, and straightaway would move on to the next phase of his life.

EPILOGUE

QUINCY RETURNED TO KANSAS City with the Marshal.
His deal with the Justice Department severely restricted his
freedom: Home confinement in his Crossroads apartment.
Modern technology ankle bracelet to allow the Feds to monitor
his whereabouts. Random check-ins with the Feds.

On Saturday, Atwell and Quincy met with Hickman and
listened to what they already knew and, additionally, what they
didn't. The full story. Chapter and verse of what Stacy Milnes
had done; how far she had been willing to go. How she pulled it
off. Hickman laid out count after count of felonies – each time
Quincy presented a false financial statement to a bank; each
time he filed false tax returns, and each time he lied under oath
in the bankruptcy process. A sad litany and with the possibility
of so many counts, Quincy lost track of the number of years
he might serve in prison.

*There are no alternatives at all. No choice. I did it. No point in a trial.
In a trial, the jury will know I did it. The presiding judge, with just a hint
of a red Windsor knotted tie sticking out from his black robe, will know I
did it. It will be a spectacle of rulings: "sustained," "overruled," "move on
counsel," "the jury shall ignore," "hearsay," "irrelevant." All of those court
rulings, while the jury will watch me every day. The jury, not believing my
lawyer. It will be the spectacle of Stacy Milnes, the criminal, taking the stand
and gleefully testifying against me. The jury believing her. The Kansas City
Star reporting all the miserable details. No alternatives from which to choose.*

In the end, Quincy allowed Atwell to try to negotiate a plea
bargain. Atwell had little to work with. All he could offer was

prompt delivery of the Swiss account assets and the crypto-currency. Yes, Atwell had succeeded in convincing Quincy to come clean about everything. The revelation of the undis-closed crypto sent Hickman into a prosecutorial orbit – as expected. It took a while, but Hickman managed to regain his composure so he could conclude the negotiations with Atwell. Judge Robertson heard about the crypotcurrency through the courthouse grapvine and let Jamie know that nothing about Witherman would surprise him.

As was the process in the federal system, Quincy Witherman and AUSA Robert Hickman came to an agreement of the charges to which Quincy would plead guilty, but the presid-ing U.S. District Court Judge would impose a sentence after confirming that Quincy was not coerced into signing the agree-ment, taking into account the plea deal, the recommendation of AUSA Hickman, and the comprehensive and complicated Federal Sentencing Guidelines.

The deal: In exchange for the immediate delivery of the formerly hidden assets, Quincy agreed to plead guilty to one count of bankruptcy fraud, one count of perjury for lying on the witness stand, one count of presenting false financial statements to banks, and a fine of $2 million, with the balance of the hidden assets to be deposited into the registry of the Bankruptcy Court and distributed to taxing authorities and then as the bankruptcy process deemed appropriate.

The money wasn't used to pay the banks as the deal with the other Debtors remained intact and as long as they made their monthly payments, the banks had no right to the concealed assets. But then, Stacy Milnes was not really after money; she just wanted to take Witherman down.

Hickman recommended a sentence of five years in a mini-mum security prison. Quincy, with the assistance of Michaela, delivered the assets to AUSA Hickman to be processed. He hoped that the delivery of so much money to the Government would be a substantial mitigating factor in the Judge's determination of sentencing. Atwell wasn't so sure. He worried a judge might see it as Quincy's inappropriate "no harm, no foul" argument and would reject it as basis to grant sentencing leniency.

First Commercial Bank promptly fired Stacy Milnes. She contended that the bank didn't fire her; she said she quit. Technically, her deal with the Government required her to quit, and she tried to. She handed her notice of resignation to the bank president, who tore it up in front of her, threw the pieces of paper into her face, and fired her. Normally a soft-spoken man, the president managed to ratchet up the decibels, and not usually a vulgar man, the president managed to use the word "fuck" time and again; "good fucking riddance." It didn't bother Milnes. It was one of her favorite words. Uncharted territory for the president, but he acquitted himself admirably.

As directed by the bank president, a security officer escorted her slowly out of the bank in full view of the other special assets officers. Once outside, she had to contend with local news crews who blocked passage to her car. Quite the spectacle. She quickly sold her small townhouse in St. Louis' Hill neighborhood and disappeared. She changed her hair color, lost twenty pounds, tried make-up for the first time in her adult life, and moved back to Philadelphia, where she worked as an after-hours inventory stocker at a local Summit Supermarket as she tried to figure out the rest of her life. *Maybe she could become a consultant or a member of The Moses Team*, she thought from time to time.

The order of restitution, a matter of public record, required her to repay First Commercial the money she authorized the bank to pay to Moses, Rome, and Hargrove from whatever sources she could muster, including her retirement accounts.

Still, full restitution wasn't something she would quickly repay on the salary of a supermarket stocker.

The bank president said over drinks with a friend, "Stacy Milnes is now about as useful as a frayed three-dollar suitcase. I rue the day I brought her on-board at this bank."

Recently, Milnes received a call from a woman who identified herself as a detective sergeant investigator with Scotland Yard, London. The DSI wanted to talk to Milnes about the man-in-the-middle attack on Michaela Huld's computer. *Will this never end?*

First Commercial's president flew around the country, and then the world, to meet with the presidents of each of the syndicate banks in a less than successful attempt to convince them to continue as banking partners with First Commercial in future syndicated bank deals, meeting a frigid reception at each bank. The value of First Commercial's stock dropped as the stock market absorbed what information it could in the public domain. If one listened closely, one could imagine hearing the entire First Commercial banking corporation breathe a long, loud sigh of resignation as it accepted the damage done by one Stacy Milnes and plotted a way to restore its image. If one looked closely, one could imagine seeing the First Commercial office building in downtown St. Louis sag ever so slightly as if the building hung its corporate head and let its corporate shoulders move down and roll into a position of surrender to Stacy Milnes and the corporate shame she had brought upon the bank.

No Federal authorities spent any time chasing down either Rome or Basil Hargrove. Rome wasn't the only low-level hacker in the world, and Hargrove wasn't the only lower level corporate employee to do something abhorrent in exchange for a bribe. Too many bigger fish.

Moses Aaronson and Michaela Huld each escaped further criminal scrutiny. Moses continued as he had been for many years – just an aging man living alone with his only companion, Emily, the rat terrier who adored him. He hoped for more assignments, just so he could return to the Madison Park benches and review information in whatever new case on which he could work. He thought about Stacy Milnes from time to time and decided that if she ever asked to join the Team, he would decline. His overriding factor in determining who joined the Team was whether the person would be part of the solution or part of the problem. He didn't think Stacy Milnes could ever avoid being part of the problem.

Michaela Huld continued her financial advisory practice, changed her VPN service, and ceased her custom of using any technology outside of her home and office. Whether her new technology protocol would thwart an attack from someone like Rome was unclear to Michaela. But it wouldn't have been unclear to Rome. *There is always a way*, she regularly thought.

And Judge Robertson? He and Jamie followed the Witherman and Milnes developments in detail as they moved on to new cases and potential rulings requiring attention. Yes, the Judge put his first notch in his commercial Chapter 11 revolver, but that notch came with an asterisk. True, the plan was confirmed, and true, most of the Witherman debtors reorganized. Hence, the notch. But he felt that an asterisk was appropriate and signified the downfall of that last Witherman debtor – Quincy Witherman himself. The Judge found Stacy Milnes in contempt of Court, and to date, has deferred assigning a penalty. The Witherman cases made for great lunch fodder when the other Western District Judges and he got together for their monthly lunch.

Brian Chimes reported to the syndicate banks the Milnes goings-on at the last bankruptcy hearing. In a moment of disbelief, one of the bankers asked him if he had embellished any of the facts. Chimes responded in his signature Texas drawl, "Friends, I cain't make this shit up." The bankers and their attorneys met and decided to put a plan administrator in place to run the Witherman companies to ensure a constant flow of payments from the building revenues to the banks. Only after payment in full would the banks return control of the companies to either Witherman or whomever Judge Robertson directed.

The lawyers – well, they did what all lawyers do. They closed files and moved on to new clients, new matters, new challenges. Perhaps unsurprisingly, 3J and Pascale added a new O'Brien's drinking rule number four – no talking about Quincy Witherman. They violated the rule every once in a while. How could they refrain? 3J spent more than a passing amount of time thinking about how Quincy almost took his life. Debt, overwhelming debt, can be … well … overwhelming. More than once, she sat in her apartment in a new, flashy, glass high-rise building near the edge of downtown and listened to Paul Desmond on his album, *Take Ten*, counterpoint with guitarist Jim Hall. Harmony between guitar and alto sax. Cool Jazz, 1963. Melodic, warm, inviting, and elegant. She reflected on her encounter with Quincy Witherman and hoped those descriptive words would somehow, someday apply to him. She knew, however, that better descriptions included aloof, distant, private, cold, emotionless, devious, and calculating. She could add to that list apprehended, and, very nearly, dead. She could also add to the list, damn fool.

Life as a bankruptcy lawyer was anything but melodic, warm, and inviting sometimes. Her chosen field. *Ain't life a bitch.*

And Quincy Witherman? Well, he awaits sentencing while he sits around his small apartment and listens to copious amounts of his vinyl music. He figures there will be little music, and certainly no vinyl, in prison. He tries to think a lot. When he does, he believes he has a lot to say, but no one to say it to –

but this is his story, so you can hear what he has to say in his own words.

§

So, now you know. I had my solution to my bank problems. And then I didn't. Lyndon Johnson once said that every complicated problem has a simple solution ... that doesn't work. Maybe I should've listened to good old Lyndon. Now I'm awaiting sentencing. Waiting in my apartment from daybreak to sunset. I suppose all of this waiting serves to get me used to a new life of endless waiting. My new life from can to cain't. And let's not forget that the Swiss money and the crypto will go to pay creditors and everyone is getting paid in full. Correct? So perhaps the Judge's sentence won't be so bad.

I know this: I'll be the second Witherman in over two hundred years to do jail time. I had good lawyers. But none could ultimately save me from the inevitable, from myself, from the path that history chose for me. Real estate was my Witherman rite of passage and now jail will be as well.

During the plea bargain negotiations, the U.S. Attorney – I think Hickman is his name – told my lawyer in a moment of negotiating tactic and unproductive bluster that I wasn't good. What does that even mean? Was he trying to refer to one component of the eternal human conflict between good and evil? That's a little too dramatic for my taste, but maybe for a Federal prosecutor that's standard fare. Maybe Hickman's world is all plain and simple. Black and white. Good and bad. Wrong and right. I've thought about this. If I'm not good, existentially not good, then I have no choice but to ask, *so what?*

Hickman also said my life was honeycombed with lies. Wrong. Not lies. Just one lie. A single, solitary untruth repeated many times over the years. That single lie, shared and cultivated with

Michaela Roston Huld, doesn't define my life. I won't let it. My skyscrapers define my life and they are resolute monuments that point to the stars every night.

But I *am* worried how the loss of the lie will effect my relationship with Michaela. It was the lie that brought us together, after all. Without that lie anymore, Michaela and I will just have to find other endeavors to share and cultivate. I hope we can. I hope *she* hopes we can. I hope we can remain an "us."

I'll be thinking of Grant Green's lyricism, and Art Pepper's pain, and Ike Quebec's soulfulness, and Chet Baker's vulnerability. And, as I do, I'll hope to plan my rebound from prison, my next business conquest, my next fortune, the rest of my life with Michaela, and my next music selection. I won't have my vinyl records, so I'll have to drop my turntable needle in my mind and imagine the music. As I conjure up my music each day in prison, I might even allow myself to dream about how to plan for my return, for the possibility of a return to success. But success is a scary thing. I've learned that it sets us up for failure.

Let's not dance around it: the truth, *the whole truth*, and nothing but the truth. Turns out, I don't do well with that second truth. I'll have to work on that in prison. It'll give me something else to do and something to talk about in the weekly group get-togethers with the prison shrink.

Have I learned anything? Not really. There's no recovery from a "do-whatever-it-takes" business mentality. It's just the way I am. Some see risk. I see opportunity. If I saw anything less, I could never survive in the real estate business. It's ironic to contemplate that I was brought down by a "do-whatever-it-takes" banker, who is now out of banking, and, I hear, working in a grocery store. She has her freedom, but she has no future. I'm about to lose my freedom, but I believe I'll have a future … somehow. I can't see into both Heaven and Earth. Not even with these ghost eyes. But if I could, would I see Ms. Stacy Milnes and have the chance to ask her if I was her fuckin' friend now? Oh, and I heard that Scotland Yard was interested in her. May she find extreme consternation as the Brits investigate her crime. Good for the Brits.

What of repentance and redemption? Repentance and redemption are overrated. Not that I'm beyond repentance – just that I'm not interested in it. At least not now and not yet. I took a calculated risk and got caught. It would be hypo-critical for me now to pretend to find a higher power and assert repentance, although I know convicts do that all the time. But I can't repent because the forces in the universe wouldn't allow me to repent. And I can't claim redemption because I have no chips to redeem at the cashier's window of life. Old Gunn couldn't redeem himself because he had no means to do so – no money to pay the bankers. I don't see myself at the redemption window because there's no purpose served by doing so. Oh, and under the deal I struck, I'll also have no money.

This might be the moment in the play when the bad guy says his life's over. That was my thinking in Laredo, but, other than 3J, I haven't told anyone about my Texas moments of dark introspection, and I think I've moved on. Now I know my life isn't over. I think, *if you're going through Hell, you put your head down and just keep going.* Thank you, Mr. Churchill, for that one. One foot in front of the other, right? But just not off the Laredo curb.

After all, it's not about how you fall down. We all do. It's all about how you get up. Not everyone does or can. Gunn couldn't – I will. I will after I get out of a federal minimum-security prison. That will be my new fresh start. Released from prison after serving my time. No head start this time, but a fresh start should be sufficient by the time I get out.

No, this is just a bump in the road. And one that I saw coming. In due course, I'll ride over that road bump and use

406 | MARK SHAIKEN

my fresh start to get back to who I am; all I do is all I am, and that's all that matters – I build skyscrapers. That's my legacy. That's what I'll leave behind. My skyscrapers.

I just need to make sure I have found a way to move forward and move on. For me, one without the other won't work.

A reporter for the *Kansas City Star* called me a few days ago. He asked me to describe what it felt like to have the Swiss account for so many years and keep it hidden from the IRS, banks and the bankruptcy court. I told him to ask this old guy, Moses Aaronson, who I've learned was the one to uncover the account. I told the reporter that Aaronson did all the background, developed the facts, uncovered the account and should have all the information a reporter could ever want. The reporter said he wanted to hear it from me. I said I couldn't help him – I couldn't talk about it because all I had done was lived it.

I asked Atwell what life would be like in prison. He said I could expect a wake-up call at 6 a.m., overcrowded bathrooms, 7:15 a.m. breakfast (not great food), work duty, lunch (more not great food), more work, headcount, mail call, dinner (same), free time, and lights out in a dormitory setting. No barbed wire. Then a *Groundhog Day* repeat. Lots of time to decide if my next building will be in Minneapolis or Salt Lake, I suppose. Oh, and contemplate how I'll finance it.

See you in five years, or whatever sentence the District Court Judge imposes. Minus time off for good behavior, of course.

AFTERNOTE

The Debtor on Saturday, March 30, 2020

BEDTIME IN MY CONFINEMENT quarters. It's been six months since I've heard from Michaela. She's moved on. I suppose, so have I. Life in prison is better without the complications of a relationship. At least I tell myself that each night as I try not to mourn her loss.

I've grown accustomed to my new life. I'm in here with a banker who embezzled from depositors to support a gambling habit, a broker who got caught making money off of insider trading, an accountant who laundered money, and a politician who was on the take. I'm the only bankruptcy criminal. The crims – my new friends and group session colleagues. A good crew, in an incarcerated kind of way.

But, as you well know, a pandemic has now descended. The entire world is now in lockdown and I worry that my imprisonment will result in my death from a COVID-19 virus, just as imprisonment resulted in Gunn's death from a Yellow Fever virus. Another debt-related Witherman death? Might I be released to home confinement? It's been more than a year since I last talked with 3J and Pascale. I suppose they've moved on but I need help. And I think, *Michael Cohen may soon be released to serve out his sentence at home. Why not me? Gunn, Gunnie, 3J, Pascale, please, get me the hell out of here!*

TUESDAY, JANUARY 26, 2021

(Acknowledgments)

FRESH START – MY fourth book, and my first work of fiction. Thanks to former colleagues and friends who were willing to take the time to talk through some legal questions. In particular, thanks to John Aisenbrey and David Bell for guiding me through the "Fruit of the Poisonous Tree" doctrine and the world of criminal law. Thanks to Nick Zluticky for listening to the plot line and helping guide me when I needed direction. Thanks to Cindi Woolery for information about the U.S. Attorney's Office and to Jane Pansing Brown for discussing with me modern day ways to restrict movement when an accused is awaiting sentencing. Thanks to Chris Lenhart for fact-checking me on suspicious activity reports.

Thanks to Zachary Shaiken for the many discussions and information about a man-in-the-middle-attack, Virtual Private Networks, and for his high-tech guidance when I needed it.

Thanks to all my banker friends and acquaintances. You are all the best and none of you even approaches a Stacy Milnes.

Thanks to all of my bankruptcy colleagues at Stinson for sharing war stories over the years and fueling my interest in bankruptcy law fiction.

Thanks to Rebecca and Andrew Brown of Design For Writers for all of their hard work, editing, design, and book publishing skills. You guys are the best.

Thanks to Michael Kahn for sharing Madison Park and the Flatiron District with me so I could get a feel for the neighborhood and include it in *Fresh Start*.

Thanks to Loren Shaiken for all of your support and love, and for letting me disappear for such extended periods of time while I researched and put *Fresh Start* down on paper. And thanks to our little sixteen-pound, canine rhinestone cowgirl, Emily. Moses is lucky to have you in the book, but we are luckier to share our world with you in real life.

Amazon Review

YOU WOULD MAKE AN author very happy if you would please consider leaving a short, Amazon review at https://tinyurl.com/49dkfs7w.

AUTOMATIC STAY
A 3J BANKRUPTCY MYSTERY

Watch for the release of my next bankruptcy novel, *Automatic Stay*, starring Josephina Jillian Jones, with her supporting cast of Bill Pascale, and a host of others.

Read my prior book –
And ... Just Like That: Essays on a life before, during and after the law.
http://aws.org/HNT9GF

Join my mailing list to stay up to date at
http://markshaikenauthor.com.

Let me know what you think at
markshaiken@fastmail.com.